Bloody Sunday

Ben Coes

CANELO

First published in the United States in 2018 by St Martin's Press

This edition published in the United Kingdom in 2019 by

Canelo Digital Publishing Limited
57 Shepherds Lane
Beaconsfield, Bucks HP9 2DU
United Kingdom

A CIP catalogue record for this book is available from the British Library.

Print ISBN 978 1 78863 526 4
Ebook ISBN 978 1 78863 018 4

Look for more great books at www.canelo.co

Printed and bound in Great Britain by Clays Ltd, Elcograf S.p.A.

Prologue

The plane was long, shiny, and black: a Bombardier Global 7000, owned by the Gustave Roussy Institute, one of the most advanced cancer research and treatment centers in the world. Part of the hospital's variety of offerings was a dramatic and very expensive accouterment: remote, on-site, fully staffed, complete diagnostic biological protocols and analysis and, in turn, determination as to whether a patient has cancer – and if so what course of action should be taken. This gave them the ability to assess any individual, anywhere in the world – provided they had the wherewithal to foot the bill.

Seven hours before, another plane from the Institute had flown the same course: Paris to Pyongang, North Korea. That plane was a cargo plane, loaded with a variety of advanced diagnostic medical equipment, including state-of-the-art MRI, CT Scan, blood, oxygen, and cellular analytic hardware, and cutting-edge radiologic equipment. All of the equipment was now in position at the Pyongang Medical College Hospital.

The Bombardier carried a team of cancer specialists, all under the leadership of Dr. Marc de Saint-Phalle. De Saint-Phalle was widely considered to be the top cancer specialist in the world. A total of ten people from the Institute were with him, among them doctors, radiologists, and nurses skilled in field work and known for their proficiency and operational precision. De Saint-Phalle had hand-picked every one of them.

The first six seats were occupied by a different group. Each man was young – mid-twenties – and stocky. Two were bald and clean-shaven. The others had longish hair and thick beards. All of them were ex-Israeli military – Sayaret Metkal to be exact, which was, along with Shayetet 13, Israel's most elite group of Special Forces operators. They were all highly-trained, skilled at counter-terrorism operations, anti-guerrilla warfare, and all manner of tight-sight envelope protection and penetration, firearms and explosives, cold weapons, surveillance, face-to-face combat, and extended field work in network dark locations. They were from a private, London-based company called Four Winds LP, known for their military skills and discretion. The Institute was an important client. What country the Institute was going to – who they were going to see – these were state secrets and the Institute had learned to trust that the soldiers of Four Winds would not leak the secrets of the world leaders they were sometimes paid to try and heal.

The trip to North Korea had taken a month to negotiate. The North Koreans didn't balk at the Institute's price: $57.2 million for two days work – but they resisted when the Institute insisted on bringing their own security. Finally, when it was clear the Institute would not relent, Pyongang agreed to allow a full-on security squad, armed to the teeth. Kim Jong-un had a reputation. If tests showed he had something wrong with him, he was the sort to order the execution of those giving the diagnosis. He might still do the same – but now Pyongang understood that many people would die if Kim attempted to harm de Saint-Phalle or one of his team. De Saint-Phalle knew the drill. It was not the first time he'd traveled to hostile territory in order to examine a dictator.

Without de Saint-Phalle, Kim would have no choice but to bring in an inferior team from China – or else rely on North Korea's own team of cancer specialists, whose knowledge and abilities were decades behind the Institute's.

De Saint-Phalle looked across the aisle. A woman, Dr. Megan Licameli, with short, jet black hair, was reading the same set of documents he was: Kim's health records going back to his childhood.

"It's in the genetics," said de Saint-Phalle.

"What is?"

"Declination of the pancreatic mechanism. Whether it's the trypsinogen gene or ataxia telangiectasia we won't know until later."

"I read it differently," said Megan. "The primary DNA structure is decaying. Hydrolysis, oxidation, or nonenzymatic methylation. The DNA is unstable. If you look at the sequences of his parents as compared to his grandparents, there is material genetic crossover. His grandmother was related to his grandfather before they married. Then his father married his first cousin. His basic indices is falling apart. Of course he has cancer. Not to mention, he's probably completely insane. Explain to me again, Marc, why are we going?"

De Saint-Phalle paused.

"If I had a dollar for every time I think I know what I'm going to find before I find something completely different – or nothing at all – I'd be a very rich man."

"You are a very rich man," said Megan. "What if you had a dollar for every time what you predicted came true? Would that pile be bigger?"

De Saint-Phalle grinned.

"Maybe," he said.

–

The streets in Pyongang were closed. All citizens not at work had been ordered inside for the four hour period of time, in the middle of the day, that Kim would be traveling to the hospital.

The motorcade began at the Presidential Palace. Five vehicles in all, four black Range Rovers and, in the middle, a long, dark red Mercedes limousine, bulletproof, steel-plated undercarriage, a driver with a small pile of submachine guns on the side seat, despite the many layers of protection along the route and within flanking range of the limousine.

Inside the hospital, the mood was hushed as Kim Jong-un, North Korea's Supreme Leader, waddled down the quiet, brightly-lit sixth floor hallway.

Other than a three-man security detail, the only individual accompanying Kim was General Pak Yong-sik.

Yong-sik was the head of the North Korean armed forces, the Korean Peoples' Army, or KPA. By number of soldiers, KPA was the largest military force in the world. But this was not why Yong-sik was here. Yong-sik was Kim's most trusted confidante, the only other man in North Korea who knew something was very wrong with the thirty-five year old Kim. Yong-sik had served under Kim's father, Kim Jong-il. Back then, Yong-sik had become Kim Jong-il's closest ally and friend. Yong-sik had been appointed head of KPA at age thirty, leapfrogging over more than a hundred more senior officers. General Yong-sik was older now but remained the second most powerful man in North Korea. If he'd been like a brother to Kim Jong-il, he was like a father to Kim Jong-un, who, at age thirty-five, was not only infected with cancer, but was also a chain-smoking alcoholic who snorted cocaine throughout the day and could not sleep unless he passed out.

Kim was his own worst enemy. He started smoking at age nine and drinking by eleven. He lost his virginity at age twelve to a stunning prostitute flown into Pyongang from New York City. He attended a highly exclusive, highly secretive boarding school in Switzerland and returned home during his last year there, expelled after attempting to rape the fourteen-year old daughter of one of the instructors at the school. Kim Jong-il's gift to the school – to keep the story of his aberrant son out of the press – was a $50 million check.

Kim's life had been one of moneyed debauchery mixed with the sudden acquisition of power in a country trained like dogs to believe their Supreme Leader was a demi-god.

At the end of the long hallway, a set of double doors was closed. Outside, two of the Israeli gunmen stood at attention, each man clutching a submachine gun, trained at the ground.

Kim approached. Rather than being angry at the sight of the armed foreigners, he smiled and extended his hand.

"Welcome to North Korea," he said in nearly flawless English, a soft accent the only giveaway that it wasn't his first language.

"Thank you, sir," said one of the Israelis, nodding politely and scanning Yong-sik and the three-man security detail. The other Israeli reached for the door handle and opened it for Kim and the others in his entourage. One of the North Korean guards remained outside the doors with the Israelis while the others trailed Kim and Yong-sik inside.

The examination room was cavernous. For the purposes of the examination, the Institute's team of medical engineers had appropriated the hospital's largest operating room. The Institute's equipment was set up in a horseshoe around a central operating table. The room was two stories high. A second floor opened up to a balcony filled with seats, now empty. Beeping and pinging from various machines provided a steady din.

Two more Israeli gunmen stood on opposite sides of the examination room. A third man was in the balcony amphitheater, standing and watching from above, a high-powered rifle across his chest.

The French medical team stood in the room, motionless and silent as Kim entered. They all wore uniforms that were light blue. Everyone had on surgical hats, except for the man in the middle of the group, de Saint-Phalle, who stood before the large stainless steel examination table.

De Saint-Phalle stepped toward Kim and bowed slightly, then extended his hand.

"Mr. President," said de Saint-Phalle. "I am Marc de Saint-Phalle from Gustave Roussy. It is a pleasure to meet you, sir."

Kim shook de Saint-Phalle's hand but though he wanted to smile, a nervous, distressed, even vulnerable look appeared on his face. He said nothing. He couldn't speak. For a moment, it appeared he might break down.

"Does it hurt right now?" said de Saint-Phalle, trying to ease Kim's fears by engaging him in a simple question.

Kim nodded, placing his right hand on the side of his torso.

"On a scale of one to ten, with ten being the worst pain you've ever felt, and one being no pain at all, how would you rate the pain?"

"Six," said Kim. "It never goes away, except with the painkillers. Can you help me?"

"We're here to determine what is wrong, Mr. President," said de Saint-Phalle. "We 're doctors and researchers who've devoted our lives to understanding and treating all forms of cancer. At this point, we don't even know what it is."

"You saw the results of the blood test."

"Yes, I did," said de Saint-Phalle. "You have elevated platelets and white blood cells, but it doesn't necessarily mean it's cancer, sir."

"Can you save me if it is?" whispered Kim.

De Saint-Phalle cast a glance to Yong-sik.

"If you can be saved, yes, we will save you," said de Saint-Phalle. "But first, let's determine what's causing the pain in your side. Your doctors were not allowed to run the sort of tests that will be needed to diagnose what is going on. We're going to run those tests."

"What if it's cancer?"

"Let's cross that bridge if and when we get to it."

"I want to know."

De Saint-Phalle looked at Megan for a moment, then back to Kim.

"One of four outcomes will come from our two days of tests," said de Saint-Phalle. "One, you don't have cancer. We find out what the pain is and recommend a course of action. Then we fly home. Two, you have cancer and it's treatable with various strategies and treatments available right here in Pyongang, with our guidance from Villejuif. Three, you have cancer and it cannot be treated locally, in which case we would advise you to come to Villejuif where we can treat it properly."

Kim nodded.

"And what is the fourth?" said Kim.

"The last scenario is some sort of advanced inoperable cancer," said de Saint-Phalle evenly. "But again, we don't know anything yet, and the fact that you walked in here and are not displaying signs that would normally signal terminal cancer is a promising beginning. Now, if you will, please sit down on the examination table and point to where it hurts."

By the end of the first day of tests, de Saint-Phalle and his team knew what was wrong. It didn't take long. With each set of test results, like a sculpture forming out of a mass of rock, they honed in on a precise picture of what was wrong. They would not need a second day of tests. The results of the four biopsies were conclusive.

That it was advanced cancer of the pancreas was immediately apparent, but the biopsies performed on Kim's liver, kidneys, and stomach showed an even more frightening discovery. The cancer was an extremely aggressive, rapidly metastasizing type of the disease that rendered any more tests unnecessary and any potential cures impossible. The team from the Institute all agreed that it was inoperable. The only thing they couldn't agree on was how long Kim had to live. De Saint-Phalle believed Kim had, at most, a month to live. Megan Licameli predicted that North Korea's leader would be dead within a week.

What de Saint-Phalle told no one was that he'd known the moment he looked into Kim's eyes. He didn't know what exact form the cancer would take, but he'd learned to recognize the look. He'd seen it so many times he could tell the difference; the difference between the normal, horrible worry that all patients emoted before knowing whether or not they were sick, and the spectral, indescribable chill of those poor souls who already knew they were dying, that they were almost dead.

De Saint-Phalle called Yong-sik at just after ten o'clock that evening.

"I think you should come to the hospital," said de Saint-Phalle.

"I'll leave right now."

Forty-five minutes later, Yong-sik entered the operating room. De Saint-Phalle was alone. The medical equipment, brought in by the Institute, was gone, already on the plane. The rest of the medical team was back at the airport. Even the Israelis were back on board the waiting Bombardier, something de Saint-Phalle insisted upon. He wanted to handle this alone.

Yong-sik was still dressed in military uniform, his chest emblazoned with colored insignia and medals. De Saint-Phalle looked at Yong-sik with a steady, emotionless stare.

"Where's the rest of your team?" said Yong-sik.

"On the plane, general. A second day of tests won't be necessary."

Yong-sik paused. His hand reached for the table to steady himself.

"Tell me."

"President Kim has inoperable cancer," said de Saint-Phalle. "It started in his pancreas and spread. It's now in virtually every part of his body, including his bones, which is likely the reason he's having break-through pain. But it's everywhere."

"Metastasized?" said Yong-sik.

"Correct. A very aggressive form of cancer."

"What about radiation?" asked Yong-sik. "Chemotherapy? What about operating on him? Right now. Tonight."

De Saint-Phalle shook his head.

"It's too late, sir. At this point, to kill the cancer we'd have to kill Kim. No amount of radiation, drugs, or surgical procedures would be adequate. It would simply be a waste of President Kim's final days. A painful waste, I might add. Because at the end of the day it wouldn't work. There's simply no way to halt the progression. I'm very sorry."

Yong-sik looked at de Saint-Phalle for several moments. His eyes became red with emotion. He sidled up to the examination table and pulled himself onto it, sitting down.

"I'd like to inform President Kim as soon as possible," said de Saint-Phalle.

"I will tell him."

"It's my responsibility as his doctor," said de Saint-Phalle. "He'll have questions you can't answer."

Yong-sik shook his head, no.

"Thank you for coming," said Yong-sik, wiping his eyes and standing. He reached out his hand and shook de Saint-Phalle's hand. "You are a good doctor, an honest man. There is only one person who can inform the supreme leader. I'll have you driven to your plane. When you're in the air, I will go see him. You might have armed men protecting you, but he is unpredictable. If he's going to kill someone, it should be me."

—

An hour later, Yong-sik stepped inside President Kim's massive, palatial bedroom. Kim was seated in bed, beneath the covers, dressed in silk maroon pajamas. He was smoking a cigarette, the ashtray was on the duvet in the middle of the bed. A lone light was on in the room, a large glass lamp on the bedside table, and it cast a gold hue across the room. A glass of red wine was on the bedside table.

Behind Kim, on the wall, was an oil painting. It showed his father, Kim Jong-il, and Kim. In the painting, Kim was a child. He was seated on his father's lap, a big smile on his face. His father was holding Kim's hand in his own, a tender look on his face as he held his young son.

Yong-sik walked across the soft oriental carpet and came to Kim's bedside. He bowed before Kim for a few seconds, then raised his head and looked at Kim. Kim took a drag from his cigarette, then exhaled.

"How bad is it?" said Kim.

Yong-sik started to talk, but then became choked up.

"Come now, general, certainly it cannot be that bad?"

Yong-sik nodded.

"I'm afraid it is, my leader," said Yong-sik.

Over the next few minutes, Yong-sik relayed the medical findings by the team from Gustave Roussy. Kim calmly sipped from his wine glass as he listened, then lit another cigarette. His face was blank as stone, though not a look of resignation or fear. It was a frightening look, a look Yong-sik recognized, when Kim wanted – needed – someone to blame, a scapegoat, a release valve for the deep, unquenchable anger that coursed through him like boiling metal. When Yong-sik was finished, he looked up at Kim. He couldn't hide his own emotion. It wasn't fear, but rather something only he knew, something he could never say to anyone, not even Kim. It was the sorrow of a father who suddenly understands his son is going to die.

"*How dare you!*" said Kim, seething. "*I'm the one dying, not you!*"

Yong-sik nodded, but said nothing.

"I… I'm sorry," said Yong-sik quietly.

Kim took another sip of wine.

"You wanted me to go see these doctors two years ago," said Kim, staring off into space, thinking aloud. "You were right. You're always right, general. You were the one who told me my father died. I would never harm you. You're the only family I have ever known. Did you know I can't even remember what my father was like? It is only through your stories of him that I have any idea."

"He would be very proud of you," said Yong-sik.

"Do you mean that?"

"Yes."

Kim put the empty wine glass down and leaned back into a big pillow. He stared again off into the darkness of the room, lost in his thoughts. His eyes abruptly cut to Yong-sik. The look had returned as Yong-sik knew it would, the anger and resentment, the fury of a man dying, a man who believed he was immortal. His black eyes flashed slashes of hatred and rage.

"No, he wouldn't be proud of me," said Kim, his voice inflecting with emotion. "But he will be. If I am going to die, I will bring others with me like nobody else has. I always knew the sign would come, the reason my father built the nuclear weapons. Finally, the sign is upon me. Don't you see?"

Yong-sik nodded, though he wasn't sure what Kim was talking about.

"I will join my father and grandfather now," said Kim. "If I am to die, it will not be in vain. It is time. It is time to show our enemy that death comes to us all. I will leave this earth an inferno. *I will light the world on fire! I will light America in flames from the North Korean sun!*"

1

LA VILLA BLEUE
SIDI BOU SAÏD
TUNISIA
NORTH AFRICA

On a small terrace outside of a hotel room on the coast of North Africa, a man stood. It was nighttime and he'd been standing in the same place for two hours. In his hand was a pair of large, silver-colored, high-powered binoculars. He kept them aimed at the ocean and a large yacht moored offshore, its lights still blazing yellow despite the late hour. He could see people inside the main cabin of the $190 million yacht.

The man slid a small switch on the side of the binoculars and all colors disappeared. This activated the binocular's thermal imaging system. He was now able to look at the yacht's heat patterns. The yacht, and everything around it, went black. Near the front, a cloud of white showed the large boat's motor as it idled. Inside the cabin, fuzzy white silhouettes appeared as if in a photo negative, as the occupants of the yacht were revealed, their bodies emitting enough heat to enable the binoculars to relay the fuzzy white carapaces. He counted eleven people on board. Several people were asleep. Some were still moving. He studied the decks of the two-hundred foot yacht. He counted two men on the stern of the boat, a man at the bow, and one other man who was walking along the near side – the port side – of the yacht.

This was the security cordon, there to guard the occupants of the yacht. It was a serious crew, all ex-military and armed to the teeth.

The man's hair was down to his shoulders and messed up, even a little oily, as if he hadn't bathed in a few days. In fact, it'd been more than a week since soap or shampoo touched him, though he'd swum in the ocean many times. A mess of moustache and beard covered his face, which was tanned a deep brown. He wore jeans and a white tank-top that showed off massive shoulders and arms, ripped with muscles. On the man's left shoulder was a jagged, wide, thick scar. On his right bicep was a small tattoo: a lightning bolt, cut in black ink, no bigger than a dime.

Beneath the man's left armpit was a worn, custom-made leather holster. Inside was a gun: Colt 1911. A long black polymer suppressor was threaded into the muzzle of the gun.

It was one-thirty in the morning local North Africa time.

He stared for a few more moments, then put the binoculars down on a table. He picked up a glass from the table. It was half-filled with bourbon.

The temperature was in the eighties, yet a stiff wind chopped from the ocean across the small town on Tunisia's coast and it was pleasant.

He'd been in Africa for a week now, in Tunisia for three days, in Sidi Bou Saïd for eighteen hours.

He took a large sip of bourbon and stared out at the black ocean. Despite the late hour, the sky to the east held an ambient bluish black, and it made the horizon visible in eerie purple.

Below the hotel, the small tourist town of Sidi Bou Saïd spread in a meandering cross-hatch of white stucco, cobblestone streets, and blue trim, inclining steeply toward the ocean's shore. He could hear music from an outdoor café somewhere nearby, a light drumbeat mixed with sitar and a soft female voice singing in Arabic. It was a sleepy beach town, peaceful, off-the-beaten-track, out-of-the-way. Everything about the little town was idyllic.

Except on this particular terrace. For here, quiet was juxtaposed to the man's eyes — two eyes of steel blue that looked cold, alert, and angry. They were eyes that hinted at violence.

Operational.

Then he saw her. Was it the alcohol? She was on the terrace, to his right. Her brown hair was being blown by the wind. She was looking at him, pleading with him, reaching her hand out…

Holly.

He shook his head, trying to push her away, clutching the glass and taking another sip, a sip he didn't want. But as hard as he fought, he couldn't stop looking back at her – at the mirage, the memory, of his wife, taken from him more than a decade before by a bullet.

"I'm sorry," he whispered as tears coursed down his cheeks. "I'm so sorry. I didn't know. You have to believe me…" His whisper trailed off as a gust from the North African coast sent his hair awry, tousling it in a sudden breeze.

Dewey Andreas took another large sip of bourbon, draining the glass. He leaned over and poured more bourbon into the glass, then lifted the glass to his lips and took another big sip. He removed a pack of cigarettes from his jeans pocket and lit one.

It had been months now since Dewey learned the truth.

The truth.

That his wife hadn't killed herself. That they'd killed her and made it look like a suicide. A unit where spouses were forbidden, an elite, highly-secret squad of operators culled exclusively from Delta and Navy SEALs, brainchild of the former director of the Central Intelligence Agency who wanted a covert kill team deployable on American soil, outside the bounds of the law. But nothing had gone as planned. He'd been charged with Holly's murder and by the time the jury acquitted him, the unit's recruiters had moved on, leaving Dewey to pick up the pieces of his shattered life without the woman he loved. He was kicked out of the military a day after his acquittal. A military, a country, he'd risked his life for. Like Holly, gone with the wind, gone forever.

All of it was visited on him like a ferocious lightning strike from a clear sky, the bolt hitting with such force it should have killed him. But it didn't. Instead, it hardened him, hardened what was already the hardest of American tough. Dewey had learned to accept his fate. Had learned to accept Holly's suicide. He fled America for the U.K., taking a job on an offshore oil platform in the North Sea, delivered by helicopter to the rig in the middle of a brutal winter storm. It was there – on that rig, then another, and still others, off the coast of Africa, Europe, and South America, that Dewey had healed. Or, perhaps more accurately, where Dewey had sealed off and destroyed every part of him capable of feeling. Working as a roughneck had not just provided an escape – it had hardened him, even beyond what the American military was capable of, for it was offshore where the only law that mattered was the law of the jungle. It was offshore where Dewey Andreas learned what an animal he could be, what an animal he was.

And then, Dewey had returned to the fold. He'd been reeled back into the government that betrayed him. A cell of Islamic terrorists had targeted America – their first target the massive oil platform Dewey was gang chief on. Despite of the way he'd been treated, Dewey risked his life to fight them. As much as he hated the government that kicked him out, that falsely accused him of murdering the woman he loved, he still loved the United States of America. He was American. Nothing could strip the red, white, and blue from his heart.

After returning, Dewey found people inside government he trusted. The U.S. government, in turn, found Dewey to be its most formidable weapon. Since returning to stop the attack on America, Dewey had led a coup in Pakistan, and stolen Iran's only nuclear device hours before it was to be detonated in Tel Aviv. He'd stopped a cell of ISIS terrorists who'd taken over a dormitory at Columbia University. He stopped an assassination attempt on the President of the United States.

But it was that last act – stopping Charles Bruner from killing President Dellenbaugh – that changed everything, for it was Bruner who wanted to recruit him a decade before. It was Bruner who'd ordered Holly's murder.

Murder.

He shut his eyes, holding back tears. He clenched his fist and slammed it into the railing at the side of the terrace. Too hard. He looked down, unclenching his fist. He hadn't broken anything, but blood coursed from the knuckle.

He took another sip.

Everything Dewey thought he knew was an illusion. The death he'd spent a decade getting over was an illusion. They'd come for him and murdered her. Murdered her just so he could serve in their secretive unit unencumbered by family.

"*Why the hell do you think I would've gone with you? Fuck you,*" he whispered.

It was the same question he'd been asking himself for weeks, for months.

I'd never join you. I would never have joined you, you arrogant sonofabitch.

Dewey had killed the man behind it all, Charles Bruner, but it did little to assuage his anger, his hatred, and his guilt. He'd gotten Holly murdered. Not intentionally, but he was the one they wanted and he was the reason the unit's henchmen had jammed his service pistol into Holly's mouth and blown off the back of her head. Now all he could feel was anger – a dark, cruel, hate-filled anger that was growing by the hour.

In four months, Dewey had done little except look for the one man remaining. It had become his singular obsession. To the exclusion of friends, job, family, Daisy. A year ago, he imagined marrying Daisy. Now, he couldn't talk to her, so deep was the guilt that occupied his troubled mind. Someday he'd explain to her why he never returned her calls, why he didn't answer the door when she came looking. But not this day. This day was for Holly.

He took another sip of bourbon, then took a deep drag on the cigarette, casually scanning the cobblestone streets that ran below the slightly dilapidated hotel, then the ocean, once again eyeing the yacht moored at the far edge of the small harbor.

"I'm coming for you," he whispered as he stared out at the yellow dot.

He took one last puff of the cigarette then flicked it from the terrace. He pushed his hand back through his hair. He watched as a young couple walked in a slightly inebriated zig-zag down the cobblestones, the woman laughing at something the man said. He looked back at the yacht. Suddenly, the lights disappeared. He picked up the binoculars and scanned the boat again. Except for a low glow from the running lights along the gunnels of the boat, all other lights were off. He flipped on thermal. Again, he counted the bodies of people inside the boat, all apparently at rest. He counted two gunmen who remained on the deck of the boat, standing guard despite the darkness.

It's time.

Dewey slammed down the rest of the bourbon then turned and entered the darkened hotel room. His eyes caught the visitor seated on the sofa in the same moment he flipped on the lights. Dewey ripped the gun from beneath his left armpit and swept it toward the figure.

"Don't shoot," said Tacoma, raising his hands and staring calmly at Dewey.

Tacoma was leaning back, both feet on the table. He wore a pair of bright white slides. He held a beer in his hand. He looked casually up at Dewey.

Dewey held Tacoma in the firing line of the suppressor for an extra second, then stuffed the gun back inside the holster.

"I hope you don't mind," said Tacoma, taking a sip of beer. "It was in the fridge. I had another one too."

"What the fuck are you doing here?" said Dewey as he moved to the credenza and placed the glass down.

"I'm here to stop you before you do something stupid," said Tacoma.

"It's too late," said Dewey. "Who sent you? Hector?"

"I came on my own," said Tacoma. "But they know you're here."

"Who?"

"Langley. I… well I sort of read something on Hector's desk."

Dewey shot Tacoma a look.

"What the hell does that mean?"

"There's a RECON team coming to get you," said Tacoma. "There's three of them in the lobby. They're waiting for you to walk out. Probably dart you up with some Tizanidine and fly you home."

Dewey found the bottle of bourbon on the counter and poured half a glass.

"I thought you said you came alone?"

"I did. I knew they were sending in a team. I beat them here," said Tacoma grinning.

"What do you want, a medal?"

"Sure," said Tacoma.

"Why should I believe you?"

"I wouldn't lie to you," said Tacoma. "Even though you're an ungrateful asshole."

Dewey ignored the taunt. He looked at Tacoma.

"Do they know you're here?" said Dewey.

"I don't think so," said Tacoma. "I have a car a few blocks away and a plane waiting at the airport. We should probably get going – we'll need to go out through the service entrance."

Dewey put the glass down and looked at Tacoma with a perplexed expression.

"Rob," said Dewey sharply. "I'm not leaving."

Dewey walked to the closet and removed a large duffel bag.

"If Langley can find you, so can whoever you came here to kill," said Tacoma, pointing to the ocean. "Whoever's on that fucking yacht. Have you considered that?"

Dewey carried the duffel to the middle of the room and set it down on the coffee table in front of Tacoma, pushing his feet off to accommodate the bag.

"How did Langley know I was here?" he asked, unzipping the bag.

"You set off a tracker a week ago," said Tacoma, "when you walked into Dulles. Then you popped the grid at Heathrow, but the tracker didn't go blue so they know you connected. They pushed every known alias against the X6 framework. You popped the grid again in Tangiers under the name Dane Walker. Three days ago you, you flashed again when you entered Tunisia."

"Impressive," said Dewey casually as he rifled through his duffel bag and removed several items and placed them on the credenza: explosives, a set of advanced, waterproof night optics, called "four-quads," a SIG P221 with a suppressor already threaded into the muzzle, extra magazines, a white nylon shoulder holster, and a long black suppressor. He took the .45 from beneath his armpit and set it down, not looking at Tacoma, who sat down.

"Who are you here for, Dewey?"

Dewey removed a tactical wetsuit from the duffel bag – short-sleeved, mid-thigh with several airtight pockets.

"Unless you want to see my ass, you might want to look away," said Dewey.

He took off his clothing and quickly pulled the wetsuit on. He started stuffing the airtight pockets with guns, ammo, and explosives. Finally, he walked to the credenza and bolted down the remaining quarter glass of bourbon.

Dewey continued to stare blankly at Tacoma, picking up one of the guns and sticking it into an airtight pocket on his right thigh.

"What do you want me to tell, you, Rob? How I found out my wife didn't commit suicide and someone in fact murdered her? How I'm going to go put a bullet in one of the motherfuckers behind it? Is that what you're wondering? Because that's what I'm doing. And anyone who stands in my way is going to die."

Tacoma leaned back. He was silent for several moments.

"So that's what this is about?" Tacoma said.

"Yeah, that's what this is about. I'm going to install some air conditioning in Peter Flaherty's skull."

"It won't bring Holly back."

"No shit," said Dewey, continuing to prepare.

"So you found Flaherty?"

Dewey shot him a look.

"There's a Tier One kill order on him," said Tacoma. "There's a right way and a wrong way to kill him. This is the wrong way."

"There's no wrong way," said Dewey. "Flaherty killed my wife. He staged her suicide then put a muzzle in her mouth and pulled the trigger."

"Do you know the operating environment?" said Tacoma. "How many men he has? Electronic surveillance, trip wires? Let JSOC send in a team of SEALs."

"No way. JSOC was who let Flaherty escape from Guantanamo in the first place. I'll take my chances."

Dewey reached into the duffel and removed two small cubes, one orange-colored, the other gray, each the size of a pack of cigarettes, along with a black object the size and shape of a double A battery. He put them in a third airtight pocket on the side of his left thigh then zipped it tight.

"You need sanction before you go out and just put a bullet in someone, otherwise you lose any sort of protection they can provide," said Tacoma.

"Bullets," said Dewey.

"What?"

"Bullets, plural. You said before I put a bullet in someone. I'm putting *bullets* in someone, plural, as many as I can."

He stuck the other gun in the airtight pocket and zipped it up.

"I'm going to stick a gun in his mouth and blow the back of his fucking head off."

Quickly, Dewey pulled on his jeans and a windbreaker. He pulled a thin backpack over his shoulders.

Dewey moved toward the door, but Tacoma intercepted him, standing in the way.

"Excuse me," Dewey said. But Tacoma didn't budge.

"Five minutes," said Tacoma.

"Why?"

"You're not right right now," said Tacoma. "You know it and I know it. You're pissed off. I don't blame you. I'd be pissed off too. But this isn't the way to deal with it. You're going to get killed. For chrissakes, you smell like a bourbon factory."

"It's the way I deal with it," said Dewey.

"It won't bring Holly back."

"I'm not doing this to bring her back. I'm doing it because there's a man on a boat who was one of the ones who killed her and he doesn't deserve to live. It's about justice. I'd rather die than live with myself if I didn't do this. If they kill me, I went out doing what I wanted to do."

"I get it," said Tacoma, pausing. "Hey, you want me to come? I know how to swim."

"No," said Dewey. "I need to do this one myself."

Dewey stepped to the duffel bag. He took out a large coil of rope. He went out to the terrace and tied the end of the rope around the railing.

"Don't wait up."

He climbed onto the railing – then disappeared.

2

SIDI BOU SAÏD
TUNISIA

Dewey rappelled down the side of the hotel in silence, dropping onto a cobblestone lane that was well-lit but empty. He walked quickly away from the hotel, favoring the shadows near the low-flung homes and shops closed for the night, a thin backpack over his shoulder.

He cut right down a thin alley only a few feet wide, passing blue shutters that were closed and locked for the night, always moving downhill in the direction of the water. After several more turns, he came to the end of a small street and was across from the water.

A long, sandy beach ran across the waterfront. It was deserted, empty, and dark, with tall wooden lifeguard stations every hundred feet. The area just in front of the beach was cordoned off for swimmers. Beyond, the waters were dotted with small fishing scows, motorboats, and a few sailboats. Looming behind them were a half-dozen larger yachts, moored off the beautiful coastal village. One in particular stood out: a long white yacht at least two-hundred feet in length, beyond the rest of the boats.

A pair of jetties stuck out from the shore to the left.

Dewey moved past shops and restaurants, skulking in the shadows until he came to the beach. In darkness, Dewey removed the backpack, windbreaker, and then his shoes and pants. Beneath, he had on a short-sleeved tactical wetsuit that came down to the middle of his thighs. He pulled on a set of waterproof four-quads, night vision optics, pulling them down over his head and leaving them dangling around his neck.

He retrieved a pair of flippers from the backpack and walked to water's edge, pulling them on, then dived silently into the water.

Dewey swam sidestroke to his right, keeping his head above water, weaving through the various boats that were moored close to shore. His quiet swim took twenty minutes until finally he passed the last line of moorings. He kept going, paddling quietly out into the dark waters way beyond all the boats.

In front of him, several hundred feet away, he could see the transom of the massive yacht. A few dim lights dotted the transom, shining a wan yellow onto the façade of the yacht where its name was painted in fanciful script. He was too far away to read it. He pulled the four-quads up over his eyes and flipped them on so he could see better.

Закон джунглей

"ZAKON DZHUNGLEY"

LAW OF THE JUNGLE

was painted on the back of the boat.

Dewey scanned the yacht with the four-quads in normal mode, the same as a set of high-powered binoculars. He saw no one. He flipped the four-quads into thermal mode. Where before he'd seen only blackness, he saw two white skeletons on deck, moving in military like fashion along the port side of the yacht looking for intruders.

Dewey kept swimming until he was several hundred feet out beyond the yacht. Then he turned, cutting left, aiming for an area far past the yacht on its starboard side, the furthest and thus darkest side of the boat. He needed to be out beyond the watchful eyes of whatever guards were patrolling the deck.

After ten minutes of silent swimming, he arrived at a point approximately a hundred feet out beyond the large yacht. He reached to a pocket on the chest of the wetsuit and removed a small silver canister the size of a cigar. This was a ditch pipe, designed to give its user a few blasts of oxygen beneath the water.

Dewey dived down and swam beneath the water toward the yacht, kicking his feet furiously. He moved beneath the water until he was able to see the white of the hull. Instead of surfacing for air, he kept swimming, putting the ditch pipe in his mouth and pressing the end. A large burst of oxygen filled his mouth and lungs. He kept moving until he was directly below the boat. He let himself float up toward the hull, taking one last kick of oxygen then letting the device drop and sink as his hands found the fiberglass of the hull. He brought himself slowly up the curve of the hull along the starboard side of the boat until finally he breached the surface, quietly catching his breath.

Dewey treaded water a few inches out from the hull. He pulled the four-quads up from his neck and left them wrapped across his forehead.

The yacht's gunnel ran a few feet above the waterline. Small red lights dotted the gunnel every ten feet or so. Above that was a shiny brass railing. A long line of porthole windows reflected above the waterline, each one dark except one to the far right, near the bow, which glowed a dull yellow.

Reaching up and grabbing the railing was out of the question – it would make too much noise.

Dewey pulled the optics down over his eyes and scanned along the railing, looking for gunmen. He didn't see anyone. He treaded gently back to the hull, placing his hands against the smooth fiberglass, cloaking himself beneath it, then inched his way toward the stern of the yacht. Suddenly, he heard a voice. It was a man's voice – deep and staccato, the words Russian. He sounded as if he was just above him. A muted response came from the far side of the boat. The other gunman, also Russian.

Dewey took a deep breath and slipped silently beneath the water. He pushed his hands against the hull to create leverage, enabling him to move lower and lower beneath the boat. When he was deep enough to kick, he pushed one last time and aimed toward the sea floor, swimming underneath the hull of the boat, which loomed a spectral white above him. When he came to the stern, he stopped kicking and let himself drift up to the surface. He reached his hand out as he arose, grabbing the corner of the yacht. A stainless steel ladder for swimming jutted down beneath the waterline. He held it for a few moments and then moved around to the front of the ladder. He held himself below the waterline, trying to look up through the water. But as he was about to surface he saw a dark figure – one of the gunmen – moving slowly along the stern of the boat. Dewey waited, still holding his breath, watching as the man moved lackadaisically back and forth. He could make out the outline of a rifle in his hands, black steel catching a glint of what little light emanated from the yacht's running lights. The gunman seemed to pause for a few moments. Dewey felt his lungs tighten. When, finally, the gunman didn't move, Dewey had no choice. He clutched the ladder and let his nose and mouth surface for the briefest of moments, exhaling quietly, taking a breath, then submerging again.

For the next fifteen minutes, the pattern repeated itself as the gunman remained poised along the stern of the ship. Had the man heard something? Finally, Dewey watched as he moved to the left and walked along the port deck away from the stern.

Dewey climbed silently up the ladder and crawled onto a low, flat teak swimming platform. He removed his fins and scanned quickly, seeing no one. Dewey unzipped one of the airtight pockets on the wetsuit, removing the pistol. He chambered a round then pushed the safety off. He screwed in the suppressor. He remained on one knee, crouching on the swim platform.

The yacht was two stories high, not to mention whatever lay below the waterline. On the roof, the spiny outline of a helicopter could be seen.

A short set of stairs led from the swimming platform to the deck, where lounge chairs and tables were neatly arrayed beneath a white sailcloth canopy. Beyond was a door.

He heard footsteps and then saw the light to the left suddenly shift as one of the gunman approached. Still kneeling, Dewey swept the gun left just as the gunman came into view. The man's eyes registered Dewey just as Dewey pumped the trigger. A dull thud mixed with the sound of the ocean. The bullet struck the gunman in the left eye, kicking him backwards. He grunted as he fell to the deck. Dewey charged up the stairs to the deck and cut right, along the starboard side of the boat, running barefoot along the thin wood gunnel. He heard a shout from the back of the yacht just as he reached an opening beneath the sailcloth canopy and cut left, charging across the deck to the port side of the boat, hoping to take the other thug by surprise. But just as he came to the far edge of the yacht he caught the faint sound of a boot hitting against a hard surface behind him. Dewey stopped, pivoted, and dropped to his chest just as the second gunman emerged from the opening Dewey had just come through. Dewey fired, two silenced bullets, a dull, metallic *thwack thwack* followed by a heaving groan as the bullets struck the man in the chest, cutting him down and dropping him over the side of the boat, where he made a dull splash.

Dewey moved to the door and stepped inside the yacht. All the lights were extinguished except for a lamp in the corner. Dewey went to it and turned it off. He pulled the four-quads down over his eyes and flipped them on, flaming the night optics. Suddenly, the yacht's interior was illuminated in eerie, apocalyptic orange.

He stepped through the room, a dining room with a massive round table in the middle. He clutched his weapon in his right hand as he stepped around the table, dripping water as he made his way deeper into the yacht.

Beyond the dining room was a large kitchen. A stairwell in the corner led to the second floor. He ascended quietly and stepped into a long, darkened hallway, guided only by the four-quads.

He counted seven stateroom doors in all, three on each side and one at the end of the hallway.

Dewey unzipped the pocket on his left thigh, removing two small cubes, one orange-colored, the other gray, each the size of a pack of cigarettes.

Explosives.

He took out the small black object. Each side of it was adorned with a button – one orange, one gray.

Detonator.

Dewey took one of the explosives and peeled off the adhesive covering the back, then knelt and stuck it against the wall just a few feet into the hallway. He moved down the hallway to the last door on the right. Dewey paused outside the door. Gently, he jiggled the door handle. It was locked. He unzipped a pocket on the wetsuit on his right thigh and removed a pickgun, then stuck it against the small keyhole and pressed the trigger. The device, designed to pick all manner of locks, made a low humming noise. He watched impatiently for several seconds, precious moments, expecting to hear the lock turn. Instead, the pickgun continued a low grinding hum and then abruptly stopped.

Dewey heard a voice coming from somewhere outside, and then another. Someone was yelling out on the deck.

Someone had discovered the first guard's body.

Quickly, Dewey took the other explosive and peeled off the plastic covering the back. He reached out and stuck the device on the door.

A second later, a shrill alarm pierced the corridor. Bright red strobe lights started flashing, flooding the corridor with light.

Dewey walked back toward the entrance to the hallway, not too fast. He removed the four-quads and dropped them on the ground, then unzipped a pocket beneath his right armpit. He removed a second handgun – SIG P226. He spread his arms, training the gun in his left hand on the entrance to the hallway and the weapon in his right hand in the opposite direction – back down the hallway toward the two bedroom doors. The detonator was in his right hand along with the butt of the P226.

He heard footsteps on the staircase to his left just as the door at the end of the hall to his right opened and a large, bald man emerged, a pistol in his hand. He aimed at Dewey, even as Dewey held him in the firing line of the P226.

A second later, a frantic gunman entered the hallway, clutching a submachine gun and training it on Dewey. He was joined by a second man, who also held a submachine gun. The two men flanked the entrance to the hallway.

Dewey was hemmed in.

Dewey stood approximately halfway down the hallway, arms spread, one gun aimed at the Russian, the other at the gunmen.

"*Turn off the fucking alarm!*" barked the Russian.

A moment later, the hallway went silent. The red strobes continued to flash. No one moved.

"I'm not here for you," said Dewey turning and glancing at the oligarch. "I'm here for Flaherty."

"*Do you have any idea who the fuck I am—*"

"No, and I don't care," said Dewey. "I'm here for Flaherty. Tell your men to lower their guns."

"*Fuck you!*"

Dewey triggered both guns, one after the other, the one in his left hand twice. Three dull metallic thuds – *spit spit spit* – echoed in the corridor. Both gunmen at the head of the hallway were hit by bullets, the man on the right in the forehead, the other in the mouth, both falling backwards. In the same moment, the oligarch let out a pained grunt, the lone bullet fired in his direction striking him in the right shoulder. He dropped to the ground, his handgun falling from his grip.

Dewey checked to make sure the guards weren't moving, then glanced at the Russian.

"I didn't kill you," said Dewey, "and I won't kill you if you cooperate. Where's the key to Flaherty's room?"

The oligarch's face was beet red. He clutched his right shoulder. Blood seeped out over his fingers.

"What did he do?"

"He killed my wife. Now where's the key?"

Dewey heard the metallic friction from behind him – the slat action of someone chambering a round.

"Drop the gun," came a voice from behind him.

It was an American, a voice Dewey recognized. Dewey didn't know Flaherty's voice, but he knew this man's. A voice from his past. Nasally and vicious.

"I said drop it," the man repeated.

Dewey heard footsteps coming from behind him. Slowly, he turned his head. The man was thin, dressed in a silk bathrobe, glasses on. He held a handgun which was aimed at Dewey's back.

"Gant," said Dewey.

Josh Gant, the former deputy CIA director, a traitor who'd tried but failed to have Hector Calibrisi – and Dewey – murdered.

"Very good," said Gant. "Now drop the guns, both of them."

Dewey lowered both his arms and placed the weapons on the ground. The oligarch grabbed his own weapon from the ground with his left hand.

"Your timing is impeccable, Josh," said the Russian, who stood slowly up and aimed the gun at Dewey.

"With your permission, Constantin," said Gant, "I'd like to be the one to kill him."

Dewey watched the oligarch's face. He nodded, staring hatefully at Dewey as blood poured down from his shoulder.

"By all means," said the oligarch. "You just saved my life."

Dewey turned to face Gant. In his hand, Dewey still held the detonator and he cupped his hand, shielding it from view. Gant trained the gun on Dewey. Gant looked nervous. His eyes fixated on one of the submachine guns. A maniacal smile crept across his lips. He kept the pistol aimed at Dewey as he slowly knelt down and picked up the MP7. He left the handgun on the ground and slowly stood up.

Dewey knew Peter Flaherty had taken refuge in the employ of the oligarch, but Josh Gant was a surprise. Gant had once been the CIA's youngest deputy director in history. But like Flaherty, Gant had chosen a treacherous path, attempting to kill Hector Calibrisi, the Director of the CIA, and take over the agency. Dewey had traveled half-a-world away to hunt down Flaherty. Before tonight, he wouldn't have traveled a hundred yards to kill Gant – but now that he had the chance, well, why not?

"Any last words, Dewey?" said Gant as he aimed the submachine gun at Dewey's head.

"Yes," said Dewey, his eyes pivoting between Gant, the muzzle of the submachine gun, and the Russian behind him. "I want to apologize, Josh."

Gant laughed – a humorless cackle.

"For getting me removed from Langley?" said Gant angrily. "Exiled? Arrest warrants issued by twenty-seven different countries? Is that why you want to apologize to me, Dewey?"

"No," said Dewey. "For this."

He clenched his fist, depressing both buttons on the detonator – and the air was abruptly pulverized. The explosions ripped the air at both ends of the corridor in a fiery burst of dust and fire. The ground shook. The noise was deafening.

Gant was just a few feet from the device when the bomb behind him detonated. He was blown hard and sideways, the bomb eviscerating his legs, tearing one off at the knee along with part of his torso and arm. He flew into the wall and down. He screamed in agony, a blood-curdling cry.

Dewey picked up the Colt from the ground. He walked toward the end of the hallway. The Russian oligarch was face down against the wall, dead, part of his back cratered away by the explosion. Blood was everywhere. The door to the suite next to the oligarch's was off its hinges, kicked inward. Dewey came to the opening and waited a brief moment, then – with the weapon extended in front of him – entered, firing. A loud scream followed one of the shots. Dewey stopped firing. He saw Flaherty on the ground. His neck was bleeding badly. The bullet had struck him dead center in the larynx.

Dewey stepped over Flaherty, a leg on each side of him. He trained his gun on Flaherty's head. A light by the bed cast a low yellow hue in the room.

Flaherty struggled to breathe. Both of his hands clutched his throat, as if he could prevent what was happening.

"That was for killing my wife," said Dewey.

"I didn't kill her," he coughed. "Kyrie did."

"Anyone who had anything to do with that program killed her."

"We were taking orders."

"Oh," said Dewey. "I didn't know. In that case, let me get a doctor."

Dewey lowered the gun away from Flaherty's head, then triggered it. The bullet ripped into Flaherty's thigh. Flaherty's eyes went wide in the same moment he let out a horrific scream.

"You know, if you had just said I'm sorry I might've let you live," said Dewey. He fired again, sending a bullet into Flaherty's chest, killing him. "Actually, that's not true."

Dewey walked down the hallway, finding the P226 and sticking it back in one of the watertight pockets on the wetsuit. He came to Gant, who was on the ground, his eyes open, dead. Dewey triggered the gun once, twice, three times, three point blank shots in the center of Gant's chest.

He moved quickly down the hallway, charging down the stairs and through the kitchen and dining room. He found his fins on the swim platform and pulled them on, then put the other gun in one of the airtight pockets. He glanced one last time at the massive yacht then dived silently into the warm water.

3

PUNGGYE-RI, NORTH KOREA

The town of Punggye-ri spread out over more than fifty square miles. Despite its vast size, Punggye-ri had precisely zero inhabitants.

A long, winding dirt road cut through an area at Punggye-ri's eastern border. The land in this part of the town was barren and flat. What little vegetation there was consisted of a few patches of scragglylooking scrub brush. Because of this, the small building at the end of the winding dirt road could be seen – on a clear day – from miles away. This was no accident.

The building was the control tower.

It was a simple, windowless structure, constructed of corrugated steel. It stood ten and a half feet tall and had a flat roof, on top of which were several large antennae. Other than a small parking area, which was empty, the control tower was the only man-made object in any direction for several miles – at least, the only man-made object above ground. Exactly four-hundred feet from the control tower was a small mound of dirt that arose a few inches in the air. This mound of dirt marked what had been the opening to a tunnel that was now plugged with sand, gypsum, and gravel. The tunnel was 772 meters deep. About halfway down the tunnel, a lead-lined canister held diagnostic equipment.

At the bottom of the tunnel sat a thirteen-kiloton nuclear bomb.

The control tower was surrounded by four massive but shallow craters in the ground, each several hundred feet in diameter. The craters memorialized the locations of North Korea's four previous nuclear tests.

Six kilometers away stood another building. This was the surface control bunker. Like the control tower, it was off on its own, at the end of a dirt road. The surface control bunker was made of concrete and had three large windows that faced the control tower in the distance. Inside, there was one room – a large observation and management area filled with tables, computers, diagnostic equipment, and more than a dozen high-powered cameras. Several dozen people stood behind the window, each with a set of binoculars, watching the control tower in the distance.

Dr. Yung Phann-il, the man responsible for North Korea's nuclear weapons program, removed the binoculars from his eyes. He looked at a young engineer who was seated before a control screen. Phann-il nodded to the man.

"You have my permission to proceed," said Phann-il.

"Yes, sir," said the engineer.

The young man reached forward and lifted a small metal compartment. Beneath was a red switch. He waited one extra moment, glanced at a digital clock on the screen in front of him, then flipped the switch.

"Ground zero in five, four, three, two, one…"

Boom.

It was less of a sound than a bump beneath them, followed by a weak tremor that grew stronger and stronger. In the distance, the air near the control tower went dust-filled and wavy. Everything inside the bunker shook and rattled. After just more than twenty seconds, everything stopped.

The entire room full of scientists, engineers, and military officials looked at Phann-il. His face was as blank as stone – and then it flashed into a wide smile.

"*Success!*" he yelled… and the room broke into a chorus of cheers.

4

U.S. GEOLOGICAL SURVEY
RESTON, VIRGINIA

Less than ten seconds later, half-a-world away, Martha Cohen was taking a sip of coffee when she suddenly heard the soft, high-pitched sound of beeping coming from one of her computers. With her free hand, she hit her keyboard, entering into one of the applications she used to monitor geologic activity. Brown, an analyst at the U.S. Geological Survey in Reston, Virginia, stared at her screen as it flashed red. Earthquake. Another few keystrokes revealed a map. In seconds, Brown's view zoomed-in to a place she'd seen before, a place that, according to her equipment, had just had an earthquake. But like the previous four, Brown knew it wasn't an earthquake.

"Oh, no," she whispered.

She lunged for her phone and hit speed dial. There were a few clicks but no ring, then a stern female voice.

"Office of the National Security Advisor," came the voice.

"This is Dr. Martha Cohen at USGS. I need Mr. Brubaker immediately. This is an emergency priority."

"He'll ask—"

"North Korea just conducted another nuclear test," interrupted Brown. "It's early, but I assess between twenty and twenty-three kilotons."

"How long ago?"

"Less than a minute."

5

OVAL OFFICE
THE WHITE HOUSE
WASHINGTON, D.C.

An hour later, President J.P. Dellenbaugh sat behind his desk inside the Oval Office. The meeting had been going on for thirty minutes.

In addition to Dellenbaugh, there were ten people in the room. They included the President's National Security Advisor Josh Brubaker, Secretary of Defense Dale Arnold, Chairman of the Joint Chiefs of Staff Phil Tralies, NSA Director Piper Redgrave, Secretary of Energy Marshall Terry, Secretary of State Mila Mijailovic, and the Director of the Central Intelligence Agency, Hector Calibrisi. Several other White House staffers were also present.

Dellenbaugh had already spoken with the President of South Korea, the President of Japan, and the Premier of the People's Republic of China.

Dellenbaugh's sleeves were rolled up, his tie loosened. He was looking at Brubaker, who was briefing the group on the explosion.

"USGS has it at twenty point four kilotons," said Brubaker. "That's more than twice as powerful as North Korea's last test."

"What are they after?" said Dellenbaugh.

"Money," said Mijailovic, the Secretary of State. "They conduct a test whenever they're running low."

"It's more than that," said Brubaker. "Kim is insane," he added, referring to North Korea's leader, Kim Jong-un. "Analysis of Pyongang cash flows through various currency markets indicates nothing at a critical point. Yes, the country is destitute – but they have cash."

Dellenbaugh looked at Calibrisi.

"This has gone on far too long, Hector," said Dellenbaugh. "They have nuclear weapons. It's only a matter of time until they figure out how to build an ICBM." He looked at Brubaker. "Josh, if you're right, if Kim is motivated not by greed but by insanity, then God help us."

"So let's do some nuclear testing of our own," said King, the hot-headed Irish chief of staff. "We can start with downtown Pyongang."

Dellenbaugh cast a hard set of eyes on King. "That's not productive."

"It wasn't meant to be, sir. Until now, Kim Jong-un has been all talk. But no more. We can't allow that to happen. A pre-emptive strike has to be on the table."

"You heard the Chinese Premier," said the Secretary of Defense. "If we attack North Korea, Xi will consider it a declaration of war on China. Trust me, that's a war we don't want to fight right now. Attacking is not an option."

"*Everything* is an option," said Dellenbaugh brutally.

Brubaker looked at Calibrisi.

"Why the hell haven't you guys done anything?" seethed Brubaker.

"You think we haven't tried?" said Calibrisi. "We have three agents rotting away in North Korean prisons and seven dead. Read your briefs, Josh."

There was a long silence. It was Dellenbaugh who spoke. He looked at the Secretary of Defense.

"I want three military options," said Dellenbaugh. "I want one of them to include tactical nuclear weapons. Coordinate with the Secretary of State. Any military action will need to be heavily pre-empted in Beijing and Tokyo."

"And Moscow," said De La Garza, the Secretary of State.

Dellenbaugh looked at Calibrisi.

"You have a week, Hector."

"To do what?"

"I don't know," said Dellenbaugh. "Something that hurts. Something that gets us closer to stopping Kim."

6

MI6 HEADQUARTERS
THE RIVER HOUSE
LONDON

Jenna Hartford was leaning back in her chair. On her desk were several pieces of paper, laid out in a row. It was the details of an operation she had designed.

Different intelligence services are good at different things. MI6 was the world standard-bearer in terms of covert operation design.

A middle-aged woman named Veronica Smythson was MI6's director general of operations design, but it was Jenna who was the small department's star. In three years at MI6, she had risen on the strength of her bold, often theatrical operations. Jenna had designed the complicated, brilliant operation to kill Fao Bhang, head of Chinese Intelligence. She was also the chief architect of an operation to expose a pair of moles inside MI6 who'd been selling secrets to the Russian government.

The operation in front of her was a simpler affair. MI6 was attempting to recruit a Saudi attorney who acted as a courier between Hezbollah and ISIS. The agent handling the recruitment believed the Saudi was now having second thoughts. Jenna's operation was originally supposed to be a simple snatch-and-grab. It wasn't that simple after all. Jenna had spent the night before analyzing various electronic data surrounding the Saudi. She was convinced he'd long since abandoned the idea of running to England. He was escaping – and somehow knew MI6 was coming.

Despite spending all night designing the now somewhat complicated operation, Jenna wasn't reviewing it. Instead, she was reading, for the hundredth time, the forensic analysis of her husband's murder. Each time, the report made her heart ache as she thought of Charles in the very moment the bomb went off. It was as if she needed the pain to make her feel less guilty. Of all the professions she could have chosen, why did she choose intelligence work? And why had she let Charles borrow her car that morning? For six long months now, the questions kept occurring and re-occurring in her head as she thought about the sight of the flames and fire on the street below the window of their flat – and her husband incinerated within.

She studied the summary:

TOP SECRET
MI6 CODE
77.c.5Tx
WITH MI5 SPECIAL UNIT AFTER ACTION INVESTIGATION AND ANALYSIS:
CHELTENHAM BOMBING – 4-APRIL
[NOTE: INVESTIGATION IS ACTIVE]
SUMMARY: Until further evidence is developed, the preliminary conclusion of the committee to investigate the events of April 4 at Cheltenham Mews is inconclusive. The explosive used was SEMTEX. Analysis of residue implicates a Philippines manufacturer whose product is widely available throughout the world. Analysis of CCT video is also inconclusive. The investigation is, per order of DG Chalmers, to be kept active and focused on individual motives related to F6-2 Hartford, whose previous actions may have motivated the event.

–

Why me? she thought to herself as she stared at the top sheet. *Fucking, why?* She put her hand to her eyes and rubbed them, slowly shaking her head back and forth.

The door to Jenna's office suddenly opened. A young black man in a dark sweater put his head inside. It was her assistant, Jonas.

"Jenna, the briefing?" he said. He said it scoldingly, but with a tender smile on his face.

"Oh, yeah," she said. She glanced at the clock on her desk. She stood up, placing the file down.

She had on a pair of tan linen pants and a sleeveless Burberry blouse. Both were wrinkled. The blouse was untucked.

Jonas scanned her up and down and shook his head. He stepped inside and shut the door. He walked toward her.

"Your hair is a mess," he said. "Did you sleep here again?"

"No," she said, lying.

"You're a bad liar. You were wearing that same outfit yesterday. Where's your brush?"

"I don't have a fucking brush," she said, her British accent sharp and precise. "Who cares anyway?"

"I do," he said.

Jonas stood in front of Jenna and reached forward with both hands, running them through her hair from front to back several times, trying to straighten out her hair.

"There," he said.

He pulled his sweater off and handed it to her.

"Put this on. We're the same size. It's Paul and Shark. It's unisex."

"Oh, for fuck's sake," said Jenna. She pulled the sweater down over the blouse. It fit well.

"Brilliant," said Jonas. "Now get going."

Jenna started to walk to the door.

"Wait," he said. He reached to her desk and grabbed the operation design. "Might be a good idea to bring this."

Jenna took it from him and looked briefly in his eyes, saying nothing. She walked to the door and stepped out.

–

Inside the operations briefing room, half-a-dozen individuals were already seated, including her immediate supervisor, Smythson, and

Derek Chalmers, the head of MI6. When she stepped inside, the conversation stopped. Jenna said nothing. Instead, she took a seat at the end of the table and looked with a blank expression around the table. All eyes were on her.

"What?" she asked. "I'm sorry I'm late. I... I lost track of time."

Smythson stood up and walked around the table, coming up behind her. She reached forward and, without asking, took the operation briefing from Jenna. Standing behind her, she read it over. After a minute, she handed it back.

"Needlessly complicated," said Smythson. "This is an exfiltration. We have assets in-theater. We know he's going to be at the train station at sometime between twenty and twenty-two hundred. The car is positioned outside. Airport, flight to London. Frankly, we didn't even need an architect on this one."

Smythson dropped the paper down on the table.

Again, there was a period of quiet as all eyes went back to Jenna.

"Why was I asked to bloody well do it then?" said Jenna, staring hard at Smythson.

"Because it was a straightforward snatch-and-grab you could've penned in thirty minutes," said Smythson. "I was trying to be kind."

"Maybe I just don't know what I'm doing anymore," said Jenna.

"Oh, for Christ sake, have thicker skin, Jenna," said Smythson, sitting back down.

"Thick skin?" said Jenna.

"Yes. Don't take it so personally."

Jenna paused.

"Fine, I agree we should all have thick skin," said Jenna. "So I hope you won't take it the wrong way if I tell you you have no bloody fucking idea what you're talking about."

Smythson's eyes grew icy.

Chalmers cleared his throat.

"Veronica, Jenna—" he said.

"Let her finish," said Smythson, leaning back. "This should be good."

"If I had written the design as you instructed, the target would have escaped and we'd be out one courier, a man we've spent two years and millions of dollars recruiting," said Jenna.

"Oh, bullshit. How do you know?"

"Because I ordered up two years of *Echelons* on the man and I spent more than an hour poring through bloody cell taps and emails. Your courier won't be at the train station. He bought a plane ticket to Cairo. He's not going to be there! He lied to you. So if we want to take him, my operation is the only way to do it. He needs to be taken at lunch – today. Otherwise we can all forget it. He'll be gone."

Jenna paused and stared at Veronica.

"I know how thick your skin is, Veronica," Jenna said, "so don't be upset by the fact that your operation would have resulted in the loss of a key MI6 courier."

Smythson was silent, as was everyone else in the room. It was Chalmers who finally spoke up.

"Give us the room," he said, looking at Jenna.

Everyone stood up from their chairs and started to leave except for Chalmers, Smythson, and Jenna. Chalmers glanced at Smythson. "You too," he said.

Chalmers and Jenna were alone, at opposite ends of the long glass table. After several pregnant moments, Chalmers smiled.

"You pretty well put her in her place, didn't you?" said Chalmers.

"She deserved it."

"Does anybody deserve anything, really, when it comes right down to it?" said Chalmers.

"What do you want, Derek?" said Jenna.

"Did you know I was the one who recruited you?" said Chalmers.

"I thought it was Burrows."

Chalmers shook his head, no.

"There's a professor at the university," said Chalmers, "a man who occasionally marks a promising individual. Anyway, he'd spotted someone, Nicholas something or other. I took him to coffee. Afterwards, he was in the finals of the Student Union debating competition. There was a large crowd. I went into the back of the auditorium and took a seat to watch our man, Nicholas, in the debate. I figured he would destroy whoever he faced."

Jenna said nothing.

"Anyway, I watched a young, pretty brown-haired girl come out onto the stage. She didn't have any notes. She was a first year at Oxford. Nicholas what's his name was president of the student union. I think everyone expected him to stomp on this young girl."

"Woman," said Jenna, barely above a whisper.

Chalmers smiled.

"Woman," he agreed. "But you weren't having any of it, were you, Jenna Bradstreet Hartford?"

A small smile, the first in weeks, came to her lips.

"I've often wondered if I should have just left you alone," said Chalmers. "After all, you'd be an MP by now. A young Margaret Thatcher, but with beauty."

Jenna stared at Chalmers for several seconds.

"Are you firing me?" she asked.

Chalmers said nothing. He held her eyes in his gaze.

"No," he said, finally. "But I'm assigning you."

"What?" she barked. "Why? I'm the... well, let's be honest: I'm the bloody well fucking best at what I do."

"You're talented, Jenna, no question," said Chalmers. "But you need a different platform than what MI6 is willing to provide. A broader platform."

"What the hell does that mean?"

"I've spoken with Hector Calibrisi and Bill Polk," he said. "They're both familiar with your work. You'll join the Directorate of Operations. They need an architect, badly. Frankly, it's in MI6's interest for Langley to have someone with your skills there."

"And am I obligated to tell you everything? I'm not going to be a rat of yours inside the Central Intelligence Agency."

"I agree. You work for them and your loyalties are to America, and, hopefully, Britain always."

"What makes you think I would even consider going to the CIA?" Jenna yelled. "Fuck them. Americans? Fuck all, Derek."

"You'll go," said Chalmers, looking her in the eyes and picking up his water glass. He took a sip. "We've leased a flat for you in Kalorama. You'll be on triple pay. Two years. That should clear your head."

"And if I don't want to go?"

Chalmers grinned.

"Don't bullshit a bullshitter," he said. "I'm giving you a license to kill. At least show a modicum of appreciation, will you?"

7

TONGHAE SATELLITE LAUNCHING GROUND
MUSUDAN-RI
NORTH HAMGYONG PROVINCE
NORTH KOREA

A long line of vehicles moved quickly through the remote hills north of Chongjin, a desolate, impoverished city on the coast of North Korea. There were seven sedans and one black limousine in all. The vehicles were guarded by two extended-cab, dark green-colored troop carriers, one in front and the other in back. Each specialized vehicle was filled with half-a-dozen armed soldiers from the Special Guard Unit, an elite division of the Korean Peoples Army.

The limousine's windows were tinted dark. Small North Korean flags stuck up from the front and back corners of the vehicle.

The motorcade sped along the thin, pothole-strewn roads of the rural coast, the dark, white-capped waters of the Sea of Japan visible in the distance. The hills and valleys alongside the road intercut between empty land, covered in dirt and rocks and the occasional shrub or tree, and shacks, small huts and houses made of scrap metal, wood, or concrete.

Inside the limousine, North Korea's Supreme Leader, Kim Jong-un, lit a cigarette and took a deep puff as he looked out his window. It gave Kim no pleasure seeing the thin, emaciated figures milling about ramshackle homes without electricity and barely any food, staring at his limousine as it passed by. Yet, he also didn't feel at all guilty or responsible for the terrible conditions of his country. The truth is, he felt nothing at all.

Kim was dressed in a black suit with a black trench coat. His hair was short except on top, like a little tuft. He was morbidly obese and needed help getting out of the limousine. Kim had the body of a sixty year old, but the face of a child. He looked at the man seated across from him, Pak Yong-sik, the highest ranking officer in the Korean Peoples Army.

Suddenly, Kim's eyes shot to the window. A skeletal dog was traipsing along the road side, searching for food.

"Stop!" barked Kim.

The limousine came to a halt. Kim pushed a button, lowering the window. He took another puff as he stared at the dog. Kim had a smile on his chubby face, like a young child. The dog stopped moving, staring at Kim with a nervous mixture of curiosity and fear. The dog had gray and black fur, with patches of punk, bare skin in places. Kim flicked the cigarette out onto the road. He reached into his coat and pulled a handgun from the holster beneath his left armpit. He flipped the safety off, chambered a round, then swept the gun so that it was aimed at the dog. The dog stared back at Kim without moving. Slowly, he seemed to bow his head and then took a step closer to the limousine. Kim fired. The sound of unmuted gunfire was shocking and loud. The bullet missed.

"Dammit!" he yelled. "Lousy gun!"

The dog started to move away but Kim fired again, then a third time. A bullet struck the dog in the side, knocking him to the ground, where he spasmed and writhed in pain as a low series of yelps came from his mouth. Kim fired again, hitting the dog in the head. The dog went quiet and still.

Kim stared at the creature for a few seconds and turned to Yong-sik. He tossed the handgun at Yong-sik.

"Terrible pistol," he seethed. "See to it we no longer buy any by this manufacturer!"

"Yes," said Yong-sik.

Kim slapped the leather seat next to him.

"Go!" he barked to the driver.

A half-hour later, they came to a security fence. It was twelve-feet high and fringed with circular razor wire. Small red signs indicated that it was electrified. A guard station stood before a set of gates. Two soldiers emerged as the limousine approached. One of the soldiers, seeing the long limo, turned abruptly and charged inside. The gates started moving aside, opening for the motorcade just in time to let the vehicles pass through.

The two armed soldiers at the entrance hut stood and saluted as the vehicles passed through.

Just inside the gates, a black and white sign read:

Tonghae Satellite Launching Ground

The motorcade rumbled in through the gates, where the road turned wider and smoother, as if it had been recently paved. The steel fence ran in both directions for as far the eye could see, disappearing behind sloping hills in the distance.

Tonghae was one of two missile test launch facilities in North Korea. Tonghae was the oldest, originally constructed in 1981 and consisting of little more than a circular concrete launch pad. Sohae, North Korea's second missile test and launch facility, was located to the west and was larger and more modern – at least, until now. For Tonghae had just completed a substantial renovation, including the addition of a state-of-the-art launch pad, with a massive flame bucket beneath the pad, four-stage gantry tower and crane, rocket assembly building, and engine test stand.

Yet, even after the renovations and new construction, it was difficult to believe that the small collection of buildings, spread out over several hundred acres of barren land, was, in point of fact, a central flash point in a growing conflict that threatened to spark nuclear war. North Korea continued to stick its finger in the eye of Japan, South Korea, the United Nations, and, most importantly, the United States of America, by launching test missile after test missile into the China Sea, testing and re-testing, working to improve North Korea's ability to send a missile anywhere in the world.

North Korea already possessed nuclear weapons. One of the many ironies of the backwards country was that it was somehow able to manage the much more difficult technological achievement of nuclear fission and yet couldn't figure out how to fire a missile more than a few thousand kilometers.

But they were learning.

With each successive launch, the North Koreans were gaining knowledge as to what worked and what didn't. It was only a matter of time before the country possessed the ability to launch a missile that could strike anywhere in the world.

All Kim Jong-un cared about was being able to hit the United States.

Kim Jong-un's hatred for America started when he was just a young boy, traveling with his father to towns that remained half-destroyed by bombs that had been dropped almost half-a-century before by America. He recalled seeing his father cry on two different occasions, both times while visiting places his government could barely afford to feed, much less rebuild. His father, Kim Jong-il, had lived through the great war but, ironically, he was not embittered toward the United States or the South Koreans. Instead, the war gave the elder Kim a deeper sympathy for not only his people, but for his opponents as well. "To see war," he once told the young Kim, "is to know there are no winners." But Kim Jong-il only saw the reckoning the war left behind. A divided Korean Peninsula. An impoverished people without enough food to eat. Elderly farmers still scarred by napalm. Kim believed it was the guilt and sadness over not being able to provide for his country that killed his beloved papa. Through the distorted eyes of a child, Kim Jong-un developed the kind of pure hatred that only a child is capable of and never had reason to abandon it. Now, this hatred guided his every move.

The three vehicle motorcade came to a large rectangle of gray concrete, elevated into the sky by at least ten feet. This was the new missile launch pad. There were several stairwells leading up to the surface of the pad. Below the concrete, a hollowed-out area – the blast bucket – was designed to create an outlet for the heat and flames from the missiles as they initially ignited.

Standing on the launch pad were hundreds of uniformed soldiers. The soldiers stood in neat lines, as still as if they were statues, each man's right hand raised in a salute to Kim as the limousine approached.

In the middle of the gathering of soldiers, at the center of the launch pad, stood a shiny white missile that jutted seventy feet into the sky, clutched on two sides by the gantry tower.

The limousine came to a stop and Kim climbed out.

General Yong-sik emerged from the opposite side of the limo. He joined Kim at his side and walked toward the crowded launch platform. Kim and Yong-sik walked to one of the stairwells and climbed slowly up. It took Kim several minutes to climb the twenty or so steps. When he arrived at the top of the platform, his face was red, though a smile appeared. He stood and caught his breath, then raised his hand, saluting the soldiers who'd gathered for him.

A loud, cacophonous cheer suddenly came from the brigade of soldiers:

"Kim! Kim! Kim!"

One of the soldiers approached Kim and handed him a wireless microphone.

"Good morning, soldiers of the Korean Peoples Army," bellowed Kim. "Today, we launch the first test missile of the Taedongo-3! It is with the Taedongo-3 that North Korea will at long last be able to attack our mortal enemy, the United States of America!"

The soldiers began cheering. They shouted, "Long live Kim!" again and again as Kim handed the microphone back to one of the soldiers and turned to walk down the stairs, followed by Yong-sik.

"Long live Kim! Long live Kim! Long live Kim!"

Kim and Yong-sik climbed back inside the limousine, which moved slowly away from the launch pad and along a winding uphill road, passing several armed gunmen. The limousine stopped at a small, two-story glass and concrete building that sat atop the highest point of land for several miles. Kim and Yong-sik climbed out and walked to the building. This was the control tower, where all controls and communication for the missile launch were managed. An armed soldier opened the door for Kim and Yong-sik, who stepped inside.

The room looked like a control tower at an airport, with various work stations arrayed with radar screens, computers, and other devices. A large window covered the front wall and offered a panoramic view of the Tonghae facility. The launch pad was below them, down a steep hill. Soldiers were moving in lock step away from the launch pad. Beyond, the Sea of Japan appeared through a haze of thin fog and gray clouds.

Three individuals were inside the control tower. Two engineers sat at tables before a wall of controls, dials, and screens, wearing headsets. A third man was standing at the large window, looking down at the launch pad. He had on thick glasses, a white lab coat, and was speaking in a low voice to someone over his headset. He was holding a clipboard.

"Dr. Cojin," said Yong-sik.

The man turned. He suddenly caught the sight of Yong-sik and then Kim. After a surprised moment, he immediately dropped to his knees and bowed.

"Your excellency," said Dr. Cojin. "It is a tremendous honor to have you here today."

Kim removed a pack of cigarettes, pulled one out, and lit it.

"Are we ready, Cojin?" said Kim. "After almost one-hundred million dollars and three-and-a-half years, I trust the answer is yes."

Cojin stood up. He nodded.

"Yes, it is all ready, your excellency."

Kim took a deep puff, exhaling, filling the small control room with smoke.

"Yes, yes, get on with it. I don't have all day."

"If everything goes correctly, as it should," said Cojin, "I would like to introduce you to the individuals who made today's launch possible."

Kim dropped the cigarette onto the floor and stepped on it.

"The state is not a place of individual achievement," said Kim loudly. "We build weapons of glory not because we want to celebrate the men who built them, but because we want to advance the great cause of the North Korean people and to be able to strike the evil enemy, the United States of America!"

Cojin bowed.

"Yes, of course your excellency. Of course."

"Tell us about Tadondo-3," said Yong-sik.

Cojin pointed out the window to the launch platform. The final row of soldiers was moving down the steps and away from the platform.

"Taedondo-3 is a multiple-stage, solid-fueled hydro rocket, capable of reaching distances of up to 10,000 kilometers. Today, we launch Taedondo-3 with an expected flight path over the Sea of Japan. It will, if all goes according to plan, land in the Pacific Ocean approximately one-thousand miles from the coast of Mexico. It would represent the greatest length achieved in flight by a North Korean missile, your excellency."

Kim nodded and smiled. A moment of child-like glee hit his face. He clapped once.

"Excellent, Cojin!" said Kim. "Now let's do it, shall we?"

Dr. Cojin turned. He looked at one of the engineers seated at the control station.

"Kawau," said Colin. "Commence firing sequence."

Without turning around, the young engineer nodded and began typing.

"Commencing firing sequence," said Kawau.

A low, soft boom echoed from down the hill. Kim, Yong-sik, and Cojin stepped to the window and looked down at the launch platform. It appeared as if nothing had occurred, and then a few puffs of smoke ebbed out from the base of the missile. A louder explosion followed, then came a high-pitched sizzling noise, followed by a cacophonous boom and all hell broke loose. Flames and smoke shot out from the missile as it started to rise in the air. The gantry tower fell back and away as the missile slowly lifted into the air, a trail of smoke and orange flames behind it, the noise deafening. The missile climbed into the air, its velocity increasing with every passing second until, at some point, a massive boom again rocked the air and the missile's speed went from fast to super-sonic and it shot up into the sky.

Kim and Yong-sik started clapping, and Kim even yelled, hooray, as the missile climbed higher and higher in the sky…

…and then something went horribly wrong…

"Oh my God," groaned Cojin.

The missile abruptly exploded. Violent clouds of red and orange flames shot in every direction as the missile exploded. The sky was filled with flames and smoke and falling debris, chunks of missile caught in burning, fuel-soaked flames, raining down from the sky into the ocean in the distance.

Cojin stepped behind one of the engineers, leaning forward, trying to read the instruments, trying to understand what had happened.

Yong-sik looked at Kim, who stood motionless in front of the window. Finally, Kim met Yong-sik's stare. He had a dumbfounded, angry look on his face. Kim turned and walked past Dr. Cojin and the two engineers, almost stumbling in shock as he made his way to the door. When he reached the door he paused. He reached inside his coat to remove his gun from his shoulder holster, but it wasn't there. He looked at Yong-sik. Yong-sik unbuckled a holster at his waist and lifted his handgun and handed it to Kim. Kim raised the gun and aimed it at the young man on the right, whose back was to him. He fired, striking the man in the back of the head. Cojin and the other engineer turned. Kim fired at the other engineer. The bullet ripped into the young man's forehead.

Cojin held both of his arms up in resignation.

"I am sorry, your excellency—"

The third bullet struck Cojin in the chest, kicking him sideways and down to the ground.

Yong-sik stood at the window. He had a blank expression on his face. He stared at Kim as Kim watched Cojin fall to the ground. When Kim's eyes met Yong-sik's, they stared at each other for several moments. Kim moved his arm to the right and trained the gun on Yong-sik. His hand was shaking as he held him in the firing line. Finally, Kim lowered the gun.

"It's not your fault," said Kim. "But now we do it the way I said. You will call the Iranians and we'll do what we should've done years ago."

"Yes, my leader," said Yong-sik.

8

RYONGSONG RESIDENCE
NORTH KOREA

Yong-sik walked down the corridor. As always, he wore a khaki military uniform adorned with medals and other insignia. He had thick glasses and short-cropped black hair.

The hallway spread a hundred feet across. The ceiling was thirty feet high. Every surface was composed of rare crimson and white marble. Great tapestries hung along the walls, interspersed with massive paintings, each one a portrait of the same individual – a young, black-haired North Korean in various settings. One painting showed him atop a horse, sword raised high, surrounded by bodies on the ground. Another scene showed the man in the cockpit of a fighter jet, flames coming out the back, missiles just fired now soaring toward the ground where a small American flag is seen. Still another portrait showed the man performing surgery on a fallen soldier in the middle of a battlefield with mushroom clouds from nuclear explosions visible in the background.

This was the hallway that led to the official residence of North Korea's Supreme Leader, Kim Jong-un.

General Yong-sik arrived at the door to the suite of rooms. Two men in military uniforms, both of whom, technically, worked for the general, looked evenly at Yong-sik, scanning him from head to toe, Kalashnikovs trained on him at all times.

The guard on the left saluted and reached for the large mahogany door handle, pulling the door open for Yong-sik.

Yong-sik stepped into the private chambers of Kim Jong-un.

Yong-sik had been head of the Korean People's Army now for nearly two decades. This was considered miraculous in Pyongang's ruling hierarchy. Kim Jong-un, like his father, had no problem beheading aides and associates close to him on sheer whim. Yet Yong-sik had somehow survived. On several occasions, Yong-sik was convinced that Kim would have him killed. But it never happened. Kim Jong-un – like his father – found something comforting in Yong-sik's quietude and calm.

Yong-sik stepped inside the suite of rooms. It was a large, luxurious room of mirrors and large paintings, white leather couches, and gold-leafed walls, ceilings, and furniture. Music was playing. The air was cantilevered in smoke. Several half-naked women were positioned about, serving drinks, lighting cigarettes, or letting Kim and his similarly obese friends grab their asses.

Yong-sik had seen this before, of course. He was as emotionless as a brick wall as he walked up to Kim.

Kim was smoking a cigarette. A short, large breasted Chinese woman was sitting in his lap.

Yong-sik saluted.

"General," said Kim, waving his arm drunkily. "Won't you join us?"

"My Supreme Leader," said Yong-sik, bowing slightly. "It would be my honor except that as your appointed leader of the army, I feel it is not in my best interest to take enjoyment as long as I am in your trust."

Kim's smile turned into a sideways scowl.

"I asked you to have a drink with your Supreme Leader," said Kim, loud enough for everyone to hear.

Yong-sik bowed.

"My Supreme Leader, if it is your insistence, then of course I will have a drink with you," said Yong-sik.

Kim Jong-un smiled.

"That is why I love you, Pak," said Kim, waving to a servant. "You are sober-minded and yet your loyalty guides you."

A glass of champagne was handed to Yong-sik, who took a large, awkward sip.

"Might I have a word, my Supreme Commander?" said Yong-sik. Kim's smile disappeared.

"Of course," he said, shoving the woman from his lap.

"Perhaps in another room?" whispered Yong-sik, glancing at the small crowd gathered inside the spacious, luxurious room.

Kim did not want to rise from his perch. Yet Yong-sik's eyes told him it was important.

Yong-sik followed Kim to a room off the main living room. It was another massive room, one wall made completely of glass, looking out onto the few lights that dotted Pyongang, North Korea's largest city and yet a place where electricity was rationed. The ceiling was two stories tall. One wall was covered in bookshelves. The other with three massive oil paintings, one of Kim's grandfather, Kim il-Sung, another of his father, and the third of him.

A large, oval-shaped leather sofa sat in the middle of the room. The two men sat down.

"I leave for Macau in an hour, your excellency," said Yong-sik.

Kim nodded, suddenly remembering.

"Ah yes. To meet with the Iranian."

"Correct," said Yong-sik. "The exchange will take place tomorrow evening. I wanted to apprise you of this, my Supreme One, and to make sure you still want to do it."

Kim took a large swig of champagne, then reached to the table, where a silver tray was stacked high with cigarettes. He picked one up and lit it, took a large puff, then leaned back and exhaled, blowing the cloud of smoke in Yong-sik's direction.

"We know how to make highly-enriched uranium," said Kim, "but our missiles fall into the sea. Iran can send a missile anywhere but they have no highly-enriched uranium."

"Correct, my excellency."

"It is a good and fair trade. I want you to go and make the exchange. When you return, we will finally have the capability to strike at our enemies. North Korea will at long last be able to attack the United States of America."

9

CIA HEADQUARTERS
LANGLEY, VIRGINIA

The briefing was already underway when Jenna walked by Hector Calibrisi's glass-walled office. A group of people – ten in all – was gathered inside the CIA director's expansive corner office on the 7th floor of CIA headquarters. She passed by and was about to take a right and go to her office but stopped. She turned around and started walking toward Calibrisi's office.

Jenna had on a thin, brown cashmere turtleneck sweater which clung tightly to her frame. She had on a pair of white designer slacks which flared at the ankle, revealing stylish white flats. Her hair brushed the tops of her shoulders and was parted in the middle. Jenna's face was chiseled and pretty. She had brown eyes that were as mesmerizing as they were cold.

In her brief time at the CIA, Jenna had made a grand total of no friends. She kept to herself and her work. She was a mystery. She arrived early, usually before six A.M., and was working when most people left the building. Several people had tried to befriend her, asking her to join the group headed out for Friday night drinks. But she invariably said no. Calibrisi and Polk were the only ones who knew her story and they ignored questions about her, especially questions from male members of the agency's senior staff. Derek Chalmers had asked them both to shield her, at least for a time, and that's what they did. But as both men realized within a few days of Jenna's arrival, she didn't need their protection.

She reached the door and pushed gently in, then shut the door behind her. She found Calibrisi, who was staring at the screen. She looked for Bill Polk who turned and subtly acknowledged her entrance.

The briefing was about North Korea. It was an operation that had been in planning for more than a year. Its design pre-existed her arrival, though she had read the details of it.

Jenna caught Polk's eyes and pointed at herself, as if to ask, with her eyes, "Is it okay for me to be here?" Polk nodded yes, then smiled.

Two large photos cut across a plasma screen in the middle of Calibrisi's office. The briefing was just getting going.

"The man on your right is, as you all know, Kim Jong-un, supreme leader of North Korea."

The speaker was a man in his early thirties with curly blonde hair: Mack Perry, the head of Special Operations Group, the clandestine paramilitary arm of the CIA.

"The man on the left," continued Perry, "is General Pak Yong-sik, head of KPA. This operation is a designed strike on Yong-sik, an action we believe is warranted and will lead to increased instability within the inner corridors of Kim's regime."

Jenna unconsciously, but noticeably, coughed. Perry turned, as did Calibrisi. She held her hand up to her neck, indicating that she had simply coughed and that it had nothing to do with her opinion of the operation.

Perry hit the remote. The plasma shot to a view of a tall building on a crowded strip of buildings.

"Macau," said Perry. "Asia's Las Vegas. This hotel, the Mandarin, is where the operation will occur. We have ascertained that Yong-sik will be in Macau this weekend, staying at the hotel. A three-man team will penetrate his security cordon and kill him in his hotel suite. Weapons are sanitized. Special Activities Division will work reporters and tell them it was Kim who ordered the kill. We believe the effect will be extremely detrimental internally."

Jenna was shaking her head.

"Is something wrong?" asked Perry from across the room, staring daggers at Jenna.

Jenna looked at Perry.

"No, I'm sorry," she said in a soft, aristocratic British accent. "I wasn't meaning anything, I apologize. It's just—"

"It's just what?" said Perry.

"It's just that this operation is… well, it's bloody awful," Jenna said.

The entire office turned and looked at her. She caught Calibrisi. He was grinning as he looked at her.

Perry looked dumbfounded though not angry.

"What's awful about it?" he said. "I'm always open to suggestions."

"Where to start?" said Jenna in a British accent. "Let's see then. Tell me, what is your name?"

"Mack. We've met like, twenty times."

"Sorry," she said. "Tell me, Mack, what is your intended goal?"

"To harm North Korea."

"If that's your goal, it will not be achieved," said Jenna, commanding the room. "The loss of Yong-sik will simply result in someone else stepping into Yong-sik's position, and the status quo in North Korea will continue on. Kim has executed countless generals over the years and, while he does have a certain loyalty to Yong-sik, the fact is he won't care that he's dead. In fact, it will expose a key vulnerability to Kim, making him aware as to the extent of our knowledge of their movements outside North Korea, possibly preventing future foreign travel and thus further reducing our ability to potentially go after North Korea."

"I disagree," said Perry.

"Really?" said Jenna.

"I've been inside North Korea," said Perry. "I know the country."

"How many of his own generals has Kim killed in the past year?" said Jenna, staring at Perry.

"Six."

Jenna smiled.

"He's killed eight in all."

"Bullshit," said Perry. "I've read the intelligence—"

"He killed two more men last night," said Jenna, interrupting. "Wonsan Province."

"How do you know?"

"There was a red flag on BULLRUN last night," said Jenna, referring to an NSA program that produced intelligence based on cracking encryption of online communications and data. "It came out a little after midnight."

The room was silent. There were a few awkward coughs. Finally, Perry spoke up. After an initial few moments of being pissed off, he was now grinning.

"Okay," said Perry. "I'm tracking you, Jenna. I hear you. So let's discuss it."

"Isn't that what we're doing?"

"So what would you do?" said Perry.

Jenna remained composed, staring icily at Perry. She glanced at Calibrisi. She took a furtive look around the room.

"What is our goal, that is the goal of the Central Intelligence Agency and thereby the United States of America as it relates to North Korea?"

"Stability," said one man.

"De-nuclearization of the peninsula," said a woman across the table.

Jenna listened impassively.

"The goal of the west is the removal of Kim Jong-un," she said emphatically. "De-stabilization should only be pursued in that context. Killing the general brings the U.S. no closer to removing Kim and in fact pushes that possibility further away. Additionally, it would be futile and likely cost us several lives. The general's traveling security regime is well-trained and deadly. My apologies, but there are few Langley agents who can both gain entrance to the Mandarin and then dispatch a scale kill team. In fact, there's only one. Though I've never met him."

"Who are you talking about?" said a man on the far side of the office.

"Dewey Andreas. I designed an operation he worked in Beijing."

"So what would you do, if you don't mind my asking," said Perry.

"Start with the fact that a wasted operation is a hated thing at all intelligence services," said Jenna. "There is a decent hook into the operation. Whomever tracked down the Macau track should be complimented. So let's start with that, shall we?"

She walked into the middle of the room and eyed the analyst who was managing the photos.

"Can you bring back Yong-sik?" she said.

A moment later, the face shot of Yong-sik filled the screen.

"Yong-sik is on his way to Macau," she continued. "Rather than kill him, permanently sidelining him, why don't we utilize him?"

"How?" said Polk. "It would have to be without his knowledge."

Jenna looked thoughtful, staring at Yong-sik's photo.

"We poison him," she said. "A neural toxin, slow-acting, doesn't kill him for a day or two. We somehow embed the antidote in Pyongang. We poison Yong-sik in Macau and ask him for something, for example, real time SOQ on their nuclear program. Give us the details of the North Korean nuclear weapons program and we'll tell you where the antidote is. We poison him in Macau and plant the antidote in Pyongang. That way he can give us the information and we can direct him to the antidote."

"Why does it need to be in Pyongang?" said Perry.

"If he doesn't believe he has a chance to live he won't give us the information."

"How the hell do we get an antidote inside Pyongang?" asked Polk.

Jenna looked at Calibrisi.

"River House has an asset there," she said, referring to MI6. "Hector, you would need to make the ask. From what I know, he's quite reliable. Whatever poison is used needs to be a one-off, something customized, otherwise they'll draw his blood and be able to antidote him before he sends the plans."

Calibrisi stood up.

"So we utilize the general to send us the nuclear plans," said Calibrisi. He looked without emotion at Jenna. "And how does that get us any closer to getting rid of Kim?"

She stared back at Calibrisi. After a moment, she shrugged innocently.

"We'll know his capability set, his strengths, his vulnerabilities," Jenna said. "When he's lying, when he's not. We'll know if he's bluffing and if he's not. I assume we'd rather not start a nuclear war based on a bluff? On the other hand, if he's not bluffing, we'll have a peremptory window. If we must remove him – in the nuclear sense – we'll know when and where to strike."

"I like it a lot," said Perry, grinning at Jenna. "It's a dramatic improvement."

"When does Yong-sik land?" said Calibrisi.

"Sometime in the next forty-eight hours," said Perry. "We won't know until his plane leaves Pyongang."

Jenna turned and went to the door. She felt her heart racing. She felt so completely alien. She put her hand to the door just as she heard her name.

"Jenna," said Calibrisi. "You and Mack design it. We reconvene in two hours."

–

Jenna stormed from the office, more mad at herself than anything. Why did she need to come in and immediately make everyone hate her? She knew her style and her opinions were an acquired taste. Derek and Veronica had understood her foibles and bitchy nature, the way a family member does. But now she was alone and no one knew her. She sat away from her desk, away from the glass wall which let people in the hallway look in.

A knock came to the door. She turned. It was Mack Perry.

"Hey, mind if I come in?"

"Fine."

Perry stepped inside her office.

"I just wanted to say, first of all, I appreciate you interrupting and fixing that," said Perry. "I think I gave you an angry look."

"You didn't, don't worry about it."

"I mean, you did show me up but then I was thinking, you're supposed to do that. What I mean is, I don't care if you do that, as long as it's making things better, which it is. The people around here who end up becoming terrible are the ones who have an ego about being right or wrong. Anyway, sorry about that look."

Jenna had a blank expression on her face. She allowed a small smile to hit her lips.

"It's fine, Mack," she said in a soft British accent.

"Can I say something else?"

Jenna nodded yes, her arms crossed guardedly.

"I know what happened and I'm very sorry about that," said Perry. "I'm not sure what to say. I'm glad you're here. Everyone is. Even if you did ruin what was a great operation."

Jenna laughed.

"Thanks," she said.

"Want to get started?"

"Sure," said Jenna. She leaned forward. "We'll need your top chemist."

"Dave Morris," said Perry. "I'll get him up here."

10

GEORGETOWN
WASHINGTON, D.C.

The motorcycle – a red and blue Suzuki *Hayabusa* – followed a meandering, leisurely course as the dull orange of dawn colored the Washington sky. The rider was a large man, his face was hidden by a black helmet and by visor glass tinted dark. He took the bike through Georgetown and Woodley Park, keeping the powerful bike in check, its low thunder barely interrupting the quietude of a Sunday morning in the nation's capital. It was five A.M.

The motorcycle rumbled along at a calm speed, its 1340cc, four-stroke, DOHC, 4-cylinder, 16-valve engine sounding like the dark clouds on the proverbial horizon, coughing and punching the air as the storm approached. The *Hayabusa* was one of the fastest production motorcycles in the world, and its rider, a big man in cut-off shorts, running shoes, and a blue T-shirt, trotted it slowly along Woodley Park's residential streets, like a cowboy atop a stallion just before the run.

It was early spring and flowers were blooming everywhere.

He passed the Omni Shoreham Hotel and put on his signal before the entrance to Rock Creek Parkway, even though there were no other cars or vehicles on the road. He cruised slowly downhill into the curving entrance to Rock Creek Parkway, glancing left, seeing no one. He entered Rock Creek Parkway and headed north, clutching and shifting as his hands worked the throttle, his leg kicked, and the *Hayabusa*'s low, impatient thunder turned into a throaty, angry roar. With every shift, the engine went high to low, then came more acceleration, more speed, until he needed to shift again, and it repeated itself, the scream of the engine echoing through the forests and canyons that bracketed both sides of Rock Creek Parkway. He kept pushing the bike harder and harder and harder, shifting and gunning it until there was no place else to go, until there was nothing more the superbike could give him.

He glanced down at the digital speedometer. In glowing blue light, he registered his speed at that moment: 172.6 MPH.

The driver took the Suzuki up the two-lane parkway with ferocious speed, slowing ever so slightly whenever the road curved, regrouping, then ripping like all hell again. The wind was like a wall against the overwhelming force of the motorcycle. The man clearly possessed advanced riding skills. He was also confident, even reckless, some would say insane, though had someone been able to read his thoughts, all they would've discovered would be an eerie calm – for the speed, the challenge of the road, the knowledge that the slightest mistake would kill him.

It was the fifth day since Dewey had returned from Tunisia. It was the fifth day he'd awoken early and climbed onto the motorcycle. In five days, Dewey had yet to see a policeman. He'd only seen a handful of cars, each time slowing and passing at a reasonable speed, before quickly opening the machine back up.

The parkway led out of Washington, D.C. into Maryland, eventually stopping in Chevy Chase. Dewey brought the bike to a stop where the road dead ended at Western Avenue, pausing to catch his breath and glancing at his watch. It was 5:30.

As he'd done the previous five mornings in a row, Dewey drove north into Maryland. The roads were beginning to fill with traffic and he kept the bike within the speed limit, moving on side roads through Silver Spring, Kensington, Rockville, North Potomac – heading west on winding roads, passing through suburban neighborhoods, with houses that grew bigger, with larger lots and land, making his way into the Maryland countryside as the morning sun warmed his back and the wind brought the familiar smells of country – fresh-cut grass, manure, wheat and pine.

On a hill overlooking a sweeping field of green, he pulled over and stopped the motorcycle. He turned the engine off and put down the kick-stand.

In the distance, down a long driveway lined with white horse fence, he saw a rambling farmhouse and, behind it, a big barn.

Dewey felt his adrenaline spiking as he stared at the house in the far distance. The barn reminded him of the farm he'd grown up on in Castine, Maine. But the land surrounding the farm was altogether different. In every direction, fields of low green grass spread in lumpy, lush hills, interrupted here and there by trees – a massive Oak, a stand of Birch, a gorgeous geometric line of Elms. It was an exquisite piece of land.

It was the same ritual now for five days in a row, and each day Dewey felt his heart beat faster. He'd just flirted with death on the Rock Creek Parkway and yet it was not until now, sitting in silence, staring at the farmhouse, that he felt adrenaline and anxiety.

Anger.

Hatred.

Dewey had killed Charles Bruner with his own gun and yet he still wasn't satisfied. He killed Flaherty and Kyrie. Yet he still felt the rage. He wanted revenge a hundred more times, a thousand more times. Above all, he wanted his wife back.

It had been Bruner who ordered her murder – and killing him had done nothing to quell the fever that burned inside Dewey's heart.

Finally, he started the motorcycle back up and kicked-up the kickstand. His hands were shaking as he fought the voice inside his head.

Do it. No one is innocent.

He started to drive away, as he had done five days in a row now, as the voice inside his head grew louder and stronger.

Do it. You'll never be free until you do.

Dewey suddenly turned the bike in a 180-degree turn. He drove back toward the driveway to Bruner's farm and cut in, entering the property of the man who killed his wife.

After Dewey stopped Bruner, the entire conspiracy had been laid out. Bruner and Flaherty had created a secret cabal inside the

U.S. Government, killing the Speaker of the House and then the Vice President. They'd come within moments – inches – of killing President J.P. Dellenbaugh. Had they succeeded, the cabal would have been in control of the White House. They would've had control over the most powerful nation on earth. In the days following Bruner's death, there was an unprecedented round-up of the conspirators. Most had been caught and now awaited trial for high treason. Several members of the cabal, including Harry Black, the U.S. Secretary of Defense, had committed suicide rather than face the public disgrace, humiliation, and punishment for their misdeeds. A handful had fled and were actively being hunted down by the FBI or CIA, with support from NSA.

Flaherty was dead.

Bruner's wife had been brought in and interrogated for more than two weeks. Dewey had forced himself to watch video from the interrogations. The woman had known about almost everything – the assassinations, the plan to seize power, the massive nuclear strike Bruner had planned for the Middle East. But she had not known about the only thing Dewey cared about, the cabal's early years, when recruits inside Delta and Navy SEALs were identified and, if married, their spouses killed, the murders made to look like suicides. She claimed not to know. At Dewey's insistence, they had even tried pharmaceuticals on her, using an advanced complex of drugs to enhance her ability to speak freely and honestly. But her story had not changed. She didn't know her husband had ordered Holly's death.

Ultimately, Dellenbaugh had made the decision not to prosecute Molly Bruner. She was 77-years old and in frail health already, having survived two bouts of cancer. No one had objected, not the Attorney General nor Calibrisi. They'd cut a deal with her lawyers. Molly Bruner could never leave her farm again in exchange for a plea of no contest. She was allowed one visitor a week, such as a cleaning person, someone to cut the lawn, someone to bring her groceries, or a doctor. She was not allowed use of any form of external communication, including regular mail, nor was she allowed to watch television. She'd been exiled within her own world.

Dewey didn't disagree with the decision, at least not at the time. Even now, he didn't care if she was locked up or free, if she was innocent or guilty. She'd been there. That's all that mattered. She'd lived with the monster who killed his wife.

Maybe it wasn't even about her. Maybe the reason he was now moving at twenty MPH up the long gravel driveway had nothing to do with her and everything to do with Charles Bruner. After all, he'd killed Dewey's wife. Why shouldn't Dewey kill Bruner's? Bruner might not be alive for Dewey to enjoy the feeling of vengeance, but did that matter? Or was he doing it not to spite Bruner, but rather for himself – to try to redeem at least some small part of the guilt that now inhabited his every moment, guilt for being the one who caused Holly's death?

All of these thoughts swirled through his head as he moved slowly along the driveway. Finally, he came to the circle that marked the driveway's end.

Dewey turned off the motorcycle and put the kickstand down, then removed his helmet and climbed off. Behind the seat was a small glovebox. He opened it and removed a pair of thin leather gloves and pulled them on. Beneath the gloves was a gun: Glock G35, sanitized, untraceable, never used, loaded.

Dewey chambered a round and then stepped toward the front door. Without knocking, he opened the door and stepped inside, clutching the pistol in his right hand and training it on the floor.

The entrance hallway was littered with piles of clothing and several trash bags. A foul odor occupied the house. Dewey maneuvered through the piles of trash and clothing and entered the kitchen. The sink and counters were crowded with dirty dishes. The kitchen table also held piles of clothing as well as half-eaten plates of food and dozens of dirty coffee cups and half-filled glasses.

The smell of burning coffee stung his nostrils and he moved to the coffee maker, where a nearly empty glass carafe sat burning on the warmer. He turned the appliance off and looked around the kitchen. The walls held several photos of Bruner and his wife, along with Bruner alongside a succession of dogs. One wall displayed older photos, each one of their young daughter, who'd been killed by a suicide bomber at age nine in Madrid. He stepped closer to the photos and looked at the girl. She had short blonde hair and wore glasses. Her smile was warm, even infectious. Dewey forced himself to look away. He passed through the kitchen and entered a long hallway, following it until he came to a door. He could smell the wood of a fire burning. He leaned toward the door and could hear the faint crackle of the fire. He took the door latch in his left hand and gently lifted it up, then pushed the door in as, in the same instant, he raised the weapon and stepped into the room.

It was a large room, filled with bookshelves and over-stuffed chairs. A big brown and white St. Bernard was asleep on the ground just inside the door. Dewey's eyes moved to the fire – and then to the corner of the room, blocked by a table. A large pile of blankets. His eyes met the eyes of a woman. She was seated in the corner, pressed back against the wall, everything but her head covered in blankets. Her hair was light gray and long, tangled and messed up. Her face looked haunted, her skin a pale gray, with dark bags beneath her eyes. Dewey stepped slowly across the room, the pistol in his right hand, aimed at the woman. He said nothing as he moved closer and closer. He came to the corner and was now in front of her. He held the gun so that the muzzle pointed between her eyes. He felt the polymer trigger beneath his index finger.

She stared up at Dewey with a confused, pitiful expression, though she was not scared.

"Are you from the government?" she whispered.

Dewey said nothing. He stared at her for several quiet moments.

"I thought you'd be coming someday."

He could see his right hand tremoring ever so slightly as he gripped the handgun.

"I told them everything," she said. "It's okay. You can do it if you want to. I have nothing left. I've been dead for so long now I can't remember when I died."

Dewey continued to say nothing, to look into her eyes, as if searching for something, some sign of guilt, some connection to the man who killed his wife, some connection to Holly. But there was nothing. Only a dull, bloodshot gray, dotted with cloudy, cataract white.

"Just… please. Please will you take care of him?" she whispered.

Dewey turned and looked at the dog, still asleep on the oriental rug. His furry head was tucked between his paws. His tongue was hanging out. Slowly, he turned back to Molly Bruner. He nodded, as if to say, yes.

"Even a call to the ASPCA. They'll find him a good home. His name is Wrigley."

"Stop talking," said Dewey.

He felt the trigger harder in his hand now, clenching it tighter. He wanted to pull it; needed to pull it.

She nodded meekly, as if to say yes.

"He killed my wife," said Dewey.

She kept her eyes focused on his, looking back up into his eyes in the moments after his words. Then, she shut her eyes for several seconds, tilting her head down. When she opened them again, she was staring at the blanket. Her forehead, brow, eyes, and cheeks all crinkled up into a wince, as if in pain. She let out a quiet sob and tears appeared on her cheeks.

She didn't say anything.

Dewey wanted to say more. He wanted to scream as he imagined what Holly went through.

They stuck a gun in her mouth and pulled the trigger. She was twenty-eight years old!

He wanted to step forward and put the gun in Bruner's wife – stick it in her mouth and fire. Blow her brains across the bookshelves. Do what they'd done to her…

But he couldn't. Instead, Dewey lowered the gun to his side. He looked at her for one more moment. She'd shut her eyes again and seemed to be swaying back and forth. He watched her for one last second – then he turned and left.

–

When Dewey arrived at CIA headquarters, he was still dressed in shorts and a T-shirt. He'd forgotten his ID but the security guards outside the main gates knew him and let him in.

Once inside the building, Dewey went through two more security check points, both of which used iris scanners to confirm his identity.

He took the elevator to the seventh floor and walked to the entrance to the suite of offices reserved for the Director of the CIA, Hector Calibrisi, and key members of his senior staff. Two armed, uniformed agents stood outside the locked, bulletproof glass doors. They recognized Dewey as he approached and let him in.

He continued down the hallway. The director's suite of offices was shaped like a horseshoe, with glass-walled offices on the external sides of the suite and a bullpen of work stations in the middle. Dewey came to the corner, where Calibrisi's office was located. As he approached, Calibrisi's assistant, Lindsay, stood up. A large smile was on her face. She stepped around the wall of her work station and approached Dewey, giving him a hug.

"Hi, Dewey," she said.

"Hi, Lindsay."

"I haven't seen you in a while."

Dewey nodded, but didn't say anything. He glanced inside Calibrisi's office. Calibrisi was seated on one of the leather sofas in the office. A woman, whose back faced Dewey, was seated across from Calibrisi.

"You look tan," said Lindsay. "Where were you?"

"I took a little vacation," said Dewey. He nodded toward Calibrisi's office. "How long's he going to be?"

Lindsay shrugged.

"Hard to say. He's with Governor Brown from New York. You didn't hear it from me, but the president is thinking of asking her to serve as vice president."

"Why's Hector meeting with her?"

"She asked for the meeting," said Lindsay. "She's one of the ones who says he's too old to be running the CIA, so maybe she's trying to schmooze him before she sticks a knife in his back."

"Okay. I guess I'll wait."

"Would like a cup of coffee? Water?"

"Sure," said Dewey, "but I'll get it."

Dewey went back to the suite entrance, took a left, and continued until he came to the kitchen. He went inside and poured a cup of coffee. He walked back along the opposite wall of offices to the end, took a left, and came to Lindsay's work station. Calibrisi made eye contact with him as he passed. There was an empty chair at the work station next to Lindsay's and Dewey sat down. Lindsay was on a phone call, a thin wireless headset over her head. She looked at Dewey, rolling her eyes. When she finished, she removed the headset.

"Members of Congress," she sighed. "They're like mosquitoes."

Dewey laughed. He took a sip of coffee and recoiled. It tasted old and sour.

"It's terrible coffee, I know," she said.

"I've tasted worse," said Dewey. "So, how are things going around here?" he added, trying to make conversation.

"Not bad," she said. "I mean, not great either. Ever since the attempted assassination, it feels like a twenty-four hour inquisition around here. Some people think we're to blame. Langley should've seen it, that sort of thing. She," said Lindsay, nodding toward Governor Brown, "is leading the inquisition. She says the president should clean house here and at the FBI."

"Why did Dellenbaugh choose her?"

"The House and Senate have to approve the president's nominee. She's the only one that'll survive a vote up there. That's why Dellenbaugh chose her."

Dewey took another sip. It still tasted like crap but it went down easier this time.

There was movement inside Calibrisi's office. Governor Brown stood up, along with Calibrisi. When the door opened, the governor of New York, Judy Brown, stepped out into the hallway in front of Lindsay and Dewey. Brown was dressed in a dark Navy pant suit. She was short and thin, with a pretty face. She had long, straight brown hair combed neatly back. She smiled at Lindsay, then registered Dewey, taking in his shorts, T-shirt, messed-up hair, and overgrown beard and mustache.

Calibrisi came out of his office and stood by Brown's side, grinning ever so slightly at Dewey.

"Hi," said Brown, reaching her hand out toward Dewey. "I'm Judy Brown."

"Hi," said Dewey, standing up. He towered over her. He leaned forward and shook her hand.

Brown looked back at Lindsay.

"Thank you, Lindsay," said Brown.

"You're welcome, Governor Brown."

After Brown had left, Calibrisi nodded to Dewey, telling him to follow him into his office.

Inside, they sat down across from each other on the sofas.

"Welcome back," said Calibrisi.

Dewey had an emotionless expression on his face.

"You're pissed because I sent a team over?"

Dewey shook his head.

"No," he said.

"That was quite a job you did on Flaherty and Gant."

Dewey nodded.

"The Russian you killed is Putin's brother-in-law," said Calibrisi.

"I didn't know."

"Everything's alright," said Calibrisi. "I had Bill clean it up. We sent in SEAL Team Four. They ripped out the GPS and took the yacht and sank it thirty miles offshore."

"I left it clean."

"I'm sure you did, but the last thing we need – the last thing you need – is another enemy."

Dewey stared at Calibrisi. After several moments, he spoke:

"I'm done," said Dewey.

Calibrisi sat back, nodding slowly.

"Done?"

"Yeah. I'm resigning."

"Okay," said Calibrisi. "You mind if I ask why?"

"I don't mind," said Dewey. "But I don't really feel like explaining."

"I need you to," said Calibrisi. "NOCs don't just walk away. It's not that simple. So either you explain it to me or you explain it to someone else."

"I want a family," said Dewey. "I want another child. I want to teach him about football and hockey. Or, if he's a she, I don't know, I'll teach her hockey but maybe not football. Hell, I'll teach her whatever she wants."

Dewey's eyes were red and sad, though he fought to keep his emotions in check.

"I liked Australia," said Dewey, barely above a whisper. "Working outdoors."

Calibrisi started to say something and then stopped. He bit his lip, trying not to utter something he would regret. If there was anyone who knew what Dewey had been through, it was Calibrisi, and beyond his duties as CIA director, a more powerful force ran through him. He loved Dewey like a son, the son he'd never had.

"How soon?" said Calibrisi.

"Today. Right now."

Calibrisi nodded. He was calm, quiet, and deep in thought.

"I have a few things to pack up downstairs," said Dewey, referring to the large subterranean training and practice facility several floors below ground that housed the Directorate of Operations, which included Special Operations Group.

"I'll have Lindsay process the release," said Calibrisi, a sad look on his face. "Give her a few minutes. I'll be in a briefing in one of the theaters. Bring it in and I'll sign it. Bill will want to say goodbye, too."

Dewey nodded. He stood up and walked to the door.

"Oh, by the way, that's yours," said Calibrisi, pointing at a package on his desk that was wrapped in red wrapping paper. "It's from the president."

Dewey walked to Calibrisi's desk. He removed the wrapping paper. Inside was a shiny, polished wooden box. A brass plaque on the top was engraved with the words:

To Dewey, my friend. Thank you for your bravery.

– President J.P. Dellenbaugh

The president's signature was also engraved.

"He's already given you the Medal of Freedom," said Calibrisi. "I think he wanted to give you something to say thanks."

Dewey opened the box. Inside was a pistol. It had an ivory handle and a patina of wear, though it was beautiful. It was an old 1911.

Suddenly, there was a knock at Calibrisi's door. Dewey turned. It was Lindsay.

"Excuse me," she said. "Hector, the briefing is on hold until you get there. They're waiting for you to start."

"Tell them I'll be right down," said Calibrisi.

Dewey ran a finger over the gun. In small block letters on the side, it read:

COL. D MACARTHUR 1917

"It was MacArthur's second service pistol," said Calibrisi. "He carried it until he died. It was at the Smithsonian. He needed to, ah, pull a few strings to get it."

Dewey picked it up and held it, admiring it. He put it back in the box and shut it, then picked up the box. He looked at Calibrisi.

"Thank him for me, will you?"

A knock came at the office door. Unlike Calibrisi's corner office, the door to this room was solid wood, ensuring privacy. Calibrisi stepped to the door and opened it. It was Jenna.

"Sorry to disturb you," she said. "It's important."

"Come in."

Jenna stepped inside the office. Calibrisi shut the door behind her. She looked at Dewey for a silent moment, but said nothing.

"Jenna, this is Dewey Andreas," said Calibrisi.

"Hi," she said.

Dewey nodded, but said nothing.

"What is it?" said Calibrisi.

Jenna glanced at Dewey.

"We've completed the design of the operation," said Jenna. "As I said earlier, the asset in Pyongang is a River House play. The request needs to come from you."

"Why me?"

"Derek will say no to me," said Jenna.

"What do we need specifically?"

"He's a reporter," said Jenna, "His name is Talmadge."

"Will he be exposed?"

"I don't know," said Jenna. "He's the intermediary. We need him to plant the antidote. I selected a busy place, a public place, a museum that sees thousands of visitors, but it's no secret Pyongang has cameras everywhere. He might get burned."

"Over here, burned means the asset doesn't survive," said Calibrisi.

"It means the same thing in London," said Jenna. "There's no other way."

Calibrisi stared for several moments at her.

"Fine. Is the briefing ready?"

"Yes. Josh Brubaker is already there."

"I'll call Derek right now."

Jenna reached for the door. She turned and looked at Dewey, whose back was turned. He was looking out the window. "Nice to meet you, Dewey."

Dewey turned his head.

"You, too."

After Jenna left, Dewey looked at Calibrisi.

"Who is she?"

"Jenna Hartford. She's an architect, on loan from England. Six months ago, her husband was killed by a car bomb intended for her. Derek asked if we'd bring her in."

Dewey nodded.

"North Korea?" Dewey said.

Calibrisi looked at Dewey but remained quiet.

"What's the operation?"

"What does it matter?" he said. "You're leaving."

Dewey grinned.

"Thanks for reminding me."

"The mission briefing is about to start," said Calibrisi. "After you pack up, feel free to come and listen. I'll sign your release in there."

11

CIA

Calibrisi walked back to his office, catching Lindsay's attention as he pushed the door in.

"I need Derek Chalmers," he said.

Lindsay nodded and put her headset on.

Calibrisi went inside his office. He remained standing, glancing at his watch.

Dewey's decision didn't surprise him. Nothing involving Dewey surprised him anymore. He couldn't exactly blame him.

A month ago, Calibrisi had dispatched Dewey to Paris in order to accompany the Secretary of State on a secret diplomatic trip. Calibrisi had sent him because he thought it would be a peaceful, straightforward three-day trip to Paris. At the time, Dewey was recovering from a knife wound to his chest, inflicted by an ISIS terrorist during a vicious fight on the top floor of a dormitory at Columbia University. Dewey and his team had stopped an entire cell of terrorists that bloody day at Columbia and the trip to Paris was meant to reward him. But Paris had gone haywire. The Secretary of State was shot in cold blood in his hotel suite and French authorities put the blame on Dewey, locking him up in a Paris terror intake unit, interrogating him. It was Dewey who tracked down the real culprit. It was Dewey who exposed a plot to assassinate the president and take over the government.

A few weeks after almost dying from a knife wound, Dewey had yet again very nearly died escaping from the French prison and hunting down the cabal behind the plot to overthrow the American government.

The feeling Calibrisi had as he waited for Lindsay to find Derek Chalmers was a mixture of guilt and deep anxiety. He felt guilty for nearly getting Dewey killed, and yet he felt an even more powerful sense of dread at the thought that the best operator he'd ever seen was about to hang it all up and ride off into the sunset.

America needed Dewey – but Dewey needed to find something he'd lost a long time ago. Dewey needed to find a sense of peace and normalcy. Family, perhaps even love. Above all, Dewey was tired of being shot at, having knives thrown at him, and running. To the outside world, Dewey seemed invincible. His actions had earned him the country's highest military and intelligence awards and his after-action reports were taught to all Tier One operators both inside U.S. intelligence as well as Special Forces. But Calibrisi knew Dewey wasn't invincible, far from it. His first wife had been murdered, and the woman who would've been his second wife had been shot with a bullet intended for him. Jessica had died in Dewey's arms, and the truth is, Dewey had never been the same since. He seemed older and sadder, a tragic figure whose unique skills as a paramilitary operator masked an individual who only wanted to be left alone.

Calibrisi looked at a photo on his desk of Dewey and Jessica. He probably should've put it away by now but he couldn't bring himself to. Jessica was on Dewey's shoulders, a big smile on her beautiful Irish face. Dewey was also smiling. They were so happy that day.

Let him go, Calibrisi thought to himself.

He reached to the photo and with a trembling hand picked it up. He opened a desk drawer and put the frame inside, then shut the drawer, steeling himself for that terrible moment when time has passed, when events have overtaken memories and the only way to keep going is to move on and close off what was.

A moment later, the phone on his desk buzzed and the intercom came alive.

"Derek Chalmers on three," said Lindsay.

Calibrisi picked up the phone.

"Hi, Derek," said Calibrisi.

"To what do I owe the pleasure?" said Chalmers in a clipped but warm British accent.

"Can't a guy call and say hello to an old friend?" said Calibrisi.

"I learned a long time ago that when you call it usually means trouble," said Chalmers, laughing.

"I prefer to think of it as adventure."

"Ha. By the way, how is Jenna?"

"She's doing well," said Calibrisi. "I think. Have you spoken to her?"

"No."

"Why not?"

Chalmers was quiet for a moment.

"You have to set them free, Hector," said Chalmers.

Hector, thinking about the photograph of Dewey and Jessica, grinned.

"She's very talented," said Calibrisi. "It's why I'm calling."

"I'm listening."

"We're making a move on North Korea. We intercepted the itinerary of their their top military commander."

"Yong-sik?"

"He's traveling to Macau, staying overnight in order to gamble," said Calibrisi.

"What's the play?" asked Chalmers.

"Honestly, initially we were simply going to put some lead in him."

"Let me guess. Jenna re-wrote the operation."

"Bingo."

"And what is the operation?"

"The basic set-up is poison him in Macau with a slow acting toxin, then give him the antidote after he delivers us information," said Calibrisi. "I'm late for the briefing. But we need to avail ourselves of your agent."

Again, a long pause took over the call.

"I knew I shouldn't have told her," said Chalmers, laughing. "A moment of weakness. Did Jenna provide you with insight as to his chances of survival?"

"Yes. She thinks he'll be exposed. Not definitely, but likely."

"Talmadge," said Chalmers. "Classmate of one of my sons. I recruited him myself."

"With all due respect, Derek, what did you recruit him for if not this?"

"I want to know details of the operation," said Chalmers, "along with any intel you get out of it. Talmadge will need to exfiltrated."

"Of course. It goes without saying."

"Who are you sending to do it?"

"I don't know – that's Bill's call."

Chalmers paused again.

"Fine, if he's necessary, use him," said Chalmers, "but I'm not happy about it. Make sure you get him out of there afterwards."

"Thank you, Derek."

12

CIA

Two floors below ground, on the far side of the building, Dewey found his locker. An empty duffel bag was inside. He filled it with those few belongings he kept at Langley. Several changes of clothing, shoes, a small bag filled with toiletries, several knives, and two pistols, both Colt 1911s.

He went back to the seventh floor. Lindsay was sitting at her desk. She looked at Dewey with a sad look.

"I wish you weren't going," said Lindsay. She extended a single piece of paper. It was on CIA letterhead and stamped:

TOP SECRET

PART 1A

I, Hector Calibrisi, DCIA, hereby approve all legal discharge requirements and Agency responsibilities, obligations, and legal protections therewith as defined in US NAT SEC ACT SX4 [889.09A] for:

ANDREAS, DEWEYNOC 2249-A

Your service is hereby ended and is done so with the Agency's appreciation. By signature below, this document is protected under extra federal protection Presidential Order A8 and your service cannot be used in any way or in any legal proceeding against you.

Sincerely,

_____

Date

PART IB

I, ANDREAS, DEWEY, NOC 2249-A, do hereby accept all legal, security, confidentiality, and statutory requirements and obligations as defined in US NAT SEC ACT SX4 [889.09A] as regards former employees.

_____

Dewey Andreas

_____

Date

Dewey read it over several times. He looked up at Lindsay.

"Thanks," he said. "Do you have a pen?"

She paused a few seconds and reluctantly handed him a pen. Dewey signed his name and dated it. He stared for an extra moment at the sheet of paper.

"You don't have to do this, Dewey," said Lindsay. "I know it's none of my business, but why don't you just take some time off?"

Dewey said nothing. He picked up the sheet of paper. He gave Lindsay a kind smile.

"Do you know where he is?"

"I never was very good at convincing people of things," said Lindsay. "He's in OPS three. Want me to walk with you?"

"Sure."

13

DIRECTORATE OF OPERATIONS
OPS C3
CIA

The CIA operations theater – one of six – was windowless, small, and highly secure. In some ways, the room resembled a home theater. An enormous plasma screen covered the wall at the front of the amphitheater. Four rows of comfortable chairs were arrayed before the screen on risers, each with a small table for taking notes. But that's where the comparison ended. On both sides of the large plasma screen were work stations, all filled with analysts, who wore headsets and stared into smaller screens. The wall to the left – across from the entrance – was arrayed in plasma screens, smaller than the one in front, but important nevertheless. The operations theaters were where Langley – and specifically the Directorate of Operations – managed clandestine activities. Once an operation was green-lighted, it was assigned to one of the theaters. Here, all activities were managed and monitored, from the time before an action began through the operation itself. The screens, the analysts, the room, were all meshed into a wide variety of intelligence inputs, including satellite feeds, on-the-ground surveillance, and any other set of data deemed relevant, such as conjoint NSA, FBI, and JSOC activities relating to the covert action.

The middle of the semi-circle was an unusual-looking table made of glass and polycarbonate.

This was the final planning and presentation of a covert action. There was still time to alter the operation. Indeed, this was one of the main purposes of the presentation: to garner feedback and critical advice.

On the front wall, the plasma showed several photographs of General Pak Yong-sik, the highest-ranking officer in the Korean Peoples Army. He had a gaunt, drawn face, with a sharp jaw, a long nose, thick, neatly combed black hair, and glasses. Several of the photos showed Yong-sik standing next to Kim Jong-un, North Korea's leader.

The screen also displayed a live news feed from CNN. Across the bottom of the screen, a red news ticker read: *Special Report: North Korea Nuclear Showdown*. A video showed North Korea's leader, Kim Jong-un, standing on a dais overlooking a military parade, with thousands of soldiers marching on a main boulevard in Pyongang. Sprinkled among the perfectly orchestrated soldiers were missiles being towed by slow-moving trucks, as well as tanks and other military equipment.

There were a dozen people in the amphitheater, including Bill Polk, Mack Perry, and several other CIA analysts and case officers. Josh Brubaker, the President's National Security Advisor, was also present, seated in the front row. The deputy secretary of defense, Pete Brainard, was sitting in the second row, to the side.

Jenna Hartford stood leaning against the far wall, arms crossed, staring up at the CNN news report. Perry was next to her. The meeting was scheduled to start at 10:00 A.M. It was now 10:25.

Polk, who was in the first row of seats, looked impatiently at his watch, then made eye contact with Brubaker.

"Where the hell is Hector?" said Brubaker.

"I don't know," said Polk.

"I have a briefing," said Brubaker.

"Is it more important than North Korea?" said Polk, pointing at the plasma screen.

"It's *about* North Korea," said Brubaker, annoyance rising in his voice. "The whole region is bracing for war. South Korea, Japan, China – the entire theater is in a state of crisis. We've got Japan and South Korea demanding the U.S. take pre-emptive military action before Kim strikes one of them, or they will. In the meantime, Beijing is telling the president that if we take pre-emptive military action they'll step in and defend Pyongang. Add Russia to the mix. They've moved half the Pacific Fleet into the Sea of China. Does that answer your question, Bill?"

Polk glanced at Jenna, who looked up. Her eyes met Polk's then went to Brubaker.

"Yes, Josh, it does. Thank you."

"I'm sure this mission means a lot to you all," continued Brubaker, "but it is an asterisk compared to the larger chess match that's going on over there. I'll be very honest: the reason I'm here is to listen. If there is any chance Langley is going to make matters worse, I was sent here by the president to kill it. It is simply too delicate a situation to be messing around with North Korea right now, especially Yong-sik, who by all accounts is the one rational man in Pyongang. We assume he's the one thing holding back Kim from catapulting the entire region into war."

Jenna was new. It was the first time she'd met Brubaker. He hadn't even shaken her hand when Perry introduced her, instead simply nodding. Jenna didn't care. She wasn't thinking about such things as who does what, and who calls the shots – probably why she always got into political trouble. Jenna saw everything through the framework of a maze she was building, a maze that was the operation, its individual parts obvious in retrospect, its gridwork very evidentiary looking back, but her job was to create the maze in the first place, thereby enabling her side to move one step ahead of the enemy, who would inevitably discover the maze.

She was an architect of the highest caliber. Every one of her missions had gone flawlessly. During her time at MI6, Jenna had designed 17 clandestine operations, each theatrical and bold, often obtuse, refined, athletic, and above all clever. She scanned the room with cold dispatch. She liked Polk, but thought Brubaker an ass. Mack was nice and she was trying to teach him how to do it – how to properly design operations – but could she teach him? Could she really teach anyone?

If Derek was like a father to her, Hector was like an uncle. He didn't have the responsibility of imposing discipline or criticism. He let her get away with anything and got a kick out of her in the way only an uncle can to an unbridled, self-confident niece. She thought she'd hate America, and Langley in particular, but quite the opposite had occurred.

And today was her first test. She knew it.

The door to the room opened and Calibrisi walked in.

"Sorry I'm late," said Calibrisi. "Let's hear what you have, Jenna."

"Of course," she said, moving to the center of the room. Jenna wore a stylish green blazer over a white shirt and a matching pair of green slacks. In her hand was a remote.

"For those of you who don't know me, my name is Jenna Hartford," she said. "As this is the first action I'm involved with, please forgive me in advance for any violations of protocol in regards to such things as names, titles, and various other things."

Jenna clicked the remote. A large photo of North Korea's leader, Kim Jong-un, splashed across the plasma screen.

"Mack and I have completed the design of an operation intended to ascertain top secret information regarding North Korea's nuclear missile infrastructure, timelines, and strength of force projections," said Jenna. "The operation is code named *Needle in the Haystack*."

Jenna glanced at Calibrisi, who nodded subtly.

"In the past month, Kim Jong-un has conducted six separate underground nuclear tests," said Jenna. "While many western analysts believe Kim is simply being provocative in regards to the West, these tests were materially greater than anything the North Koreans have attempted to date by a factor of four."

She hit the remote. A digital map appeared showing Southern Asia. She clicked it again. Suddenly, several red lines moved in an arc from North Korea into the sky, then fell into the China Sea.

"During the same time period, the North Koreans launched a total of nineteen missiles," said Jenna. "As the infographic shows, acceleration, trajectories, and acclimation have improved dramatically with each successive test. Several of the tests resulted in failure, but most were successful. They don't have ICBM capability as of yet, but they are working feverishly toward that end and it is virtually inevitable that they will achieve their objective."

"What's their goal here, Jenna?" asked Brubaker.

"Isn't it obvious?" said Brainard, the deputy secretary of defense. "They want a deterrent. Kim would like to strike the United States with a nuclear weapon – or at least have the ability to do so."

"That makes no sense," said Brubaker. "We'd wipe them off the map. They know that."

"Would we?" said Jenna, looking at Brubaker.

"Very little Kim Jong-un does makes sense," said Calibrisi. "Jenna's question is the right one. Would we wipe North Korea off the map? Put yourself in the president's position, which means China must be taken into consideration. It's naïve to assume we would simply react by destroying North Korea, especially since it is our actions – or inactions – which have enabled this megalomaniac to be in the very position he's in."

There were mumbles and a few coughs.

"How long until the North Koreans can hit the coast of California?" said Brubaker.

Jenna turned to Mack Perry, who was sitting before a computer, headset on.

"A few days ago, I would've said not for a few months," Perry said, "but the North Koreans are making quantum advances in key areas, particularly fuel cell technology. In the most recent test, one of the vehicles travelled more than twice as far as any previously documented North Korean missile. So they are improving at a non-linear pace. Even knowing that, I would still say they won't have the ability to hit Los Angeles for a few months. Unless—"

"Unless what?" said Brubaker.

"Unless the North Koreans acquire the technology," said Perry. "We have several enemies who possess scale, reliable ICBM technology and who would certainly trade with Pyongang for some Highly Enriched Uranium. It's a question of when, not if, their rockets can make the trip. But one thing is for sure: we don't have a lot of time."

"Let's get to the operation," said Calibrisi.

"Yes, of course," said Jenna. "The goal of *Needle in the Haystack* is to find out the precise stage of North Korea's nuclear missile capability in order to know if and when the United States needs to pre-emptively act to stop them before they do in fact strike Los Angeles, or another U.S. city."

She hit the remote. A map of China appeared, then zoomed in on a red star next to the word, Macau. A moment later, a night photo of Macau shot onto the screen. It showed dozens of modern skyscrapers lit up in bright neon.

To the individuals inside the Langley briefing theater, Macau needed little introduction. It was a key juncture in the world of international espionage. Crossroads to Asia. The largest gambling mecca in the world, bigger even than Las Vegas in terms of gambling revenue, all packed into a skyscraper-filled place geographically smaller than most American towns. It was a place of astounding wealth, secrecy, and lawlessness, where the elite of Asia's political, financial, military, and intelligence worlds gathered to gamble and party outside the tight boundaries of home countries – and do business. For this reason, Macau was, for the west, a cipher.

"Our operation takes place in Macau," said Jenna. "Asia's Las Vegas, but much more decadent, dangerous, and important. Macau is the entry point for contacts inside the Asian theater. In the case of North Korea, it represents our only opportunity to penetrate the closed-off world of the North Korean ruling hierarchy."

"What's the team?" asked Brubaker, looking at Polk. "How many men? Who's going?"

"We'll make that decision after the briefing," said Polk.

–

Dewey stepped into the amphitheater and stood inside the door. He caught Calibrisi looking at him. Calibrisi nodded toward the seat next to him, telling Dewey to come over and sit down, though Dewey remained standing near the door.

Dewey looked at the plasma screen, staring at the photos of North Korea's leader, Kim Jong-un.

The woman he'd met a little while ago, Jenna, was standing at the center of the room. She clicked a remote. A half dozen photos of another North Korean appeared, different shots of the same individual. He was middle aged, with short-cropped black hair and a hard, slightly sinister look on his face.

"General Pak Yong-sik," said Jenna, "top ranking officer of the North Korean People's Army."

Dewey listened as Jenna spoke.

"Yong-sik is the longest-serving KPA chief ever and a trusted aide to Kim, in fact, his most trusted aide. Yong-sik's itinerary has him traveling to Macau sometime tomorrow. He will be staying here," she clicked the remote and a large skyscraper filled the screen, "the Mandarin Hotel, under heavy security, for one night."

"Yong-sik is a devoted player of Blackjack," said Perry. "While this probably isn't the sole purpose of the trip, he will be playing. This has already been confirmed by informants we have inside the Mandarin Hotel."

"You're telling me Yong-sik walks into the casino and plays Blackjack?" asked Brubaker. "He's like a sitting duck."

"He plays in his suite at the hotel," said Perry. "A private game."

"I want live monitoring of all inbound air traffic," interrupted Polk. "Moscow, Tehran, Istanbul, Berlin. Maybe he's gambling but let's assume that's not the real reason for the trip. If Yong-sik's meeting someone, we want to know."

"Good idea," said Jenna, nodding to Perry.

For the first time, Jenna looked at Dewey.

"The operating plan is straightforward," said Jenna. "We've arranged to insert an agent into the casino's operations. He'll penetrate Yong-sik's security cordon inside the Mandarin Hotel. As Mack said, Yong-sik likes to play alone. Posing as a Blackjack dealer, the agent will hit Yong-sik with this needle."

Jenna held up a syringe. She nodded at a man in the front row.

"Dr. Morris, would you be so kind?" Jenna said, offering the syringe to a chubby brown haired man who stood up and stepped to center stage.

Dr. David Morris was the chief toxicologist at the CIA. He wore glasses and looked slightly nervous, like a professor. The former chief anesthesiologist at the Cleveland Clinic, Morris had three Ph.Ds, one from Harvard, one from Stanford, and one from the University of Moscow. It was in Moscow where Morris learned about poison.

"Digoxin, more commonly known as Lanoxin, is a heart medication," said Morris. "It derives from certain plants, such as foxglove, and helps control irregularities in the heart, such as atrial fibrillation. It's a cardiac glycoside and has a steroid nucleus containing five fused rings, and this is important. These rings allow us to attach other chemicals, such as methyl, hydroxyl, and aldehyde in order to influence the drug's overall biological activity. In other words, it's a drug that takes to chemical alterations rather easily. The drug's effects can be manipulated. Digoxin is the proverbial fox in the hen house, it gains access easily and can then be used to do whatever we want."

Morris held up the syringe.

"Unlike run-of-the-mill Digoxin, the potion on its way to Macau is lethal," said Morris. "It's been laced with a designer toxin we developed right here at Langley with help from the CDC. The poison contains two specific, time-released chemical reactions. First, almost immediately after being infected, the poison will cause its recipient to develop a very sharp fever. Heart rate will spike dramatically. Blood pressure will go through the roof. This is meant to demonstrate to General Yong-sik that the poison is real. It won't kill him, however. After a few hours, the fever and other symptoms will revert, allowing him to do what we need him to do. The second layer of toxin hits around the twenty hour mark. The same symptoms re-occur, along with new ones, including temporary blindness and sharp abdominal pain. From hour twenty on, whoever's been poisoned is on a rapid and very painful path to death, which we've engineered to occur at the twenty-four hour mark. Once Yong-sik is hit with the needle, he'll have twenty-four hours to live unless he injects the antidote."

Jenna stepped forward and stood beside Morris.

"Assuming the poisoning goes according to plan, Yong-sik will have to make a choice," said Jenna. "Die – or give us what we want in exchange for the antidote."

"I like it," said Brubaker, nodding, "a lot. Very creative, Jenna."

"Actually, it was Mack and I together, along with Dr. Morris."

Jenna clicked the remote. A photo of the front of a wide, majestic-looking limestone building hit the screen.

"This is the Victorious War Museum in Pyongang," said Jenna. "What we want from Yong-sik is in Pyongang of course, so we'll need to plant the antidote there."

"How?" said Brubaker.

Jenna looked at Calibrisi.

"British Intelligence has a deep-based asset inside Pyongang," said Calibrisi. "They've been kind enough to allow us to utilize this asset in the operation."

"An hour ago, a CIA jet was dispatched to Seoul," said Jenna, "where a handoff of the poison and the antidote will occur. If all goes according to plan, the antidote will be in the agent's hand in Pyongang sometime tomorrow. He'll pre-set the antidote beneath a bench on the second floor of the Victory Museum. Once we receive what we want from General Yong-sik and have authenticated its authenticity, we'll tell him where the antidote is."

"Why not just let the bastard die?" said Brainard, the deputy defense secretary.

Jenna shot him a look.

"Two reasons," said Jenna. "One, as Mr. Brubaker noted, Yong-sik appears to be – if not an ally – at least someone with both oars in the water. We don't want him dead, especially with tensions running so high. Second, if he lives up to his end of the bargain, we should live up to ours. We've given our word."

"It also sets up the potential for future collaboration," said Polk. "After all's said and done, the fact is, he will have committed treason. We might be able to exploit that for future needs."

The theater was silent for a few moments. Jenna's eyes scanned the rows of people.

Brubaker spoke up.

"Who's the *NOC* we're sending in, Jenna?"

Jenna looked at Perry.

"It's not finalized yet," said Perry.

"Why not?" said Brubaker.

"We just finished the design, Josh," said Polk. "That's where it starts. We'll look at manpower in the region and make the best determination. If there's no one in-theater we'll fly someone in."

"You think one agent is enough?" said Brainard.

"I think any more than one increases the risk that someone ID's one of them," said Polk. "KPA security, Chinese intelligence. We do have a non-official cover in Manila right now. He speaks Korean and Mandarin. He's straight out of central casting."

"Who?" asked Brubaker.

"Wheeler," said Polk. "He's been on a green task for the last two months."

Jenna shot Polk a look.

"Paul Wheeler?" she said in a sharp British accent.

"Yeah, why?"

Jenna crossed her arms, a blank expression on her face.

"No reason," she whispered.

"Out with it, Jenna," said Calibrisi. "There are no secrets. We don't hold opinions back."

"There was an American called Wheeler on a mission in Berlin last year," she said. "Am I right? Is it the same guy?"

"The situation in Germany wasn't his fault," said Polk.

"Wheeler killed an innocent bystander. It was in the bloody newspapers."

"And your point is?" said Polk, his face flashing red.

Jenna did not back down one inch.

"This is a delicate operation," she said. "In the wrong hands it will result in an international incident."

"Who else do we have?" said Calibrisi.

"We have agents in Seoul, Tokyo, and Shanghai," said Perry. "None are *non-official cover.*"

The room went silent. Near the door, a small shit-eating grin spread across Dewey's lips. Dewey didn't know Wheeler. In fact, now that he thought about it, he'd never even heard of him. But he loved the sight of Jenna standing up to Polk. He also sort of liked her English accent.

Now that he took the time to look at her, he liked the neat, elegant way she dressed, too, and how her shoulder-length hair swept ever so slightly behind her head as she spoke. Mainly he liked that she said what she was thinking and didn't back down.

From the other side of the room, one of the analysts interrupted.

"Excuse me," he said. "COMM flash from DIA. They're getting heat readings off General Yong-sik's plane."

"He's leaving earlier than planned," said Perry.

"We also have a confirmation of a KUDS Force jet taking off from Tehran an hour ago. According to DIA the planes arrive in Macau within ten minutes of each other."

"We're briefing the president right now," said Brubaker, pointing at Calibrisi, Polk, and Jenna. "If the purpose of Yong-sik's trip to Macau is to meet someone from Iran, this thing just got elevated. Let's go."

"We need to get an operator in the air," said Jenna. "I might not like Wheeler, but if he's all we got—"

"He's the only *NOC* we have outside of Europe right now," said Polk.

Dewey was standing just inside the doorway, dressed in jeans and a T-shirt, staring down at the release form in his hand. He kept his eyes glued to the sheet. Finally, he looked at the door to the amphitheater. Next to the door was his duffel bag, packed with his belongings, including the gun he just got from President Dellenbaugh.

For whatever reason, Dewey suddenly pictured Bruner's wife, so pathetic, lying on the floor, with nothing to live for. He'd entered the house to kill her. It was the moment he knew he needed to get out, to escape this world he'd somehow been brought into. A world, he now realized, he would have to fight in order to leave. He walked over to Calibrisi, who was seated in the front row.

"Dewey?" said Polk.

Dewey ignored Polk and extended the release form to Calibrisi.

"What is it, Bill?" said Dewey without looking up from Calibrisi.

"We need you to go to Macau," said Polk.

Calibrisi looked up at him. His look was not cold, nor judgmental.

Josh Brubaker, the White House National Security Advisor, stood up.

"I'm not going to Macau," said Dewey. "Wheeler can handle it. If not Wheeler someone else. In fact, from the sound of it, anyone can fucking handle it."

Dewey looked down at Calibrisi. Calibrisi took a pen from his coat pocket and signed the release form, then dated it.

"Your country needs you right now," said Brubaker.

Dewey returned Brubaker's look with a cold, hard stare. His eyes found Jenna. Then he turned and walked to the door, grabbed his duffel, and lifted it over his shoulder. He looked back one more time.

"I'm not doing it," he said.

All that was visible to the occupants of the room was Dewey's back. His brown hair was thick and tousled, getting longer, down to his shoulders, still straight but unbrushed. He wore jeans and a red and black T-shirt that clung to his large frame.

They all knew he'd just gotten back from Tangiers; a personal mission of revenge; in fact that he'd killed Peter Flaherty, ex-DDCIA Joshua Gant, and a brother-in-law of Vladimir Putin, along with a small army of thugs. That he'd done all that because one of the men on board had played a role in the death of his only wife, Holly, so many years before.

Even Brubaker looked at the ground apologetically. He knew. As much as they needed him, Andreas was just another human being.

Dewey turned.

"I want to be left alone. Can any of you understand that?"

He turned back and glanced around the amphitheater. There was a long, pregnant pause. Then someone spoke.

"I understand," said Jenna softly.

Dewey met her gaze, then pushed the door open and walked out into the hallway and to the stairs, then to the parking lot. As he reached his car, he winced slightly as he fought off the shame he felt at that moment, the shame of walking away from the job he loved, from the country he loved.

The shame he knew he would need to endure in order to find the happiness that, at that moment, was more important than any patriotism or duty; the happiness he needed in order to find a reason to keep on living.

14

JOINT BASE ANDREWS
MARYLAND

Dewey parked his car – a black 2006 Ferrari 575 SuperAmerica – inside a maintenance hangar near the outer rim of Andrews's labyrinthine set of runways, buildings, and land. He locked it and set the key on the back left tire.

He found Steve Owen inside the main building. Owen was dressed in flight gear. Owen politely but firmly grabbed Dewey's elbow and pushed him back out through the door. In the distance, a shiny black F-18/A loomed in the middle of the tarmac.

"You sure this is okay?" said Dewey.

"It's fine. I need hours if I want to keep my license. To be perfectly honest, I might be a little rusty."

"When was the last time you flew?" said Dewey as they walked toward the jet.

"A month or two," said Owen. "It didn't go very well. Do you have life insurance?"

Dewey didn't laugh. He followed Owen across the tarmac. He climbed up the ladder and strapped into the back seat. Owen followed him up the ladder and strapped into the pilot seat then fired up the engine and prepared to take off as he went through a quick systems protocol with the Andrews flight deck as, at the same time, he powered up the F-18/A and started taxiing toward the runway. By the time he hit the beginning of the long runway, Owen had the jet speeding forward. He turned into the barrel of the runway then slammed it forward. Dewey's head was pushed backwards for a moment as the F-18/A roared down the tarmac. In a few seconds they were airborne. Owen slammed the jet harder, ripping toward the blue sky like a missile. Dewey was again throttled back into the seat, his stomach suddenly churning. He felt like he was going to vomit. In seconds they were scorching across the sky.

"Can you slow down?" said Dewey over commo.

A giddy laugh came from Owen.

"Sorry about that," said Owen. "I forgot you haven't had extensive training in this stuff. I'll slow down and take you over to Newark. You can catch a commercial flight. I'm sure they must have hourly flights to Bangor, Maine."

Another laugh emanated from Owen as Dewey clenched his teeth and closed his eyes, trying to hold it in.

"You better hope I don't throw up—" Dewey started, just as Owen rotated the jet 360-degrees in a little over a second.

"What was that?" said Owen.

—

Owen torched the fighter up the seaboard, moving a few hundred feet above the jaggedy-edged coast that was New England. Dewey stared out the port window, looking at Boston, and then above, trying to guess where Massachusetts ended and New Hampshire began. The ocean was a beautiful shelf of dark blue, with spatters of white where the wind topped the violent currents.

Twenty minutes later, Owen brought the jet into Bangor International Airport.

As Dewey climbed down the ladder, he looked at Owen. Dewey's eyes were still slightly wavering, like marbles, as he eyed Owen.

"I should punch you," said Dewey.

Owen smiled, then acted offended, even though he was still smiling.

"What?" he said. "I thought you needed a ride?"

Dewey shook his head. He climbed down to the tarmac. He pulled the back pack off his back and unzipped it. He looked up at Owen.

"When do you need me to pick you up?" said Owen.

"I don't," said Dewey.

15

OVAL OFFICE
WHITE HOUSE

President Dellenbaugh was seated on one of two tan leather Chesterfield couches at the center of the Oval Office. Across from him, on the opposite sofa, sat the Governor of New York, Judy Brown.

Dellenbaugh was in his first term as president, having been elevated to the post following the untimely death of President Rob Allaire, for whom he'd served as V.P. A month ago, Dellenbaugh's vice president, Danny Donato, was assassinated, killed after his plane was shot down near Hawaii. Faced with the challenge of selecting a new vice president, Dellenbaugh was close to selecting Brown.

Brown was forty-six years old, with medium-length black hair and a voluptuous frame. She was attractive, though her looks were cut with a tough aspect, a look that made her appear as if she was ready for an argument. Brown had served as U.S. District Attorney for the Southern District of New York, where she focused her prosecutors on terror cells, human traffickers, and Russian mobsters. She became a celebrity, a folk hero in New York, and she rode that popularity to the governor's mansion in Albany.

Brown was from western New York, outside of Buffalo, the only child of a Buffalo policeman who was killed in the line of duty when she was nine. She was pro-life, pro-gun, pro-death penalty, and a fiscal conservative, the kind of politician who had no place in the liberal bastion of New York politics. Yet, she'd been elected governor with more than 60% of the vote. Brown was a hard core conservative who nevertheless had won the trust of moderates and even some liberals with her plain-spoken manner and her toughness. Some would even say, her fearlessness.

"How did the meeting with Hector go?" said Dellenbaugh.

"Fine," said Brown.

"Do you still think he's too old to be running the CIA?" asked Dellenbaugh.

"Yes," said Brown, "and no."

"What does that mean?"

"Mr. President, what I said was taken out of context," said Governor Brown, referring to a now well-known comment Brown had made on CNN. "What I said originally was that when I'm sixty-four I don't think I'd be able to run the CIA. It wasn't a knock on Hector Calibrisi. The assholes at CNN cut it that way."

"Judy, if I ask you to be vice president, you'll be, let's see—"

"Fifty after your second term, Mr. President. Fifty-eight after my second term, all hypothetically speaking."

"Which is young."

"Anderson Cooper took it out of context. When I'm sixty-four I want to be in Tuscany, cooking my family all the great meals I never got to cook all these years. I don't want to be doing anything when I'm sixty-four. That being said, Langley has failed to stop several material threats coming from outside our borders. I've seen the after-effects firsthand. Russian mafia. Human traffic. Terror. The time to stop these threats is when they're still outside our borders. You can blame the FBI all you want but they're just doing clean-up by the time things metastasize inside the U.S."

Dellenbaugh smiled.

"That's the most naïve thing I've heard today."

"You disagree?" said Brown.

"You might have a good idea about the war we're fighting in New York City, governor," said the president, "but it's nothing compared to the *wars* we're fighting in about ten countries scattered all over this world. You have no idea."

Brown started to say something, but stopped herself. She leaned back and crossed her legs.

"I'm actually glad to hear that," she said.

"Why?"

"It makes me feel safer knowing it's not incompetence."

"It's not," said the president. "It's us, Great Britain, and Israel. That is the final wall. We are the final wall. It's constant and it's frightening."

Dellenbaugh leaned forward and poured a cup of coffee from a silver coffee service on the table between them. He didn't offer Brown a cup. He sat back and took a sip.

Brown stared calmly at Dellenbaugh without speaking.

"Would you get rid of him?" asked Dellenbaugh.

"If I were vice president?"

"Yes."

"If I'm vice president, I will support you and your decisions as they relate to Langley and everywhere else. Who runs the CIA would not be my decision. If it was, I probably wouldn't just fire him. I voted for you, President Dellenbaugh, and I support you even if I'm not asked to be V.P. If you're saying there's more here than meets the eye, then I'd want to learn more and spend more time with Hector and his team. Who knows, maybe I have some good ideas that can help? I'm ruthless when it comes to people trying to hurt this country."

"I appreciate your honesty," said Dellenbaugh.

"Thank you."

A knock came at the door. Cecily Vincent, the president's assistant, looked in.

"They're here, sir," said Cecily.

Dellenbaugh stood up, followed by Governor Brown.

"I'm afraid I have to cut this a little short, Judy."

"No problem. If you'd like to continue our discussion, I'm glad to stay in town," said Brown.

"That might not be a bad idea."

Cecily led Brown out through a different door, what was considered the main door, though true insiders seldom used it. Cecily returned and opened the door to her office. Hector Calibrisi, Bill Polk, Josh Brubaker, and Jenna Hartford entered the Oval Office and sat down.

Dellenbaugh looked at Jenna.

"You must be new."

"I'm Jenna Hartford," she said in a clipped British accent, stepping forward to meet Dellenbaugh.

"Nice to meet you," said Dellenbaugh, smiling.

"She worked at British Intelligence," said Calibrisi.

"I couldn't tell," said Dellenbaugh sarcastically. He sat down, as did the others. "What's the latest?"

"Langley has completed the design of an operation," said Brubaker. "This is the North Korean general I discussed with you earlier."

"Yong-sik," said Dellenbaugh. "Why do you need me?"

–

Over the next ten minutes, Jenna, Polk, and Calibrisi briefed the president on the details of the Macau operation. When she was finished, Dellenbaugh walked behind his desk, deep in thought. He paced back and forth in front of the window.

"What more do we know about the Iranian plane?" he asked.

Calibrisi, who'd been scanning his phone for updates, looked up.

"It's Abu Paria's, sir."

Dellenbaugh's eyes met Calibrisi's.

"It can't be a coincidence," said Dellenbaugh.

"I agree."

"So why are they meeting?"

"We don't know if they are, Mr.President," said Calibrisi.

16

BANGOR INTERNATIONAL AIRPORT
BANGOR, MAINE

A silver Dodge Ram pick-up pulled up at the terminal as Dewey walked out. The pick-up lurched slightly a few times, until it came to a screeching stop just a few inches in front of Dewey. He chucked his duffel in the back and reached for the passenger door. Sitting in the driver's seat was a teenage boy, with longish, messy brown hair parted in the middle, a handsome face, wearing a white sweater with red and blue stripes around the collar and several visible holes as well as brown areas with large dirt stains. The boy smiled.

"Hi, Uncle Dewey," said Sam.

Dewey paused a few moments, standing in the door. Cautiously, he climbed into the truck and shut the door.

"When the hell did you get your license?" said Dewey. "Aren't you like fifteen?"

"Fourteen," said Sam. "Besides, it's easy."

"What happens if you get pulled over?"

"I've never gotten pulled over," said Sam. "The key to not getting pulled over, Uncle Dewey, is to lose them right when they start coming after you. It's easy."

Sam hit the gas and the pick-up took off.

"Where's your dad? I thought he was picking me up."

"I volunteered," said Sam.

"Volunteered?"

"I took his truck. He's going to be pissed off as hell. Can you sort of cover for me? Cushion the blow a little? I mean, I am here, aren't I? I did in fact pick you up."

Dewey started laughing.

"Alright, I'll cover for you," said Dewey, leaning back in the seat and looking out at the countryside as they drove. "Just try not to hit a telephone pole or a tree. Or another car. Just don't get in an accident, otherwise all bets are off."

Sam waved his hand dismissively through the air as he slammed the gas and weaved into the oncoming lane, passing a few cars, then zig-zagging back into the right lane.

"I've been driving since I was twelve," said Sam. "Don't worry, I got it. Just sit back and enjoy."

–

Dewey shut his eyes. He still felt a sense of guilt for walking away from the operation. But the truth was, he was tired. Four separate operations had occurred over a span of only two months. First, Cloud, the Russian terrorist, who'd nearly detonated a nuclear bomb in the busiest port in the world, just a hundred yards away from the Statue of Liberty. Then there was Damascus, and Isolda, the leader of ISIS. Destroying the cell at Columbia University, getting stabbed. When he needed the rest the most was after Columbia, and Calibrisi had sent him to Paris as a reward, a three-day junket guarding the U.S. Secretary of State. A no-brainer job. Then the Secretary was murdered – the blame put on Dewey – part of a massive inside conspiracy to kill the President and Vice President and take over the U.S. government. It had nearly succeeded, but Dewey stopped it. He didn't care about the thanks, the accolades, the medals and honors he'd been bestowed for each event. He sent them all to Maine, to his mother, who he knew would store them away someplace in the barn where the squirrels wouldn't get to them.

Dewey didn't care about the honors. He cared about his country. He cared about his perception of himself. How would he feel during the few moments that human beings feel just before dying? From a bullet or old age, all would someday know that moment. Dewey thought about that moment. How would he feel about himself? Would he be proud? That was why he took risks. He'd been given the physical gifts, but no one knew where that other element came from, that part of Dewey that also had the spirit of America's founders, the men and women who fought for independence and risked their lives so long ago. Dewey viewed himself as the modern version of the early American settler, fighting for his country.

But he was tired. He wanted a family. That much he knew. He could never move back to Castine, or even Bangor. Or maybe he could. Because the truth was, he wanted the feeling of holding a child again, a child of his own. He wanted that feeling and often woke up clutching his pillow, having dreamt about the feeling he'd once had. Maybe it was Castine. It's not that he was opposed to living on the coast of Maine, in the middle of nowhere. He just wondered if he could find someone he could love, a woman who would give him the gift of fatherhood, the feeling of holding a small child and kissing its cheek in the sun, or the rain, protecting that girl or boy from a hard world and yet bringing to that same world a potential savior.

Sam nudged Dewey, awakening him from his thoughts.

"We're here," said Sam. "You owe me fifty bucks."

"Fifty bucks?"

"UBER woulda been a hundred," said Sam.

17

ASSOCIATED PRESS
PYONGANG, NORTH KOREA

As usual, Talmadge's weekly package arrived from Seoul. Kae Myung Bin, Talmadge's North Korean assistant, placed the cardboard box on Talmadge's desk. His eyes shot to the shipping label. Usually, the box's return address said:

> **Karry McCafferty**
> **AP – Seoul**
> **3009008 Fikitake North**
> **SEOUL KOREA**

Today, the label was different, off by one letter:

> **Karry Mcafferty**
> **AP – Seoul**
> **3009008 Fikitake North**
> **SEOUL KOREA**

It was the type of small typo the North Koreans were unlikely to pick up, and if they did, was easily explained away, but Talmadge knew what it meant.

MI6 had intercepted Kerry's normal care package and sent their own. Which meant a message of some sort – orders – were hidden inside.

Talmadge, the Associated Press Pyongang Bureau Chief, was one of only three Western reporters stationed in North Korea, the result of an agreement between the North Korean government and the Associated Press, an international news organization based in New York City and owned by its member newspapers in the U.S.

Talmadge was also an agent for British Intelligence, MI6.

The AP's North Korean offices were housed inside the headquarters of the state-run Korean Central News Agency (KCNA) in downtown Pyongyang. Talmadge was one of three AP employees, and the only non-North Korean. Officially, Talmadge had editorial independence over his articles. But of course his presence in Pyongang was dependent on his articles being devoid of anything controversial or critical of the North Korean government. Every word Talmadge wrote was read and re-read by KCNA censors, though that was just the tip of the iceberg. In fact, everything Talmadge wrote – or read – news articles, emails, letters, books, newspapers, magazines, and anything else that came by mail or over the Internet was also read and re-read by government officials, who were not only deeply suspicious and wary of the possibility that Talmadge might be a spy, but oftentimes had nothing better to do.

"Did they find anything?" asked Talmadge.

Kae Myung Bin grinned.

"I saw a jar of jam on Cheol's desk," said Kae Myung Bin.

Cheol was one of several military officials stationed at KCNA for the sole purpose of watching Talmadge and inspecting any mail that was sent by him or that he received.

The box was damaged in several places. Several small holes had been punched through the top and sides, looking for anything that might have been embedded in the cardboard. The box had been taped and re-taped several times. A large red sticker on the side:

Geom-yeol doen

It meant inspected and scrawled across the sticker was a handwritten date and three different sets of handwritten initials.

After three years in Pyongang, Talmadge's weekly care packages from Kerry, his former assistant in Seoul, were expected. Still, they received as much scrutiny as ever. Nevertheless, Talmadge's minders, as well as Kae Myung Bin, looked forward to the packages. The minders because they often stole items from the packages, Kae Myung Bin because some of what the minders hadn't taken Talmadge gave to him.

Talmadge opened up the box as Kae Myung Bin looked on. Inside, the box was filled with several boxes of cookies, crackers, along with cans containing various food items, including artichoke hearts, peach halves, fruit cocktail, coffee beans, condensed milk, and soup. Several paperback books were stacked on one side of the box, along with a National Geographic magazine.

Everything in the box – every can, every box, every book and magazine – had a small, round, orange sticker on it, indicating that each item had been inspected.

Talmadge lifted a box of chocolate chip cookies. The box was already open and one of two sleeves of cookies was gone. He opened the plastic on the remaining sleeve and took a cookie, then put the sleeve back in the box and handed it to Kae Myung Bin. He handed Kae a can of peaches, a can of tomatoes, and a box of Kraft macaroni and cheese.

"For you," said Talmadge.

Kae Myung Bin smiled.

"Thank you, Ross."

–

That night, back at his small apartment, Talmadge unpacked the box. It was the first care package in more than a year that contained a message from River House.

Talmadge took the National Geographic into the bathroom. Opening the medicine cabinet, he removed what looked like a normal pair of reading glasses. He looked at the cover. In the upper right hand corner, the number "61" was written in ink that was visible only with the glasses on. He flipped to page 61. It was the third page of an article on sharks. Certain letters in the article had small dots placed above them, again visible only with the special glasses on.

VLS ADOTE MLK
TAPE 1 SUB BENCH ACRS FR G KM NAT MUS

Talmadge understood the message immediately.

**There are vials hidden in the condensed milk. Take 1
and tape it to the underside of a bench at the Victory
Museum, across from the painting of Kim Il-Sung.**

In the kitchen, Talmadge took a can opener and opened the can of
condensed milk. He poured the contents into a plastic bag so as not to
waste it. Inside the can, affixed to the side, was a piece of black plastic.
He removed it and popped it open. Inside were two small, thin glass
syringes with clear liquid inside.

Talmadge's mind raced, trying to figure out what it all meant.
Presumably, poison, or an antidote. Someone inside Pyongang was
going to be poisoned. But by whom? By him? The instructions didn't
explain. Why?

It didn't remember. He remembered his training.

Do your job. Do what you're told. There will not be time to explain.

Talmadge shook his head, as if erasing his thoughts from his mind.
He knew it was best to not think about it – to not attempt to
figure out what the operation was all about. If he thought about
anything other than the execution of the mission, he risked appearing
distracted, confused, or acting erratic, the very types of behaviors the
North Koreans are looking for. They'd spot his aberrant demeanor
immediately, resulting in interrogation.

Talmadge knew he needed to focus solely on the mission.

He took one of the syringes and went into the bathroom. Standard
procedure – they'd sent two doses in case one broke in transit. He set
it down on the sink and reached for the medicine cabinet, pulling it
out from the wall. He hid the syringe behind it. He went into the
kitchen and returned with what looked like a glass jar of mayonnaise.
He opened it and, with his right index finger, spread paint around the
perimeter of the mirror, hiding where he'd stowed the needle.

He took the other syringe and placed a small strip of two-sided tape on one side then put it inside a concealed area sewn inside the left pocket of his leather coat.

Talmadge tore the page from the National Geographic and used it to start a fire in the small coal-burning stove. He opened a can of tomato soup and ate it along with some crackers, thinking about the museum. He would go first thing in the morning.

No, you stupid fuck!

That would be precisely the sort of behavior that would tip off his minders, a sudden, inexplicable change of routine. No, that was a terrible idea. He had to come up with a better one.

18

MARGARET HILL
CASTINE, MAINE

Air Force One touched down at Bangor International Airport beneath a cloudless sky in late afternoon. It was cold out. A Coast Guard Sikorsky helicopter was waiting on the tarmac when the president's plane touched down, its rotors already humming and kicking up dust.

Dellenbaugh walked down the stairs of the plane. His tie was off. He wore a blue suit and white shirt. He climbed aboard the helicopter.

Other than Secret Service agents, Dellenbaugh was alone. As the chopper aimed for the rugged coast of Maine, he sat in a canvas fold down seat in back, staring out the window.

Dellenbaugh knew he was more than simply being cautious about North Korea. He was worried. He hated micro-managing and he trusted the CIA to execute with whatever manpower they deemed appropriate. But his gut told him something was wrong. That gut instinct had never failed him, and right now it was telling him to do whatever he had to do in order to get Dewey Andreas to go to Macau.

Perhaps it was the warning issued to him by the Chinese Premier. Even delivered through an interpreter, there was no mistaking the chill in Xi's voice.

"If the United States moves pre-emptively on North Korea, the People's Republic will respond as if you have moved on our country. We have Kim under control. You must trust us, Mr. President."

"That's Blue Hill below, Mr. President," said one of the pilots, leaning back and shouting. "We're almost there."

The hills outside were colored blue and green, then were flanged with gray rock, jagged coast, then the black blue water of Penobscot Bay, patched with sailboats, motor boats, and the occasional white cap from the wind.

The Sikorsky began a rapid, sharp descent. Fields of green were spread in neat rectangles; a farm. In the middle of the acres of land stood a large red barn, along with a rambling white farmhouse, with black shutters all around.

The chopper swirled in a slow eddy then hovered, inching smoothly down onto a field near the farmhouse. The pilots quickly shut the engines down.

"I'll be back in a few minutes," said Dellenbaugh, leaning into the cockpit.

He stepped out of the helicopter and walked towards the front porch of the farm house as a pair of dogs, one a slow-moving sheepdog, the other a suspicious St. Bernard, came marching across the low-cut grass. A teenage girl with long blonde hair came walking behind the dogs.

"I'm J.P. Dellenbaugh," said the president as he approached the girl.

She extended her hand as she approached. "I'm Reagan Andreas."

"Hi, Reagan," said Dellenbaugh. "Is Dewey here?"

"Yeah," she said, staring at the helicopter. "Can I check it out?"

"Sure," said the president. "Tell the pilots I said it was okay."

"Awesome. Thanks. Is it okay if my brother looks at it too?"

"Absolutely."

"Thanks, Mr. President."

Dellenbaugh reached a split-rail fence and swung his leg over it, then walked to the screen porch. An older man, whom Dellenbaugh recognized, pushed the screen door open.

"Hi, Mr. Andreas," said President Dellenbaugh.

"Hello, Mr. President. Please call me John."

John Andreas, Dewey's father, was, like Dewey, tall and stocky. He had a resigned, calm, happy look on his face. He reached out to shake Dellenbaugh's hand, but Dellenbaugh pulled him closer, hugging him.

"We need your son again," said the president.

"I figured that."

Dellenbaugh entered the screened porch. He saw the others: Margaret, Dewey's mom, Dewey's brother Hobey and his wife, Barrett, Sam, Dewey's nephew. They all stood up and greeted the president.

"Is Dewey here?" said Dellenbaugh.

"He's out in the barn," said Hobey. "Sammy, go get him."

"No, that's okay," said Dellenbaugh. "Just point me in the right direction."

—

Dellenbaugh crossed the gravel driveway and walked along a hundred yards of white fence. In the distance, the ocean was visible in dark blue above trees beginning to unfold with new green as spring approached. The door to the barn was open and Dellenbaugh entered. He found Dewey in the stables. He was brushing down a large brown horse. Dewey was in a flannel shirt that was covered in dirt and strands of hay. His face was covered in sweat. He caught the president's eyes. He stared a few moments at Dellenbaugh, then put the brush down.

"What do you want?" said Dewey, wiping his face with his sleeve.

Dellenbaugh entered the stable.

"I grew up in a house where you could see the concrete of the foundation," said Dellenbaugh. "It was one story. It was light blue, ugliest thing you've ever seen, right next to another house that looked exactly the same. The whole street looked the same. The reason it was light blue is because my dad got the paint free from the assembly line where he worked. It was car paint, some Oldsmobile color they discontinued."

Dewey nodded, listening with a blank expression.

"I always wanted to live on a farm," said the president. "What's it like?"

Dewey stared at him, as if considering not answering – his guard was still up. He knew what was coming.

"There's a lot of work," said Dewey. "You get used to it." Dewey put his hand up to the neck of the horse and rubbed it. "It's hard to explain how close you can feel to a horse. Or when you go inside and there's a fire going and your fingernails are lined with dirt."

There was a long pause and they could hear the horse exhaling.

"You know why I'm here," said Dellenbaugh. "We need you."

Dewey continued rubbing the horse's neck. After a while he pushed his hand back through his hair.

"No, you don't, sir," said Dewey.

"Do you think I would've flown up here if we didn't?' said Dellenbaugh.

"You might think you need me, but there are several people who can get this operation done. I heard the briefing. It's straightforward."

Dewey moved to the stable door to leave, but Dellenbaugh stood in his way. Dellenbaugh stared at Dewey as he looked at him, blocking him from leaving.

Dellenbaugh had grown up in Detroit. He played professional hockey and knew how to fight. He wasn't stopping Dewey with the power of his office. At this moment, he was challenging Dewey.

Dewey moved next to Dellenbaugh and started to push him aside, but Dellenbaugh held firm. Dewey pushed harder now – and Dellenbaugh pushed back.

"No one's watching," said Dellenbaugh, rolling up his sleeves and squaring off. "Your country needs you right now. I'd go if I could, if I understood what to do – but I don't."

Dewey shook his head.

"I'm not fighting you, Mr. President—"

"If I win, you go to Macau," said Dellenbaugh, raising his fists in a fighting stance that once sent shivers through the NHL. "You win, you can stay and we'll find someone else."

Dellenbaugh swung as he suddenly stepped forward, his fist brushing Dewey's chin as Dewey instinctively moved out of the way. In the same moment, Dellenbaugh's other fist hammered a blow to Dewey's stomach. But before the first punch was even thrown, Dewey had slashed his arm through the air beneath Dellenbaugh's swing, catching Dellenbaugh at the throat and jamming his thumb hard into the president's carotid artery. It all happened before Dellenbaugh knew what was happening. Dellenbaugh let out a pained grunt. Calmly, Dewey pushed the president back – gently but firmly – to the stable wall.

"I'm asking you," said Dellenbaugh, his voice straining under Dewey's grip.

Dewey held Dellenbaugh one more moment, then let go.

"Okay, Mr. President," said Dewey. "I'll go to Macau."

19

IN THE AIR

Abu Paria sat back in the luxurious seat inside the cabin of the Gulfstream 100 that now coursed across the sky.

With him, other than the pilots, were two younger men, both KUDS Force, both Paria's chosen traveling companions. Kaivan, 24, was a 5'8" and stocky. Farhad was 6'2" and even Paria occasionally feared his physical presence, despite the fact that he worked for him.

When Abu Paria, the leader of Iran's most elite fighting force, KUDS Force, as well as the overall boss of all Iranian intelligence forces, ventured outside of Iran, there were precautions. Paria was a target of all Western intelligence agencies as well as a motley collection of underground Iranians who wanted an end to the radical Shia regime started by Ayatollah Khomeini two generations ago. It was no secret that Paria was the mastermind behind terror throughout the West. He funded Hezbollah, Hamas, and even, very secretly, through various middlemen, ISIS. Paria had paid for and witnessed battles between two of his own forces – ISIS and Hezbollah, ISIS and KUDS, Hamas and Hezbollah – on multiple occasions. He was playing a longer game. Paria believed chaos, political strife, terror, and war were the foundations that Iran could build a superpower upon.

He ventured from Iran only when the stakes were truly large.

Despite all this, he barely fidgeted as he flew, cabin lights off, through a misty oblivion. He didn't sleep, read, or look at his phone. He stared straight ahead, at the back of the seat across from him, which was empty.

The trade was straightforward. Iran would give North Korea two Safir missiles – Iranian-made intercontinental ballistic missiles – which could deliver whatever payload was attached to it to any place on earth. In exchange, North Korea would give Iran 454 kilograms of highly enriched uranium as well as eleven nuclear triggers.

Paria knew Yong-sik. Not well, but he knew him. They'd met in North Africa, at a meeting a week after 9/11. It was a discussion amongst the intellectual and financial underpinning of the countries and organizations who all believed they were at war with America, convened by a Chinese billionaire and major funder of the anti-American diaspora. Paria and Yong-sik had talked – through interpreters – late into the night, Yong-sik telling Paria stories about Kim Jong-un and Kim Jong-il, Paria speaking of Khomeini. They were just stories, no information of value, more tales from the unique worlds from which the two came.

Indeed, Paria trusted Yong-sik enough that he'd already floated the Safir's. They were less than a day from North Korea's coast.

The plane arced slightly right. Paria finally turned from looking at the seat back. He watched through the window as the jet descended from the sky. Blue went to white and then, below the cover, was a grayish, cloudy horizon. Nevertheless, Macau's glittering silhouette cut through the mist, beckoning Paria toward it like a moth to the flame.

20

MACAU INTERNATIONAL AIRPORT
TAIPA ISLAND
MACAU, CHINA

A red and tan Dassault Falcon 8X swooped out of the clouds and descended quickly toward the airport's lone runway, a strip of concrete laid atop a man-made pile of dirt and debris adjacent to the small island of Taipa, connected by a pair of aging causeways to the heart of the airport.

The facility was only built in 1995. Somehow, the small facility showed both its youth and, at the same time, its age. At the time of its construction, Macau was still controlled by the Portugese, who China had allowed to operate the city under long term lease as a port. Along the way, gambling had been introduced to Macau. By the time the long term lease expired in 1999, Macau was a fast-growing hub of gambling, if still small compared to Las Vegas and Monaco. But now it was the world's largest gambling epicenter.

The airport's maintenance buildings and garages were dilapidated, but the central passenger terminal was glass and modern. Since taking control of Macau in 1999, the Chinese, rather than re-building the airport, had opted instead to "put lipstick on the pig," putting glass where they could but leaving the cracking concrete and ugly sight lines alone. After all, Macau's visitors weren't coming to admire the airport. They were coming to gamble.

At least, some of them were.

Yong-sik, however, was not here to gamble – at least, not until tonight, after business was completed. At this moment, North Korea's top general was here to do the opposite of take risk. He was here to trade North Korean-made nuclear materials for Iranian-made intercontinental ballistic missiles.

The jet landed at just before six P.M. Macau time.

Yong-sik sat in the front row of the sleek French-made jet. He was accompanied by a small army of soldiers and staff members. Twelve soldiers comprised his security team. Half-a-dozen other men worked for Yong-sik in various capacities inside the executive office of the KPA, including a personal assistant, a secretary, and a translator. Yong-sik had also brought along top KPA experts in the Directorate of Nuclear Activity as well as from the KPA Missile Directorate.

The Falcon taxied to the private terminal, where several long, black limousines were waiting. After the plane came to a stop next to the line of limousines, a soldier from Yong-sik's security cordon activated the hydraulic door to the jet. Once it lowered to the ground, a line of armed soldiers were the first to go down the stairs, scanning the area immediately around the jet, then inspecting the line of limousines, inside and out. Two of the soldiers removed long, thin poles which they moved beneath the vehicles, inspecting for explosive devices while two other soldiers inspected the insides of the vehicles, scanning for bombs.

The other four members of the team stood guard around the vehicles, rifles aimed at the ground, scanning for anything suspicious. As the inspection took place, several soldiers removed suitcases from the back of the jet and put them inside the limousines.

The air was humid, in the eighties, and a warm wind blew off the ocean.

The inspection took almost half-an-hour. Finally, when the security team was done, one of the men signaled to an officer at the top of the jet's stairs.

"General," the man said. "It is ready."

The line of vehicles moved out of the airport and was soon on the main road to downtown Macau.

The sky had turned to a purplish-gray with not a cloud anywhere in sight. The central district of Macau was a cluster of glass skyscrapers, each with a distinctive design.

At the sloping, blade-like curvature of the Mandarin Oriental Hotel, the limousines split. Two entered the underground parking lot while the other two moved into the circular front entrance of the hotel. Yong-sik was in the second of these. He climbed out of the limo and walked inside the massive entrance foyer of the Mandarin Hotel, accompanied by four soldiers as well as two of his aides. Standing immediately inside the lobby was a man in a black linen suit, with a beard and mustache, and dark, olive-toned skin. He walked toward Yong-sik.

"General Yong-sik," said the man, his accent Middle Eastern. He extended his arm, a friendly smile on his face. "I am Farkar," he said, shaking Yong-sik's hand.

"Where is General Paria?" said Yong-sik.

"Waiting upstairs, sir," said Farkar. "He wanted me to express his hope that if you would like to take a few minutes in order to unpack and relax, he could meet with you later. Alternatively, he is available now if you would like to meet sooner."

Yong-sik nodded.

"Now," said Yong-sik. "Later I will be playing Blackjack in my suite."

"Very good, sir," said Farkar. "Please, follow me."

Farkar led Yong-sik to a private elevator. Farkar watched as Yong-sik and four other men climbed aboard the cab. Other than Yong-sik, all the rest of the North Koreans clutched weapons.

Farkar inserted a key into the wall. The elevator shot up to the penthouse floor.

The hallway was dimly-lit. A half-dozen Iranian gunmen stood in the hallway outside the entrance to the suite. They saluted Farkar and then watched as their North Korean counterparts exited the elevators. Farkar nodded to one of the Iranians soldiers, who returned his look, then approached one of Yong-sik's deputies.

"My name is Abbas," said the Iranian. He extended his hand toward the ranking soldier. "We have a suite reserved for the traveling security party. There are refreshments, food, that sort of thing. My suggestion is we each leave a guard in the hallway, and the rest of the teams go to the suite and relax. There is too much firepower in one hallway for what should be a peaceful get-together."

The North Korean soldier eyed Yong-sik, who nodded, giving his ascent.

"Please, General Yong-sik," said Farkar.

Yong-sik, along with two of his deputies, the missile expert and the nuclear expert, followed Farkar to a door at the end of the corridor.

The door opened up into a massive suite that occupied the entire ocean half of the penthouse floor. It was vast, with windows covering three of four walls, and stunning views of the ocean as well as the lights that now glittered like jewels from Macau's skyline.

Inside, the tall, imposing figure of Abu Paria – Iran's top military leader – stood in the middle of the entrance foyer.

Paria wore a short-sleeved khaki military shirt covered in medals and military insignia. He had on matching khaki pants and steel-toed boots. Paria was 6'5" and weighed 275-lbs. but he loomed larger. He was bald, with no facial hair. As Yong-sik entered, Paria stood with his arms crossed and a blank expression on his face. After Farkar, Yong-sik, and the two other North Koreans entered, another guard shut the door. There was a long moment of silence as Yong-sik and Paria stared at each other. Finally, Paria smiled, uncrossed his arms, and stepped toward Yong-sik.

"General Yong-sik," said Paria in a deep, gravelly voice, with a thick accent. "It is very good to see you again, my friend."

Paria moved closer and bowed, then reached his hand out and took Yong-sik's hand, shaking it enthusiastically.

"It's good to see you, too, General Paria," said Yong-sik. "His Excellency, Kim Jong-un, sends his warmest regards to you and to the Most Honorable Leader, Dr. Suleiman."

Paria towered over his North Korean counterpart.

"On his behalf, I thank you for your kind words," said Paria, "and extend Imam's wishes to your Supreme Leader for a prosperous and joyous spring."

Yong-sik bowed slightly.

"Now tell me, general, how was your flight?" said Paria.

"It was very pleasant, thank you," said Yong-sik.

"I was invited to North Korea by Kim Jong-il himself, may he rest in peace. It was a most enjoyable trip, general. It was the beginning of the oil agreements."

"Two countries starving to death because of the West and its sanctions," said Yong-sik.

"Together we took the first steps to fight back," said Paria. "You needed oil. We needed guns and bullets." Paria placed his large arm on the diminutive Yong-sik and gently patted his back. "It's been a good friendship. In fact, I would have a hard time naming a more important and reliable friend to Iran than North Korea. Come, let me show you the view."

Yong-sik walked beside Paria through the expansive set of rooms. They crossed a spacious dining room with a huge black onyx table surrounded by a dozen chairs. One wall was filled with large oriental paintings and a sideboard that was shiny and gold. The opposite wall was a sheet of glass. On the table was a silver tea and coffee service. Past the dining room, another hallway fed into a palatial sitting room. A curving, modern, white leather sofa sat close to the ground. The room occupied the triangulated corner of the building, so that every wall was comprised of glass.

Yong-sik nodded subtly to one of his military aides, ordering him to remain outside the room so that he and Paria could be alone.

Paria took a seat on the sofa and watched as Yong-sik walked past the sofa to the wall of glass. He stopped next to the edge of the window and stared out at the sky.

"You like the views, I see?" said Paria, laughing gruffly.

"I remember when Macau had one hotel."

The sky outside was a steely gray, flanged with deep orange. Several planes were in the sky, inbound for the airport, visible at different elevations. The surface of the China Sea was silvery as the last of the day's light refracted across it. Closer to the Mandarin, neighboring hotels were like brightly-lit daggers of light and glass, jutting in the air alongside the Mandarin, windows visible with people inside, neon lights in fanciful script running across different roofs, a feeling of activity, of technology, of possibility and wealth.

The two men were alone. Both of the North Korean military experts who'd accompanied Yong-sik remained near the room's entrance.

Yong-sik stared out for more than a minute. Paria said nothing, instead allowing the North Korean to enjoy the view. Had it been an underling, or someone who needed something from Iran, Paria's behavior would have been very different. By now, Paria would be barking orders and making demands. But it was Paria who needed something. He knew he needed to be patient with Yong-sik. After all, what North Korea potentially offered – nuclear weapons – was more much more valuable than what Iran offered. Still, Paria's patience grew thin.

"General," said Paria, "won't you please sit down. We have much to discuss."

Yong-sik turned.

"Of course," said Yong-sik, walking toward the sofa and taking a seat near Paria. "What is the expression, General Paria? Let's get down to business?"

"Yes, precisely," said Paria. "An American expression. Ironic, isn't it?"

Paria let out a low grumble of a laugh.

"What do you mean?" said the North Korean dryly.

"As we speak," said Paria, "the Iranian container ship *Silver Dawn* idles in international waters in the Sea of Japan. I have authorized the captain of the ship to move upon our mutual agreement. On board the ship, there are two Safir intercontinental ballistic missiles, state-of-the-art, built with the latest technological capabilities and materials."

Yong-sik had a blank expression, though he allowed a slight, satisfied smile.

"That is most excellent," said Yong-sik.

Yong-sik turned to one of the soldiers standing outside the doorway and nodded. In his hand was a large stainless steel briefcase. A chain from the case was locked to his wrist. He walked to the middle of the seating area and placed the briefcase down on the table, rotated two lock dials, and popped the case open. Inside, set securely in a foam holder, was a small, odd-looking device – a sealed glass tube with four electrodes leading into its base and an arrangement of wires and of varying lengths were joined together buy a piece of black steel. Several wires dangled from both ends of the object. The object was held in place by a pair of straps.

Paria leaned forward, his eyes wide. He stared at the object for several moments.

"Is it what I think it is?" said Paria.

"That depends," said Yong-sik. "What do you think it is?"

"A nuclear trigger?"

Yong-sik nodded enthusiastically.

"Correct," said Yong-sik. "Specifically, a krytron: cold-cathode, hydrogen-filled, intended for use as a very high-speed switch. Jin," said Yong-sik to his aide, "give the general the key."

The young military aide removed a key from his pocket and stuck it into the lock at his wrist, unlocking the chain. He extended the cuff to Paria, who accepted it.

"But, I don't understand," said Paria. "We need to discuss the terms of our deal."

"Consider this a gesture of good will, General Paria," said Yong-sik, "from his excellency, the Supreme Leader. I'm told it's not the newest of technologies but it is reliable."

"It's no secret that triggers have been a challenge for our engineers."

"Yes, I know," said Yong-sik. "As we speak, the other ten triggers have moved into the waters near the Strait of Hormuz, along with the agreed upon uranium, 454 kilograms."

"It seems the possibility of a trade is imminent," said Paria.

"More than imminent," said Yong-sik. "I've been instructed to remain in Macau until we've concluded our business."

Paria gently unstrapped the trigger from the briefcase and held it in the air, looking at it with a confused look on his face.

"I don't even know how it works," said Paria, "but I suppose that doesn't matter. Let's discuss value. The question is, what are eleven nuclear triggers and a 454 kilograms of uranium worth to me, and what are two Intercontinental Ballistic Missiles worth to you, yes?"

Yong-sik smiled and nodded, yes.

"Yes, you've said it perfectly, General Paria."

"In 1997, Iran had so little cash that often we went without pay for months at a time," said Paria. "North Korea was generous with us. Iran was paid market rates for our petroleum, even though we both knew you could have insisted on paying much less. After all, there was no market for Iranian oil, yet you paid full price. Today, with our sanctions gone, we are in a better position, but you now suffer the burden that we once suffered. Am I right?"

Yong-sik looked emotionlessly at Paria, a hint of coldness in his eyes. Perhaps it was pride. Finally, he nodded, yes, without saying anything.

"Among friends, there is no shame," said Paria. "The Republic of Iran will give you the missiles, free of charge. In addition, we will pay you for the triggers and HEU. Please determine a price you think is equitable."

"That is most generous, but it's not necessary, general," said Yong-sik.

"I know," said Paria. "It wasn't necessary for Kim to buy our oil in 1997 either. But he did."

21

MACAU

Dewey flew aboard Air Force One to JFK, where Mack Perry met him on the tarmac. Perry handed Dewey a leather satchel.

"Here your papers. You're getting into Macau under a Spanish passport, the details are inside. You'll be operational once you're there."

"Why Spain?"

"It has nothing to do with the mission," said Perry. "It's a safe alias, that's all, a rich Spanish guy who did some work for MI6. We don't want you getting stopped at the border. You have a history with PRC. You're flying to Madrid then Macau."

"Got it. Is the operation still the same?"

"No. We need to get the poison inside Yong-sik's hotel room. You can't carry it in. We're figuring it out now. It'll be set up by the time you're there, hopefully."

Dewey glanced at Perry.

"There's your ride," said Perry, pointing to a black jet, stairs down, engines purring, a hundred feet away.

Dewey climbed aboard the jet, a CIA GV, which took off as soon as the stairs were back up and locked. Dewey read over the papers as the GV climbed to 30,000 feet over the dark blue of the Atlantic.

Dewey was traveling under a Spanish passport and the name Diego Escalante. Escalante was a Spanish billionaire, traveling to Macau for the first time to check it out after decades worth of gambling in Las Vegas and Monaco.

Usually CIA agents, when on assignment in a foreign land, took a role at the local U.S. embassy or consulate. This provided the agent with official diplomatic immunity, or *cover*, protecting the agent from prosecution if they were caught. An official agent, if captured, was usually escorted to the border and kicked out of the country.

But there were also agents who ventured into enemy lands without diplomatic immunity, unprotected. It was called *non-official cover*. Inside Langley, they were nicknamed *illegals*. Officially, they were known as NOCs. If captured, these operators faced severe criminal punishment, up to and including execution. They operated alone, across enemy lines, without a safety net. The reasoning was straightforward. A NOC had more freedom to roam because he or she would not necessarily be under surveillance by a foreign government, as embassy workers often were. This meant that NOCs had wide operational latitude. It was the ideal way to surreptitiously enter a country and move unhindered by the threat of surveillance and law enforcement.

Unfortunately, the risks were far greater. In the case of Macau, Dewey was on Chinese sovereign soil. This made the risk of the operation much higher. Unlike some countries, the Chinese government liked to put most foreign travelers under some sort of surveillance, especially Americans. Even though Dewey was traveling under a Spanish alias which was designed to withstand electronic scrutiny, the Chinese also used sophisticated facial recognition software at most airports and border crossings.

Dewey's last visit to China was two years before, an operation to kill the head of Chinese Intelligence, Fao Bhang. The mission was successful. China was just about the last place on earth he could afford to spend a lot of time in.

But Macau also had advantages. It was one of China's shining jewels, the epicenter of gambling in Asia. Macau now surpassed Las Vegas as the largest gambling mecca in the world. Gambling was incredibly important – and brought in hundreds of billions of dollars to the Chinese economy. If gambling was an important and growing source of revenue for China, so were gamblers, especially so-called "big fish" like Diego Escalante. Those arriving in Macau on private jets were screened on the tarmac by local Chinese customs officials. It was a far simpler and easier process than having to go through the long customs line in the main terminal.

In Madrid, he switched planes, getting on a private Airbus owned by Escalante. The plane was luxurious. There were two staterooms along with a large lounge area with leather couches, televisions, and several stewardesses. In case any of the stewardesses or pilots aboard the jet worked for Chinese intelligence, Dewey acted the role of a Spanish billionaire, or at least how he thought one might act.

A few hours out, he phoned Jenna.

"Hi, Dewey."

"Hi," said Dewey.

"Where are you?"

"Two hours out. Mack said there are changes to the design."

"Only one," said Jenna. "You'll get to the Grand Hyatt, change, and go to the Mandarin. General Yong-sik has arranged for a private blackjack game at eleven P.M. You'll be posing as his dealer. I hope you're okay with cards."

"I'll be fine."

"Bill was worried about a strip search by Yong-sik's security crew," said Jenna. "We won't want them finding the needle, obviously. We altered the protocol. The needle will be taped to the underside of the Blackjack table."

"Got it."

"There's one more thing," said Jenna. "A plane left Tehran heading to Macau and landed around the same time as Yong-sik's plane. It was Abu Paria's."

–

When the jet touched down in Macau, a pair of young Chinese customs officials came on board the plane and inspected his passport, then conducted a brief interview with Dewey. The two officials were deferential.

A limousine was waiting on the tarmac. The driver was an older man in a black uniform. He was Chinese and opened the back door of the limousine.

"Grand Hyatt Hotel, por favor," said Dewey.

"Of course, sir."

"What is the local time?" Dewey asked in Spanish.

"Nine-thirty," said the driver as the limousine started moving.

It was getting late. He needed to move quickly now.

At the Grand Hyatt, Dewey was given a key to the room. The suite was on the top floor of the hotel. Once inside, he went to the closet and found the safe. He typed in a six digit code and the safe popped open.

Inside was a large pile of cash, two silenced handguns – Colt 1911s, an earbud, two concealed weapons holsters, and a piece of twine.

Dewey picked up the earbud and placed it in his ear, tapping twice.

"This is Dewey Andreas, on COMMO, check."

He heard a few clicks, then a male voice.

"Hold on, please."

A moment later, he heard Jenna's soft British accent.

"Dewey?" said Jenna. "Are you ready?"

"Yeah."

"Was everything there?"

"Yes."

"Okay, you need to get moving," said Jenna. "Yong-sik is now at dinner. The Mandarin Hotel is next door to the Grand Hyatt. There's a tuxedo in the closet. Put it on. It should fit you."

"I don't like tuxedos."

Jenna laughed.

"As I said before, you'll be penetrating the operation as a Blackjack dealer. Two security men from the Mandarin will accompany you to Yong-sik's room. Your identification is in the pocket of the tuxedo. You're Spanish, but not Escalante, that was simply to get into the country. You're originally from Madrid. You've worked various places, Las Vegas, Dubai, and most recently, Monaco. There'll be a security perimeter around Yong-sik's suite. It's imperative that you be unarmed."

"What do you mean, 'unarmed?'"

"Leave the guns. Dewey, you're going to be scanned and patted down by experts," said Jenna. "If they find a weapon on you, they'll kill you."

"How many men are we talking about?"

"Four or five would be my guess, though we don't know for sure. Now listen up. There are two electric shuffling machines," said Jenna, "though you shouldn't even need to deal any cards. The syringe will be taped to the underside of the card table. A gun will be hidden next to it. Yong-sik gambles alone. If his goons are outside, you need to poison him without him calling for help. If any of his men stay in the suite while he plays, you need to kill them."

"Fine, I got it."

"Just remember, Dewey, be careful with the poison," said Jenna. "There's one antidote and it's in Pyongang. You can't play around."

"I'll try not to."

"Now get moving," said Jenna. "He should be finishing dinner any minute. Good luck."

"Was there anything more on Paria?" said Dewey.

"No, nothing."

–

Yong-sik took a sip of wine and looked at Paria. Paria was talking on his phone, saying something in Arabic. Every few words, Paria would take a large sip of wine.

Finally, he hung up the phone. He looked at Yong-sik's interpreter.

"The objects we discussed are moving toward the Port of Nampo," said Paria quietly. "They'll be there in a few hours."

"I will make sure we're ready to receive them."

"What about the—" Paria paused, looking around, then whispering: "objects?"

Yong-sik glanced to a table nearby. A man in a dark suit met his eyes and nodded.

"Everything has been put aboard your plane," said Yong-sik.

"Excellent," said Paria, smiling.

"I'm grateful," said Yong-sik, reaching out and shaking Paria's hand. "My country is grateful."

"As are we," said Paria. "The… objects are all capable of hitting the west coast of the United States," whispered Paria. "Just put them on the launch pad, hit the button, and say bye bye Los Angeles. Now, I must go."

"Why such a rush?" said Yong-sik.

"I am flying back tonight."

Paria quietly scanned the dimly-lit restaurant.

"Too many people want me dead," said Paria, standing. "Macau isn't safe, not for anyone."

22

GRAND HYATT HOTEL
MACAU

Dewey mixed the tubes of black hair color and massaged it back through his hair. He took the electric razor and shaved off his beard but left his mustached intact, using the last of the hair dye to color that as well. He took a quick shower, put on the tuxedo, and locked everything – weapons, commo, his real identification – in the safe.

He looked at himself in the mirror. It had been an easy set of alterations – drugstore hair color and an electric razor – yet he was surprised at how different he looked. The rich brown tan of his skin helped. He looked Spanish – like a bullfighter, or a model.

As he stepped toward the door, his eyes were drawn to a table next to the bed. There was a small pad of paper there along with a pen. He took the pen and put it in his jacket pocket, then left the room.

Always know where your weapon is.

He walked the two blocks from the Grand Hyatt to the Mandarin. As he was about to go inside, he looked at his watch. It was nine P.M. He still had half-an-hour before he was supposed to meet the casino crew chief, a man named Yao who would insert him into Yong-sik's card crew.

–

Paria said goodbye to Yong-sik and arose from the table. As he walked to the lobby of the Mandarin, he put his phone to his ear and dialed.

"Kaivan," he said. "I'm just leaving now. Have the plane ready to go."

"Yes, general," said Kaivan.

Paria walked through the lobby of the hotel. His eyes were drawn to a man in a tuxedo who was coming in through the hotel's main entrance. He was large and walked with the calm, athletic demeanor of an athlete, his eyes scanning the lobby as if hunting for prey. He had a mustache and neatly combed dark hair. He looked, for a brief series of moments, Spanish. But Paria saw through the subtle disguise. It was a man who, for three years, had crowned the list of enemies of the Islamic Republic of Iran, a man Paria's VEVAK agents had died a few months before in the French Alps trying to kill. It was the man who stole Iran's first – and only – fully operational nuclear device. An American. *The* American.

By God, it was Dewey Andreas.

Paria immediately stopped and scanned the lobby. He turned and walked toward the concierge desk, at the side of the lobby. It was a small miracle the American hadn't seen him first.

Paria turned sharply and moved past the concierge's desk, out of sight line. He pulled out his phone and dialed Kaivan.

"Get over here," said Paria. "*Immediately!*"

"What is it?" said Kaivan.

"Andreas is at the hotel," said Paria.

There was a long pause, then Kaivan spoke.

"Do you think…" Kaivan started. "Do you think he knows you're here?"

"No," seethed Paria. "He's not here for me. It's some sort of operation, perhaps involving Yong-sik."

"We need to warn him—"

"*Shut up,*" said Paria, watching from behind a pillar as Andreas walked into the Mandarin's lobby bar. "We don't need to warn anyone. We need to kill Dewey Andreas."

–

Dewey entered the lobby of the Mandarin. It was modern and elegant, busy yet hushed. On the other side of the lobby, he heard the din of voices and laughter coming from the hotel bar. He looked at his watch one more time and walked to the bar, taking a seat at the bar.

"Puedo tomar su orden, señor?" said the bartender in Spanish.

"Dos borbones Americano y dos cervezas, por favor" said Dewey.

"En seguida, señor."

The bar was crowded and, as Dewey waited for his drinks, he glanced around. It was mostly couples, along with a few groups of men. All of them, no doubt, getting ready to go out for a night of gambling.

When the drinks came, Dewey took one of the bourbons and threw it back. He then drank the beer down in three or four large gulps. He paused for a few moments, looked at his watch, then took a small sip from the second beer, nursing it as he bided time. When he was ten minutes out, he looked at the bartender.

"El baño, señor?" Dewey said.

"Allá, por el pasillo, señor."

Dewey walked through the bar to a dimly lit hallway, then entered the empty, brightly lit restroom.

At the sink across from the door, he turned on the water as he pushed his hand back through his hair. His eyes looked glassy and a little bloodshot, but he was alert.

The door burst open.

Reflected in the mirror, Dewey caught the black, murderous eyes of a very large man. He barely had time to register the man's face, barely had time to remember. He was coming too fast. Whoever it was coming to kill him.

Paria.

The Iranian lurched through the door and charged like a madman at Dewey. In his right hand, Paria clutched a knife. He sprinted at Dewey, who kept his back turned. An animalistic grunt came from Paria as he lunged across the restroom.

In the mirror, Dewey registered a second man just behind Paria, a tall, thin Iranian in a business suit. Dewey left the water running and reached to his chest, removing the pen from his blazer pocket.

Always know where your weapon is.

132

Paria raised the blade to his right and swung at Dewey – from behind – slashing the silver steel in the direction of Dewey's neck.

Dewey waited, watching in the mirror, timing his next move. At the last possible instant, Dewey ducked, rotated a quarter turn, then burst back towards Paria with his shoulder, slamming Paria just above his waist. Paria's legs went out from underneath him before he could stab the knife into Dewey. He was airborne for a second, then fell on his back onto the hard marble floor.

Dewey kept moving, surging across the bathroom toward the second killer. The man was already moving toward Dewey, swinging at him with another knife.

Dewey anticipated it, ducking sideways. The knife missed, the blade cut the air just inches from Dewey's face. The Iranian was exposed.

Dewey swung the pen viciously through the air, but the Iranian was quick, ducking, avoiding Dewey's swing. He swiped at Dewey a second time, a violent, trained slash. The blade struck Dewey at his left forearm, but Dewey struck in the same moment, swinging the pen viciously through the air. The killer's combat blade grazed Dewey's arm in the same moment the pen's steel tip thrust into his skull. Dewey gored the pen tip deep into the man's temple. The pen penetrated skin, then into skull. Blood shot left as the pen broke through the membrane.

The thug collapsed to the ground as Dewey swiveled – facing Paria.

Paria was on his feet again. He squared off against Dewey, a combat knife in his right hand. Paria flicked it at Dewey as he moved slowly toward Dewey. Suddenly, Paria lurched at Dewey, swinging with his right arm. Dewey blocked Paria's forearm with his left hand as the blade ripped toward him, then punched Paria in the nose, jerking Paria abruptly backwards. Blood shot from Paria's nostrils.

Paria shuffled back and put his fingers to his nose. His fingers came away covered in blood. He eyed Dewey with hatred.

Paria moved toward Dewey and swung again, a vicious slash at Dewey's neck. Dewey jerked his head back, evading the knife, then sent a vicious kick up into Paria's neck, snapping his head backwards.

He followed the kick with a savage strike of the pen, stabbing it through Paria's left cheek, then yanking it back out.

Paria staggered backwards, stepping toward the urinals, trying to settle down, trying to slow things down. In his right hand Paria still clutched a knife. He felt for his left cheek with his other hand. Again, his hand came back covered in blood.

"They taught you well," said Paria, breathing rapidly, his nose and cheek gushing blood. "Tell me, Dewey, why are you in Macau?"

It had been many years since the endless, monotonous training; KAPAP, Eskrima, Brazilian Jujitsu. All of it had been taught to Dewey and the other members of his Delta class by a South African named Johannes and his small team of martial arts experts. Dewey had fought for hours on end, for days on end, for weeks and months on end, with hands and face covered in blood, sometimes been beaten unconscious. He'd fought so much it eventually become part of him. It all came back to him now as he stared down Paria, whose face ran red with crimson.

Calmly, Paria wiped his blood-soaked fingers on his shirt as his left cheek ran red down to his short collar.

Dewey stared like a hunter at Paria, who was backed up against the wall.

Over Paria's shoulder, Dewey eyed the door –

Paria shook his head. The message was clear:

Only one of us leaves this bathroom alive.

Dewey clutched the pen in his right hand. He stepped back and squared off against Paria, who still clutched the knife.

Dewey clutched the pen in his right hand.

Paria came at him, holding the blade out in front of him. He took one step then another. He leapt at Dewey, spearing the knife blade at Dewey's torso. Dewey dodged left, avoiding the blade, then swung the tip of the pen at Paria's mauled face.

Paria caught Dewey's wrist with his left hand as the pen tip came within a quarter inch of his left eye. Paria's hand was big and gripped Dewey's wrist like a vice.

Paria yanked hard – his strength was tremendous – and sent Dewey tumbling to the ground. Dewey's head struck the base of corner of the sink. The pen popped from Dewey's hand and careened toward the door, away from him.

Paria descended onto Dewey, who lay on the ground face up. The blade was in Paria's right hand. Bleeding badly from his nose and cheek, Paria was smiling. He raised his right hand and took a hatchet swing from above. Dewey saw the blade as it glinted in the light. He pushed with his hand against the sink, then kicked up at Paria's head. Dewey's foot landed squarely in Paria's badly damaged nose, crushing it. Dewey felt bones break as his foot made contact.

For the first time, Paria screamed out in agony, an animal moan, dropping the knife. Blood poured from both nostrils as Paria stumbled backwards, but somehow managed to remain on his feet.

Dewey climbed to his feet. He charged at Paria, punched Paria's chest with his right fist; it was like hitting a tree. He swung again, this time lower, at his rib cage, with everything he had. But still, Paria remained standing, almost unhurt.

Paria hammered a left fist into Dewey's chest, pushing Dewey back. Paria swung again, catching Dewey in the ribcage, as Dewey flailed a punch that caught nothing but air, and then Paria swung yet again, his right fist in a roundhouse blow that caught Dewey squarely in the chin, sending his head sharply, dangerously backwards.

Dewey remained standing, his vision momentarily blurred and dizzy. He could feel it then, the surge of warmth. It started in his neck and shot out concentrically, like a drug. It was the feeling he knew. The feeling that was behind it all. It spread across Dewey as the figure of the hulkish Paria moved toward him:

No man can kill you.

Paria swung again, right fist to the ribs, then left. Dewey absorbed the blows as Paria moved him backwards, against the wall. Paria swung at Dewey's head, striking him behind the ear with a painful punch. He swung again, this time with all his might. He wanted a knockout blow to Dewey's head. Paria's feet left the floor.

Dewey ducked. Paria's fist struck the marble wall, his fingers cracked against the hard stone, and he recoiled.

Dewey kicked Paria in the groin, bending him forward, then followed the kick with a punch to the forehead, jerking Paria back.

Paria caught himself, letting the jab push his head to an upright position. He leapt at Dewey, tackling him at the waist and wrestling him to the ground. Dewey landed hard, on his back, in a growing pool of blood. Paria landed on top of him. He seized Dewey's arm and twisted, causing Dewey to wince in pain, but Paria wouldn't let go of it as he moved his other hand to Dewey's neck.

The Iranian was now on top of him, at least two-hundred-and-fifty pounds of muscle and hatred.

Paria let go of Dewey's arm and wrapped both hands around Dewey's neck now, gripping it tightly, strangling him.

Dewey tried to punch at Paria but it was useless, like striking a wall. He struggled for air as the Iranian dug his fingers deeply into his trachea, choking him, trying to break his neck. Dewey was weakening, struggling for air, and he stopped punching at Paria. He searched desperately with his hands. He felt for one of the knives, slapping at the blood-covered marble in vain.

He felt blackness coming on through the lack of air.

Through intense pain, Dewey searched with his arms. He slapped the ground, feeling along the wet floor. But he found nothing. Still, he kept searching as Paria choked him, staring with black fury into Dewey's eyes. Paria kneaded the neck, watching Dewey turn blue, choking him violently.

Dewey felt something then. It was the pen. It was there, just beyond his fingertips. It was against the wall. It was just out of reach, but he kept fingering the ground as he felt the lack of oxygen, and the sheer weight on top of him.

And then Dewey's fingers found the pen and picked it up.

He was weak now. He gripped the pen, trying to simply muster the strength to swing at Paria, but he could not.

Don't give up.

Dewey felt a strange sense of calm. He studied Paria's neck. A big vein bulged on the right side of it as he choked Dewey. Dewey closed his eyes and swung as hard as he could, slashing the tip of the pen into the side of Paria's neck. The tip gored through skin and muscle, ripping deeply into Paria's neck, penetrating flesh, veins and Dewey's target, Paria's carotid artery. Blood shot right from Paria's neck like a hose. The pen stuck out from the side of Paria's neck as blood poured from his neck. Paria's hands went abruptly weak. He let go of Dewey's neck and fell to the floor.

Dewey fought for breath, watching as Paria pulled the pen from his neck, screaming, then held his hand against his neck to try and stop the current of dark blood that flowed.

Dewey lay on the floor, barely able to move. Paria attempted to hold his neck as blood poured down over his fingers. Dewey pushed himself up. He climbed to his feet and stood. He straightened his tie and then looked down at Paria, as Paria attempted to speak.

"What is it, Abu?" said Dewey, trying to catch his breath. "Still wondering why I'm in Macau?"

Through clotted throat, Paria moved his head.

Yes.

Dewey reached down and grabbed the neck of Paria's shirt and ripped it up. He took the strip of cotton and removed his tuxedo coat. He wrapped the piece of material around his forearm, over his white tuxedo shirt, where he'd been grazed with the blade. He put the coat back on and looked at Paria. Dewey removed a cell and opened the camera. He snapped a few photos of Paria bleeding out on the bathroom floor, then texted them to Calibrisi.

"Maybe I was here to kill you," said Dewey. "Have you ever considered that?"

Paria's eyes fluttered. They turned white for a split second as they rolled back up into his head and he died.

Dewey looked to his right, at the long row of stalls, each with full doors. He dragged Paria into one of the stalls and shoved his gargantuan corpse into the corner, wedged next to the toilet. He retrieved the second man, dragged him to the stall, then lifted him up and threw him on top of Paria. He went inside the stall, locked the door from the inside, then stood on the toilet and climbed out over the door.

Dewey went to the mirror and splashed cold water on his face. He looked at his tuxedo. He could see blood in the bright lights of the bathroom. He took a hand towel and wetted it, then dabbed it where he saw blood. The jacket was also badly wrinkled, but there was nothing he could do about that. He saw a few blotches of red on the front of the shirt. There was nothing he could do about those either.

He still had some time until the meeting with Yao, the man Langley had on the inside of the Mandarin. He looked at the ground. The floor was spattered in blood, with several large pools. But there were no bodies. Someone entering the restroom wouldn't discover the corpses immediately.

With calm, his back upright, he walked back to the bar, pushing his hand up through his thick, slightly perspiring hair. As he arrived at the bar, a pair of females was standing behind his empty chair. They were in their twenties, one was blonde, the other, brunette, both had long, straight hair and wore short, stylish dresses.

"Excuse me," said Dewey, reaching for his drink. "Would you like the chair? I was just getting ready to leave."

Both women smiled, gazing up at Dewey. The brunette grabbed Dewey's bourbon and handed it to him.

"No, I've decided, you can't leave yet."

She handed Dewey the glass, rubbing his chest with the back of her hand after he took it from her.

"Thank you," said Dewey.

He took the glass and downed it, nodding to the bartender for another. When it came, the bartended handed it to him. Dewey downed it as quickly as the first.

The bartender watched him, as did the women.

"Another?" said the bartender.

Dewey looked for the first time at the blonde, his eyes meeting hers, green eyes that invited Dewey to speak to her. Then he looked at the brunette, whose brown eyes were like warm pools; she moved a half step closer, smiling seductively up at Dewey.

Dewey met their looks with a cold, emotionless glance, neither affectionate nor arrogant. It was a blank look, Dewey's blue eyes like cold Maine ocean in winter. He glanced at his watch. He still had a few minutes.

"One more," said Dewey, looking at the bartender. "And whatever these two would like."

23

BELVERDSHIRE MANOR HOUSE
ENGLAND

Chalmers's Agusta Westland AW101 descended upon a square rectangle of green manicured British lawn, its big rotors swirling the chilly autumn evening, blowing leaves an every direction.

The estate – Belverdshire – was massive, limestone in a three story spread out of picture books about England, a castle really.

Chalmers, the head of British Intelligence, watched the landing through a window. At age 51, the Eton-educated Brit had thick blonde hair, a sharp nose, and a handsome face. He had on a neatly fitting business suit, a subtle Savile Row plaid in double breast style. Chalmers was 6'4". He wore a blue striped button down shirt with no tie, a pair of brown, slightly worn John Lobb wingtips on his feet. He didn't look all that dissimilar to what he looked like twenty years before, when he was MI6's top spy in the Middle East, perhaps slightly more confident – and ten pounds heavier.

Chalmers held a leather valise as he climbed from the door of the big chopper. He crossed the lawn and was met by a man in a suit.

"Sir Derek?"

"Good evening."

"I'm William."

The man extended a phone.

"Please, your left thumb, sir."

"Of course," said Chalmers.

A moment later, the phone beeped.

"Follow me, sir."

Chalmers walked astride the man across a pebble stone driveway before the mansion's limestone portico. Ivy covered many of the walls. This was an old house, a palace really.

Chalmers barely noted the mansion's grand façade. He'd been here before.

He was ushered through the grand entrance foyer, around a large round table atop which sat a large bouquet of red Peonies and the day's newspapers. They went straight ahead. After passing through a high-ceilinged hallway with walls adorned with framed photographs and portraits, Chalmers was ushered through a large doorway into a large drawing room. The room was massive, with twenty foot ceilings, some walls lined with bookshelves, others with paintings both modern and old – Picassos, Damien Hirsts, and several Rembrandts. There were two different seating areas, each generally focused on opposite ends of the room, where tall, fanciful stone fireplaces contained roaring fires. One of the two seating areas had sofas and chairs in old, burnished leather. Above the mantel was a massive, ancient looking taxidermy of a buffalo's head, shot by the great great great great grandfather of the current occupant of Belverdshire while on a hunting trip to America in 1765. The other seating area was more formal looking, with chintz-covered George Smith Chesterfield sofas and over-stuffed chairs.

Chalmers crossed the length of the room to the far seating area, usually referred to as the "Buffalo end."

A man with a mane of gray and black hair was seated on a leather sofa. He had a thick crystal glass in his hand, which was a quarter-filled with single malt. The man wore a stylish red button down shirt and gray flannels. His legs were crossed. He was smoking a cigarette, somehow making it look elegant, even appetizing, his drags refined, his exhales blown with grace.

"Mr. Home Secretary," said Chalmers as he approached.

"Get yourself a drink," said Lord Radcliff. He didn't need to tell Chalmers where the liquor was kept.

Chalmers crossed to a bookcase and pushed it in slightly. The entire bookcase swung out. Behind it was a dimly lit copper bar, small but lined with bottles, glasses, a silver ice bucket, and a copper sink and faucet.

"Try the Irish, Derek," said Radcliff.

Chalmers grabbed the single malt. It was an ancient looking bottle of Jameson's, the label partially worn off and brown with age. He poured a glass and turned the sink on ever so slightly, creating a few small drips of water. He let one hit the liquid in the glass, turned the water off, and walked to a big club chair across from where Radcliff was seated.

Chalmers took a small sip and looked at Radcliff.

"Well?"

"Rather decent," said Chalmers.

"I would hope so," said Radcliff. "That bottle cost me fifteen thousand pounds at auction."

Chalmers stared at the glass.

"I would've been more aggressive with my pour."

Radcliff chuckled, leaned forward, and stubbed out his cigarette.

"You wanted to see me, Derek?" said Radcliff.

"Yes," said Chalmers. "It's about your niece."

"Jenna?"

"Yes."

Radcliff lifted his glass to his lips, paused, then took a sip. He smiled.

"Jenna," Radcliff said. "Your star pupil. Do you miss her?"

Chalmers looked into the hearth.

"Very much so," said Chalmers.

"And how's she getting on with the Americans?"

"From what I've heard, no complaints, though she hasn't done much. People are wondering why she's even there."

"Is that why you wanted to see me?"

"No," said Chalmers. "I spoke with Hector Calibrisi earlier today. They're running an operation in North Korea. It was her design. They needed to expose Talmadge."

"Did they ask permission?" said Radcliff.

"In a manner, yes. If successful, the price will have been worth it."

Radcliff took a silver case from his pocket and opened it. He grabbed a cigarette and lit it.

"But that isn't why you're here," said Radcliff.

Chalmers shook his head, no.

"No," he said, taking a sip of scotch. "I've come to talk about the final report on the death of Jenna's husband, Charles."

"I read it," said Lord Radcliff. "Jenna's Range Rover was blown up with a generic form of SEMTEX. A government who wanted her dead, or perhaps mercenaries. Spotless, except they killed the wrong person. It was a terrible report. Superficial, without possible explanations or reasons as to why someone should want to kill Jenna. Inconclusive. As for motive, the report was disappointingly vague."

"That's the official version, yes," said Chalmers.

"Is there an unofficial version, Sir Derek?"

"Lord Secretary, I hired an outside firm, disconnected to MI6 and the British government. Israelis I know."

"Interesting," said Radcliff, taking a puff of his cigarette. "And what did they find?"

"Charles Hartford was the target of the bombing, Lord Radcliff," said Chalmers, "not Jenna."

Radcliff took a puff and exhaled, then took a sip of scotch. His face contorted with disbelief.

"*Charles?*" said Radcliff. "Nonsense! I've known the boy since he was born. *It was Jenna's bloody Rover!*"

"Charles's cell was destroyed in the bombing, but the Israelis were able to penetrate the SBC database and find the last week's worth of text messages on his phone. The man Charles was supposed to meet, his business partner, Billy Thompson, made sure Charles would pick him up in the Rover that day," said Chalmers. "After his partner's death, Mr. Thompson liquidated the partnership's assets and disappeared. Interestingly, he wired Charles's partner's half to Jenna. He could've easily kept it all."

Radcliff leaned forward and grabbed another cigarette, then nodded to a servant, indicating he would need a refreshment on his beverage. He lit the cigarette, puffed, put the lighter down, leaned forward, deep in thought, then leaned back until he reached leather.

"I don't like where this story is going, Derek."

"I don't either, Mr. Home Secretary," said Chalmers.

"Who is this Thompson character?"

"Precisely," said Chalmers. "He's American, at least that was his cover. He met Charles at Harvard Business School. That's how he reconnected with him two years ago, an alumni group. It appears he may have paid off certain people in the business school IT department to manufacture his having gone there."

Chalmers paused.

"And?" said Lord Radcliff. "His background? Where is he from? Who are his parents?"

"There's nothing there," said Chalmers. "An only child, both parents now dead, no relatives. There's quite literally not enough there to fill an ashtray. Either he was a ghost or it's been wiped clean."

"What do the Israelis think?

"They don't know, but their suspicion is Thompson is a Russian operative."

Chalmers paused, becoming slightly emotional. He took a sip of scotch and continued.

"For Christ sake, Derek, if you're going to tell me Charles somehow got himself mixed up with Moscow—"

"Jenna," interrupted Chalmers. "That's why I'm here. What if the bombing was intended to send a message to Jenna?"

"Well, now, that's a muddy bog, isn't it?" whispered Lord Radcliff. "But how? You recruited her. She's my niece."

Chalmers said nothing.

"That doesn't seem to impress you," said Radcliff.

"Lord Radcliff, I don't believe she's mixed up in anything, but we need to make sure."

"She obviously is mixed up in something, Derek."

"I'm not willing to go to that conclusion yet."

"So why not ask her?"

"You know the answer to that, Mr. Home Secretary," said Chalmers.

"You'd tip her off, that is, if there's a connection."

"Which I believe is not even a remote possibility," said Chalmers. "Still, we need to run this down, and yes, we don't want to tip her off."

"Do you inform the Americans?"

"No. Not yet. Not until we know more. I trust Hector but no."

"What do you need from me?"

"I need authorization to run a Cambridge Protocol," said Chalmers.

Radcliff looked up. The ask was unusual – and significant. Chalmers wanted permission to investigate Jenna's father, Sir Bobby Farragut, the Earl of Ipswich, a member of the Royal family, the brother of Radcliff's wife. By British law, only the Home Secretary and the Prime Minister could allow a Cambridge authority and both needed to agree.

"Why do you need it?" said Lord Radcliff.

"As a former Circus employee, MI6 can investigate Jenna. But not her parents."

Lord Radcliff stood up and walked to the hearth. He threw another log onto the fire. He remained standing in front of the fireplace.

"It seems there should be more substance before the Prime Minister and I allow you to start rooting around in Sir Bobby's affairs."

"I'm not talking about a full-blown investigation," said Chalmers. "This is strictly sub-rosa, off the books. I would bet my life Jenna is clean. She's like a daughter to me and I think I know her. If Jenna knew I was suspicious it would destroy her. But we cannot be governed by emotion."

"And certainly not trust," said Radcliff.

"If there's a connection back-up into Moscow, we need to know. That includes everything back through birth."

"Would you use the same firm?" said Radcliff, walking to the large coffee table and picking up a cigarette, then lighting it. "The Israelis?"

"No. This is a REPO: We need to find Billy Thompson, whoever he is. To do that will require a degree of brute force. We're talking about Russia. This isn't going to be delicate."

"Who then?"

"I want to hire a firm out of Virginia," said Chalmers. "It's a Langley shop. Katie Foxx and Rob Tacoma, both ex-Special Operations Group. They have deep agency ties and if this thing gets out-of-control I want Langley there. Also, Tacoma is fluent in Russian."

"And?"

"They're expensive."

"How expensive?"

"Two million dollars a week. They don't negotiate."

"Well, Sir Derek, that's why we pay you," said Radcliff, "to make those decisions. It seems exorbitant but I trust your instincts. I know you'll protect Jenna."

"So do I have your support, Lord Radcliff?" said Chalmers.

"Yes. I'll call the Prime Minister later and brief him. Assume he'll agree with my assessment. If not, I'll call you – but you're to proceed."

Chalmers drained the glass and stood. He nodded at Radcliff and turned. He started toward the door.

"Derek," said Radcliff.

Chalmers stopped and turned back to Lord Radcliff.

"If, or I should say, *when* this turns out to be a goddam goose chase, we are to never talk of it again," said Lord Radcliff. "She is my niece. This was part of our duty as government."

"Yes, Lord Radcliff."

24

CIA HEADQUARTERS

Calibrisi received Dewey's texts of Abu Paria. They were grisly photos. Paria was lifeless and drenched in blood. He stared at them for several moments.

When Calibrisi was an agent, he'd taken similar photos after killing. In a drawer at his home, he still had a photograph of him holding a dead Pablo Escobar by the hair in the moments after he shot him. The killing of Paria was a major development and Calibrisi knew it. Paria had been one of America's and Israel's most formidable enemies, funding terror everywhere he could.

Two thoughts came to Calibrisi's mind. First, why was Paria in Macau and at the same hotel as Yong-sik? Second, there would be a power vacuum inside the Iranian military and intelligence hierarchy.

Both were urgent, but the latter was less urgent. Yong-sik and North Korea took precedence.

He forwarded the photos to a number of individuals inside the Agency.

To the head of the Iran desk, he texted:

> Paria dead. We need to know if this represents an opportunity to move on Suleiman.

Then he gathered Jenna, Polk, Perry, and a few others, passing around his phone.

"This adds a new element to what is going on in Pyongang," said Hector. "I know everyone is focused, but it's time to double-down.

Paria had to have been meeting with Yong-sik. We need to know why. We need to start worrying. Think outside the box."

–

Jenna went to her briefcase, a beat-up leather briefcase from Tanner Krolle, a gift from Charles. She removed a cell phone and powered it up. She found the number and hit dial.

After several clicks and long silences, the phone started ringing.

"Hello?"

"Hi, Jayson."

There was a long pause.

"I heard you left," Fields said. "Went to the dark side."

His accent was British but rough, a cockney accent, from London's east end.

"I did," said Jenna.

"You could've said goodbye, you know. I was left to rumors. The entire field was left to rumors. Bitchy, if you ask me."

"Tell me how you really feel," said Jenna.

"What do you want?"

"Are you still stationed in Macau?" Jenna asked.

"Yes."

"Are you working?"

"Yes," he said. "We're killing some Australians."

"I need your help."

"With what?"

"We're running an operation in the city," she said. "There might be some complications. I don't trust anyone we have there, well, other than the agent running it."

"Fuck off," said Fields. "I work for England."

Jenna paused.

"We both work for the same side, Jayson."

"Jenna," Fields said, his voice softening. "You know I'd do anything for you. I'm mid-stream in this."

"I understand. I won't call you unless it's really, really, really important, okay?"

25

MANDARIN HOTEL
MACAU

"So, how do you like Macau?" said one of the women, the brunette.

Dewey tried to remember which alias he was supposed to be working under. Was he Escalante or was he a different Spaniard? He was a different guy, a veteran high stakes dealer most recently in Monaco. He hadn't even asked Jenna his name.

"It's okay," said Dewey.

The blonde perked up. The brunette was already smiling as she stood close to Dewey and took a sip of white wine. The blonde put her hand on Dewey's shoulder.

The two women looked like models. Both were young, late twenties, with perfectly chiseled faces, dressed in sleek dresses that showed off their long legs.

Dewey looked at his watch. It was 9:44.

"I have to go."

The brunette put her hand to Dewey's torso.

"Mr. Yao sent us to retrieve you. He said you might be late."

–

Dewey was led outside by the two women. A half block away, a tall man was standing next to a long, black Mercedes limousine. He opened the door as Dewey approached. Inside, Dewey sat on the back seat. Across from him was an Asian man, older, distinguished looking, with an unhappy glare on his face. He was dressed in a blue button down shirt with no tie along with stylish pants and leather boots. He had black and gray hair. He was fair skinned, smart-looking, with a wide face and a fearless, calm demeanor. He stared at Dewey as Dewey sat down across from him and the gunman shut the door to the limo.

"You were supposed to be in my office fifteen minutes ago."

"Chill out."

"You think this is some sort of joke?" said Yao.

"Who do you work for?" said Dewey angrily. "If it's us then fuck you, Yao. Get me inside."

Yao exhaled with an exasperated sigh, but said nothing.

"I'm sorry I was late," said Dewey, quieting down. "I was attacked in the bathroom off the lobby. If you don't believe me, there are two bodies in there. You're going to need a clean-up crew."

Yao's mouth went slightly ajar. He leaned back and whispered something in Mandarin to the limo driver, who climbed out of the vehicle and moved quickly toward the hotel.

"Who was it?"

"Iranians."

Yao nodded almost imperceptibly.

"Why the bar?" said Yao.

"I needed a drink. Now if it's okay with you, can we get going?"

"Fine, just a couple things. As you're standing in front of the table – dealing – the needle is sticking forward, toward where he will be sitting. The gun is to the right. It's chambered, no safety, suppressor."

"Fine."

Yao nodded, yes.

"You should know," said Yao, "Yong-sik is a big man."

"How big?"

"Not as big as you, but nearly. He won't go down without a fight."

Dewey grinned.

"Thanks for the heads up, now can we get moving?"

–

"Yong-sik will bet upwards of a million dollars a hand," said Yao, leading Dewey back inside the hotel. "Some people think he counts cards. He's made and lost tens of millions of dollars at the Mandarin. Right now, his house account is up by more than eleven million dollars."

Near the elevators, Dewey and Yao were met by a pair of security men from the casino, dressed in dark business suits, one of whom held a large steel briefcase. Inside were two card shuffling machines, several new decks of cards, and $20 million dollars in chips, already paid for by the People's Republic of North Korea.

"They'll take you," said Yao. "By the way, the suite is soundproof."

Dewey nodded and climbed aboard the elevator with the two security men. One of the men slid a thick metal card into the elevator console, then pressed "PH." The elevator moved silently up toward the top floor. When the doors opened a minute later, they moved left, toward the end of the carpeted, dimly-lit hall. They arrived at the Presidential Suite. Four men were standing guard outside the large mahogany double doors. They were dressed in military attire – light khaki – and each man wore a black beret. Each man clutched a submachine gun.

They were North Korean special forces soldiers, positioned outside Yong-sik's suite of rooms.

Dewey stayed behind the casino security men.

One of the North Koreans – a short, wiry man in his thirties with a thin mustache – stepped forward, holding his hand up to greet one of the hotel security men.

"*Lùjūn shàngxiào*," said the Mandarin employee, speaking in Mandarin. "*Huānyíng huí dào guóyǔ jiǔdiàn*."

Colonel Pak. Welcome back to the Mandarin.

"Who's he?" said Pak, the North Korean. "I've never seen him before."

Yao nodded toward Dewey:

"This is Pablo. He's been working in Monte Carlo for several years. As you requested, he speaks neither Mandarin nor Korean."

The four North Korean soldiers all looked suspiciously at Dewey, scanning him from head to toe with a skeptical look. Colonel Pak started speaking in Korean, asking Dewey a question.

"He's Spanish," said the hotel security man. "He speaks Spanish and a little bit of English, that's all."

"Where in Spain are you from?" said the North Korean in broken English.

"Sevilla," said Dewey.

"Where?" Pak persisted.

"Montequinto," said Dewey.

Pak continued to stare at Dewey.

"Your jacket, very dirty."

Dewey nodded.

"I work all day, sir," said Dewey with a slight Spanish accent. "My apologies."

Finally, Pak nodded, saying nothing. He turned to one of the other North Korean agents, who stepped forward and patted Dewey down, looking for a weapon.

One of the other North Koreans knocked on the door. After waiting a few seconds, he opened it.

"General Yong-sik," the man said in Korean as he peered cautiously inside. "The card dealer from the casino is here."

"Send him in," came a distant voice from inside the suite.

As three of the gunmen remained outside the suite, the senior North Korean, Colonel Pak, led Dewey and the others into the massive Presidential Suite.

Behind the double doors was a gilded entrance area, with a beautiful red oriental carpet, a large, gold-framed mirror on the wall, and a stunning Murano glass chandelier – colored a light orange – hanging from the ceiling. Beyond was a larger open living room.

A blackjack table was in the middle of the room.

The suite occupied the entire corner of the hotel's penthouse floor. The outer walls were all glass. The suite was luxurious, even exotic, with curving modern sofas in plush material and comfortable looking club chairs arranged around various tables of thick glass. Those walls not made of glass were covered in ornate wallpaper decorated with green and blue bamboo trees.

Yong-sik had the lights low. Macau sparkled through the windows, the lights of the city's skyline like a wall of stars.

One of the Mandarin security guards placed the steel briefcase on the Blackjack table and opened it up. He started setting up the table.

Dewey stood behind him, looking around for Yong-sik, but seeing no one. He became aware of music playing softly over speakers in the large room. It sounded like a guitar playing high notes accompanied by a female singer in a language he didn't understand.

The card table was six feet long, four feet wide, with a half-circle cut out for the dealer to stand. The security man stacked the chips neatly on the table along with the two shuffling machines and several decks of cards.

One of the casino men looked at Dewey, nodding. Then both men left as Dewey remained standing still just inside the living room.

Suddenly, Dewey heard Yong-sik's voice coming from another room. He was speaking Korean.

The North Korean agent stepped to Dewey, still not trusting him and afraid he might eavesdrop.

"Water?" said the North Korean, in English.

Dewey shook his head, no.

Yong-sik entered through a door on the far side of the room, pocketing a cell phone. He was taller than Dewey expected, six feet two or three. He was thin but clearly in good shape – muscular, with the gait of a fighter. He was wearing a short-sleeved polo shirt and khakis. From the file, Dewey knew Yong-sik was in his fifties, but he looked younger. He stared at Dewey, analyzing him. His eyes were black and calculating. Dewey felt a slight tinge of uneasiness.

He clutched a champagne glass in his hand. He crossed the room and stood before Dewey. He scanned him up and down, just as Dewey would expect a man who'd spent his life in the military to do. Dewey remained quiet, his eyes emotionless and calm, looking beyond Yong-sik.

"What is your name?" he asked in broken English.

"Pablo."

"Where are you from?"

"Spain," Dewey said, also in bad English, with a Spanish accent. "Recently, Monaco."

"Ah, yes," said Yong-sik. "I would like very much to go to Monaco."

"It is nice," said Dewey, nodding politely and avoiding eye contact.

Dewey caught Colonel Pak in his peripheral vision. He was watching Dewey carefully, glancing back and forth between staring at Dewey and looking at Yong-sik, who looked back. They were assessing Dewey. Was he a card dealer? Was he an American spy? A British spy? An Israeli spy? It was a question they had to ask themselves every time they stepped foot out of North Korea.

"May I see some identification?" said Yong-sik.

Dewey reached into his back pocket and produced his wallet, handing it to Yong-sik as if he had nothing to hide.

Pak joined Yong-sik, standing next to him and parsing through Dewey's wallet. Yong-sik removed a laminated work visa, worn at the edges, showing that Pablo Rios, born in Sevilla, Spain, was a Spanish resident. He held the card up next to Dewey, comparing the photo of the man on the plastic card with Dewey. Yong-sik put the card back in the wallet and handed it to Dewey.

"Precautions," said Yong-sik with a malevolent grin. He looked at Pak and brushed the air, sending him away. Colonel Pak turned and walked to the suite doors, exiting and shutting the doors. Dewey and Yong-sik were now alone.

Yong-sik looked at Dewey.

"Let's play some cards, yes?"

Dewey nodded without emotion.

He stepped to the table as Yong-sik went to the bar, pouring himself a large glass full of vodka.

Dewey moved to the card table and picked up a deck of cards. It was wrapped in plastic. He waited for Yong-sik to return to the table with his cocktail. After he sat down, Dewey presented him the unopened deck to inspect. Yong-sik brushed the air, indicating the gesture was unnecessary.

"I've been to the hotel many times," said Yong-sik. "There is no need."

Dewey fed the first deck into the card shuffling machine, running his hand along the underside of the table, trying to avoid the needle. He felt the long thin plastic of the syringe containing the poison, held to the table with a small piece of double-sided tape. He moved his hand left and felt the butt of the pistol, also stuck to the underside of the table.

Dewey did not make eye contact but instead continued to watch the electric shuffler as it moved cards frenetically through the machine.

He didn't want to waste time. There was good timing and bad timing in all operations, but knowing the right moment to move on a target was less about experience and more about luck. For whatever reason, Dewey continued to feel a sense of unease. Moreover, he was still flustered from what happened in the lobby of the hotel. First, Paria, then being tricked by Yao's female agents. Both situations had worked out, but either could've gone sideways. Dewey didn't feel lucky. He wanted to get out of Macau as soon as possible…

As Yong-sik lifted the glass of vodka to his mouth one more time, Dewey reached beneath the table and grabbed the pistol. He swept the gun above the table and trained it on Yong-sik, holding him in the firing line of the vasiform suppressor. With his other hand, he removed the syringe from beneath the card table and slowly raised it, placing his thumb atop the plunger – the needle extended like a dagger. He kept the gun aimed at Yong-sik, saying nothing.

Calmly, the general looked up at Dewey, not flinching. Yong-sik raised his hands, indicating he was not going to fight.

"I'm not here to kill you," said Dewey, his English now perfect. "But if you want to live you need to do exactly what I say—"

"Central Intelligence Agency?" said Yong-sik. "And what is in the needle?"

"Poison," said Dewey. "You'll have twenty four hours to do what we ask. Although if it was me I'd try and get it done sooner. Apparently the last few hours aren't much fun. The first hour sucks, too. You'll spike a fever. That's how we teach you we know what we're doing. You go back to Pyongang, do exactly what we tell you to do, we tell you where the antidote is."

"Clever," said Yong-sik, nodding respectfully. "So let me guess, you want me to kill Kim?" Yong-sik paused. "I will not. Go ahead and shoot me. He is my leader and my God."

"Why was Paria here?" said Dewey, who took a half-step backwards. He needed to move around the side of the table to hit Yong-sik with the needle.

Yong-sik remained seated, watching Dewey as Dewey moved slowly to his right—

Suddenly, Yong-sik kicked out into one of the legs on the underside of the table. It was a brutally hard kick and the table flew violently into Dewey's waist, knocking him back. Yong-sik's abrupt move caught Dewey off guard. Less than a second later, Yong-sik kicked the table again, this time sending Dewey tumbling back. He lost his balance, falling sideways and landing on his right arm. He felt a sting as the needle stabbed into his chest during the fall. Dewey rolled to his back, clutching the gun in his left hand. He pulled the needle from his chest, registering the plunger. He hadn't pressed it in. He swept the gun toward Yong-sik, who was already leaping over the card table. Yong-sik's feet touched the table top and he caught air, left foot and fist extended as he pounced. Before Dewey had time to react, Yong-sik landed on Dewey's torso and lunged down at Dewey's head, his right fist slashing down at Dewey's neck. All of it happened in the silent half-second after Dewey hit the ground, and Dewey knew he was now on the defensive. Yong-sik's fist slammed into his neck. A second fist, from Yong-sik's other hand, followed. Dewey twisted right as a third strike from Yong-sik cut the air. His fist hit the carpet next to Dewey's head. Dewey swung the needle up at Yong-sik, but Yong-sik slammed his foot down on Dewey's elbow, trying to break it, sending a painful electric jolt through Dewey's body. The syringe went flying from Dewey's hand, rolling across the carpet. Dewey watched the needle roll along the carpet, as if in slow motion.

Dewey understood the signs. The operation was heading sideways and he knew what that meant, what he had to do.

Cut your losses.

He'd moved too soon. He should've let him drink more. He...

It doesn't matter. Get out of here before he…

If he couldn't poison Yong-sik, he at least needed to kill him.

Dewey swept the pistol and fired twice in rapid succession, two dull thuds – *thwap thwap* – hit the air, but Yong-sik had again moved too fast for Dewey. The slugs hit the ceiling as Yong-sik blocked the sweep of Dewey's arm with his left foot, following it with a vicious kick to Dewey's chin. As Yong-sik reached to wrest the pistol from Dewey's hand, Dewey had no choice but to hurl the gun away from them both, across the room, just as Yong-sik grabbed Dewey's forearm, wrestling him, twisting his wrist. Struggling to catch his breath, Dewey punched Yong-sik in the side of his ribs, once, twice, three times, as he tried to extricate his other arm from Yong-sik's clutch. After a fourth punch to the North Korean's exposed torso, Yong-sik let go. Dewey wrapped his arm beneath Yong-sik's armpit and ripped backwards, hurling Yong-sik a few feet in the air. He landed on his back and was up in no time. But Dewey used the split second to crab toward the pistol. He grabbed it and swung it in Yong-sik's direction, again acquiring the North Korean in the firing line of the suppressor.

Yong-sik's face was flush with anger, though with a confident sneer.

The room was soundproof. Maybe Yong-sik knew that – but Dewey doubted it. Either way, he hadn't even attempted to call out to the soldiers outside. As Dewey's eyes met the general's, he understood why. His face look showed hatred and confidence; he wanted to kill Dewey on his own. He was enjoying himself. Now that Dewey held him in the aim of the pistol, the North Korean didn't say a word.

But by not firing immediately now that Dewey had him, Yong-sik also understood full well how badly Dewey wanted something.

From the ground, on his back, gun trained on Yong-sik, Dewey fought to catch his breath.

The North Korean had knowledge of a type of martial arts Dewey wasn't familiar with. Which meant he was a true student; it meant any more face-to-face combat with Yong-sik was likely going to be a losing proposition.

Yong-sik took a deliberate step toward Dewey.

"Not another step," said Dewey.

Yong-sik's eyes moved to the syringe. Dewey's followed him there. The syringe was six or seven feet to Dewey's left, lying on the beige carpet.

Yong-sik took another step toward the syringe.

"I said don't move."

"If you were going to kill me you would've," said Yong-sik. "You need something."

Slowly, Dewey stood, gun aimed at Yong-sik.

"You're right," said Dewey, stepping slowly to his left toward the syringe.

"And what is it you want? Perhaps I'll give it to you without all this fighting and needles."

"All North Korean military plans," said Dewey. "Nuclear capabilities, locations, everything."

Yong-sik laughed as he took another step toward Dewey.

"And why would I give you that?" he asked. Yong-sik pointed at the syringe. "If I don't you'll poison me? Do you think I have all the plans right here? And why would I—"

Dewey glanced at the needle – and in that flash of a moment felt the hard force of Yong-sik's bare foot hitting him with a brutal kick in the neck, a kick that would've killed most men. Dewey felt his head snap back. His neck muscles could barely stop the jolting kick, a death strike intended to kill Dewey. Dewey went flying backwards, as if he'd been kicked by a mule. The gun fell from his hand and slid…

Dewey clutched his throat as he hit the carpet. He couldn't breathe. Instinctively, he turned to see Yong-sik charging for the pistol. Dewey didn't bother getting to his feet. He saw Yong-sik running for the gun and he scrambled, knowing Yong-sik was closer to the weapon and that if he didn't stop him he'd be dead in seconds.

Yong-sik reached the gun, grabbing it and sweeping it toward Dewey just as Dewey lunged. Yong-sik fired; a dull, metallic *thwack* echoed inside the palatial suite. But the shot missed. Dewey's hands found Yong-sik – he grabbed his mid-section, tackling him, slamming him down on his back, sending the gun spiraling toward the corner of the room. Dewey grabbed Yong-sik's right wrist and twisted hard

– trying to break the North Korean's arm at the elbow. But Yong-sik had already grabbed Dewey by the neck, wrapping his arms around Dewey's neck, interlocking his arms – all in a blurry moment – and suddenly had Dewey in a death hold. Dewey struggled to get out of it but it was futile, and he lost access to oxygen within seconds. He tried to use his body weight, but every lurch he made, trying to slam Yong-sik backwards as he clutched his neck, was a waste of time. Yong-sik anticipated everything. He was on Dewey's back, on the ground, holding Dewey's neck and trying to kill him.

Dewey felt his body start to send him warning signals. The lack of oxygen was killing him. With every ounce of strength he could find, Dewey sent his elbow backwards in a fierce thrust, hitting Yong-sik in the rib cage. Yong-sik grunted in pain.

Dewey fought for breath as he climbed to his feet, gulping oxygen. Dewey established strategic position before Yong-sik could attack again. He squared up and backed off a few feet, giving himself precious time. Yong-sik stood up.

The North Korean was a superior martial arts fighter. But Dewey had survived. That fact alone, he knew, was unexpected – at least in the mind of his opponent.

Dewey and Yong-sik were now squared off against each other. Both men glistened in sweat, their faces bright red.

"Who do you work for?" said Yong-sik, panting, wiping perspiration off his face.

The two combatants circled each other in the luxurious living room of the suite. Dewey ignored the question.

"The CIA?" said Yong-sik. "Calibrisi?"

Dewey glanced down. A small drop of red was visible where the needle had pricked him above the heart. He scanned for the needle, seeing it to his right. Yong-sik's eyes followed where Dewey was looking.

"Go ahead," said Yong-sik, taunting him. "Reach for the poison. I won't make the same mistake twice."

Yong-sik moved aggressively toward him, both hands raised. Yong-sik lurched forward, his right arm slashing and again, out of nowhere, came his foot, slashing air and hitting Dewey in the side of the head, near his lip. He felt his head snap right. He tasted blood and spat a red mouthful on the carpet.

Dewey knew the importance of staying on his feet now.

Yong-sik parried again, his fists flying low, at Dewey's torso. This time Dewey thrust his left arm out, guarding his neck, just as Yong-sik again kicked the air from behind. Dewey blocked Yong-sik's foot at the ankle but Yong-sik's other foot slammed below his arm, striking his chest, a brutal kick that sent Dewey backwards.

Dewey reeled, struggling to maintain his balance. But had a free half-second and as Yong-sik charged again toward him, he attacked. He surged forward, lunging left as he kicked his right foot into Yong-sik's knee, bending his leg awkwardly at the knee. Yong-sik fell forward, a pained cough his only sound. As his head was about to land on the carpet, Dewey had already spun a one-eighty with his other foot, slashing clockwise, catching Yong-sik in the chin with brutal force, taking the North Korean down.

Dewey paused, his hands squared off as he caught his breath. He looked down at Yong-sik, whose eyes rolled about in his eye sockets, like marbles. The North Korean was dazed. But he would live.

Dewey grabbed the gun then retrieved the needle. He stepped above Yong-sik, who looked wobbly up at Dewey, in a state of confusion. Dewey knelt lower, the gun in his left hand, the suppressor just inches from Yong-sik's head. He suddenly slammed the needle down into Yong-sik's neck, pushing in the plunger with his thumb.

Dewey stood back up and waited for Yong-sik to regain some semblance of recognition. The North Korean lay on the floor for more than a minute, his eyes closed. Dewey stepped to the window and opened it, tossing the empty syringe out.

Dewey stepped to the chair where Yong-sik had been sitting. The glass of vodka was on the cushion, half full. With the gun still aimed at Yong-sik, Dewey picked up the glass and chugged it in two gulps.

Finally, Yong-sik stirred. Slowly, he sat up and looked at Dewey.

"You have twenty-four hours until it kills you," said Dewey. "In a little while, you'll get a fever. It won't last, maybe a few hours. You'll feel fine, long enough to fly home and do what I told you. If you don't, things will start getting ugly at about twenty hours. Very rapid heartbeat, fever. You'll know you're about to die when you start to lose vision."

Yong-sik appeared to be more awake. He listened carefully.

"What is it?"

"Poison."

"Obviously it's poison. What kind?"

"The kind that kills you in twenty-four hours," said Dewey.

"What do you want?"

"I already told you. A schematic of North Korea's internal military nuclear force complex. That means capability set, devices, locations, how they're moved and when. We want to know how many devices there are, where they are, and where you are in terms of the ballistics. HEU count down to the pound. Make no mistake: we'll know if you're bullshitting and if you are you die. It's already in your body."

"Why do you think I would have access to this—"

"You do. We both know it. It's up to you. Either you're willing to die to protect it or you're not. We'll find out in twenty-four hours."

"So I give it to you? You'll just let me die."

"That's a risk you're going to have to take," said Dewey. "But I don't lie. There's one antidote. It's already inside Pyongang. You give us what we want, we tell you where the antidote is. It's a custom poison. There's no hospital in the world that can save you, even if you had a week – and you don't. The only way you live, general, is give us what we want."

"How do I contact you?"

"Send the information to one one at one two dot com. One one at one two dot com. Very easy to remember. Can you remember that?"

"Yes."

"Good."

Dewey walked a few feet away from Yong-sik.

"I'm going to leave," said Dewey, the gun still trained on Yong-sik, who was slowly starting to stand up. "I'll tell your men you're not feeling well. Don't try and do anything: I don't know where the antidote is. You'd be wasting your time trying to take me." Dewey looked at a mirror on the wall, straightening his hair and tucking his shirt in. "Not that you could," Dewey added. "I'd kill all of them, and then I'd kill you."

Dewey walked to the door. As he was about to open it, he turned and looked at Yong-sik, still seated on the ground, obviously in pain from the kick, but lucid enough to watch Dewey as he left.

"By the way," said Dewey, "congrats on that first hand. We didn't have time to play but I saw the cards and you had an ace and a jack. Blackjack, buddy. Tonight's your lucky night."

–

Dewey tucked the weapon into his pants as he stepped into the hall, two of the gunmen trained their weapons on him.

Dewey raised his hands.

"Where are you going?" said Colonel Pak.

"The general does not feel well," said Dewey in broken English.

Pak moved by Dewey and entered the suite. Dewey looked back to see Yong-sik standing in the foyer. He watched as the other soldiers stepped quickly inside. Dewey and Yong-sik made eye contact. One of the men asked Yong-sik a question, which he answered.

Dewey's hand moved to the butt of the pistol, tucked into his belt. But nothing happened. A moment later, one of the gunmen shut the door and Dewey moved quickly to the stairs.

26

IRAN DESK
CIA HQ
LANGLEY, VIRGINIA

Calibrisi sat on a metal chair inside the crowded room that served as the CIA's Iran desk. He was next to Lloyd Edgington, one of the agency's primary analysts.

Edgington was examining the photos of Abu Paria. It didn't take long for him to positively confirm Paria's identity. A mole next to his eye and a scar on his forehead erased any sort of doubt. Of course, it was probably unnecessary. Paria's viciousness came through even in death, as if he might suddenly leap up and attack at any moment.

"So, why was he there?" said Calibrisi.

Edgington leaned back and unbuttoned his tie.

"I don't know," said Edgington. "But I'll find out."

27

ASSOCIATED PRESS
PYONGANG

The next morning, Talmadge sat down with Kae Myung Bin, his assistant, and Lee Song Hui, the AP photographer.

"I have an idea for a story," said Talmadge.

Lee Song Hui, the AP photographer, sat up enthusiastically. She was only twenty-two years old and dreamed of someday working for AP outside North Korea, so whenever Talmadge had ideas for stories she became excited. There were only so many stories a reporter could write about North Korea that avoided controversial topics.

"Let me guess," said Kae Myung Bin, lighting a cigarette. "A story about a certain reporter's decision to donate the rest of his care package to one of his colleagues?"

Talmadge laughed.

"No, nothing so absurd," said Talmadge. "You've seen the tourism statistics. Tourism is up. Just this past week, a delegation of more than thirty people from Sweden came to Pyongang."

"We've written about the rise in tourism, Ross."

"Yes, but how about a series of articles on some of the things to do and places to go when visiting?" said Talmadge. "Starting with the National Museum."

"I like it," said Lee Song Hui.

"It's boring," said Kae Myung Bin.

"That's the point," said Talmadge.

"Yes, I suppose it will fly by the censors," agreed Kae Myung Bin.

Talmadge was brought by two operatives from the North Korean Information Bureau to the National Museum. He spent the morning walking through the entire museum. Whenever he wanted to take a photo, he asked permission.

Finally, they arrived at a large, high-ceilinged room with only one painting: a massive portrait of Kim's grandfather, Kim Il–Sung, the founder of the Korean People's Republic. Both government officials, as well as Talmadge, bowed before the painting.

"Would it be permissible if I sit down?" asked Talmadge in Korean, pointing at a bench across from the great portrait. "I would like to describe the painting as I look at it. It might take a few minutes."

The two men looked at each, then one of them shrugged, as if to say to the other, fine with me.

"Please do so," said one of them to Talmadge.

Talmadge sat down and started to write. After several minutes, he shook his pen, trying to get more ink. Mildly frustrated, he took the pen and put it in the pocket of his blazer. He removed another pen – as well as the antidote, which was in a small syringe, with an adhesive on one side. He pretended to start writing again, watching the agents, making sure they weren't looking, then quickly reached beneath the bench. He pressed the small syringe against the wood on the underside of the bench, making sure it held. Then he started writing again.

28

GRAND HYATT HOTEL
MACAU

Dewey returned to his suite at the Grand Hyatt. He went into the bathroom and took off his shirt. He leaned into the mirror and examined the spot where the needle had hit him. It was barely visible, only the tiniest of red marks, like a mosquito bite.

He took his phone and punched in a three-digit sequence.

#8+

He hit send. The message would convey a simple fact. Yong-sik has been poisoned and the ultimatum spelled out. Operation successful.

He stripped off his pants and climbed into the shower. He took a long, relaxing shower, gradually lowering the temperature of the water, from warm, to tepid, and finally to cold, as cold as the hotel could offer. It wasn't Maine cold, but it was cold. He was trying to cool down and stop the sweating from the fight.

Dewey finally climbed out of the shower and dried off with a towel. He stepped to the mirror. His face was redder even than before. Soon, his dry face was wet again as he started sweating. He stared into his own eyes in the mirror – then glanced down at his chest, registering the small red mark where the needle had accidentally dragged. It had only been a few minutes, and yet the red mark was no longer small. It had spread out and was the size of a quarter. The redness was turning into a deep purple. The colored area was also elevated, puffed-out a small bit from his chest.

You didn't press it. It's not possible. You injected it all in Yong-sik!

He told himself it hadn't happened, yet his eyes couldn't look away from the growing purple patch on his chest.

He took his phone and opened a proprietary agency application called Vision designed to enable the phone to conduct a number of basic diagnostic medical functions. The screen lit up and he pressed an icon shaped like a square, then placed the phone's camera against his neck. A few moments later, the phone made a low beep. Dewey looked at it.

HEART: 149 BPM
BP: 244/165
TEMP: 105.2 F

Dewey stared at the screen an extra moment, then hit speed dial. A dull monotone came on and Dewey spoke:

"Twenty-one."

A second later, a voice came on the line.

"Andreas," said a man. "What's the problem, sir?"

"I need Jenna Hartford immediately," said Dewey, walking slowly, indirectly toward the bed.

"Hold, sir."

Dewey sat on the edge of the bed. Suddenly, the room was reeling, spinning around, and he felt unbearably hot.

"Dewey?" came Jenna's aristocratic British accent. "We received the message. Excellent job."

Dewey fought to hold onto the phone. It wanted to drop to the ground.

"Jenna," Dewey said calmly, as calmly as he could. "How much of the poison does it take to infect someone?"

"Why? Did you not hit him well enough? Don't worry – we'll know soon enough. In fact, we know Yong-sik's jet was just powered up at the airport. He's getting ready to leave."

The words were meaningless to Dewey as he fought to remain lucid, despite the sweat that now poured over his body and the fever which had grabbed him in a noose.

"Please just answer me," said Dewey.

"Oh, right. A drop. A fraction of a drop."

"Why did I need to inject an entire vial?"

"Insurance," said Jenna. "But in case all you could do was nick him, even then his goose would be cooked."

"What are the first signs?" said Dewey, already knowing the answer.

"Fever. A sharp fever. It was manufactured that way. That way, Yong-sik knows the toxin is real. It stops after a few hours. He has time to retrieve the documents. Then it kicks in again, in case he has second thoughts."

Dewey slipped off the bed, landing on the floor.

"Dewey?" said Jenna. "Are you still there? Is something wrong—"

The sound of Jenna's abrupt, pained moan hit Dewey's ears.

"Dewey," she said. "You've spiked a fever, haven't you?"

"Yes."

"How bad is it?"

"I'm okay."

"What's your temperature?"

"A hundred and five. But that was a few minutes ago. I'm about to lose consciousness."

The phone went quiet.

"*Jenna*—"

"I warned you, Dewey," said Jenna. "Why don't operators ever listen? *I told you*. I made it *so* clear. There's one antidote. It's in Pyongang."

"Can't they make another?"

"Not in time," said Jenna. "It was a proprietary strain. A one off. We needed to be sure Yong-sik couldn't simply walk into a hospital and take care of it."

Slowly, Dewey leaned down toward the carpet. The lights in the hotel room were still on. He was naked. He held the phone to his ear as he felt the first spike of deep, flu-like chills in his spine and neck.

"Dewey, if you're still listening, you don't have an option," came Jenna's soft, polite but firm English voice. "I need you to get to the airport."

"Why?"

"Because you're going to need to go to North Korea. You'll need to get to Pyongang. It's that simple. If you want to live, you must find a way to get to Pyongang. In the meantime, you have precious little time. Can you stand up?"

Dewey lay on the ground, his body shivering and convulsing.

"I'll try."

"I'll have a plane ready by the time you get there. Just stand up, get dressed, and get a cab to the airport. Can you do that for me, Dewey?"

Dewey tried to speak, but felt his hand shake, and then came numbness, a horrible sense of dizziness, and the phone dropped to the floor.

He heard Jenna's voice, shouting for him from the phone, but he couldn't move. She was shouting something, her words coming through in painful bursts. He shut his eyes, awakening a few minutes later to the loud, insistent sound of his phone being off the hook, of the terminated call. He felt as if his entire body was on fire. He shut his eyes again as he fell into unconsciousness.

29

CIA

Jenna stood still, her eyes transfixed on the phone in her hand. She felt her heart racing and then a strange sensation, a cold shiver that ran through her head and body.

She picked up the phone on her desk.

"I need Dave Morris," said Jenna. "It's urgent."

"Hold please."

Jenna's office was small, with a desk, a credenza, and three chairs, one where she sat, and two in front of the desk, pressed against the glass wall that looked out into the horseshoe-shaped set of offices that for CIA senior staff. The outer walls were lined with offices while the area in the middle was like a bullpen where various assistants worked. Jenna's desk had several neat stacks of papers and files, along with the phone console. Behind her were bookshelves. They were largely empty. The only personal item was a framed photo of Charles, an old photo of him on a beach in Marbella, where they had gone on their honeymoon.

"Hi, Jenna," said Morris. "Any news?"

"Yong-sik has been poisoned, but Dewey somehow pricked himself. He—" she paused, trying to keep her emotions under control. "He's spiked a fever."

There was a long silence.

"Oh no," said Morris. "Jenna, I made it clear—"

"I know, but it happened. First if all, did you save any? Can we dispatch a jet with another antidote?"

"The poison was custom," said Morris. "The antidote is created with the poison. The only way to create a new antidote would be if we had more poison."

"And do we have more poison?"

"No. I explained that. I can try and re-create the strain, but even then the odds of achieving the precise compound needed to create an effective antidote… my God, Jenna, it's small. Too small. There's timing, temperature, and a million other factors."

"So the only way Dewey lives if he goes to Pyongang and gets the antidote before Yong-sik? There's no chance – Yong-sik will get there first."

"Can you call the agent who planted it?" said Morris. "He could move the antidote."

"And if Yong-sik sends what we ask, he dies?"

"It's better than Dewey dying."

"It's moot," said Jenna, thinking aloud. "We can only reach Talmadge by mail. We wouldn't have the time."

"Wait," said Morris. "I just realized. We may have sent two antidotes."

"Two? Why? Why didn't you tell me—"

"We sometimes do," said Morris, "if there's a break in the custody chain. In case of breakage in transit. Hold on."

Jenna shut her eyes, shaking her head back and forth, waiting for what seemed like an eternity. Morris came back on the line.

"Harvey sent two," said Morris.

Jenna breathed a sigh of relief, then realized it meant practically nothing if Dewey couldn't get to it.

"The problem is," continued Morris, "we send two because they *do* often break in transit. What will the agent do if both survive?"

"Hide it," she said, "at least that's what he's trained to do."

Across the bullpen, she could see into Hector Calibrisi's office. She couldn't tell if he was in there, but she moved to the door and walked quickly around the edge of the bullpen. She looked inside, seeing no one.

"Do you know where he is?" said Jenna.

"He went to the State Department," said Lindsay. "Is everything okay?"

"No."

Jenna ran back to her office. She found her old cell phone, the one from MI6, and dialed. This time, it started ringing almost immediately. It rang for half a minute then went to an automated voice mail message. Jenna dialed again. This time, it only rang once before Fields picked up.

"Jenna," said Fields. "It didn't take you long, did it?"

"I need your help, Jayson," she said.

"And I told you, I'm mid-stream. I can't."

"Please," said Jenna softly. "It's a guy just like you. He would do the same thing. He's in trouble. Please, Jayson."

Jenna's voice was filled with desperation and emotion.

Fields let out an exasperated groan.

"Fine," he said. "Where is he?"

"At the Grand Hyatt."

Yong-sik was carried to the elevators, his eyes closed, his clothing drenched in perspiration. One of the soldiers inserted a white card in the elevator console and the elevator descended without stopping until it reached the basement, where a black limousine was idling, the back door open. Yong-sik was carried to the limousine and set down on the back seat. Three soldiers climbed in with him and the limo screeched forward, moving quickly through the parking garage and shooting from the hotel.

Fifteen minutes later, Yong-sik's jet was moving down the runway, skirting above the blue water of the South China Sea. North Korea's top military commander was clinging to life. His temperature was 104 degrees. His body was wracked by convulsions.

An hour into the flight, Yong-sik regained consciousness as his temperature abated. Then he remembered the man at the hotel. He looked out the window and realized that nothing would ever be the same, that in the next twenty-four hours he would either die or commit treason.

"You have lost everything," he whispered to himself. "All for a game of blackjack you didn't even get to play."

–

Jenna entered Polk's office on the second floor of CIA headquarters. It was one of three offices Polk kept inside the sprawling facility that housed the agency. As head of the Directorate of Operations, he had responsibility for both Special Activities Division and Special Operations Group, the two prime pieces of the Directorate of Operations. The other offices were in the basement, inside the two separate directorates. This was where Polk went for more formal meetings with military leadership, senators and key congressional staff, and visiting high-rank from foreign intelligence services. Polk also used the space to come and do paperwork – and to think.

Polk was seated in a white leather chair when she entered. He didn't need to ask. He could see the urgency on Jenna's face.

"What happened?"

"Dewey's been poisoned."

Polk was a short man. He was bald and wore glasses with tortoise shell rims. He wore a yellow Brooks Brothers button down shirt, gray flannels, a green and silver striped rep tie, and cordovan loafers. A product of Nobles and Yale, Polk would have looked at home in the faculty lounge at any number of New England boarding schools – but appearances were deceiving. It was Polk who ran the CIA's vaunted kill teams, the individual charged with executing covert missions across the globe.

Polk had never warmed to Dewey. He was against Calibrisi bringing him in-house and he hated the lack of predictability that came with everything Dewey did. But he understood full well the value of Dewey's involvement. Calibrisi was close to Dewey on a personal level; Polk was unmarried and had few personal attachments to people. Yet, something connected Polk to Dewey in a way even he refused to admit. Dewey somehow took operations to places they were never meant to go to – places Polk originally joined the CIA to find. Trouble always seemed to find Dewey but in that trouble oftentimes lay the seeds of darker truths the agency's analysts could never see.

Not only was Polk thinking about Dewey, and what a recurring headache he was, he was also still getting used to Jenna.

–

Jenna explained the situation, including the fact that Dewey was now on a plane bound for Osan Base in north South Korea, near the border with the enemy, and that a second antidote existed – and may or may not have survived the long trip to Pyongang.

"What will Talmadge do with it, if it survived?" asked Polk.

"He would've hidden it inside his apartment."

"That's a start. What are you thinking?"

"The only scenario I see is infiltrating the border and hijacking a vehicle," said Jenna. "There's no other way. He can't enter under some sort of tourist visa. He's barely alive right now. It needs to be something where he can move on his own. He'll stand out like a sore thumb. By the time they finish interrogating him, even with a decent cover, he'll be dead."

Polk nodded.

"I agree."

Jenna sat down in one of the two leather chairs in front of Polk's desk.

"I don't know what to do."

Polk stood up and walked to a filing cabinet. He opened a drawer and sifted through various files until he found what he was looking for. He removed a red bordered manila folder with the words "EYES ONLY" printed diagonally across the cover. The tab said "Operation Achilles."

"Driving won't work," said Polk. "There's not enough time. Look at this. We never used it. It was designed twenty years ago, a contingency plan for taking out Kim's father."

Jenna took the file and started reading. Polk sat in his desk chair, reading through a stack of papers with a pen in his hand, occasionally writing something down or signing his name, then flipping the page, all the while watching as Jenna pored through the file.

When she was done, she looked up at Polk.

"It's brilliant," she said. "Did you do this?"

Polk had a blank expression on his face.

"No," said Polk. "We had another architect back then, that is, another architect on your level, Jenna."

Jenna blushed.

"My level, that's ridiculous…"

Polk smiled. He took a piece of paper and scrawled a phone number down.

"Call Bill Prestipino. He's in charge of Osan. Tell him I told you to call. Also, tell him this a *Category Four Directive*."

30

GRAND HYATT HOTEL
MACAU

A tall black man moved swiftly through the sleek, well-lit lobby of the Grand Hyatt Hotel. He had short hair, and wore a striped polo shirt, jeans, and running shoes.

His name was Jayson Fields.

He climbed aboard an empty elevator and hit the button for the 18th floor. At 18, he got off the elevator and moved down the hallway. He went around the corner and came to room 1844. He looked both ways to make sure nobody was looking, then inserted a thick white plastic card which had a wire extending off the back. He inserted the other end of the wire into his cell phone and pressed the "start" icon and waited as the screen became green lines of numbers, scrolling from top to bottom in dizzying fashion.

After more than ninety seconds, a light on the door handle suddenly turned green. He grabbed the handle and twisted the knob, removing the card and putting it in his pocket along with his cell.

He entered the suite, removing a thin stainless steel case from his back pocket. He came into the living room, but it was empty. He went through a door into the bedroom and turned on the lights. Dewey was on his side, tucked into a fetal position. His eyes were closed. His body appeared red. The man could see him shivering.

He stepped in front on Dewey and knelt down.

"Dewey," said Fields, reaching over and lifting one of Dewey's eyelids.

Dewey reached out and grabbed Fields by the wrist, but his grip was weak and Fields continued to examine Dewey's eyes.

"My name is Jayson Fields. I work for British Intelligence. Jenna sent me. How you feeling?"

"Not too good," Dewey whispered.

Fields removed a syringe from the thin case.

"It'll sting," said Fields.

In one fluid motion, Fields jammed a needle into Dewey's neck, then pressed the plunger.

"What is it?"

"Adrenaline. Enough to get you on a plane."

Dewey cringed as the liquid hit his bloodstream. He closed his eyes as it took effect. When he opened them again, he was breathing rapidly.

"Where's your clothing?"

Slowly, Dewey sat up, then climbed to his feet. He found his jeans and shirt in the bathroom, pulling them on. He found his leather weekend bag and reached inside and took out his knife, inside a leather ankle sheath, and put it around his left leg. He stuffed his gun and a few other belongings inside the bag.

"How long was I out?" said Dewey.

"I have no fucking clue, but we need to get going."

Dewey stared blankly at Fields.

"Where?"

"The airport, that's all I know."

31

PRIVATE RESIDENCE
PRESIDENTIAL PALACE
PYONGANG

Kim stumbled awkwardly into the bathroom. He was drunk, but that's not why he was stumbling. The nausea was overwhelming.

The bathroom was huge, with marble everywhere, two bath tubs, a large open glass-walled shower, and four separate sinks. Kim made it to the first sink by the time he started vomiting.

With every passing hour, Kim felt the cancer coming on. The one thing that got him through it was the thought that perhaps it was all in his mind, that the cancer didn't exist, that he would live forever.

He finished throwing up. His face was drenched in sweat. He looked down into the sink. Blood streaked the brownish liquid from his stomach.

When Kim accepted the fact that the cancer was real, the blood his own, the pain that which approaches before death, he found the strength to keep going in a different thought, a more powerful idea. He thought of America. The country that looked down on him, that sought to control him as it had sought to control his father. Democracy, a word America used to colonize the world with as much death as any dictator. It was the thought of America that guided Kim. He wouldn't destroy America. He couldn't destroy it. Only America itself could do that. But he could rip into the very fabric of the country in a way that would last indelibly, as 9/11 had. He would get the blame, but Kim saw it as credit. He would be one of the last to fight back against the coming Americanization of the world.

He saw movement in the mirror. He saw his wife's face.

"What do you want?" he said.

She was crying.

"I want to know if you need my help, my leader, my brave one."

Kim shook his head, no.

"Leave me," he said. "*Now!*"

32

IRAN DESK
CIA

Lloyd Edgington's phone started beeping as he stared at his computer
screen.

DIA Parizeau, W

An hour before, Edgington had called Parizeau, the top satellites
expert at the Defense Intelligence Agency, requesting re-tasking of
one of DIA's satellites. Parizeau wanted to scan above the Yellow Sea
and the Sea of Japan north of the DMZ, the demilitarized zone that
separates North and South Korea. Edgington had also asked Parizeau
to have DIA's computers sift through archival satellite feeds from Iran
over the past month. Edgington needed Parizeau to see if there was
any unusual activity. He needed to find out why Paria was in Macau
to meet with Yong-sik.

Edgington picked up the phone.

"Hi, Will," said Edgington. "Do you have anything?"

"I think I might," said Parizeau. "So I called NSA. They keep track
of all planes and ships that go to or come from Iran, down to the GPS.
I ran the coordinates of every ship or plane coming out of Iran for the
past month. I was able to locate the plane that arrived in Macau, Paria's
plane, I guess. It's still sitting on the tarmac. But there's something else.
A container ship left Hormuz. It popped the algorithm."

"What does that mean?" said Edgington.

"The ship is in the Yellow Sea. It's in Nampo, a city on the coast. It arrived last night."

"Can you take some decent pics?"

"Shouldn't be a problem."

33

OSAN AIR FORCE BASE
SOUTH KOREA

Colonel Mark Prestipino felt one of his cells vibrating. It wasn't the one he usually used. It was his private cell, the number unknown to most people. In fact, only three people knew the number, his wife, back in Chicago, General Torey Krug, commander of JSOC Pacific Theater, and Bill Polk at the CIA.

He looked at the screen.

URGENT

"Presto," he said.

"My name is Jenna Hartford, sir, and I work for the Central Intelligence Agency," came Jenna's soft, aristocratic British accent. "Bill Polk said to call you."

"How is Bill?" said Prestipino, his voice gruff.

"Fine. It's a *Category Four Directive*, colonel."

"Oh, shit. Let's hear it."

"Colonel Prestipino, we are mid-stream in a *Tier One* operation involving North Korea. The operation has been complicated and we need your help."

"How do I know you're CIA?"

Jenna ignored the question.

"We have a priority asset who needs to get inside North Korea without being killed," said Jenna. "He needs to get to Pyongang."

"Good luck," said Prestipino.

"He's an American," said Jenna. "In fact, he was a Ranger, like you, colonel. He's been poisoned. The only antidote is in Pyongang."

Prestipino stepped to the window and looked north, toward North Korea.

"Jenna, the border is extremely well-guarded," said Prestipino. "Remember that war we fought? There are no weak points."

"Actually, that's not true," said Jenna. "There's a stretch of coastline south of Haeju, on the west coast. Enter correctly and you have some time."

"As you would expect, every inch of border is on SAT," said Prestipino. "It's all tied into the KPA missile defenses. We might be able to get someone near the shore – but they're shooting everything from the DMZ all the way out to international waterline. The only way to deal with that is an SDV, which we don't have."

"There's a difference between being seen and being shot," said Jenna. "A helicopter moving due East at this particular place will be seen on satellite immediately. But it will have approximately seventeen minutes until a missile hits it. We need to drop our asset as close to Pyongang as we can."

"So we fly inside the border, drop him, and turn around? It doesn't work. They'll hit the chopper way before it's back over the border."

"That's why we called," said Jenna. "I have an idea. Actually, it's Bill's idea. We're going to have to sacrifice a helicopter. We'll also need a corpse or two."

34

KOREAN PEOPLE'S ARMY HEADQUARTERS
PYONGANG

Yong-sik uploaded the two key documents the Americans wanted.
His hands shook. He'd started to feel the fever coming on again. He
needed the antidote. There was no time to fuck around with the CIA
if he wanted to live. He did want to live. On Yong-sik's innermost
level, he thought Kim was mad. He would have died for Kim's father,
his mentor. But Kim Jong-un, Yong-sik decided, wasn't someone he
was willing to die for. He was a madman. His father and grandfather
would be astonished and deeply embarrassed if they could see him
now.

The two documents were North Korea's most closely held secrets,
a report entitled:

**KPA MILITARY POWER ASSESSMENT AND
STATE OF READINESS**

And a thinner document:

SUPREME LEADER'S DECISION MATRIX

Both documents were updated in real time, throughout the day. The
first laid out in precise detail all assets of the Korean People's Army in
terms of manpower, weapons, border vulnerabilities, missile program
assessment and data, and, perhaps most importantly, nuclear program
assessment and data. Everything was there. It was a virtual blueprint,
for a capable military planning group, on how to attack North Korea.

The second document was ten pages long. Nine of the pages each had a small map on top. Each page displayed a different location: Los Angeles, Las Vegas, Phoenix, San Diego, and other cities in the American southwest. The map showed each city with circles on it, with numbers.

The numbers were casualty estimates, the circles blast and fallout zones. How many Americans would die from a nuclear strike in each area.

The last page was a photo of Kim. Beneath his photo was a paragraph.

Statement by his Most Excellency, Kim Jong-un.

The word DRAFT is next to it.

"It is my decision that we will strike the Great Satan, America. I now await a sign of when, not if. But make no doubt in your mind, the decision has been made and it will be on a Sunday. It will forever be called 'Bloody Sunday.'"

As Yong-sik prepared to hit send, he remembered one more thing. He found a folder on his desktop and attached a document entitled:

HEALTH RECORDS OF THE SUPREME
LEADER – CONFIDENTIAL

He hit send as he felt his face flushing red with heat. It was unmistakable. The poison was beginning to take hold. He looked at his watch. His hand was shaking too much to read the time.

35

CIA HEADQUARTERS
LANGLEY

One of Jenna's email programs abruptly chimed. The message had no sender. Three documents were attached. All were in Korean. She opened a separate program on her computer called CYPHER. It was a CIA language translation engine. A minute later, the documents appeared in English:

> **KPA MILITARY POWER ASSESSMENT AND STATE OF READINESS**
>
> **SUPREME LEADER'S DECISION MATRIX**
>
> **HEALTH RECORDS OF THE SUPREME LEADER – CONFIDENTIAL**

"Bloody Christ," said Jenna softly to herself. "It worked."

She looked around the half-empty operations room.

"It worked!" she yelled, clapping her hands.

"What is it?" said Perry.

"The documents from General Yong-sik," said Jenna.

"Forwarding right now. Could you get them to everyone you think should see them?"

"Yes, of course."

Jenna re-read the three titles. She opened one of the documents:

> **SUPREME LEADER'S DECISION MATRIX**
> Updated: CURRENT DATE

List of cities: LA, Phoenix, Houston, San Diego, Dallas

Decision:

Transcript:

"My decision is made. I want both missiles capable of reaching the United States to be on active alert and prepared for launch." KIM

"The process of arming the two Iranian missiles is nearly complete. Theoretically, they will be ready tomorrow (Saturday)." YONG-SIK

"Make preparations for Sunday. It will happen Sunday. It will be called Bloody Sunday." KIM

"Yes, your grace." YONG-SIK

RECORDED BY Lt. Col. Ghan

"My God," she said, a horrified look on her face as she scanned the plans to strike America.

Jenna began to open the assessment of North Korea's military power, but her eyes were drawn to the third document.

HEALTH RECORDS OF THE SUPREME LEADER

It was short – only five pages long. She scanned it quickly, staring in disbelief. Then, her mouth went ajar. She knew what it meant. It all made sense now.

PROGNOSIS: STAGE 4 PANCREATIC CANCER

In our estimate, the Supreme Leader has between two weeks and one month left before the cancer proves fatal.

"Oh my God."

It all crystallized in that moment. Jenna understood. Kim was dying and he wanted to live in infamy, forever known as the man who detonated a nuclear device on American soil. History would write of America destroying North Korea for what had happened.

Kim was a madman. He was actually going to do it. It wasn't a bluff. He had terminal cancer and why not.

"Oh God," Jenna whispered again. She lurched from her chair and started running down the hallway.

36

DIRECTOR'S OFFICE
CIA
LANGLEY

Calibrisi returned to his office at Langley from the State Department, where Secretary of State Mijailovic was in a virtual shitstorm of putting out fires – all of them somehow related to North Korea.

The documents from Yong-sik had been distributed within the highest levels of the U.S. government. The fact that Iran had delivered ICBMs to Pyongang was front and foremost. That Iran was skirting agreements to end its nuclear program was a secondary issue, a large issue, and yet it paled in comparison to Kim and the fact that he was preparing to strike a city in the United States imminently with nuclear weapons.

What had been a planned coffee between Mijailovic and Calibrisi had been interrupted by Jenna Hartford. An hour's trip to Foggy Bottom turned into four. The picture the Yong-sik documents painted was alarming. Not only did the North Koreans possess the capability to hit the United States with nuclear-tipped ICBMs, there now existed a rationale for why they actually might: Kim Jong-un was dying.

What intrigued Calibrisi the most was the fact that Yong-sik had included Kim's health reports. It wasn't part of the exchange. Yong-sik was warning them; there could be no other explanation. Kim was about to die. He was living his final days. That those final days coincided with an underground nuclear weapons test and a sharp increase in activity at two of North Korea's key missile bases made it clear. Yong-sik was warning them. He was asking for help.

Or was he? Was he warning the West or was he daring the West? Was it a ploy like so many of the other ploys by Kim – a ploy to get money, for example? What if the health records were a fabrication?

Calibrisi opened a drawer in his desk and removed a small device. It was a blood pressure monitor. He wrapped it around his wrist and turned it on. As he felt it tightening around his wrist, he stared out the window. He was used to feeling anxious. He'd been a highly-placed agent, had worked in counterterrorism at the FBI, and now was in charge of the world's pre-eminent spy agency. He was used to the feeling of the unknown, the feeling of worry for people he put at risk. But today he felt different. It was an altogether worse feeling and it gave him a rapid heartbeat and a sharp, acid-like pit in his stomach.

It was because of Jenna, he knew. Her design had pushed America into something hideously dangerous. It was information that never would've been discovered in time by Langley's agents, yet even so, Calibrisi wished for a simpler time. He wished in a way they hadn't discovered it all. But they had – and it was impossible to ignore. Indeed, the operation – if they could figure out the right response – could end up saving millions of American lives.

Calibrisi had agreed to bring her in at Derek Chalmers's request, and now he had misgivings. The operation to poison Yong-sik was brilliant, but part of Calibrisi wished they'd simply stuck with the original plan: kill Yong-sik. Yes, they'd extracted valuable information – even critical information – but what if it wasn't even true?

But it had to be true. The information was damning. There was nothing exculpatory about it. North Korea was moving into attack scenario. For whatever reason, Kim believed striking the United States made sense. Even though much of the information was already known to the U.S., Kim's health status was not. Yong-sik didn't have to include it. Without Jenna's creative operation, they would never have known Kim was about to die.

"Why did you do it?" Calibrisi whispered.

A simple needle prick to Dewey's chest made it all so meaningless. Why didn't they just kill the sonofabitch?

British Intelligence was renowned for its complex, elegant, operations, but Calibrisi felt as if he was untethered, out over the tips of his skis, flying down a sheer cliff of ice and no idea what lay below.

But of course, it was Dewey that was behind it all. He was the cause of the pit in his stomach. Dewey was going to die. Calibrisi never counted him out before, but there was no way he could walk into Pyongang without being seen. Even if he could get there, he needed an antidote that may or may not still exist. They couldn't reach Talmadge, the only man who knew if the two vials had survived the trip to Pyongang and if so, where the second one was.

His worry about Dewey mixed with his reflections on Kim. If the documents were true, if North Korea was moving closer and closer to a nuclear strike on the U.S., there was only one way to stop it. America would have to strike first. A pre-emptive nuclear strike.

The two thoughts collided and he understood that even if by some miracle Dewey made it and found the antidote, he might die anyway. He might end up being one of the millions the United States might have to annihilate in order to prevent the annihilation of Los Angeles, or Houston, or Phoenix, or some other American city.

Why didn't you just kill Yong-sik?

Calibrisi picked up his cell and called Jenna.

"Can you come down here?"

"Be right there," she said.

Calibrisi looked at his watch. He stood up and packed some papers into his briefcase and then put his cell phone to his ear. He dialed Polk.

"Bill, you need to come with me," he said. "Meet you on the roof."

Calibrisi hung up and pocketed the phone as Jenna approached the door and stepped inside. He looked at her with a blank expression.

"Let's go," he said.

"Where?"

"The White House. We're briefing the president."

As Jenna and Calibrisi walked down the corridor, a tall man with a mop of frizzy, curly blonde hair came out of one of the elevators. It was Lloyd Edgington.

"Hector," said Edgington.

"I don't have time, Lloyd."

"We found the connection," said Edgington. "A cargo ship from Iran pulled into the Port of Nampo last night."

"Nampo?"

"On the Yellow Sea, south of Pyongang. DIA captured still photos of the ship being off-loaded. Missiles."

Calibrisi shook his head in exasperation.

"Send a flash to the War Council," said Calibrisi, turning and moving to the stairs that would take him to the rooftop helipad.

37

THE WHITE HOUSE
WASHINGTON, D.C.

Hector Calibrisi, Bill Polk, and Jenna Hartford climbed aboard a helicopter on the roof helipad at CIA headquarters. They choppered from Langley to the White House, landing on the South Lawn. It was Saturday at just after five o'clock in the morning. The group from the CIA was met by several Secret Service agents along with Josh Brubaker, the president's National Security Advisor. As the agents, escorted them on a speedy walk across the South Lawn and through the Rose Garden, Brubaker pulled Calibrisi aside.

"I just got off the phone with the director of the Gustave Roussy Institute," said Brubaker, stopping Calibrisi in the middle of the Rose Garden. "They were the ones who made the diagnosis on Kim. They were in Pyongang. The document is real. Kim is dying of cancer."

Brubaker wore jeans and a navy blue V-neck sweater. His blonde hair was tousled and a layer of stubble was on his face. He had a concerned look on his face.

"What's the temperature in there?" said Calibrisi.

"What do you think it is? Hot. The Secretary of Defense is in there along with the chairman of the Joint Chiefs. They want to turn Pyongang into an ink stain."

"That's understandable," said Calibrisi calmly. "The question is, how much time do we have? We need to understand if our satellites can pick-up when the North Koreans start fueling the missile."

"Or missiles," said Brubaker.

"Or missiles," agreed Calibrisi.

"It's not going to be a friendly crowd, Hector. General Tralies is blaming you guys for not knowing Abu Paria was in Macau until this morning and not knowing Kim was dying of cancer."

Calibrisi nodded.

"Fair questions," said Calibrisi. "Though I would point out, we know about them now."

–

Accompanied by two armed, plain-clothed members of Department of Defense internal security, Will Parizeau crossed the lobby of the Watergate, went outside, and climbed into the back of an idling black Chevy Suburban.

Parizeau had only been to the White House once before – as a twelve year-old while on a vacation to Washington, D.C. with his parents. That time, he didn't come anywhere near the Oval Office.

Parizeau was the Pentagon's top satellites expert. Out of a highly-secure suite of offices in the U.S. Navy Yard in southwest Washington, he managed a a team of analysts whose job was to direct America's high-altitude satellites and spy on friend and foe alike in order to create as accurate a situational awareness as possible as to threats potentially facing the U.S. and its allies. The deployment and movement of the Pentagon's satellites was done by a different department, but Parizeau and his team aimed the cameras. More importantly, Parizeau was the interpreter of what the resulting photos showed. And what they showed was nuclear weapons.

The call from the Secretary of Defense had come in at 4:47 that morning.

"Will, this is Dale Arnold."

Parizeau thought he was dreaming – or perhaps having a nightmare. He reached for his glasses as he sat up in bed.

"Yes, Mr. Secretary."

"There are two DIS agents on their way to your apartment," said the Secretary of Defense. "They'll escort you to the White House."

"Ahh… okay, sir," said Parizeau, wiping his eyes, trying to wake up. "Can I ask what's going on?"

"North Korea."

"Is everything okay, sir?"

"No, it's not. Get dressed. I'll see you in fifteen minutes."

38

IN THE AIR

The jet was a specially-designed Gulfstream GV. It was almost ten years old but still one of the fastest – and most luxurious – of Air America's fleet of jets. Dewey sat on one of the brown leather seats in the main cabin. The jet had its own master bedroom suite, but Dewey took one of the regular chairs and quickly fell asleep.

Dewey was dressed in jeans and a T-shirt.

Halfway through the flight, Fields shook Dewey's shoulder several times, trying to wake him up. He did it as gently as he could, not wanting to be the one who woke Dewey up too abruptly.

"Dewey," said Fields, shaking his shoulder. "How you feeling?"

Dewey looked up as if awakened from a dream, its haze remaining even after his eyes opened. Pain from the fever still hung in his bones. It took him a few seconds, then he looked at Fields.

"Who are you?"

Fields stared at Dewey, not responding.

"Where are we?"

"Over the Sea of Japan."

"How long until we land?"

"A couple hours. Here," said Fields. "Take these."

Fields reached his hand out. There were two small pills, one oval and red, one light green and round. He dropped them into Dewey's hand.

"Am I being taken hostage?" said Dewey, still not understanding where he was.

Fields grinned.

"I work for MI6. Jenna sent me to help you."

Dewey nodded, a dazed, confused look on his face.

"Oh, yeah. It's coming back now."

Fields pointed at Dewey's hand, holding the pills.

"It's called a stat-pak," said Fields. "If we were ever shot down and captured behind enemy lines, we're supposed to take them. I don't know what it is. All I know is, it's designed for torture. Before they torture you. It's not an opioid. It's a nerve block."

"No one's torturing me," said Dewey.

"You were poisoned," said Fields. "It's a way to deal with pain that doesn't sideline you."

Dewey looked at the pills.

"At least put them in your pocket," said Fields, pushing the pills into Dewey's hand.

Dewey took the two pills and stuffed them in his jeans pocket.

"Is there a plan?"

"I have no fucking idea," said Fields. "Technically, I'm AWOL from an operation we're running back in Macau. I don't know how Jenna got me wrapped up in this, but she did. This seems like it's more interesting. I figure Jenna can call Derek Chalmers afterwards and get me my job back. Anyway, Jenna wanted to talk to you when you woke up."

Dewey stared at Fields for a few seconds. Then he picked up a phone attached by wire to the wall.

"Name?"

"Andreas."

A small click.

"Yes?"

"Jenna Hartford."

"Hold, sir."

A few moments later, Jenna's soft British voice came on.

"Dewey?" she said.

"Yeah."

"How are you?"

"Fine," said Dewey. "Is there a plan?"

"It's coming together."

"Is there really an antidote in Pyongang?" said Dewey. "Because if there isn't, don't put me through this bullshit. I'd rather go drink a few beers before I die."

"There *is* an antidote," said Jenna, "in fact there are two. A back-up was sent. General Yong-sik sent the documents, but we haven't given him the location yet."

"Why not?"

"Because if one of the vials broke during transit, that would leave only one. We'd let Yong-sik die so that you can get it, Dewey."

"No," said Dewey.

"What do you mean, no?"

"I gave him my word."

There was a long silence.

"Is the information helpful at least?" said Dewey.

Jenna bit her tongue. She knew the answer to the question, the fact that it was not only helpful but crisis stage material – that Kim was dying and about to drop a nuclear bomb on a city in the U.S. But she didn't tell him that. She knew he had to focus on one primary, sole objective: getting to Pyongang.

"It was helpful," said Jenna, "but we need to discuss your situation. The other antidote will be in Talmadge's apartment. He will hide it. You need to get to Talmadge's apartment."

"Is he expecting me?"

There was a pause.

"We've been unable to establish contact with the agent in Pyongang," she said, finally.

"Oh, great," said Dewey.

"It doesn't mean he's not there."

"Or maybe they caught him," said Dewey. "Killed his ass, found the other antidote and poured it down the drain. Or maybe it broke."

"Maybe," said Jenna, her British accent turning slightly sharper, with an edge. "Listen, I feel bad, but I'm not the horse's ass who stuck the needle in his chest."

Dewey grinned, saying nothing.

"We're working on a plan," said Jenna after a long silence. "By the time you land, it will be in ship shape, promise."

39

OVAL OFFICE
THE WHITE HOUSE

Brubaker, Calibrisi, Polk, Perry, and Jenna stepped into the Oval Office. The aroma of coffee was in the air. A small group was already gathered. Everyone was seated in the central seating area, a pair of long, light tan Chesterfield sofas that faced one another across a stunning red, white, and blue needlepoint carpet. In addition to President J.P. Dellenbaugh, five other individuals were present: Secretary of Defense Dale Arnold, Chairman of the Joint Chiefs of Staff Phil Tralies, NSA Director Piper Redgrave, Secretary of Energy Marshall Terry, and Secretary of State Mila Mijailovic.

President Dellenbaugh was seated in a leather club chair at one end of the sitting area. He was dressed in shorts, a T-shirt, and running shoes, holding a cup of coffee.

These were the top national security, intelligence, diplomatic, and military officials in the United States Government. The Yong-sik documents were causing the country's war council to drop everything and focus on North Korea. Until now, the Kim threat was theoretical. Kim was a maniac – but his constant threats to the U.S. had inured the government in the same way as a boy crying wolf too many times. Either a way for Kim to look strong inside his own country or a not-too-subtle form of extortion. But the documents sent by General Yong-sik changed everything, and they all knew it.

A secret plan to launch a nuclear missile on the U.S. was now operational. Moreover, Kim had cancer and was going to die soon. Kim wanted to go out with an historic attack on the U.S., an attack that would be self-destructive and result in most of North Korea being wiped out. Kim knew it. He wanted it. He wanted to live in infamy, even as a monster, but someone who would one day be written about in history books, like Hitler or Bin Laden. A perverse desire for fame.

America faced imminent threat. A nuclear device falling on Los Angeles would be devastating. Upwards of a million citizens would die.

Dellenbaugh and the war council were sent into high-alert.

Brubaker, Calibrisi, Polk, and Perry sat down on the large sofas.

"Coffee, Hector?" said the president.

"I'll get it," said Calibrisi.

Jenna was the last to enter the sitting area, and when she did all the seats on the sofas were gone. Only one empty place remained, in a leather club chair next to the president. Jenna glanced around and sat down in the chair. She stared down at the ground and then looked up to see Calibrisi holding out a cup of coffee to her. He smiled at her as she took it.

"Thank you," she mouthed.

Calibrisi was on the left sofa, next to Dellenbaugh. He glanced around the room as he took a sip of scalding hot coffee.

"We've all seen the documents," said Dellenbaugh, looking at Calibrisi. "First of all, are they real?"

All eyes were on Calibrisi. He didn't answer but instead glanced at the NSA Director, Piper Redgrave.

"Yes," said Redgrave. "We were able to analyze the metadata in the documents to look for possible alteration since Yong-sik returned. There was none. Either the North Koreans kept fakes on hand, anticipating such a circumstance, or they're real."

Dellenbaugh looked at Calibrisi.

"Are they real, Hector?"

"Yes."

"We are potentially going to kill millions of people based on these documents," said Dellenbaugh. "You better be goddam sure."

Calibrisi didn't move. He took another sip and looked at Jenna, then back to Dellenbaugh.

"I believe they're real, Mr. President," said Calibrisi. "If the military documents had come by themselves, I'd have my doubts. But the health records indicate Yong-sik wants us to know the truth. He's reaching out to us. There can be no other conclusion."

Phil Tralies, the Chairman of the Joint Chiefs of Staff, was seated diagonally and across from Calibrisi. He leaned forward, a distempered look on his face.

"How the hell did we miss this?" said Tralies, an angry look on his face. "It's your job to know the state of the North Korean and Iranian missile programs! It's your job to know Kim's health! And it damn sure is your job to know we're about to get blown up!"

"Then we did our job, general," said Calibrisi. "Thank you for the recognition."

"We have fifteen hours, maybe less!" barked Tralies, pointing at Calibrisi.

"Sorry," said Calibrisi, "I didn't realize the greatest military power on earth needed more time."

Tralies started to stand up, irate, but Dellenbaugh held up his hand.

"Sit the hell down, Phil," said Dellenbaugh sharply.

A few silent moments of tension and animosity hung in the air. Calibrisi glanced at Jenna and gave her a small grin.

Don't be afraid. Don't let anyone bully you around.

Across from Tralies, Secretary of State Mijailovic shot Tralies a cold look, then turned her head to the president. She caught his eye. Then she looked at Jenna.

"It's a miracle we have this level of intelligence," said Mijailovic. "Had we simply killed Yong-sik," she looked at Tralies, "as you wanted to do, general, we wouldn't have found out. We certainly wouldn't have fifteen hours."

Mijailovic, at forty-one, was the youngest secretary of state in United States history. She was an academic, with Ph.D.s from Columbia and Stanford. Dellenbaugh had appointed Mijailovic following the death of Secretary of State Tim Lindsay, gunned down in a Paris hotel room just a few months before.

Mijailovic again looked in Jenna's direction, then sat back on the sofa and crossed her legs.

There was a tense silence as Tralies looked at the secretary of state.

"Mila's right," said Tralies apologetically. He glanced to Calibrisi. "My apologies, chief. Your team deserves a ton of credit. I'm just concerned, that's all." Tralies paused and looked around the room. "I don't need to tell you all, we don't have the manpower to invade North Korea, and even if we did, they could still launch bombs. That leaves us with precious few military options. We could wait and hope that the North Korean missiles fail – or pray that THADD will shoot them out of the sky."

THAAD stood for Terminal High Altitude Area Defense, America's most advanced anti-ballistic missile defense system, designed to shoot down short, medium, and intermediate range ballistic missiles in their terminal phase. THADD worked by attempting to intercept missiles with a *hit-to-kill* approach, smashing enemy missiles from the sky. It was advanced, but it wasn't foolproof.

"The last thing I want to do is drop a tactical nuclear bomb on Pyongang, but I don't think THADD is reliable enough to take the risk of allowing Kim to launch a missile," continued Tralies, looking at Mijailovic. "But the secretary of state is right. Thank God we know. So let's figure out what to do."

"Before we begin, Mr. President," said Jenna, "we need your authorization to release the location of the antidote to General Yong-sik."

"Why the hell would we do that?" said Secretary of Defense Arnold. "Yong-sik's death might buy us time. It would create chaos at the upper end of the North Korean military."

"Kim doesn't need Yong-sik to press the launch button," said Jenna. "We made a bargain. He lived up to his end of the deal."

"When it comes to the threat of nuclear war, there are no bargains," said Arnold.

Dellenbaugh held up his hand. He looked to his right, at Calibrisi. "Hector?"

"I think letting him die would be foolish," said Calibrisi. "He's trying to signal us as to Kim's state of mind. He might even be an ally. I doubt it, but there's a chance he's working from within to stop

Kim. It's the only thing that explains the health records. With Yong-sik dead, we have nothing. With him alive, who knows, it might be a small hope but I'd rather have him there than not."

"Yong-sik is a thug," said Arnold.

"We deal with a lot of thugs," said Dellenbaugh.

"We either wipe out Pyongang or we don't and run the risk of a million Americans dying," said Arnold, the Secretary of Defense. "This is the fault of Kim Jong-un, no one else. He's the one killing his citizens, not us. The North Koreans are getting ready to launch a nuclear strike on the United States. We need to move *now* to stop them. Let the guy live, let him die; but we need to move right now."

Dellenbaugh stood up. He walked past his desk to a wooden cabinet, pulling open a drawer. He took out a bottle of bourbon and poured some into a glass. He lifted it to his lips and downed it.

"Mila," said Dellenbaugh, speaking to the secretary of state, "what about China? I assume we've briefed them."

"I've spoken with my counterpart in Beijing, yes, Mr. President," said Mijailovic. "I have not, however, revealed the fact that we're this far along, only that all options remain on the table. If, it's as it seems, Kim is dying of cancer and wants to go out in a big way, involving China only creates risk for the United States. The moment Beijing calls Kim and attempts to talk him out of launching missiles, Kim will know that we know his intentions and could launch the missiles immediately, before his self-imposed deadline. Our greatest asset right now is the element of surprise. We need to keep this in the dark. If Kim has gone off the deep end, the last thing we want is for him to know we know."

"You need to find out more, Mila," said Dellenbaugh. "Quietly, off-the-record, but we need to know how Beijing is going to look at things if we attack."

The door to the Oval Office opened and Cecily Vincent, the president's executive assistant, stepped inside.

"Mr. President, there's a gentleman from the Pentagon at the East Gate. He says he's supposed to be at this meeting. His name's Will Parizeau."

"I invited him," said the secretary of defense. "Please show him in, Cecily."

Dellenbaugh looked at Arnold.

"The satellite expert," said Arnold. "Mr. President, before we do anything, we need to know if we can somehow detect activities the KPA might be doing which would indicate that they're preparing to launch. If we cannot detect with reasonable confidence that they're getting close to launching, through movement of missile launchers or some other activity, then I must agree with General Tralies. We can't take the risk – based on some document – that Kim is going to do it on a Sunday. He might launch his missiles at any moment."

The door to the Oval Office opened and a tall, blonde-haired man with thick glasses stepped into the room. For a moment, Parizeau resembled a proverbial deer in the headlights as he glanced nervously around the room, which had gone quiet.

"Hello, everyone," he said somewhat shyly.

"Sit down, Will," said President Dellenbaugh, pointing to a chair at the other end of the sofas.

"Yes, sir. I'm Will Parizeau, sir. It's an honor, Mr.—"

"This is real simple," said Dellenbaugh, cutting off Parizeau. "Can we detect when North Korea is getting ready to launch a missile?"

Parizeau sat down. He pushed his glasses up on his nose.

"What kind of missile?"

"Does it matter?"

"Yes."

"An intercontinental ballistic missile with a nuclear warhead."

"How far in advance, sir?"

Dellenbaugh turned to the secretary of defense.

"What's the flight time on a missile from one of our submarines until it lands in North Korea?" asked the president.

"About three minutes. But there needs to be a margin for error."

Dellenbaugh looked at Parizeau.

"Ten minutes," said the president. "Can we figure out if they're going to launch a missile ten minutes out?"

Parizeau stared at the president and then leaned back, deep in thought. He pushed his glasses back as he seemed to be calculating numbers in his mind.

"The answer is, I'm not sure, sir," said Parizeau. "We're very good at the part that comes after they take off. We can detect a launch within seconds, even when our satellites aren't necessarily looking at the launch site. Within a short period of time, we can calculate precisely where the missile is going. But right before, well, that's hard. Ten minutes before, I... I just don't see how, sir."

"What about radiological imprint?" said Brubaker. "Are we tracking North Korea's nuclear devices?"

Parizeau took a deep breath.

"We have the ability to analyze air quality down to a molecular level," said Parizeau. "Thus, once we establish a nuclear device is there, we can lock onto the device's radiological imprint. This is how we knew a device had been moved from the Ukraine last year. But we need human intelligence to come up with a confirmed siting. We need to know where it is within a few feet, otherwise environmental factors make it impossible. Nukes don't glow in the dark, sir. With North Korea, we have no on-the-ground intelligence telling us where their devices are. Both missile facilities are large. Furthermore, the North Koreans have seventeen mobile missile launchers, most of which we have no clue where they are. Without knowing precisely where a nuclear device is, it would be like trying to shoot ants with a BB gun from a hundred miles away."

"So if they were to launch a missile, we would only know after it took off?" said Dellenbaugh. "Is that correct, Will?"

"Yes, Mr. President."

Tralies looked at Dellenbaugh.

"Mr. President, isn't it obvious?" said Tralies. "We won't know they're attacking until it's too late. Imagine the devastation even one nuclear bomb would do. Sir, it is my recommendation that we launch a pre-emptive nuclear strike targeting both missile facilities as well as Pyongang and other population centers, before it's too late."

"We have fifteen hours to figure this out," said Polk, disagreeing.

"That's what you think," said Tralies. "But none of us knows when this crackpot is going to hit the button."

"So what you're saying is 'don't trust the documents as it relates to when Kim is going to launch a nuclear missile, but do trust the documents as it relates to everything else?'" said Calibrisi. "You can't have it both ways, Phil. If the docs are real, we have fifteen hours."

"Mr. President," said General Tralies, ignoring Calibrisi. "You asked the Pentagon to come up with three attack scenarios. This is the only one I feel prepared to recommend. I repeat, it is my strongest recommendation that we move *Ohio*-class ballistic missile submarines into the Korean theater and prepare to launch a pre-emptive nuclear strike on North Korea. The difference between fifteen hours and fifteen minutes is irrelevant in the grand scheme of things. We cannot risk the lives of so many innocent Americans. It is your job as commander-in-chief to protect them."

Dellenbaugh looked at Tralies.

"Move the subs," said the president. "General, you have an hour to develop a second attack scenario. We have manpower in the area. I want to know what our soldiers could do in the event we want to pursue a non-nuclear strategy here." President Dellenbaugh stood up. He looked at Parizeau. "Will, get to work on a way to detect when they're getting ready to launch. Improvise. Be creative. We need to know. We'll reconvene in an hour in the Situation Room. Meeting is adjourned."

Everyone stood up to leave. Dellenbaugh pointed to Jenna as she started walking to the door.

"Jenna," said Dellenbaugh.

"Yes, Mr. President?"

"Release the location of the antidote to Yong-sik. It seems to me he lived up to his end of the bargain."

"Yes sir. But do know that an agent in the field has been poisoned, the same agent who succeeded in getting to Yong-sik. If there's only one antidote, and Yong-sik uses it, the agent will die."

"I'm aware of the situation, Jenna," said Dellenbaugh. "Dewey will be fine. I'm sure the other antidote is in the man's apartment. Get Dewey into North Korea. He'll figure out the rest."

40

NATIONAL MUSEUM
PYONGANG

The museum was closed when General Yong-sik's black Range Rover pulled up in front. There were two gunmen in the front of the vehicle, both members of Yong-sik's security detail.

"Wait here," said Yong-sik as he climbed from the back and walked toward the museum's elaborate entrance. As he moved up the steps, he felt desperately weak. Each step made him winded, as if he couldn't quite catch his breath. It was mixed with dizziness and a feeling like a hangover from the fever, a feeling of nausea, as if it was returning.

The front door to the building opened just as Yong-sik took the last step up the wide granite stairs. A man in a suit was standing in the entrance. He had glasses on and a kind smile. He bowed as Yong-sik entered the building. This was the museum's director, Han Yu-min.

"General Yong-sik," said Yu-min nervously. "What a great honor, sir. How can the museum be of service? Would you like to see the recently installed portrait of our Supreme Leader?"

"Stay here," said Yong-sik. "Call security. Tell them to turn off all security cameras immediately. Do you understand?"

"Yes, sir. Right away, sir."

Yong-sik walked through the immense portico and took the stairs to the second floor, finding the room. He went inside, looking for the painting of Kim Il-Sung. When he found it, his eyes moved to a bench across the large, high-ceilinged gallery. He walked to the bench and slowly sat down. He stared at the painting for more than a minute without reaching beneath the bench. He trusted no one. Even though he'd ordered the cameras shut off, there could be no assurances, and no one could see him do what he was about to do. No one could know that he'd just committed high treason in order to save his own life. After staring up at the massive, colorful painting of Kim Il-Sung, dressed in a military uniform, his hand moved beneath the bench. He felt around for the syringe, sliding his hand along the underside of the wood. Finally, he felt the object. It was stuck to the wood with tape. Gently, he pulled the syringe away. He cupped it in his hand and stood up. He left the gallery and walked to a restroom down the hallway.

Inside, he flipped on the lights then placed the syringe on the sink. He rolled up a sleeve and stabbed the needle into his forearm. He felt an immediate sensation of coldness, ice-like, and wondered if perhaps he'd been double-crossed. But the cool feeling soon ebbed into something different, a slight euphoria, and he closed his eyes as the fever-like hangover, the soreness, the indescribable fatigue – all washed away. He broke the needle off and flushed it down a toilet, then pocketed the empty syringe and plunger.

Downstairs, Yu-min was standing in exactly the same spot.

"Take me to the security room," said Yong-sik.

A floor below, Yong-sik followed Yu-min to the security room. It was small, dimly lit, and windowless, with a checkerboard of TV screens. Every one of the screens was shut off.

"As you requested," said Yu-min proudly.

The security guard looked up at Yong-sik, immediately recognizing him, then bowed several times in obedience.

"Put them on again," said Yong-sik.

The guard flipped a series of switches and the screens came to life. They were small, black-and-white, and showed live footage from various points both inside and outside the museum.

"Show me the cameras in the portrait gallery."

The guard pointed to one of the screens. The camera slowly swept across the empty room where Yong-sik had just been.

"There," said Yong-sik just as the camera came to the bench where the antidote had been planted. "Stop it. That view. I want the last seven days of tape sent to my office at once."

41

OSAN
SOUTH KOREA

The flight from Macau took a little under four hours. Dewey turned
off his phone the entire trip. It was Fields who awoke him, shaking
his shoulder gently.

"We're getting ready to land."

"How long?"

"Ten minutes," said Fields. "They'll have a pack waiting for you.
You're leaving for North Korea immediately after we get there."

Dewey shook off his sleepiness. He felt better. The fever was gone.
But in the back of his mind he knew that meant he was getting closer
to dying.

"How am I getting inside the country?" said Dewey, rubbing his
eyes. "Truck? Car?"

"Chopper," said Fields.

Dewey had a slightly surprised look on his face.

"How's that going to work? They'll shoot it down."

"I don't know the details, but you're getting briefed on the tarmac.
I need to go land this thing."

Dewey wasn't worried about dying. Truth be told, he wasn't
thinking – not much, anyway. He was trying to live his life in
minutes now, trying to focus on every second as it passed, rather than
contemplate what he would need to do if he wanted to stay alive. He
had to infiltrate a dead zone – a hostile country where he'd stand out if
anyone saw him. He needed to get to Pyongang and somehow make

contact with the in-country asset, Talmadge, who'd apparently gone missing.

Dewey had infiltrated China two years before. He'd been disguised a Chinese agent. At the time, the idea of penetrating China had seemed incredibly challenging, the odds of success frighteningly small. He now realized China had been easy compared to what North Korea would be like. After all, there were Westerners all over China, millions of them. In North Korea, Westerners numbered in the hundreds, if that.

There was no time to devise a disguise, certainly not a good one. More than six hours had passed since the needle hit his wrist. That meant less than eighteen hours until he was dead. There was no time for clever disguises and complicated operations. He needed to get to Pyongang – and quickly.

The jet touched down at Osan Air Force Base at six in the morning. The sky was a gray yellow. The jet came to a loud, fast stop and taxied down the runway, stopping next to a helicopter, whose rotors were cutting slowly through the air as Dewey climbed down the jet's stairs: SH-60 *Sea Hawk*.

Two men, both in military uniforms, approached Dewey as he took the last steps onto the tarmac. One of the men – the older of the two – extended his hand.

"Hi Dewey, I'm Mark Prestipino," he said, yelling over the din of the jet's engines and the helicopter's now slashing rotors, which blew a steady wall of wind at the three men.

Prestipino was bald with a large nose. The other man looked younger. He had blonde hair that looked a little too long for a military uniform.

"Charlie Macavoy," barked the younger man. "I'm your pilot."

Dewey shook their hands.

"How you feeling?" said Prestipino.

"Okay," said Dewey.

"You're leaving right now," said Prestipino. "There's a ruck in the back of the chopper with SAT, guns, grenades, food, water, and some basic first aid. You're flying north. Charlie will set the course, put the chopper on auto-pilot, then jump before the chopper reaches the border. You and the chopper will fly for about fifteen minutes. You'll be crossing into a remote area. KPA will pick you up on radar immediately. They'll launch missiles. But by the time the missiles reach you, you'll be inside the country and close to Pyongang. They *will* shoot you down, so you're going to need to get off by the fifteen or sixteen minute mark, got it?"

Dewey nodded.

"Seventeen minutes is an estimate," added Prestipino. "That means, keep your eyes peeled for SAMs, Andreas. Don't assume we're right. After you jump, the helicopter will keep going for a few more minutes, before they either shoot it down or it crashes. After twenty minutes, autopilot will turn off. The helicopter will begin an uncontrolled descent and crash at that point."

"If they don't find any bodies, they'll start looking for me."

Prestipino glanced at the chopper and then at Macavoy.

"They'll find bodies," said Prestipino. "Two of them, in fact. They're already on board. The chopper should get you within about fifty miles of Pyongang. You need to get going."

–

Dewey and Macavoy climbed into the SH-60. Dewey climbed into the cabin in back, behind the cockpit.

The helicopter's interior lights were extinguished but Macavoy rotated a knob that illuminated the cabin. A body was strapped to a canvas troop-carrier seat along the far wall. He was olive-skinned, his head leaning to one side, limp. He was already dead.

"There's another strapped up front."

Dewey looked at Macavoy with a blank look on his face. He didn't need an explanation.

"They were flown in from Manila," said Macavoy. "Part of an Al-Qaeda cell. They go down with the chopper. KPA will think they killed two men."

Macavoy pulled the helicopter door shut.

"By the time they do any sort of forensic work you'll be long gone."

Dewey reached for one of the corpse's mouths, opening it. He took a cursory glance.

"Are you kidding? Any idiot will know that guy's not U.S."

"It's the best we could do," said Macavoy.

Dewey patted Macavoy on the back.

"You're right," said Dewey. "It's not bad. It's just not perfect."

Macavoy exited the cabin, climbed into the cockpit, and strapped himself in. A moment later, the fearsome whirr of the rotors took over the air. The chopper lifted from the tarmac and quickly arced right, moving away from the airbase toward the north.

Dewey sat down on the floor of the cabin and pulled the rucksack in front of him. In the cabin's low light, he inspected the bag. On the outside was a small parachute, barely bigger than a bed sheet. This was a specially designed parachute made for extremely low jumps, from choppers, enough to cushion the blow but not much more. He reached inside the duffel. There were two handguns along with several extended magazines. A bottle of water was in the bag along with a few plastic bags filled with food – dried fruit mostly, along with some carrots, crackers, and nuts. A first aid kit was stuffed into a larger Ziploc bag, bandages, a suture and needle, small packs of medical alcohol, and a few pre-made, pinky-sized plastic needles, caps on, which held morphine.

A pair of knives were attached to the outer part of the duffel. Both were SOG, both were SEAL Pups. One was fixed blade combat, the other was a folding SEAL Pup.

Dewey went to the window and looked out. Macavoy had the running lights off and all Dewey could see was blackness below, an occasional small cluster of lights around someone's home in the uninhabited northwest corner of South Korea.

Dewey watched as the pilot seat was lowered to allow Macavoy access to the cabin. Macavoy climbed over the pilot seat and back into the cabin near Dewey, hunched over. He tightened the parachute on his back. He looked at his watch.

"Thirty seconds," said Macavoy, stepping to the door and pulling it open. Wind rushed in.

Macavoy looked at Dewey, then at his watch again.

"It's on auto-pilot," said Macavoy. "Start timing now. KPA will pick you up immediately. They'll launch missiles. Seventeen minutes is when the missiles will reach the helicopter. You need to jump before seventeen minutes, in fact, if it were me, I'd get out of here at fifteen or sixteen. And just to remind you, at twenty minutes, the chopper'll drop to the ground like a pile of rocks."

Dewey nodded, saying nothing.

Macavoy handed him a small tin of eye black.

"Thanks."

"Good luck, Dewey," said Macavoy, reaching his hand out and shaking Dewey's. "See you on the other side."

Dewey said nothing, watching as Macavoy turned and charged toward the open door, jumping out into the black sky. He opened the tin and started rubbing his face with war paint. He looked at his watch. Then he stepped to the door. He looked down on the passing carpet of trees and uninhabited land.

No one knows how they're gonna die and this might be how you die. It might not be there. But it might be there. Until you know it's not there, you have to believe it is.

Dewey leaned into the cockpit and glared down at the dead jihadi strapped into the co-pilot chair.

"So, you here on business or pleasure?" said Dewey.

42

KPA AIR FORCE HEADQUARTERS
KAECH'ON AIRFIELD
KAECH'ON

A male officer in a tan military uniform stared down at a screen. He wore a headset. The screen displayed live radar of the North Korean border with South Korea. The screen was black with digitally-imposed bright green markings, showing North Korea's borders. A small red light caught his eyes. The light was flashing. It was in South Korea but appeared to be heading directly toward the North Korean border. It was approaching near the western end of the border with South Korea, over a small inlet of water at the eastern edge of the Yellow Sea, into a province known as South Hwanghae.

The officer, Rhee, a lieutenant in the KPA Air Force, typed quickly, zooming in on the approaching light. He double-clicked the light. In small lettering, the words appeared:

HELICOPTER/mil
SPEED: 261kmh
DIR: NNW .087

This was not unusual. He assumed it was American. The Americans constantly tested the North Korean air defenses, but the location was unusual. Normally, the Americans came from the central part of the border, north of Osan Air Force Base. They liked to fly along the No Fly Area, but never crossed into the Demilitarized Zone.

Rhee locked the satellite group against the approaching chopper. It went deeper into the DMZ and came closer and closer to the border.

A low, dull alarm started ringing from his work station. Just when he expected it to turn, the American helicopter continued on, crossing the border. A low, dull alarm started ringing from his work station. Rhee typed, shutting down the alarm, then pressed his headset just above his right ear.

"This is Rhee, KPAF border systems control. We have a breach of the border at thirty-seven degrees north, one-twenty-five east, near the Yellow Sea. The violator is a military helicopter moving in a northeast vector at two-five-zero KMH and is in violation of Korean sovereign airspace."

"Roger," came the voice of the top ranking KPAF on-duty officer, Colonel Rok. "Lock-in missile defense systems and initiate warning."

"Yes, sir."

Rhee typed quickly, locking the nearest KPA surface-to-air missile battery onto the helicopter, which was now more than twenty kilometers inside North Korean airspace. He heard a high-pitched beeping noise, signifying acquisition of the target.

He typed again, then hit enter. This command broadcast an emergency message – in English – across all frequencies to the helicopter cockpit.

"You are in violation of North Korean airspace. Turn around immediately or you will be shot down."

Rhee analyzed the surface-to-air missile battery. The computer estimated a flight time of six minutes.

He broadcast the message three more times. The helicopter continued on a straight northward course.

He hit his headset.

"Colonel, the target is locked into the missile defense protocol."

"And you issued the warning?"

"Yes, sir. There is no reaction from the American helicopter."

"Very well," said Rhee's commander. "Fire two missiles, when ready."

"Affirmative," said Rhee. He pressed three buttons in succession on the work console just below the satellite screen, waited for a monotone, then prepared to flip a pair of switches. "Firing in three, two, one... and fire."

43

KPA HEADQUARTERS
PYONGANG

Yong-sik paced behind five men, each of whom was staring at their computer screens, watching the same thing: video from the portrait gallery. Their job was simple. Capture and print a screen shot of every individual who sat on the bench where the antidote had been planted. Everyone.

Yong-sik didn't tell them who they were looking for. He suspected it would be a Westerner, but there was also the possibility the Americans had an actual North Korean on their payroll.

It was the middle of the night. Yong-sik hadn't gone home. He wouldn't go home until he found his quarry.

The men fast-forwarded through their respective sections of tape. Certain sections of tape were crowded with visitors. Every time someone sat down, the photo was printed and given to Yong-sik, who studied each one carefully. But no one looked suspicious. Virtually every man or woman who sat down on the bench was elderly.

After several hours, one of the men stood up.

"General Yong-sik, sir," he said.

"What is it?"

"A Westerner."

Yong-sik walked behind the man. On the screen was a man with neatly combed blonde hair. Yong-sik made him rewind the tape, then watched as the man sat down and slipped his hand beneath the bench.

"Can you get closer?" asked Yong-sik.

"Yes, sir."

The camera zoomed in on the Westerner's face. Yong-sik recognized him. There were a total of sixty-one Westerners allotted work visas and allowed to live and work in Pyongang. He was familiar with them all, if not by name at least by photo. Yong-sik was one of the people who approved the visas and then reviewed them every month. But he knew this one by name. Yong-sik had sat for an interview with him a few years before. The man was a reporter for the *Associated Press*.

Talmadge.

44

DIRECTORATE OF OPERATIONS
OPS C3
CIA

Half-a-dozen people were now inside the mission theater, all of them focusing on *Operation Haystack*.

The large screen in front showed a digital map, black with various lights, symbols, and words. This was the border of North Korea, the De-Militarized Zone demarcated in bright red. A yellow light was flashing on and off and moving toward the border. This was Dewey's helicopter. It was displayed in real time, a mirror of the same screen that was running at that very moment on the USS Benfold, an *Arleigh Burke*-class destroyer currently deployed in the Sea of Japan.

The sound of voices from the ship could be heard as the chopper was tracked. The scratchy, sometimes garbled words came through on the amphitheater's speakers.

Jenna paced back-and-forth in the center of the room, watching the screen nervously, glancing at her watch despite the fact that a digital clock was imposed on the screen, and despite the fact that she'd just looked at her watch less than a minute before.

"What's that?" she yelled, pointing at a new flash of light south of Pyongang.

There was a pause, then someone spoke over the intercom.

"That's a plane," said someone on board the *Benfold*.

"I want to know *precisely* when we detect a missile," Jenna said.

"That's the third time you've told me that, ma'am. I heard you the first time."

"No reason to be snippy about it," whispered Jenna to herself.

A moment later, the voice came on speaker again.

"We have activity," he barked. "38 26 55 degrees North, 126 12 47 degrees East. That's a pair of missiles."

"Where?" Jenna yelled, reaching for her phone. She hit speed dial.

"I'll raise them," said the officer. "Hold. Look for a pair of green lights, moving quickly."

Jenna placed the phone against her ear as, on screen, a pair of bright green lights suddenly flashed. The two lights were moving quickly in the direction of Dewey's helicopter.

"*Answer*," Jenna pleaded into the cell as she watched the North Korean missiles streak through the sky.

45

APARTMENTS
PYONGANG

Talmadge awoke with a start, his body drenched with perspiration. His shirt was damp. He sat up and looked at his clock. It was 3:44 A.M.

It was the second night in a row he'd awakened inexplicably. He lifted the covers and swung his legs over the side of the bed. He pulled off his T-shirt and dropped it on the floor. He stood up and stretched. He walked into the small bathroom and flipped on the lights. He looked at himself in the mirror for a moment, debating whether or not to take a sleeping pill or just get up, make tea, read a little, then go to the office early.

He knew why he was startling himself awake at such an ungodly hour. But he tried to put the thoughts out of his mind. He did his job. He planted the antidote. No one had seen him. Who was it for, he wondered? It didn't matter. He didn't want to know. He did it, it was over, and that was the end of it.

Talmadge turned on the cold water and leaned down, splashing his face several times. He grabbed a towel from the shelf next to the mirror and put it to his wet face, drying it. The cool water made him feel better. He felt awake. He would get up and get an early start to the day. He finished drying his face and glimpsed at the mirror. He needed a haircut. Maybe he'd go to Mr. Gheng's down the street from the office for a trim before work? As he finished drying his face, he kept staring into the mirror, feeling an odd sensation. Something was wrong. What was it? He put the towel down just as his eyes saw something in the mirror, just a small wisp of movement.

No, not movement. He'd seen another set of eyes, just behind his. Someone was standing behind him.

Talmadge turned in shock, gasping. There – lurking just behind him – was a man.

It was General Yong-sik.

My God.

"Hello, Mr. Talmadge," said Yong-sik.

"What are you—"

At the same moment two things occurred. Talmadge started talking to attempt a distraction as he slashed his right arm forward at Yong-sik, hoping to catch him by surprise. At the same time, Yong-sik raised his left forearm and easily deflected Talmadge's punch as, with his right hand, he smashed Talmadge in the throat and, a half-second later, delivered a brutal clenched fist into his nose, breaking bones, crushing Talmadge's nose, blood spilling like a dam bursting from both nostrils as he groaned and reached for the sink, trying to recover, but Yong-sik didn't give him time. Yong-sik charged one step then leapt raising his right foot almost to eye level then kicking. The sole of his boot struck Talmadge in the mouth, snapping his head back and breaking his jaw. A handful of teeth dropped like Chiclets to the floor. Talmadge was sent sharply back, ricocheting off the sink, tumbling to the bathroom floor. Blood already covered much of the floor. Talmadge landed on his side, trying to move, his hands scratching at the crimson covered tile as he attempted to crawl toward the shower.

On his way to Talmadge's apartment, Yong-sik had debated to himself whether or not to bring Talmadge to one of the prisons and try to elicit information out of him before killing him. But he decided against it. Yong-sik knew Talmadge either worked for the CIA or MI6. Which one? It didn't matter. He also knew that torture would probably get information out of Talmadge, but he doubted there would be anything of use. Whoever Talmadge really was, whoever he was working for – he was deep cover. It meant he would have little information of value. Deep cover – especially in a hostile zone – was an island. Its lonely agents were told little if anything, and that was by design. If they got caught, as Talmadge had, it was precisely their lack of knowledge that kept secrets safe.

It was how North Korea worked. It was how all intelligence agencies worked. North Korea had agents scattered throughout the West – across Europe, in Central and South America, Mexico, Canada, and especially the U.S. They were there to provide intelligence and follow orders, even if an agent didn't know why.

Talmadge reached the shower and reached his hand up to grab hold of the side of the tub. Yong-sik watched him from the door as Talmadge tried to lift himself up, but couldn't. In addition to bleeding profusely from his shattered nose, his mouth seeped blood down his chin. He made a low gurgling noise as he fought to stay alive, to fight back. The kick had broken one of Talmadge's vertebrae, Yong-sik knew, perhaps both.

Finally, Talmadge let his hand go, slumping to the floor on his back as blood trickled from his nose and mouth. He looked up at Yong-sik, as if expecting Yong-sik to ask him something. Where are you from? Who do you work for? But Yong-sik stood watching in silence. He wouldn't give Talmadge the satisfaction of thinking Yong-sik even cared.

Talmadge coughed, trying to say something, like a drowning man. Yong-sik moved closer as Talmadge's eyes shut for several moments. When he opened them one last time, he looked calmly into Yong-sik's eyes.

"I worked alone," whispered Talmadge through clotted throat. "I chose to come here. I stayed after they said I could go home. I'll always be grateful for the kindness of the North Korean people."

Yong-sik watched as Talmadge fought the blood now filling his lungs. When his eyes shut, he turned and went back into the apartment.

He opened the door to the apartment. Outside stood two men, both dressed in suits.

"Ransack the apartment," said Yong-sik, rubbing his hand, still sore from hitting Talmadge. "I want a complete inventory. Put his colleagues under surveillance, but quietly."

"Yes, General Yong-sik," said one of the agents.

Yong-sik walked down the hallway toward the elevator. He pressed the button and turned.

"One more thing: return the body to its owners."

46

FOREST COUNTRY SOUTHWEST
NORTH KOREA

Dewey had on a custom designed watch made for the CIA – hard black Titanium with a bezel made of infinitesimally small pieces of diamond, heated to an air-like transparency, almost impossible to break. The dial was obsidian black with glowing numbers and glowing second and minute hands, using small traces of radioactive particles. It was an operational timepiece. Operators were not to wear the watches for long periods of time.

Macavoy had jumped seven minutes ago. That meant the closest possible missile was ten minutes out. Nine minutes from the point in time when he needed to jump. The chopper itself was set to detonate, to be found later by North Korean military, two charred bodies evidence of the mission's failure.

He felt a sudden shot of flu-like feeling rush over him. He'd forgotten – just for a moment – that he was infected. That he had less than a day before he'd be dead – if he didn't get to Pyongang and find the second antidote, the only one on earth. It was a small syringe that Dewey needed to live. Hopefully, it was in the hands of the reporter, Talmadge. With any luck, Jenna had reached him by now.

Wind rushed in through the door of the helicopter. Dewey stood near the opposite wall. He wore a black Kevlar vest, jeans, and boots. On his back, a backpack loaded with weapons, satellite phones, and water. Above the backpack was a parachute designed for extremely low altitude jumps. His face was painted black. If he survived the jump from the chopper, his only hope was to be invisible.

Right now, Dewey was in North Korean airspace. At that moment, he thought about the fact that he could've been back in Maine. He hated the feeling. He'd quit and yet something convinced him to come back in. It wasn't just Dellenbaugh, he knew. Sure, part of it was duty, but a more powerful force ran through Dewey and only he understood it. It was a need to be on the outermost point of what he could do, physically and mentally, to stop those who would do harm to the country he loved. He hated the feeling – but he needed it. Once again, it had found him.

"Stop," he said aloud. "Stop thinking. There's one objective. *Get the antidote.* It's all that matters. Don't think about anything else."

He looked at his watch. Seven-and-a-half minutes out. He had time to relax.

Dewey caught the burst of light coming from in front of the chopper, now on auto-pilot.

Dewey lurched toward the cockpit, looking ahead into the distance. It was unmistakable. A missile, in wavy orange lines, was moving toward them. He glanced at his watch. Six minutes out. Someone had fucked up the calculation. Or the North Koreans had better technology than we knew...

He heard one of the sat phones ringing – Langley calling to tell him to get off the chopper.

All of this – every thought – crossed Dewey's mind in a handful of seconds. The missile was accelerating with almost exponential velocity. It would hit long before it looked like it.

Jump when you can see the white of the missile.

Dewey charged for the open door, grabbing the ruck-sack in his right hand and leaping out the open helicopter door just as the roar of the incoming surface-to-air missile shook the air. The missile struck with awful violence – slamming hard just feet behind Dewey – and then the chopper exploded into smoke and fire.

Dewey fell, clinging to the bag, kicked by a furious wind, with no time to throw out the low-drop chute. The incinerated chopper was barely above the tree tops, just a few feet from him. He fell holding his hands and arms up, trying to avoid breaking a leg. He could get to Pyongang with a broken arm. But a broken leg was a death sentence.

Dewey slammed, chest first, into the branch, a brutal meeting of moving object with immovable force. There was a sharp crack upstream from where Dewey hit the branch as it broke. Dewey kept moving, trying to cling to something instead of falling from the tall pine, at least a hundred feet in the air.

At some point, he managed to grab hold of a thick branch, the palms of his hands scraping along the wood, ripping flesh, but he held on.

Dewey clung to the branch and swung for a few moments, relaxing for a brief second, though he was barely holding on, and was high in the branches of a towering pine within a thick forest.

Then the light awakened him. His head turned, his eyes focused: the helicopter's smoldering exoskeleton dangled just a few trees away, the flames catching the pine needles like they were doused with gasoline. The forest erupted in fire.

They would be coming.

Move.

Dewey put the ruck sack over his shoulder and moved down, from branch to branch, climbing with raw hands toward the ground. When he stepped foot on soil, he looked at his hands in the light from the inferno just a hundred feet away. There was no blood. What had been raw was now covered in dark patches of Pine sap, congealed on his hands, like tar.

He glanced once at the fire and turned to the North. He took a last gulp of breath and began running.

47

SIGNALS INTELLIGENCE DIRECTORATE
NATIONAL SECURITY AGENCY
FT. MEADE, MARYLAND

Bruckheimer was standing behind his desk, smoking a cigarette. In addition to being against NSA rules, it was illegal. Bruckheimer had an air filter machine and an open window, but his office still smelled a little.

The speaker on the console of his hard line desk phone made a short buzz, then his assistant, Kerry, came on:

"Will Parizeau from DIA is on two-six," she said.

Bruckheimer hit the speaker.

"Hi, Will. Let me guess. New Zealand? Argentina?"

Parizeau let out a small laugh.

"Good one," said Parizeau. "Jim, it's devolving and we have a serious situation on our hands."

"I know," said Bruckheimer. "I saw the *Green Flash*. How can we help?"

"We believe Kim is getting ready to launch one or more nuclear missiles. They're on missile vehicles and we have no way of knowing where the heck they are at any moment in time. I've racked my brains and the brains of everyone here trying to figure out a way. We'll be able to pick them up the second they launch, but not beforehand."

"So the Pentagon can't zero in on them and blow them up."

"Exactly. We don't know where they are."

"Which means the only option left is to wipe out North Korea," said Bruckheimer.

"Yes," said Parizeau. "I just came from the White House. In addition to not wanting to kill a million North Koreans, we have people *inside* Pyongang right now. We need to know where they're going to fire from. We can then take them down with sidewinders and avert a nuclear war."

"You'll never know where they're going to fire from, Will," said Bruckheimer, "unless you have reliable in-theater knowledge. The North Koreans are detached from the cloud. They have their own network. It's pre-historic. We simply cannot know where the missile vehicles are going to be. We've tried."

"Is there anything we can exploit?"

There was a pause as Bruckheimer lit another cigarette.

"There is one thing," said Bruckheimer. "SID has been able to hack into certain sections of the North Korean electric grid. In turn, we're running an experimental appliance that translates electronic signals into symbols that we can then correspond to words. It's DARPA shit, but we have it and it works. It's called *Rolex*. Anyway, we ran it against North Korea for the past six months. We don't know where they're going to launch a missile from, but we know when."

"So someone gives the order—"

"And we start tracking. The North Koreans send the orders hard line. They travel through a switch. What *Rolex* has learned to do is isolate the signals pattern from when a launch order is given."

"What if the order comes from some area you guys don't cover?" said Parizeau.

"All that matters is Pyongang," said Bruckheimer. "We have coverage in Pyongang. The orders come from Pyongang. Every one is the same: the order is issued electronically and precisely thirty minutes later the missile is launched."

"Can we set it up so that an alarm goes off?" said Parizeau. "It's one thing to look at past behavior. We need to know when the order is issued in real time."

There was a pregnant pause.

"I get what you're trying to do," said Bruckheimer, thinking aloud. "The algorithm works by parsing through historical data, in other words, it aggregates data from events that already happened. We need to parse through it in real time, before it's aggregated. I honestly don't know, but I'll find out."

"We need to know, Jim," said Parizeau.

"I'll get my best hacker working on it."

48

NORTH KOREA AIR FORCE
COMMAND CENTER
PYONGANG

Commander Rok stood above a large rectangular screen which displayed live radar of the moving helicopter – as well as the inbound missile. The two objects were on a collision course.

Several other senior KPAF officers and staff were standing around the satellite console.

"Are back-up missiles locked?" said Rok.

"Yes, colonel. We're locked and loaded. But the first two missiles are tracking for a direct hit."

"Nevertheless, I want the back-ups ready. The Americans have various evasion technologies."

"Yes, sir. Three missiles are prepared to move at a moment's notice."

Rok put his finger against the digital red box – the estimated collision point between missile and helicopter. He drew a line from the estimated collision point to Pyongang: 92 kilometers.

"Dispatch a heavy brigade from the reconnaissance unit," said Rok, without looking up. "I want a full capability set on site as soon as possible. That includes fire teams, forensics, emergency medical care, and of course recon. If there's anyone alive, we are to use all efforts to capture them – alive. Is that understood?"

"Yes, colonel. I took the liberty of ordering just such a precaution, sir. They are in route to estimated control point."

"Very good."

The voice of Rhee came over loudspeaker.

"Colonel, we are under twenty seconds until impact," said Rhee.

The group stood before the screen and watched as the two objects grew closer and closer. Suddenly, they merged.

"Target in five, four, three, two, one…"

A moment later, the screen flashed once, then both lights disappeared.

"We have an affirmative hit," said Rhee.

49

DIRECTOR'S OFFICE
CIA

Jenna ran from the elevator down the hallway to Calibrisi's office.
Calibrisi was standing outside, speaking with Lindsay, his assistant.

"Dewey's helicopter was just hit," she said.

Calibrisi started to say something, then stopped. A look of anger
appeared momentarily on his face. He didn't say anything.

"No calls," said Calibrisi, looking at Lindsay, "unless it's the
president."

"Please, Hector," she stammered.

Calibrisi went inside his office, leaving Jenna standing outside. He
moved to the chair behind his desk and sat down.

Jenna went inside his office and shut the door.

"We attempted contact when we first saw the missile flare," said
Jenna. "He didn't answer. I'm sorry."

"Sorry about what?" said Calibrisi.

"That I may have got Dewey killed."

Jenna looked at Calibrisi with a deer-in-the-headlights look. Her
mouth was open but she didn't say anything, though her lower lip
quivered ever so slightly. In that moment, Jenna felt lower than she'd
ever felt, lower even than the day her husband was killed. Not because
this was worse. The two were completely different. But it didn't
matter. She felt as low as she'd ever felt. She was out of place here.
Out of place and without anyone. She had no friends, no family. She
had nothing.

Calibrisi's face was red with sadness. He stared at Jenna.

Jenna considered saying something, that it wasn't her fault Dewey had gotten pricked by the needle. But she didn't say anything.

"I'll quit if that's what you think would be a good idea, Hector. I never wanted to cause problems."

–

Calibrisi sat back, running his hand through his hair, looking at Jenna. Her operation had exposed Kim. Beyond his nuclear capabilities, her operation had exposed his cancer.

"Dewey knew the risks," said Calibrisi. "And, he's not necessarily dead, either. What would *you* do if you saw a goddam missile coming at you? Jump. Jenna, you need to focus on what's going to happen next, not what just occurred. We still have Kim and nuclear bombs that in a few hours are going to be on their way to America."

"I don't think the North Koreans know there's a second antidote," said Jenna. "I didn't even know until Morris told me. They've undoubtedly ransacked Talmadge's flat but in all likelihood they were looking for papers, documents, computers, that sort of thing. Not necessarily a second antidote."

"You might be right."

"Unless they suspect he's in-country," said Jenna. "But, hopefully, the corpses on board the helicopter convince him otherwise."

Calibrisi stood up from his chair. He walked to the cabinet at the opposite side of the office. He pulled open the door to the cabinet. Inside was a mahogany shelf with a mirror behind it. Atop the shelf was an assortment of liquor bottles, a silver ice bucket, and several crystal glasses.

Calibrisi picked up a bottle of *Elijah Craig* bourbon and poured two glasses a third full. He dropped a single ice cube in each then walked over to Jenna and handed her one.

She studied it, then took a small sip.

The seating area in Calibrisi's office was comprised of two large red leather sofas across from one another and two red velvet chairs at either end, with a rectangular glass coffee table in the middle. Calibrisi and Jenna sat down across from one another on the ends of the two sofas.

"Bourbon," said Jenna. "The only truly American liquor."

Jenna put the glass to her mouth and took a healthy sip. Calibrisi watched with mild amusement, then bolted the glass down.

"I don't want you to leave," said Calibrisi. "You may have, in fact, saved millions of lives. I'm upset at myself more than anything. Dewey tried to resign. He did resign, now that I think about it. Dellenbaugh flew to Maine to ask him to do this."

Jenna finished her glass and set the glass down.

"All successful operations have flaws," Calibrisi continued. "People die. The problem is, you don't know which ones are successful and which ones are failures until they're over. If Dewey dies but we avert a nuclear attack on the United States, it will have been a success. But it's a steep price to pay."

50

FOREST
NORTH KOREA

With the orange light of the smoldering chopper behind him, Dewey broke into a desperate run. He glanced at his watch for direction, then moved in a north line into the dark expanse of tall trees.

The KPA would be coming soon. He needed to create as much distance as he could, as quickly as possible.

Just as important, Dewey had to get to Talmadge. He had to reach Pyongang before the poison kicked-in again and killed him.

The light from the fire became more and more diffuse as he moved, gradually disappearing behind the tall pines that seemed as if they would stretch on forever. Dewey was soon crossing a pine needle-covered forest floor in almost total darkness, his eyes acclimating to the dark gray that the trees let in from the sky above. He ran as fast as the conditions would allow, stepping high to avoid the thick roots that carpeted the desolate forest. For the first fifteen minutes, Dewey sprinted hard, using his hands to guide him by trees. He fell twice after kicking into roots. His lungs burned. But he didn't stop and he didn't slow down. He couldn't.

Then he heard the telltale electric din of a helicopter somewhere in the distance to the north. Soon, the whirr of a second chopper was discernible. He recognized the low-pitched, bear-like growl of Mi-26s, no doubt a full-on recon team rushing to see what the North Koreans shot down. He saw white light in the sky far out in front of him. Like search lights, the under-mounted halogen spotlights on the choppers abruptly cascaded down, framing the tree canopy and splashing white in bright patches that cut through the trees and washed over the forest floor. Dewey tucked against the dark side of a tree and remained still as both helicopters passed just above the treetops. Light suddenly hit the tree he was hiding behind, then moved on. He resumed his run.

He remembered words from Ranger School:

Step high. Shut your eyes. Let your hands guide you.

There were so many simulated night missions, ad hoc crisis exercises, and just plain long runs that it all finally blurred into a dark, exhausting continuum. That was the point. Without equipment to guide them, on clear nights and during horrendous storms, they were taught to operate at night.

You must learn. War is waged during day. It's won at night.

Everyone hated the night runs. Dewey did, too, at first. He suffered a high ankle sprain less than a week into Ranger School, on a dead-of-night, low chute drop, simulated exfiltration exercise followed by a ten-mile run through North Carolina farmland back to the base. He still winced when he thought about the way his ankle had turned as he hit the ground that night, nearly snapping. But there was little sympathy for those who got injured during training; it was purely sink or swim. If you couldn't handle the training, you sure as hell wouldn't be able to handle the real thing, at least that was the thinking.

Then, as now, Dewey found a way to compartmentalize the pain. He drew a picture of a box in his head, then took the excruciating feeling of his ankle and put it inside, then shut it off. The pain was there, but locked away.

Pain had always been Dewey Andreas's greatest weapon – how to inflict it, how to endure it.

The first five miles were grueling. Dewey felt as if he was going to die. But he pushed through it, and then each footstep began blending into the last footstep, and suddenly the pain all went away and he was transported and he could've run for days. The feeling beyond the pain.

As his eyes grew more accustomed to the night, he recognized the size and pattern of the forest around him. The pines were tall and thin, spaced every dozen yards or so, as if the trees were planted in a pattern. Dewey ran for an hour without stopping, leaving the burning helicopter and the KPA recon teams far behind.

After an hour, Dewey could only think about water. He wanted it, needed it, but he kept running, telling himself he would stop after the next five minutes, and soon the next five minutes became an hour, and then he ran on for one more.

He came to a small break in the forest where the trees abruptly ended. Across an overgrown field of tall grass, shrubs, and rusted-out farm equipment, he made out a cluster of dilapidated buildings. He looked for power lines, seeing none, and then moved through the field at a half-run, breathing hard. As he came close to the buildings, he skulked within a hundred feet of the buildings. They appeared abandoned, but the odor of manure was strong. There had to be people there. A dirt road led from the cluster of shacks, winding away to the north back into the forest between two dark walls of trees on both sides. Dewey picked-up the road and fell into a hard run, pushing his pace, constantly checking the compass on his watch to make sure he was still heading toward Pyongang. He ran hard for half-an-hour and when the road bent west he cut east, back into the forest. Dewey fell into the same steady routine as before, running in the darkness, guided by a spectral slate gray that barely allowed him to avoid the trees, step after step and mile after mile of a marathon he thought might never end.

It was after three hours when he came to a small stream and he collapsed, falling to the ground and crawling to water's edge. He put his entire face in the slow-moving water, nearly choking as he tried to catch his breath and drink at the same time. The fever had started to return, and it mixed with the pain from the run and he lay on the ground next to the stream for several minutes, struggling for breath, wracked by pain and exhaustion. He felt a temperature coming on.

Then he heard the voice.

This is not how it ends. Not here. Not now. Get up.

Dewey climbed to his feet. He pulled the ruck-sack off and fumbled around until he found the SAT phone. He hit two digits. It took almost a minute until he heard a series of clicks, then a short ring.

"CENCOM, go."

"This is Dewey Andreas. I need Jenna or Hector."

"Hold, please."

A few seconds later, Jenna came on:

"Dewey?" she said.

"Lock me in," said Dewey. "I need to know where I am."

"Hold on." He heard Jenna typing. "Alright, I have you. You're thirty-one miles from the crash site. How did you get there?"

"How far away is Pyongang?" he said, ignoring her question.

"Approximately twenty miles. You went slightly off course. You need to move northeast from where you're located."

"Where am I meeting Talmadge?"

There was a slight pause.

"We don't have a way to contact him," said Jenna.

"He doesn't know I'm coming?"

"No. Which is why you need to get to his flat. I'll get the location of the apartment and upload it."

"Got it."

51

PYONGANG

As Yong-sik's chauffeured Range Rover drove through the night toward his compound in the hills, one of his cell phones chimed. He picked it up.

"General, this is Bahn-ni."

Bahn-ni was one of several generals who reported to Yong-sik. He was in charge of air defense for the KPA.

"What is it?"

"We had an intrusion from the south," said Bahn-si. "A military grade helicopter came from the Yellow Sea west of Haiju. We acquired it immediately, targeted it, and launched two surface-to-air missiles. The helicopter continued in a northwest path toward Pyongang. At approximately twelve minutes in, one or both of the missiles struck the helicopter. Teams are on the way. The satellite shows a large fire in the forest north of Ba-do. It will take a while to get through."

"Send a helicopter to my home," said Yong-sik. "I'm going there myself."

–

The Soviet-made Mil Mi-26 helicopter flew across seemingly endless miles of thick forest, interrupted occasionally by small patches of rooftops. There were no lights because there was no electricity. Only the stars on this cloudless night illuminated the homes.

The smoke was visible from a long way away, then, as the chopper came in closer, the wreckage, flames that still burned a bright orange, and a clearing where the fallen craft had left a charred crater.

Yong-sik's pilot found a patch of ground large enough to land on just a few hundred yards away, settling the helicopter down on the forest floor.

Yong-sik, Bahn-ni, and two other soldiers, moved through the tall pines toward the crash scene. The heat from the still smoldering chopper could be felt immediately, and it grew hotter as they came closer to the wreckage. A first team of KPA reconnaissance specialists were already on the scene. Two large vehicles were off to the side – water trucks – and the soldiers – each dressed in bright orange, flame retardant fire suits – were spraying the burning skeleton of the helicopter, trying to preserve any evidence.

Yong-sik waited a few minutes as the reconnaissance team hosed down the burning chopper. One of the men dragged a burning corpse from the cockpit, which another man sprayed with water. A few moments later, a second corpse was hauled from the ruins. As they sprayed him, Yong-sik walked across the scalding ground to the cockpit.

When he got there, he looked into what was left of the destroyed cockpit. Then he walked to the two corpses, both of which were still emanating heat and smoke.

"Bring everything to Kaech'on," said Yong sik, kneeling next to the bodies.

"Yes, general."

Yong-sik stood and walked quickly to the waiting helicopter and climbed in. The chopper's rotors picked up and soon they were in the sky. From a window, Yong-sik watched as two men lifted one of the corpses and started carrying it.

"Wait!" he barked to the pilots. "Bring it back down, now!"

Yong-sik jumped from the helicopter as it was bumping down on the ground. He moved toward the wreckage.

"Put the bodies down," he ordered.

Yong-sik pushed one of the men aside. The heat was intense, but Yong-sik seemed not to notice. He stepped to one of the corpses, reaching to the man's face, the skin still smoking. Yong-sik opened the man's mouth. He felt what was left of his teeth. He repeated the examination on the other corpse.

He took out his cell and walked back toward the chopper.

"This is General Yong-sik," he said. "Patch me through immediately to Colonel Phyun."

Yong-sik understood the moment he felt the teeth. The flames had yet to destroy them, insulated by flesh and bone. They told a simple story. Neither man had ever been to a dentist. Both were missing teeth in several places, and those that did remain were crooked. He couldn't imagine where they'd gotten the dead men from, but they were no doubt already dead by the time they climbed aboard the helicopter to play the role of a lifetime.

Yong-sik thought back to the moment he sent the documents; the moment he sent one document he didn't need to, the key to it all: Kim's health report.

The burning helicopter could only mean one thing: America was coming. To kill Kim or to try and destroy the nuclear missiles. One or the other – or both. To do either, though, they would first attempt to reach…

Talmadge.

"Talmadge!" he seethed.

Perhaps he shouldn't have done anything so provocative as dump the body inside the DMZ. Now they knew. They knew he knew.

It was a chess game and Yong-sik preferred Blackjack.

A voice came on his cell.

The radio crackled.

"Colonel Phyun," came the voice.

"Get a team to the reporter's apartment immediately, colonel," said Yong-sik. "I want men in the lobby, on the stairs, and I want eyes in the buildings within sight line."

"It will be done immediately, General Yong-sik."

"Capture anyone who attempts to enter the building. Kill them if necessary. Do not allow them into the apartment. Is that understood?"

"Yes, general."

"I also want a forensics unit to go back through the reporter's apartment," said Yong-sik. "This time, tear up everything. Cut the pillows apart. Break into the walls. Rip the mattress, the ceiling, the floor."

"Yes, general, I will dispatch a team immediately."

"Bring anything you find to me."

Yon-sik pocketed his cell and walked to Bahn-si.

The air remained clotted in smoke. The heat was intense. Dozens of men were fighting to put out the last flames from the destroyed chopper.

"I want search teams moving by ground," said Yong-sik. "Between here and the capitol."

"How wide would you like the perimeter, General Yong-sik?"

"A mile wide. Every farm, every building. Tell your men to have their fingers on the trigger at all times."

"What are we looking for?"

"Americans."

52

CIA HEADQUARTERS

Jenna hung up the phone and walked to Calibrisi's office. She knocked on the glass door. Calibrisi was standing behind his desk, stuffing papers into his leather briefcase. He waved her in.

"We need to get back to the White House," said Calibrisi. "Are you ready?"

"I just spoke with Dewey," she said.

Calibrisi paused.

"Thank God," said Calibrisi. "Where is he?"

"South of Pyongang. He's on foot."

"What did you tell him?"

"To get to Talmadge's apartment. If the second antidote survived, that's where it will be."

"I want you to start thinking about how we extract Talmadge and Dewey," said Calibrisi. "Whether the two of them make it or not is beyond our control at this point. What's not is having a plan to get them out of there. Work directly with General Tralies."

"Okay," said Jenna.

They were thinking the same thing. What if Talmadge wasn't there? What if the second dose *was* destroyed in transit? One of the worst aspects of operations was the unknown and the sense of powerlessness for those people not out in the field, like, at this moment, Calibrisi and Jenna. Watching from afar with little information.

"We need to focus on Kim and the nuclear threat," said Calibrisi. "Dewey is on his own. You can't beat yourself up and you can't worry about him. It won't help but it will distract you from the bigger threat.

Dewey is tough and he's resourceful. Put a plan in place to extract him if we get to that point."

Calibrisi shut his briefcase and buckled it.

"Now get your stuff. We leave in—"

Suddenly, there was yelling in the hallway outside Calibrisi's office. Mack Perry came running to Calibrisi's door and pushed in the door.

"You two have to see this."

They followed Perry to one of the conference rooms down the hallway. A small group was seated around the conference table. This was the task force working under Jenna's command and attempting to monitor what was going on in North Korea as it related to Dewey, not only trying to figure out if he was still alive, but making plans for his extraction.

A large OLED screen on the wall showed a grainy live feed of an American. He was bald and wore a khaki military uniform. This was Colonel Nate Smith, the senior-ranking American in the DMZ, the strip of land buffering North and South Korea. Smith was standing in some sort of building that looked like a barracks.

"Go ahead, colonel," said Perry.

"We discovered him inside one of the Joint Security Area buildings ten minutes ago," said Smith.

As the camera followed Smith, he walked through a door into a building that was painted bright blue. Inside was a plain looking table with chairs on both sides. All the chairs around the table were empty – except one. In it was a man, seated, his head tilted to the side, almost on top of his shoulder, limp. A rope was tied tightly around his neck. His face was badly bruised. Beneath his nose, running down his chin, neck, and the front of his shirt, was a large patch of dried blood, damp-looking, as if still fresh.

Jenna gasped.

"Who is it?" said Smith.

Jenna started to say something, but it was Calibrisi who answered.

"His name is Talmadge," said Calibrisi. "Take care of him, will you, colonel?"

"Of course. Should I send him back to Andrews?"

"No," said Calibrisi. "Clean him up and send him to Heathrow."

"Roger that."

Calibrisi turned and walked out of the conference room with Jenna just behind him. On the elevator to the rooftop helipad, he spoke:

"Let Derek know," said Calibrisi. "River House should send a greeting party to meet the body."

"What about Dewey?" asked Jenna. "If he finds out Talmadge is dead—"

"Let him know. Get Dewey the location of the apartment and make sure he understands: if they found Talmadge out, they'll be swarming the apartment, searching for other stuff. He's going to need to come in hot."

53

CHAERYONG
NORTH KOREA

Four platoons of KPA soldiers – more than 140 soldiers – were dropped in a ten mile corridor along an East-West line of territory near Chaeryong, to the south of Pyongang. The soldiers were on the ground by two A.M. The orders were simple: find the invader.

Each platoon was spread out along the geographic line, each North Korean soldier approximately one hundred meters from the next, moving on foot.

A dozen or so trained dogs, German Shepherds, moved out in front of the line of soldiers, sniffing for unusual smells, trained to stop and alert their masters upon the discovery of any number of unusual odors, including explosives, blood, food, and human beings.

Each dog was managed by a handler, whose job it was to stay close to their dog. The dogs moved in a fast, zig-zag pattern, searching the woods for any recent signs of human activity.

Three-and-a-half hours after being dropped in the woods, Woo, a junior lieutenant in the KPA, heard barking from his dog, Podo. He found Podo next to a tree, still as a statue. Woo shone his headlamp down on the base of the tree. There, he saw a slight indentation in the shelf of pine needles that looked like a footprint. Podo stared at it, unrelenting, until Woo released him.

Woo searched the area around the tree. Several feet behind, he saw a similar imprint on a rotting clump of leaves.

Woo cued the mike on his radio.

"This is Junior Lieutenant Woo. I may have found something."

54

HWANGJU, NORTH KOREA
SOUTH OF PYONGANG

Morning had come and with it not only light but the increasing realization that he was running out of time. He'd struck Yong-sik sometime after ten P.M. He forced himself to look at his watch. It was almost eight in the morning.

Since talking to Jenna, Dewey had run for another hour. Finally, he saw sky in the distance open up and knew the forest was done. He came to the end of the tall pines. The trees stopped at a tall chain-link fence. Down an embankment, across a wide dirt shoulder, a paved road cut east–west.

Dewey crouched, holding the rust-covered fence with one hand as he tried to catch his breath.

There wasn't much traffic, but there was some. Cars and trucks rumbled slowly in both directions. Dewey watched for several minutes, trying to figure out what to do.

Perhaps Talmadge owned a vehicle, Dewey thought. Langley could lock-in his location again and Talmadge could meet him. It was risky, he knew. As a Westerner, Talmadge was likely followed wherever he went. A better plan would be for Talmadge to bring it with him and leave it somewhere nearby. Even packaging the antidote so that it wouldn't break and driving by and dropping it from the window would work, if Talmadge did it right. That way, Talmadge would not need to risk exposing himself. Yes, there was a chance the syringe might break if it wasn't packaged correctly, but it was Dewey who'd be taking the risk, not Talmadge. Dewey was willing to take that risk.

"Sonofabitch," he said.

As his breathing calmed, Dewey realized that the fever had returned. Running for so long – the pain from the running – had cloaked its return, but there it was. He felt like he was on fire, a flu-like heat that occupied every part of his body.

Not any more, he thought, trying to collect his thoughts and gather the energy to keep going. *Please, no hotter than this.*

He reached for the SAT phone and was about to dial when his vision suddenly blurred and then went black. He instinctively lay down on his back, in case someone looked over from the road. He put a hand on the fence, squeezing hard, as if doing so might make his sight return. He waited, trying not to panic, yet feeling torched by a high fever and now blind. Talmadge would have to come and find him. There was no alternative. Either that or he would… die.

He felt for the keypad on the SAT phone and dialed the two digits he thought would connect him to Langley. A steady chirping noise indicated he'd misdialed and he tried again. This time, he heard a half-ring, then a voice.

"CENCOM, go."

"I need Jenna."

"Hold on, please."

A moment later, Jenna's even, aristocratic British accent came on the line.

"You're getting closer. You're within a few miles of the city."

"I can't see, Jenna."

"What do you mean?"

"The fever's back. I blacked out. You need to have Talmadge come and get me."

There was a long pause. Finally, Jenna broke the silence.

"I have very bad news," she said. "Talmadge was found out and they killed him. His body was just recovered in the DMZ."

Dewey lay on the ground, phone against his ear, breathing in short, rapid bursts. He was burning up. With his other hand he rubbed his eyes.

Suddenly, Jenna started to cry. Dewey remained silent.

"It doesn't matter how they found out," he said finally, a touch of resignation in his voice. "It's irrelevant. We can't change what happened."

"Dewey, I'm so sorry."

"It's okay," said Dewey quietly. "I have to go."

"No," said Jenna, stiffening. "So Talmadge is dead? That's simply a piece of the puzzle we don't have to figure out. Thank God we know. Otherwise you'd be searching Pyongang for him."

"Good point," said Dewey derisively. "I can't fucking see! *I'm blind!*"

"It will pass," said Jenna. "Any minute, I promise. The blackouts are designed into the poison. They last a few minutes and then go away."

"Where am I?"

"You're in a town called Hwangju," she said, "south of the city. I've mapped out the route to Talmadge's apartment. It's uploaded to the phone."

"Describe it," said Dewey. "Where is it, what floor is he on, where's his door. Got it? Right now. That's what I need."

"Will you be on foot?"

"I don't know."

"Well, either way, you keep going north until you reach the river. It runs right through the city. Move along the river continuing north. There are three islands in the river. They're all large, with buildings. When the river splits for the third island, that's when you need to cross. His apartment is behind the triumphal arch. The building is off the main road, south of the arch. It's called Moranbong. The buildings all look the same but this one has green lettering on the front door. The number is forty seven. His flat is on the fourth floor, second door on the right. There's a Star of David scratched into the upper corner of the door. Talmadge would've hidden the second antidote somewhere inside the flat. All of this is uploaded to the phone."

Dewey saw vague traces of light, like stars, and soon he was looking up at the fence. His vision had returned. Slowly, he pulled himself up, crouching, phone to his ear, staring at the road.

"I have to go."

"There's one other thing," said Jenna. "The flat is likely under watch. Expect KPA there. As for the antidote, Talmadge was well-trained. You're going to make it and you're going to find the antidote."

55

SIGNALS INTELLIGENCE DIRECTORATE
NSA
FT. MEADE, MARYLAND

Samantha Stout sat at her desk. A wall of large computer screens – eight in all – faced her. Each screen looked as if a child had sat down and started typing random letters and numbers into it, except for one screen that had a tile of news feeds from various parts of the world running with the volume down.

Samantha was the individual inside the NSA who was responsible for testing and integrating the new software program that had been developed by DARPA. DARPA stood for Defense Advanced Research Projects Agency, an agency inside the Department of Defense responsible for the development of cutting-edge technologies for use by the military. The program, called *Rolex*, was raw but potentially very powerful. DARPA had developed a way to capture certain non-intelligent electronic signals and convert them into symbols that could then be translated into words. In other words, it could grab pure data streaming through the sky from pre-Internet forms of technology and convert it into words. It was Samantha who'd figured out how to aim *Rolex* at North Korea and specifically certain electronic frequencies that the NSA knew were being generated by the military. By writing an algorithm that was layered on top of *Rolex*'s algorithms, Stout had trained *Rolex* to be able to know what the signals pattern looked like when the North Koreans launched missiles. The problem was, *Rolex* only worked with historical data. It was a sort of armchair quarterback, able to pinpoint when a launch had taken place. Her challenge: get

Rolex to parse, assess, and react in real time. *Rolex* needed to be predictive versus reactive in order to know when the order to launch by the North Koreans had taken place – and therefore how long the U.S. had before the missiles actually left the ground.

Samantha called a classmate of hers from the California Institute of Technology, a woman named Kami Gray who worked at a hedge fund in New York City. Kami, she knew, wrote algorithms that the giant hedge fund used to look at patterns in the stock market and then predict what was going to happen next based on those patterns. Kami had already done with different software what Samantha needed to do with *Rolex*: read Terabytes of real time data in nanoseconds in order to predict the future.

Without telling Kami any classified information, she explained the challenge.

"You need to be able to know the pattern in the first few seconds," said Kami. "You need to slice off the first few seconds of the signals events you've already catalogued, then isolate them versus all other signals."

"Exactly."

"I'm going to send you an access key to an algorithm I wrote that enables us to see certain patterns in commodities prices and then drive a reaction, a trade. It's designed to react to the pattern within a fraction of a second. If the pattern is the one we trained it to watch out for, our computers automatically start buying or selling, as the case may be."

"Sounds perfect," said Samantha.

"Do you know your way around MATLAB?" said Kami, referring to the computing environment her algorithm had been built in.

"Yes," said Samantha.

"Obviously don't tell anyone."

"I won't. I owe you dinner next time you're down here."

56

SITUATION ROOM
WHITE HOUSE

One floor underground was the White House Situation Room, a windowless, high-tech conference room where the President of the United States and his most trusted military, intelligence, and diplomatic advisors convened during crisis.

The walls of the room were covered in OLED screens, eight in all, all lit up with a variety of maps, live satellite feeds, news coverage, and inter-agency, multi-party communications. The same group that had briefed President Dellenbaugh in the Oval Office was gathered in the room, along with several mission, technical, and intelligence experts.

The president sat at the head of the table, again with Calibrisi on his immediate right. Next to Calibrisi was Jenna.

Phil Tralies, chairman of the Joint Chiefs of Staff, sat the opposite end of the table from Dellenbaugh. Tralies was presenting the three military attack scenarios the president had ordered up. Tralies had a small device that enabled him to control one of the OLED screens. The screen showed a digital map of North Korea. Tralies clicked it and the number "1" appeared on the screen. As Tralies spoke, the OLED displayed digital representation of the military scenario.

"First scenario, Mr. President, is a non-nuclear option. Without getting too specific, this would involve an all-hands-on-deck pre-emptive air bombing campaign, using every available military asset the United States has in the Pacific Theater. Missiles and bombs."

The screen showed a swarm of red digital lines representing missiles as they moved toward North Korea. Hundreds of lines crossed the screen.

"Final targeting protocols are being run right now and will be live by the end of this meeting," said Tralies. "We're talking about military installations and population centers, sir. Casualty estimate: thirty to forty thousand. The downside is, the North Koreans keep their missiles on missile vehicles, so we don't know where their nukes are at any given moment. We're going to have to bomb pretty much everywhere – and even then we might not stop the North Koreans, especially if they're going to use a missile vehicle."

"What are the odds we blow up the devices?"

"My rough estimate, one in six."

Tralies clicked the device in his hand and the screen was wiped. The number "2" appeared.

"Two," continued Tralies, "is also a non-nuclear option. This involves infiltration of North Korea using manpower, delivered by water, with one primary objective: removal of Kim Jong-un. Within the last hour, a fire team of Navy SEALS has been moved to the *USS Benfold*, currently off the eastern coast of the Korean Peninsula. The SEALs would be inserted along the coast somewhere with the goal of getting to Pyongang and assassinating Kim."

The screen showed a digital representation of the *Benfold*, then a smaller craft moving to the North Korean coast.

"As you can imagine, the odds on this working are not great. As confident as I am in these guys, it's going to be hard to move into the country without detection, not to mention finding the guy."

"How much time would this require, general?" said Dellenbaugh.

"From the time we say go, at least six hours. That's without complications."

"And the odds of success?"

"One in twenty."

The room was silent. Dellenbaugh nodded, indicating he wanted Tralies to continue.

"Finally, option three is a nuclear-based attack scenario. This scenario involves a pre-emptive nuclear attack on military and population centers. The targeting would be optimized to try and destroy where we predict the missiles will be coming from, though we won't be sure and for this reason Pyongang is the primary target. That's where the order will come from. If we wipe out the people giving the order before they give the order, then they can't give the order, can they? As with option one, we won't know if we've succeeded, but the odds are much higher. We believe option three has an eighty percent chance of averting a nuclear strike on the U.S. Unfortunately, as you might expect, the casualty count is dramatically higher, somewhere between one-and-a-half and two million people."

"How many devices and which ones?"

"Nine Trident II D-5 nuclear missiles, Mr. President. This would be accomplished by two *Ohio*-class submarines now within tight range of North Korea: the *USS Tennessee*, and the *Nevada*."

The OLED suddenly showed two red objects on the map representing the submarines, spread out in the Sea of Japan, off the coast of North Korea. Then, bright green lines shot from the subs ad flew into North Korea. There were nine lines in total. Silent digital explosions appeared on the map, then circles showing the range of the nuclear fallout.

"What about THADD, general?" asked Dellenbaugh, referring to the Pentagon's Terminal High Altitude Area Defense system, designed to shoot down incoming missiles.

"THADD defenses are as ready today as they were a week ago," said Tralies. "I've instructed the Missile Defense Agency to raise their internal alert levels to the highest echelon and be prepared at any moment for activity. In addition, Aegis BMD, or Ballistic Missile Defense, is on high alert, as are various other systems designed to shoot down enemy ballistic missiles."

Tralies hit the remote and a larger, more regional map hit the screen, showing the entire world. Tralies hit the remote again. A series of bright light blue lights appeared, showing the locations of the THADD arsenal. "We have a total of sixteen active delivery vehicles with eight missiles each, a total of one-hundred twenty-eight defensive objects that can be used to shoot down enemy missiles. We don't believe KPA will have dummy rockets, but we do anticipate the possibility of more than one ICBM. In addition to THADD, we've activated all Ground Based Missile Defense Systems, or GMD, in a state of *Active Priority*. Our missile defenses are as prepared as they've ever been. That being said, when you're playing defense you're not playing offense. There has never been an authentic real battle test involving enemy ballistic missiles and THADD, BMD, or GMD."

"And what's your recommendation, general?" asked Dellenbaugh

"It hasn't wavered, sir. We are at imminent risk of nuclear attack. My recommendation is an immediate pre-emptive nuclear strike, option three."

Dellenbaugh nodded. He looked at Brubaker.

"I agree with General Tralies," said Brubaker. "Kim is going to attack. I think we have until Sunday North Korea time. That's eight hours. We have time – but we can't let the clock pass midnight. We – you, Mr. President – we all have an obligation, sir. If a nuclear bomb – and God forbid more than one – hits an American city, it would be catastrophic. We knew about it and yet we waited too long? We need to act before midnight in Pyongang."

Dellenbaugh pointed at Dale Arnold, the secretary of defense.

"Where are you on this?" said Dellenbaugh.

"I agree with Phil," said Arnold, "but I want to hear what Will has to say. If we can reliably count on knowing when Kim is fueling up the rockets, I'd be okay with waiting. I don't want to destroy North Korea but it really isn't the U.S. who's responsible for this situation. It's Kim."

All eyes went to Will Parizeau from the Missile Defense Agency. He was seated across from Jenna.

"You said there was no way to use your satellites to know when the North Koreans are getting ready to launch," said Dellenbaugh. "Has anything changed?"

"Well, yes and no, sir," said Parizeau.

"Why no?" said Dellenbaugh.

"There's simply no way to know where the North Koreans are going to launch from, Mr. President. "We can't simply scan looking for radiation."

"So why the yes?"

"The NSA might have a way of knowing when they're getting ready to launch," said Parizeau. "They're working on it as we speak. If they can figure it out, we would potentially know when the order to launch is given. Thus far, their launch timing pattern has been the same for more than a decade. The order is made and thirty minutes later the missile takes off."

"But if we don't know where they're coming from, what's the point?" said Brubaker.

"The point is, if we know when the order is made, we know how much time we have," said Calibrisi. "It allows us to work on a solution up until that point."

"Then what?" said Tralies. "So we know when they're going to launch but if we don't know where, it's irrelevant."

"It means we have time," said Calibrisi. "We're talking about millions of lives."

"If a North Korean nuke hits Los Angeles, millions of Americans would perish," said Tralies.

"I'm not suggesting we let them launch the bombs," snapped Calibrisi. "I'm saying if the NSA program works, we have until they give the order to launch to try and stop them."

"Will, when will we know if the NSA can do it?" said President Dellenbaugh.

"I don't know, sir," said Parizeau.

Dellenbaugh turned to Mila Mijailovic, the secretary of state.

"I'm curious, Mila," said Dellenbaugh. "What have you been doing for the last hour?"

Mila grinned, though ever so slightly, a Cheshire-cat grin. Mila was something of a mystery inside Dellenbaugh's cabinet, plucked out of academic obscurity in part due to her traveling to the world's hardest destinations in order to understand them and how they thought.

"Without divulging information as to Kim's health or our belief Kim is getting ready to attack, I spoke with someone high up in the Chinese politburo," said Mila. "Someone who could let me understand where the Chinese government stands on this. Someone who could deliver a message if necessary."

"Interesting," said Dellenbaugh.

"The Chinese government will not tolerate a nuclear attack. They will move into war condition. It doesn't mean they will respond, but it signals they might. They will however tolerate a non-nuclear bombing campaign. They'll obviously come out screaming but they'll let it go. I even get the sense they encourage it."

Mila glanced at Calibrisi, then Tralies. Her face was as emotionless as stone.

"What about Seoul?"

"I wouldn't worry about South Korea, Mr. President," said Mila. "They'll go along. It's China who matters."

"So you think we shouldn't use nuclear weapons?" said Dellenbaugh.

"Actually, no, I don't," said the secretary of state. She looked at Tralies, the chairman of the Joint Chiefs of Staff. "I agree with General Tralies. We're at imminent risk. One of the things my Chinese contact shared is that multiple efforts have been made to speak with Kim. All have been unsuccessful. He's burning bridges. He no longer cares. He's dying. He *is* going to launch missiles. We need to act immediately. The Chinese might respond, as my source warned, but how? America will be prepared. They don't want to get in a firefight with the United States, certainly not over North Korea. Mr. President, we need to strike right now, sir. American lives are at stake. People *you* pledged to protect. There's no good reason to wait."

Suddenly, Jenna stood up, shooting up from her chair. Dellenbaugh leaned right, slightly surprised.

"You, ah, wanted to say something, Jenna?" said the president.

"*There is a bloody well good goddam reason to wait!*" Jenna said, her British accent rising. "*Dewey Andreas is still in Pyongang! He'll be killed! That's why we're waiting!*"

The room went pin drop quiet. All eyes were on Jenna, who was the only one standing. Even staffers off to the side were awe struck.

"How do you really feel, Jenna?" said Dellenbaugh, smiling. He scanned the room.

"I... I'm sorry, Mr. President," said Jenna.

Dellenbaugh chuckled. He looked around the conference table.

"I agree with Jenna," the president said calmly. "We're not abandoning Dewey. It's that simple."

"We have no choice," said Tralies, pointing at Jenna in frustration. "The North Koreans are going to drop a nuclear bomb on the United States, probably more than one! Is Dewey Andreas's life more valuable than the lives of a million people in Los Angeles or San Antonio or Phoenix or Guam or wherever these crazy bastards decide to target?"

"We have eight hours," said Jenna. "We're talking about the man who risked his life for this country in order to retrieve this information. We have eight hours until it's Sunday in Pyongang."

"What if he decides to launch it earlier?" said Brubaker. "You heard Parizeau: we don't know where their missile vehicles are! We won't be able to detect it and then it's a live operation! We're relying on untested technology!"

Jenna looked around the room, a slightly confused look on her face.

"What if there was another way, Mr. President?" said Jenna, glancing at Calibrisi, then turning to President Dellenbaugh.

The Chairman of the Joint Chiefs started speaking, his face going red.

"We can't—"

Dellenbaugh held up his hand, shutting Tralies up.

"Go on," said Dellenbaugh, looking at Jenna.

"Dewey is *in* Pyongang," she started. "He's *inside* the city. What if Dewey could get to Kim?"

"And do what, talk him out of it?" said Tralies.

"Kill him," said Jenna coldly.

The room was silent.

"How exactly would Dewey do that?" said Dellenbaugh.

"I don't know. Not yet anyway."

Tralies shook his head in disgust.

"This is ridiculous," said Tralies. "Kim could be fueling up those missiles as we speak. You heard the secretary of state."

"It's not Sunday," said Jenna.

"What does that mean?"

"Did you read his statement, general?" said Jenna sharply. She slid the document across the table. "It will be on a Sunday. Only on a Sunday. *Bloody Sunday.*"

"I know what the damn document says," barked Tralies.

"Enough, general," shot the President. He stood up. "Everyone listen carefully. We will not allow the North Koreans to strike the United States. Make no mistake: if we get to Sunday, option three is the obvious choice. But we're not moving earlier. At midnight Pyongang time, we strike – unless the NSA can allow us to know when the order is made to launch from Pyongang. In that case, we play this out until the last possible minute. Dewey Andreas is in Pyongang and – as long as we're objective about it – we'll wait until the last possible moment before we strike. Is that understood?" He looked at Jenna. "Jenna, design an operation to take out Kim. Will, keep on top of the NSA. We'll re-convene in half-an-hour – unless the shit hits the fan before that."

–

Jenna walked outside and sat down on the South Lawn. She went past a tall, manicured hedge, out of sight from the Oval Office and West Wing. She removed a pack of cigarettes – Marlboro Lights – and lit one. She hadn't smoked in over two years but she bought a pack at lunch.

How can we kill Kim? Think, Jenna.

Her cell phone started beeping. She looked at the number. It was Derek Chalmers. She took another puff, exhaled, and answered.

"Hello, Derek," said Jenna.

"Hi, Jenna," said Chalmers.

"How are you?"

"I received your email," said Chalmers evenly.

"Talmadge is being flown to Heathrow," said Jenna. "I'm very sorry, Derek."

"He was my recruit," said Chalmers quietly.

"I know."

"Was his life worth it?"

"Yes," said Jenna. She held up her phone and brought up the email client.

"I'm sending you the results of the operation. Please don't share with anyone. Kim has cancer. He's getting ready to launch a nuclear attack on the United States. Talmadge was critical and he executed his role perfectly. But they caught him. He deserves an agency wreath of arms, Derek."

"I'll see to it. Now what happened?"

Jenna told him everything. The Macau operation, the documents, Dewey being poisoned.

"You were right to use Talmadge," said Chalmers, "as much as it saddens me. So what's wrong, Jenna?"

Jenna told Chalmers about the operation she now had approximately ten minutes to design.

"I don't know what to do, Derek," she said, her voice trembling. She looked as if she might cry. "I've fucked it all to hell. Not only Talmadge, Dewey."

"He knew the dangers of being exposed to the poison," said Chalmers. "In the meantime, I'm going to send you a document."

"I don't have time—"

"In 1972, Kim's grandfather built a series of escape tunnels from the palace," said Chalmers, cutting her off. "He was concerned about a possible coup. The design is simple. Get Dewey into the tunnels. He moves to the palace and kills Kim."

"It'll be heavily guarded," said Jenna.

"If you want to kill Kim, it's the only option, other than leveling Pyongang. Dewey knows how to penetrate a crowded security knot. Just lay out the design to Hector and President Dellenbaugh. They're the *only* two in that room that matter. *They* will make the call. Trust yourself, Jenna."

57

PRIVATE RESIDENCE
THE WHITE HOUSE

Dellenbaugh stepped off the elevator inside the private residence. He was still dressed in his running gear along with the blue sweater. He could smell himself. He needed a shower.

But he had to get back downstairs.

His daughters were seated inside the large central living room, across from one another, lying down, Summer looking at her phone while Sally held a large book above her, reading. They didn't even seem to notice as their father entered the private living quarters of the White House.

Dellenbaugh said nothing, instead walking through the living room and down the hallway into the large master bedroom. Amy Dellenbaugh was in bed, reading a book. She looked up. Instinctively, she knew something was wrong. Their eyes met. But Dellenbaugh said nothing. He looked shell-shocked.

Amy put her book down and sat up.

"Is everything okay, J.P.?"

He met her eyes with a distant stare. He said nothing.

Amy threw the blanket aside and stood up. She walked toward him. He stood still, staring into Amy's eyes.

"What is it?" she said. "North Korea?"

Dellenbaugh nodded, yes.

"The North Koreans are going to launch a missile. We don't know where it will be aimed. Los Angeles, San Diego, Houston. We don't know. There might be more than one."

"How do you know they'll really do it?"

"We don't, not until they actually launch it."

Amy put her hands around him.

"The only way to prevent it is to..." Dellenbaugh paused, "...to do something horrible, Amy."

"To bomb them first, right?"

He nodded, yes, as she leaned closer and kissed his neck.

"You'll know what to do. It's why you're the president. It's the reason Americans elected you. Why they love you."

Amy put her hand to his cheek, comforting him.

"Dewey is there," said Dellenbaugh, looking at Amy.

"Oh, J.P.," she whispered.

She took his hand and moved it to her cheek.

"Go back down," she said. "You can't rest, not now. You'll figure it out. You always do."

58

HWANGJU, NORTH KOREA
SOUTH OF PYONGANG

Dewey crouched at the fence and looked in both directions, searching. He saw something far in the distance to his right, perhaps a mile or so, a tiny object alongside the roadway. He stepped back into the trees and started moving parallel to the chain link fence, hidden from view. He ran at a medium paced jog, trying to will himself to go faster but he couldn't. Still, he kept going until he was close. Through the trees, he saw a small gas station on the side of the road. It looked like it was built in 1950, a simple concrete building and a pump. He watched as a young North Korean man walked to a car and began pumping gas.

He started to climb the fence when he overheard the distant hum of a helicopter. Dewey quickly climbed back down and sprinted to the line of trees a few dozen feet behind the fence, lunging for cover behind the trunk of a tall pine tree. He looked up and saw the black apparition as it approached from the east, moving low over the roadway. The helicopter grew louder; several cars moved to the side of the road as it coursed just a few dozen feet above the lanes of traffic. The chopper slowed as it came to the gas station. It hovered overhead for several moments, circling and searching. Then it bent left and swooped back above the road, continuing on its mission.

Dewey waited until the chopper was out of sight. He moved until he was behind the station, out of view from anyone who might be in the station. He climbed the fence and jumped down to the other side. He reached for one of his guns but then looked in both directions, watching as vehicles sped by. He didn't pull the gun out. Instead, he walked with his head aimed down, slouching, trying to not look as tall as he was, or as big as he was, above all hiding his face. He crossed a hundred yards of dirt and gravel, making it to the back of the gas station. When he got there, he didn't hesitate. He pulled out his gun from beneath his left armpit and stepped to the side of the small building. He went around the corner and walked along the front of the gas station, then ducked quickly into a grubby garage, swinging his gun in the air, scanning for other people, but there was no one. He pivoted, looking at the gas station attendant. He was still at the gas pump, his back to Dewey.

Dewey looked around. He saw a cardboard plate with a small, half-eaten sandwich on it. He broke off a piece of it and stuffed it into his mouth. He glanced back outside through the front window. The attendant was hanging the gas nozzle back on the pump. He went to the driver's window, took some money, and turned. He walked back toward where Dewey was.

Dewey stood just inside the door, blocked from view by a wall. He raised the gun. As the attendant entered, he didn't notice Dewey. Dewey wrapped his arm around the man's neck, then lifted him up, squeezing tight. It would have been easy to simply snap the man's neck, but Dewey didn't. He held him up in the air for a dozen seconds, restricting his air flow. When he felt him go limp, he let him drop to the ground, then moved through the door. He walked to the small, light yellow sedan waiting at the pump. It was an older man, frail-looking and thin. Dewey raised his gun as he came to the window, pressing it against the man's neck. He reached inside the car and opened the door, keeping the end of the suppressor pressed tight into the old man's neck. He grabbed the man by the collar of his shirt and pulled him up from the seat. Dewey led him into the garage – suppressor jabbing into the man's back – then wrapped his arm around his neck and tightened, holding the man as he tried to kick and punch at Dewey. After several seconds, the man weakened and fell unconscious. Dewey dropped him to the ground next to the gas station attendant.

He bound both men's hands and feet and gagged them. He walked back to the car, climbed in, adjusted the seat, and started driving.

The car was old, small, and slow, with a standard transmission. Driving it reminded Dewey of his father's tractor, though the car was slightly faster.

Darkness was coming and Dewey searched for the vehicle's headlights. He punched on the SAT phone and brought up the map Jenna had uploaded, with Talmadge's apartment pre-set as the destination. He was just a few miles away. He fell into the slower lane of traffic and slouched down, assiduously avoiding eye contact with other drivers. The road took him to the Taedong River, which Dewey followed along the southern bank. The road was crowded and he slouched down even further in the seat, trying to hide his face as best as he could. When he saw the third island in the middle of the river, he took a left and drove across a bridge. He saw the arch in the distance.

Dewey went left a block away from the building. He drove for two blocks and saw a two-story parking garage. As he pulled in, he began to feel his eyes become foggy again, then saw patches of black as the poison returned. He sped to the back of the half-filled garage and parked in the corner just as he went into total blackness. He shut off the engine and lay down across the front seat of the car, gun in hand, praying for his sight to come back before it was too late.

Half-an-hour later, Dewey felt strong enough to move. He climbed from the stolen vehicle and skulked along a series of alleys until he arrived at the back of Talmadge's building. He spied around the corner, waiting until he didn't see any pedestrians. The sun had set and dark shadows intermingled with headlights on the busy city street where Talmadge's building was located. Dewey was within one block when he caught something out of the corner of his eye. Parked across the street from Talmadge's building was a white sedan. Four passengers were seated inside. One of the men was looking up into Talmadge's apartment building with binoculars.

59

SITUATION ROOM
THE WHITE HOUSE

As members of America's national security leadership filed into the Situation Room, Jenna received a quick tutorial from General Tralies on how to use the remote.

Dellenbaugh entered the room and looked at Will Parizeau.

"Well?" said Dellenbaugh.

"Nothing yet, Mr. President," said Parizeau. "The NSA is continuing to work on a way to know when they will launch – but they're not done."

"How much time do we have?"

"Six hours, Mr President."

Dellenbaugh nodded and looked at Jenna.

"What's the plan?" said the president.

Jenna hit the remote and one of the OLEDs – to the left of Dellenbaugh – lit up. On the screen was what looked like an old architectural blueprint.

"What you're looking at is a series of underground tunnels built by Kim Il-sung in 1972," said Jenna. "The tunnels begin directly beneath the presidential palace and lead away from Pyongang. Kim Il-sung was extremely paranoid. He built them in case there was ever a coup or a popular uprising in North Korea. They lead directly to the presidential palace."

Dellenbaugh stood up and moved to the blueprint. He studied it for more than a minute. Finally, he looked at Jenna.

"I'm not sure I get your point."

"If Dewey gets to the antidote," said Jenna, "he will still be in Pyongang. We will have a *real* asset there. If Dewey can get inside the palace, he can kill Kim."

"So let me get this straight, Dewey needs to find the antidote, then somehow get into these tunnels, which will be loaded with soldiers, kill Kim, and pray Yong-sik stops the nuclear attack?" said Tralies incredulously.

"Something like that," said Jenna. "All I'm asking for is time. Give Dewey the time to try. You're absolutely right, he might not find the bloody antidote, but we can afford to give him the time to try. Then, if he does find it, we try and kill Kim. If Dewey can kill Kim, we solve all of our problems. The only one who dies is Kim."

"And Yong-sik launches the missiles anyway," said Tralies.

"He wouldn't have sent the health report if that were the case, general," said Jenna. "Yong-sik is reaching out."

"Are you willing to bet a million lives on it?" said Dellenbaugh.

"Yes," said Jenna.

Dellenbaugh scanned the room, looking for reactions.

"Remind me, how much time do we have until Sunday in Pyongang, Jenna?" said President Dellenbaugh.

"Six hours, Mr. President," said Jenna.

"I want operations run out of the Situation Room from here on in," said Dellenbaugh. "Subs should be at attack ready, highest alert levels. There should be direct link-up between DIA and the sub commanders. The moment we see evidence of an imminent launch, we wipe them out –but not until then. Until then, we give the NSA time to work and Dewey time to find the antidote and kill Kim."

Tralies nodded, agreeing to the plan, even though he disagreed.

"I might not agree," Tralies said, "but if we're going to try and do this, Andreas will need support."

"What do you have in mind, Phil?" said Dellenbaugh.

"Let's get the SEALs into the theater," said Tralies.

60

47 MORANBONG STREET
PYONGANG

Dewey skulked along the darkened street, coming to the side of Talmadge's building, cloaked by the shadow of the concrete as light from a cloudless sky cast a greenish, cold hue along the empty neighborhood.

He was across a side street from the building. Dewey counted two entrances to Talmadge's building, next to one another, at the front of the building.

The sedan Dewey had seen earlier was gone. He scanned for surveillance, but didn't see anyone. But he knew it wasn't possible. KPA had already found Talmadge out and killed him. Of course they would have the building under high-level watch.

But what if they didn't know Dewey was in North Korea? What if the bodies on the chopper served their purpose?

He felt his vision suddenly start to darken.

No, he thought. *Not now.*

But it was unstoppable. The poison was taking hold. He was already past twenty hours. Dewey was on borrowed time and he knew it. Yet the blackness came in the same moment a rush of flu-like fever swept through his limbs.

He crouched back against the building's shabby concrete façade, letting the blackness come. It was the fifth or sixth time. Each time, the blackness was getting longer. He knew he just needed to wait… it would go away after a few minutes. He felt his heart racing. He was drenched in a cold, greasy sweat. As hot as hell yet wracked with strange chills.

He saw the dim blue and then his sight started to come back. He looked around and got ready to move for the front door. Then he saw something: a flash of green light. He scanned, then found it. On the second floor of the building directly across from Talmadge's building, Dewey saw a green light. It came on again and lasted no more than a second. It could have been a light flash created by the fever, yet he saw it. Bright green and low. An LED, perhaps attached to a camera.

Dewey was in the shadow of an apartment building across the side street from Talmadge's building, protected by the dark. But if the North Koreans were sweeping with thermal equipment, the shadows were of little use and they would see him. He got on all fours and crawled along the wall of the building, moving slowly out of range of the window where he'd seen the light.

Behind Talmadge's apartment building was an alley. It was neat, with a row of garbage cans on one side. Across the alley from Talmadge's building was another apartment building, also made of concrete, as generic and anonymous as every building in Pyongang, at least every building Dewey had seen.

He looked at his right hand. Blood was oozing out from his pinky. His palms were raw, but covered in black from the pine. They ached. But it was lost in the fever that now gripped him. He was drenched in perspiration.

Dewey got to his feet, waited a brief few moments, then sprinted cross the street for the alley.

He ran past the line of garbage cans and came to the end of the alley, where a concrete wall closed off the two buildings. Atop the wall was razor-wire, no doubt electrified.

He found a steel door to the building across from Talmadge's building. He tried to open it but it was locked. Dewey pulled off the backpack and found a pick-gun. He put the tip into the lock and pressed a button on the pick-gun. He heard a faint jingling of metal then the device stopped. He reached for the door handle and pressed the latch. The door opened. Dewey stepped inside.

The space was musty and dark. An old fire stair. Dewey shut the door and was in blackness. He started climbing up the stairwell, using his hands to guide him, going rapidly, step by step. He acclimated to the layout and by the third floor he didn't need his hands. He charged up until, suddenly, his head hit a ceiling, hard enough for Dewey to wince.

Dewey was at the top of the building. He was in utter darkness. He felt along the ceiling. It, too, was made of concrete. One area seemed sandy and concaved in. It was concrete, started to rot and weaken. Dewey punched up at it, feeling shards of material rain down on his fist. He punched again, listening as larger chunks fell. He punched with both hands, groaning as his knuckles went bloody, but he kept going until, suddenly, a whole section tumbled down around him. He stepped back, trying to avoid the falling concrete, his arms over his head. When it stopped, he stepped onto the concrete covered floor and leapt up toward the light. His fingers found the edge of the roof and he lifted himself up onto the roof.

He stood and looked around. He could see rows of similar-looking apartments in every direction, bathed in a greenish light. He was at the side of the building. He looked toward Talmadge's building. The roof was the same height.

A waist-high eave ran along the perimeter of the roof. He reached out and felt it, wrenching it back and forth, trying to see how strong it was. The eave didn't budge or crack. It was stable.

The alley was a different matter. He was at least ten stories in the air. It was a long distance, perhaps two cars wide. It didn't matter anymore, though. Nothing mattered anymore, except for finding an antidote that quite possibly wasn't even there.

Dewey walked to the center of the roof just as he felt the numbness in the back of his eyes, a numbness he'd learned to recognize. Dark patches of black crossed into his vision. He studied the roof in the last few moments he still could see, then began a desperate run for the eave of the building. His feet moved along the concrete as his vision flickered in and out. Blackness took hold before he was at the edge of the roof, but it didn't matter any longer. He needed to get to Talmadge's apartment. Dewey charged as fast as he could, in total blindness, trying to remember, knowing that jumping too soon – or too late – would be fatal. He suddenly leapt up. His front foot landed on the waist-high eave at the edge of the building. He kept going, touching down and pushing off, leaping out into the open air as his arms and legs kicked furiously in the dark oblivion. His vision was gone. Dewey's only guide was his memory.

He flew in the air ten stories above the concrete alley, then hit the edge of Talmadge's roof. His chest struck first – a hard, punishing collision – and he grabbed with both hands, reaching desperately above him for something to hold onto. Dewey's fingers clutched the top of the roof as he absorbed the brutal force of his body striking hard into the side of the building. He held on for dear life, both hands clinging to the roof. Slowly, Dewey climbed onto the roof. He flopped down on his stomach, struggling for breath, waiting for his vision to return. After several minutes, he began to see patches of light. Soon, he could see again.

The roof of Talmadge's apartment building was empty and unlit. There was a door near the middle of the roof. He took off the ruck-sack pack and removed two silenced handguns, making sure both mags were full. He chambered a round in each gun, moved the safeties off, then moved quickly to the door.

Dewey holstered the gun in his left hand and reached for the door. He turned the doorknob ever so slowly until he heard a faint click. He trained the tip of the suppressor of the gun in his right hand against the crack in the door. With his left hand, Dewey quietly opened the door, inch by inch, his pressed against the small but growing opening.

There was nobody in the stairwell on the other side of the door.

Dewey slipped into the stairwell and shut the door silently behind him. He removed the second gun from beneath his armpit and started descending. He climbed down the stairs as if in slow motion, focusing on not making a sound – both guns trained out in front of him. After two floors, he saw the beginnings of a faint, yellow glow somewhere down below. He slipped against the wall and– while still clutching the gun – touched his finger against the concrete, using it to guide him as he stalked his way down the stairs toward Talmadge's apartment.

After one more set of stairs, Dewey saw the top of the gunman's assault helmet. The man was dressed in black tactical gear. He was looking at a cell phone. Its dim light illuminated a high-powered rifle – an AR-15 knock-off.

Dewey moved slowly to the bannister and leaned down, the silenced 1911 in his right hand. He aimed it down at the agent outside the door and fired once. The bullet struck the man in the ear, kicking him sideways. He tumbled down the stairs as Dewey took the last flight of steps and positioned himself outside the door.

Dewey knew he should have searched the agent for information, but it was too late for that. He had one goal. One objective. He needed the antidote.

The door was steel, with a small slat window crossed with wire. He looked through it for other gunmen, registering two tactical agents at the end of a long, dimly-lit hallway. Dewey opened the door a few inches and then abruptly slammed it shut. He watched through the small window as both men turned. They spoke for a moment, then one of the men started walking toward the door.

Dewey watched as the soldier approached. When the gunman was just a few feet away, Dewey stepped to the side of the door and crouched low, next to the door frame. Dewey knelt on the stairs, against the wall, below where the soldier was about to enter. He tucked the gun in his left hand into a shoulder holster beneath his right armpit, then pulled his combat blade from a sheath at his ankle. There was a pause of a few seconds. Then the door opened. The agent stepped into the stairs. As he did, Dewey stood and slashed the knife in a fluid, surgical strike. The blade ripped deep into the gunman's neck before he knew he was being attacked. Dewey tore the blade across the front of the man's neck and quickly lifted it back out. The gunman tumbled to the stairs. Dewey sheathed the knife and then threw the dead agent down the stairwell, where he landed aside the first corpse.

Dewey opened the door and moved into the apartment hallway, both guns raised and trained ahead. As he entered, he fired each weapon. Two bullets spat from the guns – a dull, metallic *thwap thwap* – hitting the gunman in the forehead and neck. The man dropped to the floor.

Around the corner, Dewey heard a voice. The dead gunman was visible to anyone around the corner from where Dewey stood. Dewey charged down the hallway, knowing that someone was around the corner – outside Talmadge's door – and they were moving…

As he came to the corner of the hallway, Dewey dived over the dead man, training both guns down the hallway. In the half-second he was airborne, Dewey found another gunman as he sought to escape. Dewey triggered both guns simultaneously. Bullets spat from the guns – *thwack thwack* – one bullet hitting the soldier in the back of the thigh, the other sailing wide. Dewey landed hard but fired again, before the agent could scream. The bullet shattered the side of the man's head, throwing him backwards, washing the walls in a blood-spattered mist.

From the ground, Dewey swept both guns across the hallway, searching for other soldiers, finding no one. He climbed to his feet, then heard footsteps at the far end of the hallway. A black-clad gunman rounded the far corner, alerted by the noise. Dewey pumped the trigger. The slug struck the soldier squarely in the neck, dropping him.

Dewey's fever was growing worse and every step felt like a battle. As he moved down the hall to Talmadge's doorway, the blackness returned.

"No," he said aloud, his whisper raspy with desperation. "No. Not now."

He felt it coming on as he charged for the door. He memorized, in that last moment, the layout of the hallway, how far it was, the position of the dead soldier outside the door, the blood spattered across the wall next to Talmadge's door. Blindness came suddenly, precipitously, cutting off everything with brutal finality.

Every part of Dewey's body ached. The fever was rising with each passing moment. His head felt like it was on fire.

It will all be over soon. One way or another, it'll all be over.

Dewey moved down the hallway with his left hand against the wall to guide him. He found the door and then the doorknob. He held onto the doorknob as he waited, his vision completely taken by black. He clutched the doorknob with his left hand, aiming the .45 in his right to the door, in case anyone came outside the apartment, praying the poison would abate at least one more time before he died.

In the blackness, he turned the doorknob. It was locked. Dewey got to his knees and, like a blind man, searched the soldier, finding his arms, then his hands. He found a key in the man's hand. Dewey waited, praying his vision would come back, that he would have one more chance...

It will all be over soon.

Then he saw gray and yellow around the edges of his eyes. Slowly, his vision came back.

He tried to stand up but it felt like his legs were disconnected from his body. He couldn't stand.

Dewey looked down at his boots, dirt covered and scuffed. The right one was torn.

This is not how it ends.

He remembered the words from training:

"You're never dead. Never! The moment you think you're dead, you already are. You're not dead."

Dewey closed his eyes. He willed himself to stand up, climbing to his feet, wracked with fever. Without warning, his stomach convulsed. He started vomiting on the floor, a watery, yellow liquid, bile from his empty stomach, he had nothing left to give.

He put the key into the lock and braced himself an extra moment, trying to count the slugs he'd used so far. Each mag held fourteen. But he couldn't count how many he'd used. His mind was turning into jelly. It didn't matter anyway. Dewey couldn't have done anything. He was too far gone. He had one thing left in him. A single minute. A last chance, before he was gone. He threw up again. Then, he turned the key. He paused. A moment later, he pushed the door in.

A brightly-lit hallway. A soldier seated on a chair. A submachine gun on his lap.

Dewey entered the apartment as the soldier turned, his eyes went wide, and he swept the submachine gun through the air. Dewey fired once – *thwack* – and the bullet ripped into the gunman's eye, spitting blood and brains across the wall. The man was kicked off the chair, where he dropped to the floor.

Before the soldier had even hit the ground, Dewey was inside the apartment, both guns raised. He acquired the two targets immediately – one a soldier, the other a man in a suit – and pumped each trigger as fast as his fingers could move. He hit the soldier in the mouth as he yelled, then targeted the man in the suit, but he was moving and Dewey missed. The agent lurched, sweeping a handgun toward Dewey as Dewey continued firing. A bullet struck the agent in the stomach in the same instant another tore into his shoulder. The agent groaned but remained standing. Dewey fired again – this time, the bullet hit the agent in the forehead and kicked him backwards, off his feet. He fell onto a small coffee table, breaking it as he collapsed.

Dewey swept the weapons back and forth across the room, looking for movement, listening.

The room was destroyed. A sofa was ripped into shreds. Large swaths of wallpaper were torn from the walls and there were big holes in the walls. Floorboards were ripped up.

Dewey went back to the door. He removed the key and pocketed it, pulled the man outside into the room, then shut the door.

He stepped into the living room, scanning quickly, analyzing the layout of the small apartment. Everything appeared destroyed. The North Koreans had destroyed every square inch of Talmadge's belongings. A galley kitchen was to his left, empty, broken glass littered the floor. He saw a doorway to the right. It was open. A dangling lightbulb in the ceiling shone down on a mattress, cut up and destroyed. With both weapons out, Dewey moved into the bedroom, a small, plain-looking room. Drawers from a dresser were scattered and clothing littered the floor. To the right was a doorway. He could see the toilet, then the mirror.

Something moved. Was his mind playing tricks? In his peripheral vision. Through the open door to the bathroom, he could see the sink and, above it, mirror. It was where something had crossed his eyes. A small, barely perceptible flicker of shadow. Movement.

Someone was standing against the wall across from the mirror. It had to be. There was no other explanation…

Dewey studied the wall of the bedroom, strips of wallpaper hanging down, several holes cleaved into the cheap sheetrock. He trained both guns on the wall and started firing in a horizontal line across the wall, a fusillade of dull, metallic *thwack thwack thwack*, a chorus from a gunman's choir. After a half-dozen shots, he heard a terrible scream. He charged for the door and knelt as he reached it, sweeping the pistol into the door and firing blindly just as unmuted submachine gun fire erupted from within, but above Dewey's head. Dewey triggered the gun just as the line of slugs cut down toward him, then heard another pained grunt and the automatic weapon fire ceased. Dewey stood and stepped into the bathroom, guns trained on the tub, making eye contact with a man in a suit who now lay on his back, the walls splattered in crimson. He stared up at Dewey, trying to say something. Dewey fired one more time, striking him between the eyes.

Dewey stared an extra moment or two, then looked at the mirror. His face was deep red, with almost a bluish hue. His hair, his face, everything was sopping wet with perspiration. He'd been here before, staring into the eyes of a dead man.

Help me.

He turned and stepped back into the bedroom. Yong-sik had obviously found Talmadge. What had his men been searching for?

Dewey walked slowly through Talmadge's apartment, stepping over bodies, looking around. The agents had thoroughly ransacked the apartment. The floor was exposed and several large axe holes had been slashed into the floor, looking for a secret compartment. The kitchen counters had been ripped out and lay on the floor in piles.

In a way, the North Koreans made Dewey's job easier. The obvious places – drawers, a desk, inside the mattress, the floor – could be ruled out.

Dewey felt his knees begin to wobble involuntarily and he reached out for the wall but it didn't matter. He fell to the floor. Again, his stomach convulsed, and he dry-heaved violently. As he continued to heave, he pulled off the backpack, unzipped it, and removed the cell phone. He hit a single number and held it in, then lay on his back, listening as the phone made several clicks and beeping noises. Then Jenna's soft British accent came on the line.

"*Dewey?*" she asked. Her voice had urgency and emotion in it. "It's nearly twenty-five hours. I thought… I thought you were dead."

"I can't find it," he whispered hoarsely. "Do you know if he had a hiding place?"

"I don't know."

"Are your agents trained to hide it in a particular—"

"No," said Jenna.

"Are you sure you sent two?"

Jenna's voice trailed off as Dewey's arm became weaker. He heard her talking but couldn't understand what she was saying, so intense was the pain now. He couldn't walk a mile. He couldn't ten feet. She didn't understand. He heard her sobbing.

"You have to keep searching," she begged. "Please. I know you can do it."

As blackness swept across his eyes, dropped the phone. He curled up in a fetal position, his sight cloaked in pitch black, and again he started convulsing and throwing up. Guttural, throaty moans came involuntarily from deep in his throat as he coughed and dry-heaved onto the dirty floor.

When, finally, Dewey's vision returned, he crawled to the bathroom, using every ounce of strength he had left. He grabbed the front of the sink and pulled himself up, looking in the medicine cabinet behind the mirror. It was empty, its contents thrown to the floor by North Korean agents. Dewey looked at the toilet. The top was off. They'd searched there too. The ceiling, walls, and floor were hacked with violent axe cuts.

Dewey stared at the mirror. The wall around it was a filthy brownish tan. A small line around the edges appeared cleaner, as if Talmadge had scrubbed it. Dewey grabbed the door of the medicine cabinet and ripped backwards. A dusting of sheetrock tumbled from the wall around the steel cabinet. He pulled even harder, yanking the entire cabinet from the wall, letting it fall next to the sink and smash.

In the recess where the cabinet had been, Dewey saw something. It was a long, thin syringe. A thin needle jutted from the end. Dewey reached for it just as his legs again went weak. He clutched the syringe as he fell to the ground, slamming the needle into the center of his chest and pressing the end of the plunger. A sharp, electric burn shot through him. His eyes went back in his head as his skull fell to the hard linoleum floor, motionless, unconscious.

61

KPA HQ
PYONGANG

Yong-sik paced back and forth inside his office at KPA headquarters. Every once in a while, he looked out the window. In the distance, he could see the lights adorning the roof of the Presidential Palace across the city. Pyongang was dark, but the palace's lights stayed on no matter the time, and no matter what the cost. The rest of Pyongang was forced under penalty of law to abide by energy saving rules prohibiting lights after ten P.M., but not the palace.

KPA was also allowed to keep the lights on, no matter the hour.

Yong-sik was consumed in thought. He remembered an expression he had read, something said by the Englishman, Churchill.

"A riddle, wrapped in a mystery, inside an enigma."

That was how he felt at this moment as he juggled so many thoughts and feelings.

Will someone find out about what happened in Macau? Will they find evidence of the documents I sent?

Yong-sik knew that, if discovered, he would be executed immediately. He didn't understand technology and computers as some did, and knew that the government computer investigative teams might – probably would – find out he'd sent the email.

Now, the helicopter. It only added to his sense of uneasiness and frustration.

On his desk was the initial report from the crash site. There were more than thirty photos of the two badly burned corpses. The bones themselves were so charred the reconnaissance team couldn't even

281

estimate the size of the two dead individuals on the helicopter. It seemed so straightforward, and yet it wasn't. His mind went back to the dental work. There was just no way either of the dead men were Americans.

It had to be related to him. But how? Was it the documents? Were they trying to send a team to kill Kim?

It didn't matter any longer. If the Americans attempted to stop Bloody Sunday, it would soon be too late. Midnight would soon be here. All Kim would have to do is issue the final order.

Yong-sik had no one he could confide in. How could he explain to anyone what he'd done? He was a traitor. To save his own neck he'd given them everything he knew and he wanted to tell someone, to ask for guidance, to confess. But he could not. He was utterly alone.

His eyes flashed to the window. He stared at the Presidential Palace. A sharp wave of anxiety swept over him.

Bloody Sunday.

Yong-sik shuddered as he realized it wasn't the helicopter that worried him now. He could care less if the Americans were here. It didn't matter. It would all soon be over. Everything would be gone. Kim would launch the nuclear device. It was inevitable now, and when that happened Pyongang would be erased from the earth. The Supreme Leader wanted to start World War III but all that would happen is the destruction of North Korea and then it would all be over.

He put his hand on the side of his desk to steady himself as he finally allowed himself to admit the truth. That Kim was mad. Yong-sik understood this now. He had terminal cancer and he would soon be dead and now he believed the only way to live was in infamy. Kim would destroy his country to live in infamy. Was it really so surprising?

Should I do something, he thought? Should I try to talk to Kim?

You already did something. You sent them everything and now they know.

"I did it to save my country," he whispered.

He shut his eyes and rubbed them. He felt ashamed for what he did. He'd sworn an oath to live and die for his Supreme Leader.

But did everyone have to die for Kim? Did an entire people need to die for Kim's... insanity?

Bloody Sunday.

Yong-sik's mind swirled with emotion, confusion, and a sense of helplessness. At this moment, he wished he could simply be a citizen, that he didn't know what he knew. He usually liked making decisions. But the conflict that faced him now was one he wished was someone else's. What did love of country mean? Did it mean blind loyalty to the Supreme Leader?

A panicked knock at the door. Kim looked up.

"*Enter!*" he barked.

One of Yong-sik's deputies, Kwon, entered. He was breathing rapidly, his face flush with excitement.

"General Yong-sik, the apartment of the reporter—" Kwon stammered.

"What about it?"

"They stopped communicating, sir," said Kwon.

"Every one of them? That's impossible."

"Yes, general, every man."

The red phone on Yong-sik's desk rang. Yong-sik and Kwon's eyes went immediately to it. Kim was calling.

"Send in a team *immediately*," barked Yong-sik before placing his hand on the phone.

Yong-sik did not pick-up the red phone even as it pealed for the fourth time.

"Yes, sir."

"Every available man. Bring the dogs. Search the building and then fan out from there."

"What are we looking for?" said Kwon.

"*Get out!*" yelled Yong-sik, purposefully ignoring Kwon's question. He picked up the phone, covering the mouthpiece.

"*Now!*" he screamed, waving his hand, telling Kwon to leave.

"Your excellency," he said into the phone.

"I must speak with you," said Kim. His voice was hoarse and his words a little slurred.

"Yes, your excellency."

"Have the nuclear devices been attached to the missiles?" said Kim, barely getting his words out before he started to cough – a violent, phlegmy cough that sounded as if Kim was choking. It continued for nearly half-a-minute.

"Yes, your excellency."

"I'm dying, Pak. Please, come to the palace."

62

CVN-76 USS RONALD REAGAN
OFF THE COAST OF NIIGATA, JAPAN
SEA OF JAPAN

Rear Admiral J.J. Quinn entered the hangar bay. Other than the aircraft carrier's small exercise room, the hangar bay was the best area on board to exercise. For several minutes, he watched. Sixteen men were running wind sprints. The pattern would vary – one lap, then a short rest, followed by three laps and a rest, then sit-ups or push-ups. They looked like they'd been doing it for at least an hour.

The pace was intense. The men were struggling. Yet not one of them stopped. It didn't surprise Quinn. After all, all of them were from SEAL Team 6.

The frogman running the exercises was also participating. His name was Mark Fusco. He barked out orders that he and the others then followed.

Finally, Quinn stepped toward the group. Fusco saw him as he and the fifteen other SEALs were running across the length of the big bay. When Fusco reached the wall, he leaned over, hands on knees, catching his breath.

"Take a break," yelled Fusco to the other SEALs.

"Hi, Mark," said Quinn.

"Admiral," said Fusco, straightening up. "What can I do for you?"

"I need you to pick three guys," said Quinn. "You're going to the *Benfold*. Osprey leaves in ten minutes."

Fusco nodded.

"Unless I'm mistaken, the *Benfold* is in the Yellow Sea?" said Fusco.

"That's right. From the *Benfold*, your team will boat to the coast of North Korea then move by land to Pyongang. You're meeting up with a guy from Langley named Andreas. He'll have in-theater command control, but not until you meet up."

Fusco wiped perspiration from his face.

"J.J.—" said Fusco. "What are we doing?"

"That's all I know," said Quinn. "That being said, American missile defenses were raised last night. This is an *Emergency Priority* order. I'd take your best three men – and some ammo."

"Understood, sir."

Fusco turned to the group of SEALs now hanging out near a stack of tires.

"Truax, Barrazza, Kolackovsky: get your shit. We're going to see the Rocket Man."

63

47 MORANBONG STREET
PYONGANG

Dewey heard the faint click of a door latch. Slowly, he opened his eyes. His face was against the wooden floor. He was lying in the hallway just outside the bathroom.

He took a few seconds to look around. He saw a dead soldier, then his chest. The syringe was still sticking into the center of his chest, but he was alive.

There was a voice, then shouting from the entrance to the apartment.

Dewey felt around for his gun, finding it on the floor near his leg. He heard footsteps and more voices, all speaking Korean. There was more shouting – orders being barked – shock.

He reached to his chest and yanked the syringe out, then picked up the gun and slowly turned his head just as a voice came from the bedroom, just a few feet away. Dewey lifted his head and focused his eyes, seeing legs. The soldier started shouting. Dewey wheeled the gun and fired, hitting the man in the stomach just as another soldier stepped into the room behind the first man, who was kicked backwards, doubling over and letting out a pained groan. Dewey triggered the pistol a second time, the gun spat a silenced bullet into the second man's forehead, knocking him sideways before he crumpled to the floor in an awkward spiral.

Dewey climbed to his feet and put another bullet into the first soldier's eye, killing him. He walked through Talmadge's apartment, stepping over bodies, calmly surveying the carnage.

He was dazed. How long had he been asleep?

One of the men's radios squawked and a voice spoke, again in Korean.

They would be coming. Any minute.

Go.

For the first time, he heard sirens.

They're coming.

He ran through the apartment and charged into the corridor then sprinted down the hallway. An apartment door was cracked open and it shut quickly. Dewey kicked the door open and a woman was standing inside. She was old, dressed in a nightgown, and her hands went reflexively above her head in terror.

Dewey moved by her and went to the window. He looked down on the street. Several military vehicles were just pulling up to the building. He watched in stunned silence as soldiers leapt from the vehicles. A block away, he saw yet more vehicles rolling in.

He had to get away.

Dewey moved back through the apartment without saying anything, shutting the door and running back down the hallway. He reached the fire stairs and moved up, climbing three steps at a time, passing the two men he'd killed earlier. He kept close to the outer wall of the stairwell as he suddenly became aware of the faint sound of steel-toed boots several floors below: soldiers moving up to find him.

When he reached the roof of the building, he stepped to the edge, carefully looking down. A dark sedan pulled into the alley, its headlights illuminating the alley. The vehicle's doors opened and two men in dark suits rushed from the car, each man clutching a weapon, leaving the lights on and the engine running. He saw the men run down the alley and enter the building across the alley from Talmadge's apartment building.

Overhead, Dewey heard the telltale electric whirr of rotors cutting the air somewhere to his left, then spotted the lights on a helicopter, cutting through the sky.

"Fuckin' A," he muttered.

Dewey surveyed the rooftop across the alley – the one he'd leapt from. He had no choice. He would need to make the jump again.

288

The chopper grew louder and louder and then a set of powerful halogen lights flashed brightly from its underbelly, lighting up the dark sky in a white search light that swept across the sky and found the roof – and then Dewey.

He went back to the stairwell door – he needed to go back down. But bullets suddenly erupted from inside the stairwell. A high-pitched staccato from a submachine gun. Dewey ducked and lurched out of the way just as slugs ripped the steel door. He slammed the door shut and looked for another place to hide from the chopper.

A thunderous series of booms as the chopper's minigun began firing. Bullets rained down in a line that cut across the roof in his direction.

Dewey charged for the roof edge, running as fast as he could just feet ahead of the quickly moving line of bullets. He needed to get up enough speed to make the jump. But just as he was about to leap he watched in shock as a swarm of soldiers emerged onto the rooftop across the alley – his only escape. He was barely able to stop due to his momentum. He diverted at the last second, lurching left, diving to the ground and rolling. He trained his gun up at the chopper and fired, pumping bullet after bullet. Bullets pinged the chopper, making loud metallic thwangs and then glass shattered. The mag clicked empty just as the minigun stopped and the chopper wheeled up and back, getting away from Dewey's bullets, but moving into a new attack position.

The assault was furious – gunfire drowned out by the mad whirr of rotors chopping air. Sirens from the streets below. It was chaos.

Dewey was on his back, shielded by the eave of the roof as the soldiers across the alley fired just above his head. He reached into his ruck and searched for another mag. He slammed it into the gun and removed the second pistol from the ruck just as the door to the roof of Talmadge's building opened and the helicopter swooped back in and the spotlight from the chopper again found him.

With one gun, Dewey pumped bullets at the doorway as the first soldier barreled through, hitting him in the chest. He triggered the second gun at the chopper overhead, dinging and banging the fuselage, causing the chopper to again spin around and carve left, out of the way.

Another soldier emerged from the doorway and Dewey fired, striking him squarely in the forehead. When a third soldier attempted to duck back inside the stairwell, Dewey fired twice, missing the first time, hitting the back of his head with the second bullet.

He reached into the ruck and pulled out a grenade just as the chopper spun around again and lit him up in bright white. He pulled the pin and hurled the grenade toward the roof across the alley, then triggered the gun at the chopper. The chopper's minigun erupted, pelting the roof just feet from where he lay tucked against the eave. He heard glass shatter and then a faint scream. The chopper lifted up – and then the air shook as the grenade exploded on the other roof. Screams and shouting echoed in the wind-chopped air. A man emerged onto the rooftop near Dewey – he fired, ripping a slug into the soldier's chest, dropping him.

Dewey looked over the parapet for a brief instant, again registering the idling sedan in the alley.

Dewey was surrounded by chaos, trying to simply last until the next second, but he was outnumbered and out-gunned.

He fired at the chopper but heard the click of the spent mag. He popped it out and reached into the ruck, searching for another mag. He found the last one. He pulled it out and slammed it in.

Gunfire started up again from the neighboring roof. Bullets thudded against the concrete and whizzed just over his head. The grenade had killed a few of them but there were more.

Dewey was out of options and would soon run out of ammo.

He crawled along the roof, hidden by the eave, a dozen feet from where the gunmen on the neighboring roof thought he was. He reached into the ruck and grabbed the low-jump chute he hadn't had time to use in the forest. He quickly attached the chute to a steel ring on his weapons vest, then stood – both guns out and trained across the alley, just as the chopper again lit him up and the minigun erupted above. In that brief quarter-second of surprise, Dewey counted four gunmen across the alleyway. He started running toward the roof edge, pumping both triggers as fast as his fingers could flex, surprising the men, who swiveled their rifles toward Dewey but too late. The *thwack*

thwack thwack thwack thwack thwack thwack thwack of silenced bullets sang as he cut down the remaining gunmen even as he gained speed, reaching the eave of the roof, hitting it with his right foot and leaping out into the open air just as the minigun pelted the ground near him with bullets. Dewey tumbled out into open air – falling toward the ground – gaining speed – then ripped the chute. It popped open even as he descended faster and faster toward the tar below. The chute ruffled a sec then burst open, arresting Dewey's descent just as he reached the ground. Bullets rained from the sky as the minigun tried to kill him in the alley, but Dewey was already running, yanking off the chute and diving into the open front door of the idling sedan. He slammed the gas just as two soldiers charged around the corner, rifles out, firing at the car. Dewey ducked as bullets tore into the windshield, then felt the car strike one of the men in the same moment a terrible scream came from below. Dewey turned the wheel as the car hit the main road and then sat up, weaving through the military vehicles and then tearing down the dark Pyongang street.

64

MOSCOW, RUSSIA

Tacoma's flight from Paris landed at 8:40 Moscow time. He rented an orange Lamborghini Huracan and drove into Moscow. He didn't need a map.

After checking into his suite at the Four Seasons, Tacoma opened the folder. He studied the information available about the man.

Derek Chalmers had hired Tacoma's and Katie Foxx's firm to investigate him. According to available data, he was American. Billy Thompson, Stanford, Harvard Business School. The problem is, he wasn't Billy Thompson, Stanford, Harvard Business School.

"*Your job, Rob, is to find this man,*" Chalmers had said, holding out a photo. "*Is he Russian? Is it mistaken identity? If he is Russian, is he high-level? GRU? The most important thing: did he kill Charles Hartford? That is really all that matters because if he did, all the other questions answer themselves.*"

Tacoma put the folder down and undressed. He looked in the mirror. His skin was a deep tan. After going to Tangiers, Tacoma had spent the last two days in Portugal – Praia Do Norte Nazaré – surfing with a couple teammates from his UVA lacrosse team. He took a shower and dried off. He wrapped the towel around his waist and sat on the bed, picking up his cell and scrolling through his contacts, finally finding the one he was looking for.

"Rob," came the voice. "It's been too long."

"Grigor, I'm in Moscow."

"You're fucking kidding me! Why the fuck didn't you tell me you were coming?"

"It's business," said Tacoma.

"You're obviously calling for a reason? What can I do for you?"

"Can we go out to a nightclub?"

"Seriously? That's what I'd do with you if it wasn't business."

"A place that has a certain clientele," said Tacoma.

"Government?"

"GRU. Operators. Assets."

The man on the line started laughing.

"I know the places," he said.

"I'll swing by and pick you up," said Tacoma.

"I'll send a car, Rob."

"I rented one. Besides, I might need to get out of here quickly."

Grigor Sarkov was the third wealthiest man in Russia. At 33, Sarkov had acquired mining rights in an area of Siberia that was thought to hold oil. Sarkov had not only discovered massive quantities of oil, but had – somewhat accidentally – found rich gold deposits and, in a separate part of the 900,000 acre piece of land, struck a diamond vein, now the most productive single diamond mine in the world.

Sarkov was now 54. A year ago, his fifteen year-old daughter had been kidnapped from a Swiss boarding school while getting a drink of water during a field hockey match. Sarkov was a close friend of Putin and the government had searched high and low for the girl. They were unsuccessful. The ransom note had come in after three weeks. It was an email – with a chilling proof of life video showing Sarkov's daughter, Irina, strapped to a ladder, and a demand for $250 million.

Through intermediaries, Sarkov heard about Katie Foxx and Rob Tacoma. RISKON, their firm, was exorbitant. For this matter, their cost was $3.5 million a week with a six-month minimum engagement along with expenses. They also required a $30 million success fee. Sarkov didn't care. He just wanted Irina back.

They told Sarkov to wire the money to the anonymous Swiss bank account the hostage takers had given for the payment, a 22-alpha-numeric account that was not traceable due to Swiss banking laws.

From there, it had been relatively easy. RISKON's hackers had long ago penetrated the Swiss banking system and all its member banks. They detected when the wire arrived, when it was moved from the central bank balance sheets and was in the member bank's possession, and finally, when the funds were placed in the account owner's possession. There was no way to know who the account owner was, but they didn't need that. Instead, they tracked the account and awaited its first disbursement – an electronic wire to an account in Barbados for a local real estate firm. The amount was material: $18 million.

Within twelve hours, Tacoma, alone, was in Barbados. A quick conversation with a local realtor revealed the information he needed, was there a property that recently went under contract, a rather large property? Tacoma waited until dark to come up from the ocean. The former Navy SEAL loved the feeling of being in the water. He'd swum to the property two miles, swimming along the coast of the island fifty feet offshore. He had on a mid-thigh black and blue tactical wetsuit, a pair of SIG P226s in water-tight pockets at his left waist and right thigh. There, inside an astonishing, huge, boldly modern, all-glass house, Tacoma had found the man – a Russian – sipping a glass of vodka as two naked women kept him company and music blared. Tacoma didn't have to break in. The glass door was open to the Caribbean air.

Tacoma had entered with only one gun. He would need his free hand. He was still wet, his face flushed. He walked in and for a few moments the three drunken partiers didn't even notice him with the music blaring. Tacoma had told the two girls to disappear, then shot the Russian in the knee. As he screamed, Tacoma worked out of him the country, then town, then address of the house where his co-conspirators had the girl. Tacoma shot the man in the head and called Katie, who was waiting in Geneva, near the boarding school the girl had been taken from. Within two hours, Katie entered the house in Stuttgart, shooting the three other hostage takers and freeing Irina.

Grigor Sarkov liked Tacoma. More than liked. Tacoma had saved his daughter.

The first two nightclubs were equally packed with people, dancing under strobe lights, and loud music. It took Tacoma an hour to sweep each one. He didn't see Billy Thompson at either. At the third club Sarkov took him to, a place called Troyka Multispace, Tacoma spied Thompson in the first five minutes, seated in a booth near the bar.

Tacoma crossed the dance floor to the bar, closer to his target. His mind flashed to someone in his fraternity at UVA – James Godfrey – who went to Harvard Business School after Virginia. Even though Thompson's story was fabricated – he never attended Harvard Business School or even stepped foot in the United States – all Tacoma could think of was what an asshole Godfrey was. A small grin crossed his face as he thought about finding Billy Thompson.

Still, Tacoma needed to be smart. Thompson was GRU or some other branch of the Russian military/intelligence world. They fired first and asked questions later, or else they didn't even ask the questions. They were highly trained in all manner of weapons – firearms, cold weapons, explosives. But it was their training in martial arts, compounded by their large size, that made them truly dangerous. Fortunately, thought Tacoma as he reached the bar and ordered a vodka, there was one country with slightly tougher soldiers.

He was seated in a round booth with three other men, smoking cigars and drinking. He was laughing. Tacoma watched him from the mirror behind the bar, sipping his vodka as he waited.

When Thompson got up, Tacoma moved ahead of him, walking where he could tell Thompson was headed, down a dark hallway lined with women to a set of stairs that led to a lower level of the club. A few people were scattered about the stairs, smoking cigarettes and talking. The music from below echoed up the stairs. Tacoma descended, looking for egress, eyeing Thompson in his peripheral, seeing a door at the bottom of the stairs. He pushed it open. Outside was an alley filled with exotic sports cars, parked while their owners partied inside. Tacoma shut the door to the alley only part way, leaving it slightly ajar, and turned around and started moving back up the stairs. He passed Thompson, then turned around again, following

295

Thompson down the stairs. When Thompson was at the bottom of the stairs, Tacoma took two running steps down and charged. His shoulder slammed Thompson in the middle of his back. Thompson's head struck the door, he let out a pained grunt, and the door pushed open. Tacoma followed with a sharp kick to the back of Thompson's knee and he fell down into the alley. Tacoma slammed the door shut and the two men were alone in the alley.

Tacoma removed his leather coat – which held both his gun and blade – and dropped it on the tar just as Thompson got to his feet and lunged. Tacoma didn't have time to react. Thompson slashed a blade which Tacoma ducked. Thompson slashed again. This time, Tacoma blocked Thompson's forearm and kicked him in the torso, sending the Russian back.

Thompson's dark eyes found Tacoma as he spat. He lurched again, blade extended, stabbing at Tacoma's head. Tacoma ducked his head to the right, barely avoiding the blade, then slammed his left fist into the Russian's neck. As Thompson tried to absorb the brutal strike, Tacoma slammed his right fist into Thompson's exposed chin, sending him flying back into the brick wall. Thompson's head struck the wall and Tacoma lunged, but the Russian absorbed it. He used the wall as leverage, and as his head slammed into wall, he immediately pushed forward, getting a precious half-second. Tacoma was several feet away. Thompson hurled the knife at the charging Tacoma.

The blade somersaulted toward Tacoma's chest but he lurched right. The knife hit his forearm, spiking in and then bouncing to the alley, but it had struck. Blood surged from the gash. It caused Tacoma to reel slightly. Thompson surged, moving closer, both fists in the air, then he lay into Tacoma. Thompson slammed a left fist into Tacoma's stomach and a right into his face, striking just below Tacoma's eye, bumping him back. Tacoma swung but by then the Russian unleashed a vicious kick to Tacoma's stomach, followed by a series of punches Tacoma could only absorb as he stepped backwards, his back suddenly hitting the brick wall. Thompson reared back and swung for Tacoma's neck, going for the kill. But Tacoma ducked. Thompson's fist struck the brick wall just as Tacoma lashed out desperately, delivering a hard right fist to the Russian's neck, then a left to his chin, and another right, sending Thompson back on his heels. But Thompson caught his balance almost immediately, charging at Tacoma, his fist covered in blood.

Tacoma had a few feet and saw the space between them. He ducked right and swung his leg in a trained wheelhouse 270. His boot swept the air. By the time it hit the Russian's jaw it was moving fast and had power. The boot hammered the Russian's jaw. Thompson let out a pained grunt as he stumbled sideways and fell to the tar, face down, blood bubbling up from his mouth and nose. Tacoma didn't wait. He pounced on the Russian and slammed his boot on his neck. He stepped down hard, pressing him against the alley as his hand shot to Thompson's mane of black hair, grabbing it and tugging to the point just before breaking his neck.

"I want information," said Tacoma, breathing hard, trying to catch his breath.

"Fuck you," said Thompson, coughing up blood.

"I'll let you live," said Tacoma.

The Russian let out a pained laugh.

"Bullshit."

Tacoma ripped up on his head, pulling it to a ninety-degree angle.

"I'll walk away," said Tacoma. "I don't care if you live. But if you don't start talking I will kill you and then I'll go through your phone and your wallet," said Tacoma, as the Russian bled in crimson trickles from his nose and mouth. "I'm guessing within an hour we'll have everything and then some. You, meanwhile, will be dead as a goddam doornail, Ivan. I'm interested in one thing. You tell me and I won't kill you."

Thompson's eyes were swirling around in the sockets. The kick from Tacoma had done serious damage. Tacoma didn't need to kill him. He was dying no matter what.

"What?" he said in a slurred mumble.

"Why did you kill Charles Hartford?"

"I was told to."

"Why him?"

"I don't know. I liked Charles. I was told to kill him, that's it. That's business, isn't it?"

"Was he GRU?"

The Russian coughed as he laughed.

"No."

"Was Jenna the target?"

"Yes, but not to kill her. It was a warning."

"Why? Is she involved with Russia?"

"Even I don't know why," said the Russian, looking up at Tacoma with lifeless eyes. "Please," he whispered.

Tacoma dropped the Russian's hair and put his right hand beneath his forehead, still on top of his neck, the yanked up. A dull snap echoed in the alleyway.

"I had my fingers crossed," Tacoma said as he let the dead man's head drop to the pavement. Tacoma found his coat and pulled it on, covering his wound. He pried the door to the building back open and moved quickly up the stairs. He found Sarkov in a booth, already surrounded by several beautiful women.

Tacoma came in front of the table and caught Sarkov's attention.

"I need to go."

One of the women to Sarkov's left, a gorgeous brunette in a sheer white blouse, leaned forward.

"Please, have a drink with us."

Tacoma ignored her.

"Can I borrow one of your planes?" said Tacoma.

Sarkov, who was leaning back, relaxing, leaned forward with a serious look.

"Of course. Where do you need to go?"

"London."

"Anything, Rob, you know this."

Tacoma felt his arm growing wet beneath the leather jacket from the knife wound.

"Is there a medical kit on board? I need sutures."

"Yes," said Sarkov. "Do you want me to get a doctor?"

"No."

"Will you have one more drink with me, Rob?" said Sarkov. "Whatever it is, I'm sure it will wait."

Tacoma eyed the brunette and smiled at her.

"No, I'm gonna go," said Tacoma as, somewhere behind him, a scream arose over the music of the club, then shouting from the stairs. He reached out and shook Sarkov's hand, gripping it for an extra moment. "You might want to leave too, Grigor. It's about to get a little hectic around here."

65

CHUNGSAN, NORTH KOREA

Two miles from North Korea's coast, four men sat on the edge of a custom-built, heavy duty tactical Zodiac. Each man wore tactical combat wetsuits, light-duty scuba packs, and carried an airtight weapons cache. One of the men nodded to the other three. This was Mark Fusco. He was team leader. He knew the other three men – Moses Barrazza, John Kolackovsky, and Nick Truax – better than he knew his own brother.

They were U.S. Navy SEALs.

Fusco leaned back over the edge of the Zodiac and let gravity deposit him in the cold, dark waters of the Yellow Sea. Barrazza, Kolackovsky, and Truax followed Fusco into the water. A second later, the Zodiac's pair of 350-HP engines revved hard and the boat ripped away, speeding west, back to the USS Benfold.

Fusco and the three frogmen moved a few feet beneath the surface of the black water toward the rocky shore. They were invisible, relying on GPS that was illuminated in the upper left corner on the inside of the scuba glass. Each SEAL was as black as the water itself. The commandos kicked their flippers in a steady rhythm, moving rapidly toward North Korea's dark, unpopulated coast.

Fusco, Barrazza, Kolackovsky, and Truax ranged in age from twenty-four to thirty-two. Fusco was the oldest, a veteran of operations in more than twenty countries across the globe. Some on land, including desert and tundra, more parachute drops than he could remember, but mostly missions having something to do with water.

At twenty-four, Truax was youngest of the four. Barrazza and Kolackovsky were both twenty-eight. They had thick beards. Kolackovsky, at 6'6 was the tallest of the bunch. At thirty-two, Fusco was considered a middle-aged man within the teams, though he was still a 5'11"205 lb. beast. They were the leading edge of America's covert operators, men who could operate virtually anywhere in the world, under extreme duress, with little support.

Tonight, Fusco, Barrazza, Kolackovsky, and Truax were entering a dead zone.

They swam into a dark stretch of rocky coast several miles from the closest town, Chungsan. They moved along the wave break, scanning for signs of life. As they reached the slippery rocks, each commando removed his fins then climbed up the rocks to a dark field. They sprinted toward a tree line, ducking behind the first cluster of brambles.

Cloaked in the shadows, the four American removed the scuba masks, tanks, weapons caches, and wetsuits. Each man unstrapped a waterproof ruck from his chest. Inside was everything they needed for urban combat, including lightweight boots, tan tactical clothing, weapons vests, and ammo. Each SEAL strapped on nylon ankle sheaths that held combat blades. Each man removed an MP7A1-Z customized fully-automatic submachine gun, retractable stock, Zeiss RSA reflex red dot sight on top, suppressors screwed into the muzzles, then strapped the weapons over their shoulders and across their chests. They did the same with the M4s and strapped them across their backs. They fastened nylon ammo belts around their waists and stuffed them with as much ammunition as they could carry. Finally, Kolackovsky took a tin of eye black out and rubbed it into any part of his face not covered by beard and mustache. Fusco and Truax did the same. Moses Barrazza, who was black, didn't need to.

It took each of them only a few minutes to get ready. They did it all in silence.

Finally, they put in specialized ear buds. Kolackovsky wore a device connecting the buds to one another as well as to a communications specialist aboard the *Benfold*. Kolackovsky turned the device on.

Fusco had an extra set for the American they were meeting up with in Pyongang.

"This is Lieutenant Kolackovsky," he said. "*Benfold*, can you hear me?"

"Affirmative, officer."

"I have you, *Benfold*. We're on shore and moving."

"Roger that."

Kolackovsky pressed his bud, nodding at the others.

"Commo check."

Fusco tapped his ear.

"Check."

"Got you," said Barazza.

"I'm good," said Truax.

Fusco tapped his ear bud twice.

"*Benfold*, this is Fusco. Can you patch me into whoever is running this at the CIA?"

"Yes. Please hold."

A half-minute later, a voice came over the ear buds of the three Navy SEALs.

"This is Mack Perry at CIA. Is this Captain Fusco?"

"You have me and my team. I was told we're to meet up with Andreas. Where is he?"

"He's already in Pyongang."

"What's the operation?" said Fusco.

"You guys need to get to downtown Pyongang," said Perry over commo. "The route is uploaded and we'll be live in real time to guide you. Andreas will brief you when you get there."

"How far are we from Pyongang?"

"About thirty miles," said Perry. "You'll need to borrow some transportation. Luckily there are plenty of Mercedes and BMWs scattered around the North Korean countryside."

Fusco and the other SEALs – who were listening in – all laughed.

"On a serious note, we've been scanning and it looks like there's a vehicle about two clicks from you guys, due east."

"Got it, Mr. Perry."

"It's Mack," said Perry.

A half-hour later, Fusco, Barrazza, Koloackovsky, and Truax came to a small, darkened home. They didn't need their night optics to see. The moon was almost full and cast a bluish light down. The home was one-story and made of concrete. There was one window on the back side of the building. A stack of firewood was piled up high. An old pick-up was sitting next to the home.

Truax opened the door quietly and put the truck in neutral. The four commandos pushed the old truck down a dirt road for a mile or so. Truax opened the door and climbed in.

"Which one of you guys remembers how to hotwire a car?" said Fusco.

"I do," said Barrazza. "In fact, I knew when I was ten years old."

Fusco and Kolackovsky laughed.

The engine suddenly made a diesel coughing sound and then came to life.

"Actually, no need," said Truax. "Keys are in it."

66

PYONGANG

Dewey extinguished the lights of the sedan. He drove for several blocks, acutely aware of the sound of sirens, roaring in the distance. He needed to get as far away from Talmadge's building as he could – but even more important was not being seen, and when he heard the sirens – multiple now – getting closer, he started looking for a place to dump the car. He saw a flashing blue and yellow light, reflecting down an alley, off a window above the alley as a police cruiser searched just a block away. Ahead on the left, he pulled into a rickety-looking parking garage. A waist high chain-link fence was shut and padlocked across the entrance. He floored the sedan and accelerated, smashing through the fence, then stopped and got out, quickly shutting the fence and trying to make it appear as if nothing had happened. He took the sedan into the dark garage and went to the third floor, parking in a dark corner behind a van. He shut off the engine and dialed Jenna.

"Dewey?"

"Yeah."

"Are you okay?"

"Yes, but I need an extraction. What's the plan?

A long pause settled over the line.

"Well, actually," said Jenna in a lilting British voice. "There's been a change of plans."

"What the fuck does that mean?" barked Dewey. "I'm in Pyongang and I need to get out."

"North Korea is about to launch a nuclear strike on the United States," said Jenna.

"All the more reason to get me the fuck out of here," said Dewey.

"You don't have time to get out of there."

"How the hell do you know—"

"Listen to me, Dewey," Jenna shouted. "The documents that Yong-sik sent say they're attacking today. As of midnight your time, we're past the point of no return. The bottom line is, he's going to launch at any time."

Dewey was quiet.

"We have two choices. Either we turn Pyongang into a glass parking lot or we kill Kim Jong-un. You're there. If you want to live, you need to kill Kim before the president launches a pre-emptive nuclear strike."

Dewey looked out the front of the windshield. All that was visible was a concrete wall.

"Why haven't we attacked yet?"

"Because you're still there."

Dewey was stunned. What had been exhaustion turned into a sense of frustration and anger. Mostly at himself.

"You have to get moving, *now*."

"How much time do I have?"

"I don't know the answer," said Jenna. "If Kim starts fueling the missiles…"

"Okay," said Dewey, stopping her. "Where he is?"

"In the palace."

"I need a route in."

"We have a route in. It's an escape tunnel that runs straight out from the palace."

"Do they know about it?"

"Yes."

"Then it will be guarded, Jenna," said Dewey, an edge in his voice.

"Without question," she said. "Probably several dozen men."

"I'm running out of ammo," said Dewey. "For chrissakes, maybe you should just nuke the fucking place."

"You're not giving up. We sent in a team. They're in country and en route to Pyongang. You meet-up in ten minutes."

"Let me guess. An 87 year-old MI6 agent with a magic umbrella that shoots darts?"

"Very funny," said Jenna. "They're Navy SEALs. Captain Mark Fusco is in charge. It's a four man team. You have in-theater command. I'm uploading a map that'll guide you to the meet-up point. Now go!"

—

Ten minutes later, Dewey crouched in the low hanging eave of the building. A digital map was imposed on the phone screen. According to the map Jenna had uploaded, the building across the street held one of a half-dozen entrances to a set of highly guarded tunnels that ran beneath the city. Built by Kim's grandfather, the tunnels were intended for escape from the palace – if the country was under attack or a coup had taken place.

He was two minutes early for the meet up with the SEALs who were supposed to be here. Dewey had worked with a lot of SEALs. His best friend was a former SEAL. Still, he didn't see any signs of life on the empty street. Were they late? Had they been captured? He needed a team if he was going to kill Kim. There were simply going to be too many people with automatic weapons for one man to make it through.

Dewey heard sirens in the distance. He put the phone back in his chest pocket. In the dim light of the alcove, he re-checked his weapons set. He needed to understand – to be absolutely positive about – the number of rounds he had, down to the last bullet.

Dewey had two guns: a 1911 and a SIG P226. Both guns had suppressors threaded into the muzzles. He popped the mag on the Colt. It was an 8-round extended mag. There were six bullets left in the mag, along with another already chambered. He slammed the mag in and ejected the SIG's magazine. There were four bullets remaining plus another bullet already chambered.

He had twelve bullets left.

On his left calf, Dewey's Gerber combat blade, eight inches of black Japanese steel, double-serrated, a patina of scratches and wear, his initials engraved into one side; the word "Gauntlet" on the other.

The sound of sirens grew louder.

From the dark alcove, Dewey stared left and right. The thin city street was empty for the night. He studied the windows of the apartment building across from him, looking for signs of life in the building – someone watching or a light on – but he saw nothing but darkness. In the dim reflection from the building's windows, he tried to see into the building above him, searching for lights, seeing none. Both apartment buildings seemed abandoned, the gray concrete and small glass windows lifeless and spectral.

The sirens again, closer this time. He needed to move.

He saw movement to his right. A faint shadow of a glimmer in a window. He raised the Colt and moved silently to the corner of the building. He waited ten seconds, and then ten seconds more. Then the glimmer again. He was closer now and he heard to faint whisper of a shoe on concrete.

Dewey lurched around the corner, gun high and trained straight ahead. The end of the suppressor found the forehead of a man who was clutching an MP7, now aimed at the ground.

"I'm Fusco," said the individual whose forehead Dewey was holding a gun against.

Dewey swept the pistol aside. Fusco appeared calm but was breathing rapidly.

"Where the other three?" said Dewey.

"Hidden," said Fusco, pointing to three different points of egress within a block of where they now stood, two doorway alcoves and behind a garbage dumpster. Dewey couldn't see any of them. "Let's get inside first. Here."

Fusco handed Dewey an ear bud. Dewey put it in his ear, then tapped.

"Commo."

"I got you," said Fusco quietly. "Guys, you hear that?"

"Check," said Truax.

"I'm good," came the deep baritone of Barrazza.

"Check," said Kolackovsky.

Dewey nodded and moved ahead of Fusco.

They walked across the empty street, a lone lamppost hitting their dark silhouettes, casting shadows along the façade of the building. They came to the building entrance – a set of double glass doors – Fusco scanning the street as Dewey looked through the glass, inside the building. They saw no one. Dewey took two steps back then charged, right foot thrusting forward, kicking viciously. The doors buckled slightly inward and he repeated the kick, two, three, four times, each time sending the doors a little more inward. Finally, the lock snapped where the two doors met. Dewey yanked one of the doors open and stepped inside, followed by Fusco, who closed the door quickly, in silence.

"Okay, I want ten second staggers on my go," said Fusco. "Moses, Nick, then John. One, two, three… *move.*"

The lobby was empty and dark and Dewey held a gun in each hand. The forced entry was loud enough to be heard, though he saw no one, just a set of stairs, a wall covered in mailboxes, a table against the wall. He charged across the lobby, past an elevator, and came to a steel fire door with Korean writing on it. He saw light at the seams of the door. He pressed his ear against the door, listening.

One of the commandos, a stocky black man – Barrazza – came in behind him, clutching a submachine gun. Dewey glanced at him, then looked back at the door. He gripped the knob and started to turn it but heard the faint scratching of footsteps on the other side of the door. He stepped quickly back, raising both guns just as the door opened. Someone was opening it, slowly and deliberately, trying to be quiet. Dewey took two running steps and kicked the door just above the doorknob. The door ripped back, striking someone in the head. The man let out a high-pitched, pained yelp as Dewey followed the door in, swinging his right arm through the air and training a pistol on the man. He was a soldier. As he lay on the ground, blood was coursing from his nose. Dewey pumped a silenced bullet into the man's forehead, as he swept the other gun – and his eyes – across the brightly-lit room.

The dead soldier confirmed the intelligence. Jenna was right. This had to be the entrance to the tunnels. A second door was near the far corner of the room.

Dewey knew the importance of acting quickly now. If there were more soldiers posted in the building, killing them before they could warn their superiors was critical.

He heard yelling from beyond the second door, then the pounding of steel-toed boots on concrete.

"We got life," whispered Dewey over commo.

He moved across the interior door, holding the 1911 in his right hand. He signaled for Barrazza to stand behind the door, against the wall, hidden. The other commandos moved along the wall behind Dewey. The five men now surrounded the door, Barrazza on one side, Dewey, Fusco, Truax, and Kolackovsky on the other. The frogmen raised their submachine guns and trained them on the door, which was closed. Dewey held his suppressed pistol in his right hand as, with his left, he reached for the door knob, turned it, and pulled the door open before standing back just as automatic machine gun fire erupted from inside the second room, pocking the concrete of the far wall. The gunfire continued for several moments.

Dewey crouched and looked at Truax, who took a grenade from his weapons vest and handed it to Dewey. Dewey took it in his left hand, still crouching. As bullets continued to fly from inside the other room, he pulled the pin out and waited until there was a brief pause in the gunfire, then hurled the grenade inside the room.

"Shut it," said Dewey over commo.

From behind the open door, Barrazza kicked hard. The door went flying shut. A second later, a loud explosion rocked the ground, kicking the door back open, as screams suddenly came from inside the second room. Dewey crabbed forward and swept his gun around the corner, firing as fast as his finger could flex. He was joined by Fusco, who stood next to him, still out of the way of the door opening. Fusco put the muzzle of his MP7 also around the corner of the door opening and unleashed a fusillade of bullets, spraying blindly into the other room.

Smoke and dust clouded the doorway.

As Fusco continued to blast into the room, Dewey holstered the Colt and pulled out the SIG P226, which had a full mag. He held a finger up, telling Fusco to hold his fire. Still crouching, Dewey abruptly dived down into the doorway, pistol in his right hand out, finger against the trigger, landing on his stomach. His eyes scanned the destroyed room, looking through the smoke and debris. He counted three men, all dead. Then he caught movement in the corner. Black hair, then a face, covered in blood. The man was back against the wall, trying to push a new mag into his submachine gun. Dewey fired. There was a low, metallic *thwack* as the gun spat a suppressed bullet at the soldier, catching him in the top of his head, blowing a small chunk from his skull. Blood washed the gray wall behind him as the soldier was kicked backwards.

"Clear," said Dewey.

They entered the room, barely registering the dead soldiers. The room was large, with several OLED screens on the wall, now shattered, as well as desks with computers on them. All of it was destroyed by the grenade blast.

They searched the room for the entrance to the tunnels. Near the soldier Dewey had just gunned down, Truax found a steel door in the floor. It was painted in bold red and covered in black Korean letters, no doubt warning trespassers away. Truax searched for a door handle, but there wasn't one – only a small digital screen.

"Scanner," said Truax.

Dewey looked down at the dead soldier. He grabbed the man's wrist and dragged the corpse to where Truax was kneeling. Truax took the man's thumb and pressed it to the scanner. After a few seconds, a lock made a dull noise, then the door cracked open. Dewey lifted it up. It was a ladder that led down into a dimly lit tunnel below.

Dewey searched the room until he found a .45 caliber pistol in one of the soldier's weapons belts. Dewey popped the mag and grabbed an extra from the man's belt, stuffing them in the pocket of his vest.

He looked up at Fusco and the others.

"I'm Dewey," he said.

"Moses," said the black man, Barrazza.

"I'm John," said Kolackovsky.

"Nick," said Truax.

"What's the plan?" said Fusco.

Dewey held out his SAT phone, displaying the layout of the tunnels that led to the Presidential Palace. He handed the phone to Fusco, who held it so that the other three SEALs could see. The tunnels resembled a maze. Leading from the palace, the tunnel divided into three tunnels, each going in different directions. These three routes then divided into yet more paths, spreading out beneath Pyongang, offering Kim a variety of ways to escape the city. Some of the tunnels criss-crossed each other at points.

According to the map legend, approximately one mile of tunnel lay between where he'd entered and the palace – if the direct path was taken. According to the map legend, approximately one mile of tunnel lay between where he'd entered and the palace – if the direct path was taken. It was confusing – but Dewey knew they didn't have a lot of time. They needed to go direct.

"How many men will they have?" said Truax.

"There's no way to know," said Dewey. "Assume it's heavy, a dozen or two."

"Looks like there are three different tunnels that reach the target," said Fusco. "Question is, which one do we take?"

"We take the shortest route," said Dewey. "A couple of you stay here. They're going to come looking."

Fusco pointed at Kolackovsky and Truax, who nodded.

"You and I move on point," said Dewey, looking at Barrazza. "Left, right formation with cover. We're entering in the middle of one of the tunnels so you," Dewey nodded at Fusco, "need to cover behind us. Obviously, we all need to watch our fields of fire."

Dewey looked at Kolackovsky and Truax.

"Kill anything or anyone who tries to get in here," said Dewey. He pointed at the dead soldier. "That soldier has some sort of check-in, every hour, half-hour, whatever. When he misses it, they'll come looking. If they bring a bunch of people, you need to blow the entrance and come and meet-up with us downstairs."

"Got it," said Kolackovsky.

"Let's go," said Dewey.

"What's the route?" said Fusco. "We don't need a briefing sheet but we do need a plan."

"We take the main tunnel," said Dewey. "That's the shortest route."

"It might also be the most heavily patrolled."

Dewey nodded.

"Do you guys understand what's happening?" said Dewey.

"Actually, no, we don't," said Fusco. "It obviously involves Kim. I assume we're going to capture or kill him, but all we were told was to meet-up with you and provide support."

"Kim Jong-un is about to launch a nuclear strike on the U.S.," said Dewey, "unless we kill him."

The SEALs exchanged glances, all in silence. Dewey turned to the stairs that would take them to the basement. He paused and looked back at the commandos.

"By the way, something you should know," added Dewey calmly. "As soon as North Korea begins their launch sequence, the United States is going to destroy Pyongang. Our only option is to kill Kim before he launches his missiles. There's no time for a mission plan or anything like that. We move now. We kill everything we see. We run through these tunnels like our lives depend on it, because they do. And then we kill that motherfucker Kim."

Every one of the Navy SEALs nodded in agreement.

"Let's go," said Dewey.

–

Dewey looked down into the tunnel. A dull gray light shone up from somewhere below. Steel ladder rungs were embedded into the concrete wall of the tunnel. Dewey climbed down into the small space, trying not to remember Columbia University, though he couldn't help it. He'd been trapped in an abandoned water pipe beneath New York City, unable to move and barely able to breathe. He fought to push the memory away. He started climbing down, remembering why he was here:

"If you want to live, you need to kill Kim before the president launches a pre-emptive nuclear strike."

67

SIGNALS INTELLIGENCE DIRECTORATE
NSA
FT. MEADE, MARYLAND

Samantha Stout finished constructing the algorithm. She sat back and stared at the screen.

Bruckheimer was now coming into her office at five-minute intervals, checking her progress. Will Parizeau had called her half-a-dozen times.

"Well, here goes," she said.

In order to test her work, Samantha ran the raw data from a single order to launch, selected at random from the catalogue of launch sequences *Rolex* had learned from. It was a launch order made four months ago by the North Koreans, exactly thirty minutes prior to the test missile lifting off and flying into the Sea of Japan.

She started the feed of data, this time with *Rolex* looking at it armed with the new algorithm.

Her heart was racing as the line of code that demarcated the order to launch appeared on the screen, a series of zero's and one's which scrolled down the screen in rapid formation. She looked at the timer on the computer screen, counting the seconds, praying.

After a minute, she stood up, too anxious to watch anymore. What had she done wrong? It should have triggered the algorithm by now.

"Come on you little bastard," she whispered.

The first minute turned into two, then three. She finally moved over and, in resignation, got ready to type. She needed to go back into the algorithm and understand why it wasn't—

A sharp chime sounded on the computer just as the entire screen started flashing. The word ALERT flashed in bright red. An automated voice came on the computer speaker.

"*Sequence active,*" came the voice. "*Twenty-six minutes, twenty-nine seconds until missile launch.*"

Jenna sat back in shock. Just then, the phone on her desk buzzed.

"Will Parizeau is on and he says he's with the president," said Samantha's assistant, Rudy.

Bruckheimer suddenly stepped into her office, his tie off, sleeves rolled up, and a layer of perspiration on his face.

Samantha grinned and leaned forward, hitting a button on the phone.

"Hey, Will," she said as Bruckheimer stepped to the side of her desk.

"Sam," said Parizeau on speaker. "I'm in the Situation Room. Unless you found out a way to do this, they're about to wipe out North Korea."

"I got it," said Sam. She scooched her chair in and started typing. "We can now detect as of three minutes after they give the order to launch. Every launch sequence from the North Koreans has a thirty-minute fail-safe."

"So we have twenty-seven minutes," said Parizeau. "Excuse my language, but are you fucking sure?"

"Yes," said Samantha.

"What if they decide to just launch, without the fail-safe?" said Parizeau.

"That's a risk," said Samantha. "But every missile launch they've ever done has the thirty minute fail-safe. I don't have an electrical engineering doctorate, but the delay might be structural. They might not be able to do it faster than thirty minutes."

"That's a big risk," said Parizeau.

"You don't understand risk then," said Samantha. "It's never happened before. I do have a doctorate in economics. From a risk perspective, there is none, other than a Black Elephant. Now let me go. I need five minutes to upload it to the satellite. It'll be live then."

"Live wire the priority feed into Janus 49, that way we can see it when it happens. Oh and Sam?"

"Yes?"

"Nice work."

Samantha continued typing, glancing up at Bruckheimer, who looked relieved. She continued typing. Bruckheimer didn't say anything but he didn't need to. Samantha understood how proud he was.

"I nailed it," she said.

"Yes, you did," said Bruckheimer, patting her shoulder.

68

SITUATION ROOM
THE WHITE HOUSE

Jenna watched the scene with fascination. She had lived through other operations but never one with such incredible ramifications. She was observing people, trying to figure them out. Tralies was a huge presence. His words carried meaning and he was straightforward and tough. She didn't agree with him on the idea of hitting immediately, but she agreed with the macro idea Tralies was fighting for: that the country's citizens must be protected and that saving American lives was all that mattered.

Jenna wanted to save American lives, but it was Dewey Andreas and the four Navy SEALs who were foremost in her mind.

The president was as she'd heard and read – a cool operator with a hard nose for details, willing to listen, to take risks, to shut down people he thought were being arrogant. Dellenbaugh was the first true leader she'd ever seen during a crisis and, without showing it, Jenna was impressed.

But the one she thought about the most was Hector. What he had shown her as anger after Dewey was poisoned transformed itself, and she understood now it wasn't anger. Calibrisi simply didn't like seeing the agents who risked their lives for him die. He was the one who refused to let her quit, either the agency or more importantly, the operation. Hope. That's what it was. He looked for the fraction of possibility in dire circumstances. All of it would likely be over by now had he not forced her to look for that fraction of hope.

And the president listened to him. He trusted him.

Jenna glanced across the table at Calibrisi. He was looking at his phone but looked up.

"What's up?" he said.

"Nothing."

Suddenly, Parizeau stood up.

"NSA figured it out," said Parizeau. "We can track when they hit the launch code. From that point forward, we have twenty-seven minutes."

Jenna's phone vibrated and she read the text. It was from Dewey.

> Entering tunnel. Out of range

Jenna frantically dialed. She needed to tell him. But the message was returned with a red exclamation point.

No coverage

69

PRESIDENTIAL PALACE
PYONGANG

Yong-sik entered presidential palace. Kim was alone in one of the sitting rooms, a massive room at least a hundred foot long by fifty feet wide, with four humongous chandeliers. Luxurious chairs, sofas, divans, and chaises were interspersed with tables atop which sat large vases filled with fresh flowers – roses, lilacs, and peonies. The room was coffered and two stories high, adorned with paintings in gold frames. Classical music played in the background. It was Beethoven.

Kim was seated on one of the sofas, clutching a glass of white wine and smoking a cigarette. There was no ashtray; several small piles of ashes sat on the table next to where Kim was sitting, as well as on the carpet and sofa.

Yong-sik walked to Kim.

"You wanted to see me, my grace."

Kim smiled, then coughed. It was a small cough but it grew louder and more wet and clotty. When he finally stopped, he took another drag, exhaled, then took a large sip of wine.

"You've confirmed that the nuclear missiles are ready to fire?" said Kim.

"Yes, Mr. President."

"How many?"

"The Iranians gave us two ICBMs," said Yong-sik. "We have attached weapons to both of them."

Kim nodded, smiling.

"Very good, general," said Kim.

"Thank you, your excellency."

"And how long from when I order their launch until they... take flight?"

"From the point of initiating the launch sequence, precisely thirty minutes."

"What time is it?" said Kim.

"Almost midnight."

"Order the launch sequence," said Kim.

Yong-sik nodded, but said nothing.

"Do you not agree, General Yong-sik?" snapped Kim.

Yong-sik took a moment. The air was tense. Kim looked angry.

"Do you know, your excellency, that I was the one who introduced your mother to your father?" said Yong-sik.

Kim took a sip of wine, a nasty, drunken look on his face. He took another puff of the cigarette then put it out on the arm of the leather sofa.

"Yes," continued Yong-sik. "Your father was visiting my father's home. They were friends. My father was also a general. I knew your father had yet to find a bride. There was a girl down the road. Anye. The most beautiful girl in all of North Korea. I went and pulled her by the arm to meet your father. She was your mother."

Kim stared at Yong-sik.

"Your father always said to me, 'tell me what you really think.' When I first served on his staff, I would try to deflect his questions by agreeing with everything he said, but he refused to allow me to flatter him. He made me tell him what I thought. He said, 'If you won't tell me your opinion, what good are you to me?'"

"Some would say this is insolence," said Kim, threat in his voice. "Treason. Do you know what treason is, general?"

Yong-sik met Kim's glare with a steady, blank look.

"It is whatever you say it is, my excellency."

Kim shifted his wine glass from his right hand to his left, then reached to a drawer and removed a handgun. He trained it on Yong-sik.

"I can kill you right now," said Kim.

"Yes, you can," said Yong-sik. "But if you launch the nuclear missiles, it won't matter. America will destroy us. They will destroy Pyongang and North Korea. I will be dead anyway. You may shoot me but I'll be dead anyway if you launch the missiles. You are destroying your country. But you know that."

Kim's nostrils flared with a hint of anger.

"So what would you have me do?"

"Simply don't do it," said Yong-sik. "I will obey whatever order you command, my grace. If you order it, it shall be done. I care not how I die – by your gun or by an American bomb – but I will not disobey my Supreme Leader."

"And what happens when I die?" said Kim.

Yong-sik bowed his head.

"I don't know the answer to that question," said Yong-sik. "Appoint a temporary magistrate whose job it is to select another leader in your honor."

"You, I suppose," said Kim derisively. He put the gun down and lit another cigarette.

"No," said Yong-sik. "I am a soldier, not a leader."

Kim stared into Yong-sik's eyes. They were red.

"I'm sorry, Pak, my friend," he said in a soft voice as tears started running down his cheeks. "Thank you for all that you did for me."

"It was my honor, sir."

"Initiate the launch sequence."

70

KPA HEADQUARTERS
PYONGANG

Bahn-ni felt the vibration of the cell phone on his chest. He removed it and looked at the screen. It was General Yong-sik.

Bahn-ni was in Room 111. At KPA headquarters, mission control, a large room covered in digital screens and filled with work stations where young analysts monitored and controlled all military-related activities of the North Korean government.

"Yes, general," said Bahn-ni.

"The Supreme Leader orders the missiles launched," said Yong-sik.

"Yes, sir. As per protocol, I am required to ask you: what is the code sequence?"

"Eight one nine zero four one."

"Very good," said Bahn-ni.

Bahn-ni turned and looked at a young analyst sitting before a work station.

"Are the targets locked in?" said Bahn-ni.

"Yes, colonel. Los Angeles and San Francisco."

"Fire when ready, lieutenant."

71

PALBONG
NORTH KOREA

Jung-hoon steered the big rig along a dirt road. The vehicle was big and eerie looking. A camaflouged truck with a missile on top. It was a missile vehicle, a mobile weapon designed to be mobile and thus untrackable to enemy satellite systems. This one was a Russian-made MZKT 79221, with sixteen massive, rugged wheels that could absorb explosive blasts and keep moving.

On top was an ICBM, an Intercontinental Ballistic Missile, tipped with a nuclear warhead.

Jung-hoon steered the rig down the abandoned country road. After several minutes he stopped. He was next to a field. He steered into the field, then backed up, then went back into the field and backed up again, turning the MZKT around in case he received the orders to move again.

This was his job. Jung-hoon drove all day, moving the missile vehicle around a quadrant of territory in the middle of nowhere. He drove for twelve hours and then handed the keys to Sung-ho, who performed the same ritual day-in and day-out: keeping the launchers undetectable.

He did a circuit check on the communications device that linked him into the men above him at KPA who made the decisions, then sat back. He turned off the lights and crossed his arms, waiting for his next orders. He thought about his wife. He would see her in only three hours. He envisioned her as he stared out at the blackness.

When the communications device started beeping, he looked down. There were six digits running in red across the small screen. He knew what it meant.

Jung-hoon unbuckled as an odd expression crossed his face. He opened the door and began the process of getting the missile ready to fire.

72

PYONGANG

Dewey climbed down the ladder, as a dim, grayish light glowed from below. He took the ladder several rungs at a time as, above him, Fusco and Barrazza followed him down. Soon, his foot struck concrete.

Dewey pressed his back against the wall, glancing around. He saw nobody – just tunnel in both directions, lit by single light bulbs dangling from wires every fifty feet or so. Dewey pulled the two pistols from the shoulder holsters. He popped the mags without looking and slammed fresh mags into each gun as Barrazza and Fusco stepped off the ladder one after the other.

The tunnel ran in the dark in either direction. It was well-constructed and clean, like a mine shaft that had never been used. The ceilings were eight feet high and the walls were at least fifteen feet wide.

Dewey holstered one of the guns and took the SAT phone from his pocket. There were no messages. They were now out of range, though their ear buds would continue to work in-theater. They could talk to each other.

Dewey stared at Fusco, then Barrazza.

"Welcome to North Korea," he said.

Barrazza laughed. Fusco grinned slightly, then cut to the chase.

"Nick, John, you guys commo?"

"Yeah."

Fusco looked at Dewey. All the SEALs were listening.

"So what happens if you get shot?" said Fusco.

"I get shot, leave me," said Dewey blankly. "Anyone gets killed, you leave them. We'll come and get you later. There's only one objective. Kill Kim. Got it?"

Fusco nodded. He looked at Barrazza.

"Set a threader," he said. "Over there." He pointed at the tunnel in the opposite direction of the palace. "We can't blow up this section otherwise Nick and John won't get through."

"Got it," said Barrazza.

Barrazza took two grenades from his vest as he walked up the tunnel, away from where they were going. He took a spool of thread and looped one end around one of the grenades. He set it down along the base of the floor. He set the other grenade on the other side of the floor then took the thread and wrapped it around that grenade until there was tension – enough to keep the thin, nearly invisible thread in the air above the concrete. Finally, and very carefully, he pulled the pin from one of the grenades. He went to the other grenade and, as gently as he could, pulled the pin from that one as well.

Anyone coming from behind him would run into the thread, causing both grenades to explode. It wouldn't do much to the tunnel itself – but it sure as shit would fuck someone up.

Barrazza pocketed the pins and ran back to Fusco and Dewey.

Dewey looked at Barrazza.

"One by ones," said Dewey. "What side do you want?"

"Left," said Barrazza.

Dewey looked at Fusco.

"You ready?"

"Yes. I have your back."

"You guys upstairs, we're moving."

Dewey clutched the silenced SIG P226. He started a fast jog down the tunnel with the gun out in front of him, toward the palace. He ran for several hundred yards, seeing no one, and came to another tunnel that shot off to the right. He stopped and crouched as, behind him, Barrazza approached. Dewey took a step, sweeping the weapon across the other tunnel as Barrazza sprinted by him and took point, charging down the tunnel.

Barrazza's eyes caught a momentary modulation in the light in the distance, someone passing beneath one of the halogens. There was someone ahead. They were a good distance away, but it was unmistakable. He stopped and held up his right hand, warning Dewey.

Barrazza could see the opening into another tunnel up ahead. He tucked flat against the wall and skulked forward until he came to the opening. He waited, then snapped his fingers as he put his finger to the trigger of his silenced MP7. Afer a few long, quiet moments, the sound of steel-toed boots came from the side tunnel. Barrazza moved in front of Dewey, against the right wall, pushing against the wall, out of view of the oncoming soldier.

The soldier didn't say anything – he didn't call in whatever he suspected the noise was – but he heard something.

The steps along the concrete grew louder. A shadow crossed the tunnel light. Barrazza heard a dull, almost imperceptible metal friction: a safety being moved off. Then came a few more steps, getting closer. The moment was coming when the North Korean would cross the opening into the main tunnel, just inches from where Barrazza now lurked.

Whatever weapon the North Korean was carrying was no doubt trained on the opening in front of him.

As the first patch of leg crossed into the opening, Barrazza fired, hammering the soldier before he knew what hit him, lighting him up in lead. The soldier crumpled to the ground as blood sprayed the concrete behind him.

Barrazza looked at Dewey.

"Delicate," said Dewey.

73

SITUATION ROOM
THE WHITE HOUSE

Every OLED screen in the Situation Room started flashing red. The word "ALERT" cut on and off across the screens.

A moment later, the screens cut to a live cam. Samantha Stout from NSA was on screen.

"The North Koreans initiated the launch order," said Samantha. "Mr. President, you have twenty six-and-a-half minutes until the North Korean missiles take off."

Dellenbaugh stared into the screen. After a moment, he turned to the table.

"Once again," Dellenbaugh said, "what is the flight time from the submarine to the target for our missiles?"

"Three minutes," said Tralies.

Dellenbaugh looked at his watch. He took a pencil from the conference table and grabbed the closest piece of paper he could find, a newspaper. He started scribbling down numbers.

"We launch at ten minutes," said Dellenbaugh.

"But sir—" yelled Tralies. "They issued the order!"

Dellenbaugh gave Tralies an icy stare. The president said nothing, waiting for Tralies to finally understand the order.

"Ten minutes," said Tralies. "In the meantime, per protocol, we need to open the football, sir. There are a number of logistical steps—"

"I know how it works," said Dellenbaugh. "In the meantime, convene a call with Putin and Xi. Invoke the *Emergency Council* if you have to."

The *Emergency Council* was created by Woodrow Wilson more than a century ago. It was the leaders of three countries. One of the most secret programs in the world, an agreement existed that superseded political boundaries and could be initiated only by its members, the leaders of the three countries, even in times of war between the parties. When a council member called for a meeting, the other two members were obligated to drop whatever they were doing. The three members of the *Emergency Council* represented more than ninety-percent of all the world's wealth and most of its land. It was the last bastion of protection, a council at the end of the day committed to fighting true threats to mankind. There weren't many members: China, Russia, and the United States of America. In essence, the *Emergency Council* was the big kid on the playground.

Dellenbaugh understood that he needed to let them know he was about to wipe out a country. He wasn't asking permission, but he was taking the time to notify them.

Two minutes later, a voice came over the phone console.

"This is Scarlett four four blue," came a European-sounding female voice. "You have the President of the United States, the President of Russia, and the Premier of the People's Republic of China."

Dellenbaugh stepped to the table as all eyes were on him.

"Vladimir, Xi, nice talking with you," said Dellenbaugh. I'll keep it brief. In a few minutes the United States is going to initiate a pre-emptive nuclear strike on North Korea. It's our only option at this point. Thank you for your time."

74

PYONGANG

Dewey and Barrazza plowed down the tunnel, taking turns running point, switching when they come to a side tunnel.

Fusco moved backwards. He'd switched weapons, taking out the M4, sweeping it across the tunnel behind them, looking for lurkers.

Fusco stepped over the bloody corpse of the dead soldier. He kept moving back but saw a shadow. He stopped. He crouched down low and pressed against the wall of the tunnel, waiting. He heard the faint scratch of material, the sound of someone inspecting the dead man. A moment later the silhouette became clearer, the dull light illuminating him. Fusco aimed the rifle and, as the soldier stepped into his sight-line – swinging his gun toward Fusco – fired. Fusco's slug ripped the North Korean in the middle of his forehead, dropping him.

Dewey and Barrazza were now a good distance from Fusco at the back. They moved past another tunnel opening without seeing anyone and Dewey took point, running down the tunnel, gun extended. They hadn't even come to another opening when they both heard the sound of a soldier speaking Korean.

The words were incomprehensible. The tone was frantic.

Dewey tucked his gun in the shoulder holster and reached to his leg, taking out his combat blade. Just as the soldier stopped talking, Dewey broke into a desperate sprint. He swung the blade and charged, slashing the knife from left to right as, with his outstretched left hand, he reached for the muzzle of the submachine gun, trying to re-direct any bullets the gunman might fire. In the same flash of seconds, Dewey sent a brutal kick to the soldier's groin. Dewey's blade caught the soldier in the neck in the same moment his hand grabbed the muzzle. Dewey ripped the blade sideways as the soldier panicked, attempting to react. But the kick was far too brutal and the soldier's hands let go of the gun and reached for his neck, trying to stop the knife. He let out a low, pained groan just as the blade tore horizontally across the nape of his neck. He went tumbling down to the concrete, unable to trigger the gun even once. The gash was deep and jagged, severing half the gunman's neck. Blood started flowing immediately, as if an envelope suddenly opened up and spilled out a gurgle of crimson.

Dewey's left hand held the submachine gun by the muzzle as the gunman let go. The man wriggled on the ground and then died. Dewey slung the gun over his back.

"We're getting closer," said Barrazza. "Lighting's better, more soldiers."

As they started to continue down the tunnel, there was the squawk of a walkie talkie: words in Korean. Dewey stopped walking. He went back to the soldier and took the radio from his belt. Someone was calling the soldier. It didn't sound urgent – until the second squawk a few seconds later. Dewey put the radio in his pocket.

"We need to move faster," said Dewey. "There's no more time."

Dewey and Barrazza started a hard sprint up the tunnel, in the direction of the palace, running into the path of a wall of gunmen that stood between them and Kim.

A bolt of cold fear hit Dewey. He realized that the North Koreans knew they were there, and why they were there. Talmadge, the dead men at Talmadge's apartment, the take down of the tunnel entrance. They understood that an invader was in their midst. An invader with one objective: Assassinate Kim. Kill the Supreme Leader.

"Faster," said Dewey, pushing the pace of their hard run. "*Faster.* We need to move faster!"

75

PYONGANG

Truax heard it first. A door moving. He looked at Kolackovsky. A half-second later they bolted for the door hatch that led to the tunnel, just as automatic gunfire sprayed the door and the sound of steel-toed boots echoed in between the low-pitched din of the submachine guns.

They went through the interior door and slammed it shut. Truax pulled a small object from his vest pocket the size of a pack of cigarettes as Kolackovsky ripped a spider web of red, green, and black wires from his pocket. Truax tore off a layer of black, wet-looking plastic from the object. Beneath was a small brick of SEMTEX. Enough SEMTEX to take down the first three floors of the building. He placed it gently against the seam of the door hatch and pressed slowly against it, smashing the clay-like material in place. Kolackovsky inserted the wires, one of which was attached to a tiny copper switch. He taped the wires next to the steel hatch so that when it opened, the wires would fall. He pressed a small button on the side of the copper switch, initiating a single-purpose motion detector.

Then they fled.

Down the tunnel ladder, Kolackovsky in front, each man scrambling as the sound of automatic weapon fire grew louder above them. They could hear shouting in Korean, high-pitched orders punctuated by yet more gunfire.

Kolackovsky and Truax reached the concrete floor of the tunnel and started sprinting, just as the explosion mauled the air. The air pressure threw each man off their feet, kicking them forward in violent, fast tumbles. Then the tunnel behind them collapsed beneath the weight of the falling apartment building. The sound of bending metal and the choke of slurry dust washed over them.

Kolackovsky was the first to his feet. He grabbed Truax by the front of his weapons vest and pulled him up.

"Let's go," he yelled.

76

PRESIDENTIAL PALACE

Fusco felt a small rumble and heard a distant thunder. Someone had triggered the grenades, he guessed.

Barrazza, on point, stopped mid-run, holding up his hand.

He smelled the faint aroma of cigarette smoke somewhere ahead. He kept moving, going slower, taking each step in silence. He saw a shadow dance across the concrete wall ahead. It was the soldier smoking. He was just past a slight curve in the tunnel ahead.

Barrazza switched weapons and got down on his stomach. He skulked slowly along the ground, inching around the bend, holding the M4 out in front of him as he crawled. Before he saw the gunman he saw the entrance to the side tunnel. The soldier was stationed there, absent-mindedly guarding the juncture between the main artery to the palace and the side tunnel.

He heard the low din of a radio playing some sort of music.

Then, the walkie talkie in the man's pocket crackled. Someone came on and started speaking in a panicked voice.

Barrazza knew what it meant.

They know.

He got to his feet and charged forward just as the soldier swung his submachine gun toward him and triggered the weapon. But Barrazza was already triggering the rifle by the time the soldier reacted. The suppressed bullets spat from the rifle – *thwap thwap* – and they ripped into the soldier's stomach, kicking him forward. Barrazza pumped one more bullet at point blank range into the soldier's forehead.

"Very nice," said Dewey, looking down at the mangled, bullet-ridden corpse. "Martha Stewart-esque."

Dewey and Barrazza both shot their eyes down the tunnel in the same moment. They heard the faint drumbeat of footsteps coming from somewhere ahead. They stepped into the side tunnel, taking a few steps back in order to get out of the direct light. They again heard the crackle of the walkie talkie, this time the one in Dewey's pocket. The words were urgent. A man was yelling into the walkie talkie. The phrases short and clipped: orders.

Dewey understood soldiers were coming from somewhere ahead – somewhere closer to the palace.

He looked at his watch. If he and Barrazza ran tried to take an alternative route through the side tunnel, they might get away. But time was their enemy. Time was all that mattered now.

"Follow my lead. Get your HK."

Dewey went to the dead soldier and flipped him onto his stomach. He lifted the dead man by the material at the back of his neck. The North Korean was light. Dewey held him up with his left hand, facing the corpse at the soldiers he could now hear running down the tunnel toward him.

Barrazza switched weapons again, bringing out his MP7, a long, round suppressor jutting from the muzzle. He moved behind the dead soldier as Dewey held him up. Barrazza aimed up the tunnel, tucking the suppressor beneath the arm of the dead man, trying to conceal himself behind him.

The sound of boots grew louder. The point soldier ran headlong into the tunnel just fifty feet away. Barrazza held his fire. As the soldier yelled something to the dead man, a second soldier came into view, and then a third.

Barrazza triggered the silenced submachine gun. The dull metallic *rat-a-tat-tat* of the weapon was like thousand hornets as Barrazza sprayed the tunnel in a methodical line. There were pained groans and a sharp scream, but it all was drowned out by the sound of weapon fire. Even suppressed, it cut through the din.

The tunnel was quickly clogged in dust and debris from the pulverized concrete, from the soldiers' uniforms as they were shredded, and from blood and body as it sprayed the air and walls. Other than a short burst of bullets from one of the gunmen which struck the ceiling, none of the men had time to do anything as Barrazza mowed them down. Barrazza stopped firing when he heard the *click click* of the empty mag.

"You're in a bad mood, aren't you?" said Dewey to Barrazza.

Dewey and Barrazza started running again, as fast as they could. Dewey was on point when suddenly...

A black flash – a lightning bolt – a dark ember—

It came at him from an egress in the wall, an alcove to the left.

Dewey saw the glint of the blade just as it darted from the wall. It was trained at his torso, and he was moving so fast he was running directly at it. Dewey lurched, trying to block the arm the blade was attached to. It was a soldier, lunging, slashing at Dewey. Dewey slammed his left wrist down on the hand clutching the knife just as the tip of the blade struck Dewey's stomach, cutting through material and skin before Dewey could do anything. Dewey groaned and slammed the butt of his pistol into the killer's skull, a vicious swing so hard he could hear the crack of bone breaking.

The soldier dropped, still clutching the blade. Dewey finally could make him out in the low light. He was young, with an angry look. He wore a black uniform, a more elite branch. His hand clutched a silver steel blade. He suddenly lunged again, this time at Dewey's neck. Dewey ducked, grabbed the man's wrist, and twisted it hard, snapping it at the elbow. Dewey wrapped his other arm around the killer's neck. He yanked back, snapping his neck.

Barrazza watched as Dewey let the corpse drop.

"You're one to talk."

They were getting closer to Kim.

They ran for another few minutes without seeing any signs of life. Suddenly, two soldiers emerged from the shadows. Dewey fired twice as Barrazza stepped clear of Dewey and added a second round of slugs. The man on the right was hit in the neck, kicking him backwards. The man on the left took Dewey's shot in the middle of the forehead and dropped to the ground.

Dewey opened his jacket and saw a large pancake of red.

"You okay?" said Barrazza.

"Fine," said Dewey. "Let's go."

77

SITUATION ROOM
THE WHITE HOUSE

The president studied the countdown clock on the wall:

00:10:47

Dellenbaugh's face was drenched in sweat. He looked calm but nervous. He caught Calibrisi's attention.

"Is Dewey even alive?"

"We have no way of knowing," said Calibrisi. "He and the SEALs are in the tunnels. There's no way to know if they'll make it to the palace. He has more than a mile of tunnel. It's guarded, and they probably know he's there."

Dellenbaugh smiled.

"It's Dewey," the president said. He looked at Phil Tralies, Chairman of the Joint Chiefs of Staff. "He has until the three minute mark. That leaves us plenty of time."

"But Mr. President," said Tralies, his voice rising. "We're cutting it too close! If anything goes wrong – if our calculations are off – we risk the possibility of a nuclear bomb destroying Los Angeles or some other city."

"What is the status of our missile defense systems?" said Dellenbaugh.

"All defense systems are hot," said Arnold, the secretary of defense. "All tracking protocols are live and the entire THADD battery is unlocked and loaded. But Mr. President, it's not a fail safe option. I can't guarantee we can take it down."

"Understood," said Dellenbaugh. "Dewey has seven more minutes."

"Mr. President, waiting any longer is unacceptable—" said Tralies. "We—"

"The last time I checked, general, I was the commander in chief," barked Dellenbaugh, cutting him off, leaning forward, throwing him a brutal look. "He has until the three minute mark."

"Very good, Mr. President," said Tralies.

78

PYONGANG

Dewey and Barrazza came to the central guard station beneath the palace.

The KPA might have a greater concentration of gunmen the closer the tunnels got to the palace, but they'd also expended many soldiers trying to hunt down the invaders. The smart thing for the North Koreans to do would be to remove Kim from the palace. But no man was brave enough to inform Kim his tunnels had been breached.

Dewey clutched two handguns. One had a full mag, the other a half-filled one.

He looked at Barrazza.

"What do you think?"

"Let me soften 'em up with a few 433s," said Barrazza, referring to a particular type of grenade.

"Do it."

Barrazza took a grenade from his belt and put it into the under-mounted launcher on his rifle. He took aim and fired. The grenade launcher made a low popping noise as it hurled the grenade down the hall into the guard station. The explosion was like a concussion, breaking glass, blowing out lights and parts of walls. Screams and howls of pain came from inside the destroyed room. Barrazza quickly reloaded and fired another grenade into the guard station. A loud, ear-splitting explosion rocked the ground and cracked the ceiling.

Dewey and Barrazza moved quickly to the guard station. It was carnage – a half-dozen bodies torn up into pieces – along with clouds of dust and debris.

Dewey's eyes shot left. A soldier was charging from one of the other tunnels. Dewey fired, striking him in the mouth, kicking out the back of his head – dropping him.

They cut through the station to a doorway.

"That's it," said Dewey, reaching for the knob.

79

SITUATION ROOM
THE WHITE HOUSE

The Situation Room was packed. On two side-by-side screens was live video feed, black-and-white, each screen showing live feeds, taken by satellite, of two missile vehicles – each vehicle holding a large missile across its back. Puffs of smoke could be seen around the base of each vehicle.

The countdown sequence for each missile was illuminated in red digital numbers in the upper left corner of each OLED.

00:05:04

Parizeau's voice came over the speaker system.

"We're approaching five minutes until launch," said Parizeau. "I repeat, we are at five minutes out."

The president was standing at the end of the conference table. His arms were crossed as he looked at one of the OLEDs.

General Tralies was pacing on the side of the table opposite from the OLEDs, his face red with frustration and desperation.

"*Mr. President!*" Tralies barked, pointing at the screens. "*We are at five minutes out! We cannot wait—*"

"All defense systems should be in a state of emergency priority," said Dellenbaugh, interrupting Tralies. "THADD batteries, mid-range defense systems."

"*For the love of God, Mr. President,*" yelled Tralies, practically begging. "*You simply can't wait any longer!*"

"General Krug," said Dellenbaugh, leaning into the speaker phone, cutting Tralies off. "Remind me again of flight times for U.S. missiles."

"Three minutes, sir," said Krug, the Commander of the Pacific Fleet, piped in over speaker, patched in from the *U.S.S. Forrestal*. "Three minutes."

00:04:47

"I want all missiles launch-ready, on my go," said Dellenbaugh.

"*Those numbers are guesses!*" said Tralies.

The president looked at Tralies, then back to the closest screen. Bursts of small, controlled flames came from one of the two missiles, though it remained on the launcher. He put his hand to his forehead and pushed it back through his thick brown hair.

00:04:29

"We're going longer!" barked Dellenbaugh, shooting Tralies an angry look. "We have until three minutes – we're going to three goddam minutes!"

80

PRESIDENTIAL PALACE
PYONGANG

As Dewey and Barrazza went through the door into the palace, a red light on the side of the SAT started blinking, indicating that a message had come through from Jenna. He opened it.

> KJI/KPA INITIATED LAUNCH SEQUENCE
> EST TIME ZERO = 27 MINS
> POTUS RESPONSE **WILL OCCUR** AT 17 MINS =
> 10 MINS **BEFORE** 27 MINS
> USS SUBS IN SEA OF JAPAN
> EST FLT TIME OF US MISSILES = LESS THAN 3
> MINUTES
> TRALIES ON ATTACK: "OVERWHELMING AND
> DEFINITIVE"
> NK MUST ABORT BY 5:33

Dewey's eyes shot to his watch. It was 5:31 A.M. He looked at the time stamp on the message. 5:16 A.M. He looked one more time at his watch. It was now 5:32. He had one minute before the United States military launched a nuclear attack.

"Uh oh," said Dewey.

"What is it?" asked Barrazza, standing behind him.

"We have one minute to stop them."

"What the hell are you waiting for?"

"You asked me a fucking question," said Dewey.

They ran quietly up a set of stairs that led into the palace. A door led into a small room barely bigger than a closet. Dewey could hear voices. He reached to the door knob and slowly twisted it. He pulled the door until it was ajar. He peered in through the crack.

The room was massive, some sort of sitting room with high, coffered ceilings large windows, chandeliers, chairs and sofas. He saw the back of a man's head in a chair in the middle of the room. The man was talking to someone rapidly, his voice rising. Kim. The other individual was out of Dewey's sight line. Dewey opened the door further – pulling it slowly, without a sound. He pulled the second pistol from beneath his armpit and nodded to Barrazza.

"Whatever you do, don't kill Yong-sik," Dewey said quietly.

"Got it."

"On my go."

Dewey pushed the door slowly in and stepped into the room, training one gun on the back of Kim's head and the other on the man he was speaking to. Dewey recognized him. It was Yong-sik.

Yong-sik didn't see Dewey at first. Instead, he was standing near the doorway, dressed in a military uniform. Another soldier was behind him and slightly to the side, clutching a Kalashnikov which was aimed at the floor. As Yong-sik began to speak, the soldier saw Dewey and pulled up the rifle.

Keeping one gun on Kim, Dewey triggered the other pistol. A dull metallic thwack interrupted the din as a silenced slug spat from the Colt. The bullet ripped into the soldier's eye, kicking away the back of the man's skull, spraying blood and skull across the door. Dewey stepped between Yong-sik and Kim, holding both men in the firing line as Barrazza moved diagonally across from Dewey, training his weapon on Kim Jong-un.

"Don't move," said Dewey to Yong-sik.

Dewey turned and for the first time met eyes with Kim.

Kim was seated on a large wing chair, his face drawn and gray. He looked smaller than the photos. The cancer was ravaging him, though his hair remained a thick block of oddly manicured black and he was still a fat load.

For several moments, there was a silent stalemate, as Dewey held Kim and Yong-sik in the muzzles of his guns.

"Either you do it or I will," said Dewey, nodding at Yong-sik.

"I would not ever do harm to my leader," said Yong-sik.

"The United States knows, general," said Dewey. "Your missiles won't make it off the ground. We're about to destroy North Korea. Do you really want that to happen? I know you don't."

Yong-sik glanced at Kim, who was staring at Dewey.

"*How dare you even consider it!*" shouted Kim at Yong-sik. He lurched for a phone. Dewey pumped the trigger. The bullet ripped into Kim's head, knocking him sideways. He slouched into the chair, his destroyed head leaning awkwardly over the arm.

Dewey moved to his right and fired just as Yong-sik dived down to the floor. The bullet missed Yong-sik – but by the time he could reach for his gun Dewey stepped over him and aimed both guns at his head, moving closer and closer, moving the tip of the suppressors down toward Yong-sik, until finally he had one of the suppressors pressed into the socket of his eye. Dewey pushed until he felt resistance from the eyeball, as if it might pop.

"You wouldn't have told us about the cancer if you agreed with that nutjob," said Dewey calmly. "Make the call. *Now!*"

81

SITUATION ROOM
THE WHITE HOUSE

All eyes were on President J.P.Dellenbaugh as he stared at the clock, as if by staring at it he could somehow get the clock to slow down.

00:03:07

The room was pin drop quiet.

General Tralies was standing in the far corner of the room, slouched in the corner, in total silence. Dellenbaugh looked at him. They shared a complicated look; from Tralies to the president, hatred for pushing it this far, respect for the knowledge that Dellenbaugh had warrior guts. Dellenbaugh looked at Calibrisi, seated in a chair, hands clutched together, biting his lip. He saw Josh Brubaker standing next to Dale Arnold along the wall, both men silent, both staring at him as he pushed everything to the last possible moment.

Dellenbaugh forced himself to look at the clock.

00:03:02

"On my go," said Dellenbaugh.

82

PRESIDENTIAL PALACE

With the suppressor still pressed to his eye, Yong-sik felt for his walkie talkie and lifted it to his ear.

"*Stop the missiles!*" he yelled. "*Now! Stop them! Cancel all launch sequences, per order of the Supreme Leader!*"

Dewey lifted the pistol from Yong-sik's eye socket as, with his free hand, he picked up Yong-sik's walkie talkie and pocketed it. He kept Yong-sik dead center in the firing line of the pistol. He tapped his right ear three times.

"Alpha."

"Get me the president," said Dewey as he looked at Yong-sik. "This is Dewey Andreas."

As Dewey waited, he walked over to Yong-sik, who Barrazza held in the firing line of his submachine gun. Dewey motioned for Barrazza to lower it, signaling that now Yong-sik could be trusted – even though he knew it wasn't true. Yong-sik was still on his back, on the floor.

Dewey came up to Yong-sik and crouched down.

"Hey, general, don't be so down," said Dewey, patting Yong-sik's shoulder as gently as he could. "You just saved at least a million lives, including yours and more importantly mine. Buck up, hombre. You got fucking Blackjack, buddy. You see, today *is* your lucky day."

Dewey heard a click in his ear and stepped away from Yong-sik, looking around the room, catching the eyes of Fusco, Kolackovsky, Truax, and Barrazza as he waited for the president to come on. The four SEALs held the room in a tight cordon, weapons moving slowly across the air, surveilling.

"Mr. President," came a voice over Dewey's commo. "We have Dewey Andreas."

83

SITUATION ROOM

The intercom abruptly cut in.

"Mr. President, we have Dewey Andreas—"

The signal was bad, and static could be heard.

"Kim is dead," came Dewey's voice. "The missiles have been cancelled. I repeat, the missiles have been canceled."

"By who?" said Tralies.

"Yong-sik," said Dewey. "Kim is dead. General Yong-sik is now in charge. Whatever you do, don't fire."

84

PRESIDENTIAL PALACE

With Barrazza's gun aimed at all times on Yong-sik, Dewey went to the door. He reached down and pulled the dead soldier into the sitting room then shut the doors. He picked up the Kalashnikov and tucked the pistol beneath his armpit.

Dewey walked to Kim as Barrazza continued to train the MP7 at Yong-sik, still on his back on the floor.

"May I get up?" said Yong-sik.

"No."

Dewey stood in front of Kim. He was slouched over, the side of his head destroyed, the chair covered in a riot of blood. Dewey took the phone and took a few photos.

"I'm sending photos of Kim," said Dewey. "I need a RECON team in here immediately. We're inside the palace. You should have my phone locked in. We're in the living quarters somewhere. I don't know how long I can hold the theater."

A voice came through the phone.

"Dewey, this is General Krug. We'll get a team there in about fifteen minutes, but you need to make sure they shut off air defenses."

"Roger that," said Dewey.

Dewey turned. He walked to Yong-sik.

"Get up," he said.

He pointed with the gun at a sofa near the far wall.

"Over there."

Dewey held Yong-sik's wrist and guided him to the sofa. Dewey remained standing. He tapped his ear.

"CENCOM, I need a Korean translator on this call," said Dewey.

"I speak Korean," said Krug.

"Make sure he's telling them to stand down," said Dewey.

Dewey looked at Yong-sik. He handed him the KPA walkie talkie.

"Tell them to expect inbound helicopters, general," Dewey told Yong-sik. "They are *not* to be fired on."

"How would I possibly explain that?" yelled Yong-sik.

"How the fuck should I know?" said Dewey. "You're the boss. Figure it out."

Yong-sik stared at the walkie talkie. He looked at Dewey.

"Why are they coming?"

"We don't want to run your country, general, if that's what you're thinking," said Dewey. "But we are going to take your nukes. All we want is stability."

"And Iraq?" shot Yong-sik. "Afghanistan? How about Vietnam?"

Dewey nodded.

"Those are the three primary reasons we don't want to run your country," said Dewey. "You're in charge now. You wouldn't have told us about Kim's cancer if you didn't give a damn about your country."

"Where are they coming from?"

"It doesn't matter," said Dewey coldly. "Tell them to turn off the goddam air defenses."

Yong-sik whispered so that nobody else would hear.

"So I can tell them they're friendly?" Yong-sik asked.

"Sure," said Dewey. "Just understand that if those choppers get fired on, you get a bullet in your stomach." Dewey paused. "It's over, general. We don't want to kill anyone and we don't want to run your country. We just don't feel like getting nuked."

Yong-sik nodded. He lifted the walkie talkie and hit the mike.

"This is General Yong-sik. The Supreme Leader is welcoming guests. They will be coming from multiple places and possibly both coasts. Expect several helicopters. They are not to be fired upon. I repeat: do not fire upon the helicopters. They are friends. I don't have to tell you what will happen if any of the helicopters are shot at."

Yong-sik handed Dewey the walkie-talkie.

"Sounded good," said Krug. "We'll see you in fifteen minutes, Dewey."

Dewey hung up the phone.

"Now that wasn't too bad," said Dewey, taking the walkie talkie. "I can see why you're such a good general."

Yong-sik shook his head.

"So, do you have senior officers you trust?" said Dewey.

"Of course."

"And ones you don't?"

"Yes, those too."

"I've been through a couple of these before," said Dewey. "Change in government. For what it's worth, some advice. You're going to need some support. Get the ones you trust over here."

"And the ones I don't?"

"They need to be locked up," said Dewey. "You can let them out later if you want. When you assume power you need to immediately start thinking about preservation of power. That means right now."

Slowly, Yong-sik extended his hand. Shyly, he said: "Thank you for saving my country."

85

PRESIDENTIAL PALACE
PYONGANG

The palace was soon teeming with people.

Five American choppers landed on the palace roof, carrying inside them a small army of Navy SEALs as well as high-level JSOC political, military, and logistics officers, including General Torey Krug, the U.S. Commander of the Pacific Fleet.

When Krug entered the sitting room, he was trailed by several SEALs in tactical military gear. Krug registered Kim, lifeless and untouched on the chair. He saw Dewey standing at the far side of the room, talking with Yong-sik.

"Take Dewey's position," said Krug to one of the frogmen. "I need to talk with him."

The SEAL walked to Dewey and introduced himself.

"Dewey, I'm Nick Smith from the U.S. Navy. General Krug wants a word. I'll stay with General Yong-sik."

Dewey nodded and walked to Krug.

"Hi, Dewey," said Krug.

"General."

"How you feeling?"

"Fine."

"Hector is on his way here along with some planners from the Pentagon and State," said Krug. "It's going to be awhile. Why don't you take one of the choppers and go back to the ship. I'll have them set you up with a cabin, warm shower, a good meal."

"I'd rather wait," said Dewey. "I'm fine. Let's make sure this thing holds."

"Have it your way," said Krug. He nodded at Yong-sik. "Is he going to work with us?"

"I think so. But I don't know."

Krug reached out and patted Dewey on the shoulder.

"Good work."

"Thanks."

–

The additional American Special Forces enabled them to quickly take the entire palace under armed guard. As soon as that was accomplished, Yong-sik reached out to a list of seven senior officers from the KPA. Each man was brought alone to the room where Yong-sik was under guard – learning of the situation only after being disarmed and entering the large sitting room. Kim's corpse was allowed to remain front and center; a warning to them all.

Krug waited until Yong-sik's most trusted senior military staff were present. He went to Yong-sik and spoke in flawless Korean.

"I want to say a few things to you and your men," said Krug. "I think you should, too, General Yong-sik."

Yong-sik nodded and stood up. He waved the other North Koreans closer. The mood was tense. There were nine commandos inside the room and three times as many in various positions around the Presidential Palace.

"You are all here because you are the men I trust," said Yong-sik. "The Americans assassinated our Supreme Leader."

A low grumbling from the North Koreans as they exchanged glances.

"The Americans did this because the Supreme Leader was going to launch a nuclear attack on the United States," Yong-sik continued. "I helped the Americans stop him. I did this because I knew that if we launched nuclear missiles at the United States, they would destroy our country. I didn't want to see my fellow countrymen die. I didn't even want to see innocent Americans die. Kim had cancer. He was at death's door. He wanted to leave a lasting mark. In a way, he did. We now have the chance to create a better country, because of him."

Krug stood next to Yong-sik and spoke after he finished:

"I'm General Torey Krug," he said, looking across the line of North Korean officers. "The United States has no interest in being in North Korea any longer than we have to. We don't want to run North Korea and we don't care if you remain a dictatorship. In fact, for the next few years it probably makes sense to keep the existing political infrastructure in place. The United States will leave as soon as North Korea is de-nuclearized. We also stand ready to be of any assistance you need in terms of rejoining the civilized world. As you know, America believes in democracy, but we honestly don't care what you do. *It's your country, gentlemen*. The reason we're here is because we didn't want to be attacked with nuclear missiles. That's the bottom line. We'll leave when we're sure it'll never happen again. In the meantime, no one leaves the palace and no one communicates outside the palace unless we tell you to."

86

PRESIDENTIAL PALACE
PYONGANG

Several planes arrived from the United States, including a large blue-and-white Boeing 777 that resembled Air Force One. It wasn't – this was the U.S. Secretary of State's plane.

Secretary Mijailovic was accompanied by a finely curated group from State, the CIA, the Pentagon, Energy, and the White House. The group included a deep bench of America's top Asia and North Korea experts, as well as crisis teams schooled in post-military conflict.

Hector Calibrisi and Jenna Hartford were on the plane, as was Josh Brubaker, the National Security Advisor, and Dale Arnold, the Secretary of Defense.

With Torey Krug serving as translator, the tension of the first few hours had lessened, though it wasn't completely gone. Krug had an easy, direct way and the North Koreans, led by Yong-sik, were cooperating. The main focus was on the country's nuclear infrastructure, though Krug – thanks to the Yong-sik documents – already knew all there was to know. Instead, Krug engaged them because he knew these were the crucial hours. He understood that something could go sideways at any moment and North Korea still had the largest number of soldiers of any army in the world. The more he could gain their trust – and have Yong-sik and his men see him as a reasonable, kind partner, their desire to try and do something would weaken.

At some point, Krug ordered Kim's corpse – as well as the dead soldier's – be taken to another room and covered and the chair removed.

When the group from the U.S. arrived, there were introductions. It was Calibrisi who spoke first.

"It's been almost sixteen hours and I apologize for the level of secrecy," said Calibrisi.

A CIA translator repeated Calibrisi's statement in Korean.

"Are there members of the military trying to find out what's going on?" Calibrisi asked, looking at Yong-sik.

"Yes."

Calibrisi looked at Jenna. She opened her leather valise and removed a piece of paper. She handed it to Calibrisi, who handed it to Yong-sik.

"That's Kim's handwriting," said Calibrisi, "or at least as close as we can get to it. He wrote it to you on his deathbed, as he was dying from cancer. That's the story. General, you are being appointed by Kim as his heir and the country's new leader."

Yong-sik inspected the letter.

"This isn't true," said Yong-sik.

"General Yong-sik, it's imperative North Korea not be seen as having been taken over by the United States," said Calibrisi. "We believe it's absolutely imperative that your countrymen not know what really happened."

Yong-sik nodded.

"I understand."

"It doesn't mean we want you to be a dictator," said Calibrisi, "though if you do, we'll have no control over it. This note simply covers up the fact that Kim was killed. It's for the masses. It buys you time to plan a smooth transition and to maintain stability, that's all."

Calibrisi looked at Mila Mijailovic, the secretary of state.

"My name is Mila Mijailovic and I'm the United States Secretary of State," she said. "Thank you for having us, for safe-guarding our arrival, and most of all for listening. I want to tell you, first of all, that we are acutely aware of the dire circumstances regarding the North

Korean treasury and economy. That is why the United States and several other nations have joined together and are preparing to make an immediate injection of cash into the North Korean treasury. The amount is five billion dollars and it will be wired as soon as we have the correct information. I should tell you that the group of nations includes Great Britain, Germany, Canada, and South Korea. We will help you. We want to help you. We want to do it quietly. When the money runs out, we will be there for you."

Yong-sik looked down at the floor, then scanned his lieutenants. Yong-sik looked at Krug.

"May we have a few minutes to consider what you said?" Yong-sik said politely.

"Of course," said Krug, nodding at a pair of men clutching rifles near the door, telling them, without words, to keep their eyes fixed on the group. Krug stepped away, along with Mijailovic, Calibrisi, and Arnold.

Yong-sik and his top lieutenants moved to the side of the room and spoke for less than ten minutes. When they returned to Krug and the others, a nervous smile was across Yong-sik's face.

"We will do it," said Yong-sik. "We are unanimous in our decision. It is the right thing for our people."

87

RIVER HOUSE
MI6 HEADQUARTERS
LONDON

Tacoma entered Derek Chalmers's 3rd floor office. He was still dressed in a leather coat and white T-shirt from Moscow.

"That was quick," said Chalmers.

Tacoma said nothing.

"Where's Katie?"

"Paraguay," said Tacoma.

"You were alone? That was worth two million dollars a week?"

"You get what you get and you don't complain," said Tacoma. "Are you interested in what I found or should I come back another time?"

"Touché."

"I found Billy Thompson. Definitely GRU. He admitted to killing Charles Hartford."

"Admitted to it?"

"Yes."

"Freely?"

"I exerted a little pressure," said Tacoma. "I asked him why. He said it was a warning to Jenna."

Chalmers's brow furrowed as he realized the implication.

"Jenna?"

"Yes," said Tacoma. "When I asked him why, he said, 'Even I don't know that.'"

Chalmers stood up and walked to the bar in his office. He poured himself a Scotch.

"Rob? Do you want something?"

"No, I need to go," said Tacoma, standing up.

Chalmers took a sip.

"How far does this go?" said Chalmers.

"You pay for confidentiality," said Tacoma, "unless it's something that the United States needs to know. If she's working at Langley—"

"I'll call Hector," said Chalmers.

Tacoma walked to the door.

"Derek, don't jump to conclusions," said Tacoma. "Assuming Jenna's bad is the same thing as everyone who assumed Billy Thompson was good. You recruited her. Someone might be setting her up."

"What did you do with Billy Thompson?"

Tacoma smiled.

"Broke his neck. See you later, Derek."

88

PRESIDENTIAL PALACE

As the conclave broke up, Jenna glanced around the large room. She hadn't seen Dewey, but her eyes found him on a sofa along the far wall of the gigantic, ornate room. It was a fancy, extra-long sofa, with gold-covered fabric. Dewey was sprawled out on his back, weapons vest still on. He was sound asleep.

Jenna walked to the sofa as Krug, Arnold, Mijailovic, Yong-sik and the other North Koreans sat down around a large table on the opposite side of the room and began the process of working together.

Jenna took a sat next to Dewey's head. Slowly, Dewey opened his eyes and looked up.

"Hi," she said.

"Hi."

"There's a plane for you over at the airport," said Jenna, brushing her hair out of her face. She smiled. "Whenever you want to go. I think this thing is under control."

Dewey looked discombobulated and exhausted. He shut his eyes. Within a few seconds, he was asleep again. Jenna stared down at him, shaking her head.

"Dewey, get up," she said, nudging him with her elbow.

"Why?" he mumbled, eyes closed.

"Because we're done. You're done. Let's get out of here."

89

PYONGANG INTERNATIONAL AIRPORT
PYONGANG

A silver Gulfstream G650ER was idling at Pyongang International
Airport, engines humming.

A few seconds later, a gray Sikorsky SH-60 descended toward the
tarmac and touched down next to the jet. The side door opened and
Dewey and Jenna stepped down onto the tarmac. They walked to the
G650, Jenna in front. They both climbed on board. Inside, Dewey
pressed a button and the hydraulic purred, pulling the stairs shut.
Within a minute, the CIA-owned jet was barreling down the runway,
climbing rapidly into the dark sky.

It was a luxurious jet. There were sixteen seats in all in the cabin,
along with several state rooms with en suite bathrooms in back. The
seats were large white leather captain's chairs, facing one another on
either side of the aisle. Dewey found a chair and sat down then reclined
fully and kicked his feet up on the chair across from him. Jenna took
a seat across the aisle from Dewey, facing him across a diagonal line.

Jenna looked at him, for the first time noticing his shirt, which
was torn in several places. He still had on his weapons vest. She noted
the butts of two guns tucked beneath his armpits in holsters. His jeans
were a grayish brown – dried dirt and mud – and ripped at both knees.
His face had a layer of stubble, dark, and, in places, stained in dirt and
– beneath his mouth – blood. His hair was messed up, but still parted
roughly in the middle. He was brown with tan. Finally, her eyes met
his. He was looking at her.

"What are you looking at?" said Dewey, his voice weary.

Jenna looked into Dewey's eyes, noticing for the first time how blue they were. She averted her eyes.

"Nothing," she said.

Dewey shut his eyes and leaned back, pushing his head against the window to go to sleep.

"If it's alright, I'm getting a drop off in England," said Jenna.

"It's fine," said Dewey without opening his eyes.

"It's my father's 70th birthday," she continued, despite the fact that Dewey was trying to sleep. "There's a party for him. They definitely aren't expecting me."

"That's great," mumbled Dewey, his eyes remaining shut.

"He'll be very surprised," said Jenna, trying to engage Dewey in conversation. But Dewey said nothing. Instead he adjusted his position in the seat, trying to stretch out and find a comfortable position for his head between the seat and the window.

"Are you trying to sleep?"

Dewey opened his eyes. They were bloodshot from exhaustion.

"How'd you guess?" he said. He immediately shut his eyes again.

After a minute or so, Jenna re-opened the conversation.

"It's my first time in England in six months," she said in a soft British accent. "My husband was killed by a car bomb in London. It was intended for me."

Slowly, one of Dewey's eyes opened.

"Can this wait?" he said.

"Yes."

Dewey shut his eye as if he was about to go back to sleep. Suddenly, he opened both eyes and sat up. He shook his head, as if trying to wake himself up. He looked at Jenna.

"Hold on," he said.

Dewey stood and walked up the aisle to the bar. He opened the refrigerator and took out two cans of Budweiser and set them on the bar. He opened both cans and chugged them, one after the other, crushing the cans after he was done and leaving them on the bar. He started rifling around the bar area, opening drawers and cabinets, finally finding an unopened bottle of Jack Daniels. He unscrewed the top and took a sizable chug. He looked back down the aisle.

"Do you want something to drink?"

"Whatever you're having," said Jenna.

Dewey took two glasses and poured each one half full with bourbon. He took two beers from the refrigerator and walked back down the aisle. He handed Jenna the glass of Jack Daniels. She took the glass with a look of disbelief and shock at the volume of brown liquid, just as Dewey extended the beer. She took that, too. Dewey sat down, put his legs up, and brought the glass of bourbon to his lips and took a big sip.

"So, your husband died?" said Dewey, leaning back and taking a sip.

–

For the next two hours, Jenna did most of the talking. Occasionally, Dewey went bar to the bar for refills, all of them for himself. It was as if Jenna hadn't spoken to anyone in six months. She told him about Charles, about the investigation, about MI6, about London. Eventually, Dewey's eyelids simply could not remain open any longer. He fell asleep during a story about an operation Jenna had designed, her first operation, a rescue of a British diplomat who'd been taken hostage in Belfast.

When they landed, Dewey awoke. He looked at Jenna. Her eyes were closed.

"Hey, Jenna," he said.

Jenna looked at him through drowsy eyes.

"We're here."

She looked out the window and stood up.

"See you back in Langley," she said, making eye contact with Dewey.

He nodded.

"Yeah," he said.

After dropping Jenna Hartford off in London, Dewey found one of the state rooms and climbed onto the bed with his boots still on and blood still staining his shirt, arm, and hair. He collapsed and fell asleep until, five hours later, he felt a hand shaking him.

"Dewey," came the female voice of the pilot. "We're here. We're back in the United States. You're home."

Dewey arose slowly from the bed. He moved past the pilot and walked to the left front of the fuselage. He hit a button and the stairs descended to the tarmac. He stepped down onto the ground. It was warm out, mid-sixties. Summer was coming. Dewey was tan already. That part of his face not darkened in stubble or covered by hair that was too long and thick was brown. He wore a red T-shirt that clung to his thick chest. His jeans he'd had on for almost a week now. He stepped down the stairs and onto the tarmac.

Dewey walked into a small gathering of on-duty Air Force men, killing time, hanging around in one of the hangars.

They stopped talking and looked at him.

"Hey," said Dewey.

All of the men stood up. One of them saluted him.

"We heard what happened," said the officer. "Nice work, Mr. Andreas."

Dewey nodded but said nothing. He kept walking until he found the parking lot where he'd left his car. It was a dark, silvery gray Ferrari 575 Superamerica, a gift from Rolf Borchardt. Dewey didn't necessarily like expensive cars, but he was starting to like this one. He stood back and stared at the sports car for a few moments, then put his hand on the back left tire and found the key he'd left there. He climbed inside and hit a button that caused the glass roof to unhitch, lift up, then tuck behind him. It was a warm night. Dewey pressed the ignition switch and the Ferrari roared to life.

90

BUTCHER
LUBYANSKIY DRIVE
MOSCOW

The man, Nemkov, walked into the restaurant. It was crowded, the mood festive. Moscow's best steakhouse on a Saturday night.

He cut through the crowd. He arrived at a leather-bound booth, a luxurious but private table in the back, out of any sight lines from the window. He sat down and placed his valise to the side, inside the booth.

Nemkov looked at the man seated in front of him, Ilyitch.

"Ya izvinyayus. Ya prishel tak bystro, kak tol'ko mog."

I apologize. I came as quickly as I could.

"Vasili is dead," said Ilyitch.

Nemkov's mouth went slightly agape, his only emotion.

"How?"

"Last night, at a nightclub. He was beaten to death, then they broke his neck. This is Vasili we're talking about."

Nemkov nodded. He reached to the other man's glass of vodka.

"Do you mind?" he said.

"No."

Nemkov took large sip, then put the glass down.

"And you think he talked?"

"Can we take that risk?" said Ilyitch. "Why else would someone kill him? More important, who *could* kill him? This is not a man who loses a bar fight."

"So someone is digging into the death of her husband?"

"If she is exposed, she knows a great deal," said Ilyitch.

Nemkov stood up.

"I understand," he said.

Nemkov grabbed the glass of vodka and polished it off. He put the glass down and gave Ilyitch one last glance – then turned and walked quickly to the door.

91

POOLESVILLE, MARYLAND

Dewey took a circuitous route home from Andrews, driving through the Maryland countryside. He knew the route well by now. Fields of deep green spread out on each side of the thin, winding country road. Spring was here and hints of summer came through in the fresh, flowery scents of the country plain. When he came to the crest of a hill, he slowed. There, in the distance, was Bruner's farm.

As he drove closer, he suddenly registered the line of vehicles, including an ambulance, several police cars, and a few dark sedans.

Dewey took a left into the long gravel driveway. When he came to a uniformed Maryland state trooper, he showed him his government ID. The policeman waved him on. He steered the Ferrari past the line of cars and parked in the circular driveway in front of the rambling mansion, next to the ambulance, whose back doors were open.

Several people were milling about. There wasn't a sense of urgency, though the mood was somber.

Dewey climbed out and walked up to a group of men in dark suits standing at the front door, which was wide open. He held out his ID.

"What happened?" said Dewey.

One of the agents, a middle-aged bald man, nodded to the other two. They walked away.

"She died last night," said the FBI agent. "Housekeeper discovered her."

"How?"

"Old age, heart attack, whatever."

Dewey nodded and started to move past him.

"We're not letting anyone inside," he said.

Dewey glanced at him. He reached into his pocket and again showed him the CIA ID.

"Learn your protocols," said Dewey.

"Sorry."

Inside, a pair of paramedics had Bruner's wife on a gurney. She was already zipped up in a black body bag. Dewey went past them, walking slowly around the ground floor of the house. Every room was cozy and elegant, with beautiful paintings in large frames adorning the walls, gorgeous antiques, and oriental carpets festooned in subtle, amazing patterns. He came to a closed door and turned the knob. Inside was the living room. It was eerily quiet. He looked at the place she had been sitting when he came to kill her. He stared for several seconds, as if she was still there. Then he saw movement and glanced to his right. Lying down in the corner was a large St. Bernard. He was sound asleep.

Dewey started to turn around to leave but paused instead. He walked to the big dog and crouched next to him. Dewey put his hand on the dog's head and rubbed it. After a few moments, the dog opened his eyes and looked up at Dewey.

"Hey," said Dewey.

Dewey ran his hand along the dog's soft back, scratching him gently. The dog lifted his head and leaned toward him, licking Dewey's other hand.

"You feel like going for a ride?"

Dewey stood up and looked at the dog, then nodded. The St. Bernard stood slowly up. They walked out of the room, down the hallway, and went outside, the dog trailing Dewey the whole way.

Dewey stared briefly at the FBI agent as he walked to the car with the St. Bernard at his side. He opened the passenger door. The dog stared for several moments at the seat. Dewey leaned down and patted the seat.

"Get in," he said. "It's a Ferrari."

The dog lifted a paw and put it on the seat and lumbered in. Dewey shut the door and walked around to the driver's side and climbed in. He pushed a red button on the console and started the car. The engine howled. Before he hit the gas, Dewey looked over at the dog. His head was nearly as high as Dewey's.

"I'm Dewey," he said, patting the dog on his shoulder. "Wrigley, right?"

The dog's big, furry, square head turned left and right. His mouth was open and he seemed to be smiling. He held Dewey's gaze for a moment. A large drop of drool emerged from his mouth and dribbled down onto the leather dashboard.

Dewey burst out laughing.

He hit the accelerator and sent the Ferrari tearing up the dirt driveway.

"You're gonna love Castine!" yelled Dewey over the full-throated roar of the Ferrari, wheel in one hand, patting Wrigley with the other as the dog attempted to stick his head up above the windshield so as to feel the breeze. "Sure, it's a little cold sometimes but you're basically wearing a fur coat so you'll be fine."